BLACK MUSTARD SEED

by

EMEKA ANIAGOLU

To Geof on his birthday,
With great respect &
appreciation,
Brenda

FOURTH DIMENSION PUBLISHING CO.

First Published 2002
Fourth Dimension Publishing Co., Ltd.
16 Fifth Ave., City Layout. PMB. 01164, Enugu, Nigeria
tel: +234-42-459969; fax: +234-42-456904
email: fdpbooks@aol.com, info@fdpbooks.com
website: http://www.fdpbooks.com

ISBN 978-156-487-3

CONDITIONS OF SALES

FOURTH DIMENSION PUBLISHING CO. LTD., ENUGU. NIGERIA

DEDICATION

To

Chinua Achebe--
The Father of Modern African Literature

Emeka Kalu-Ezera—
Pan-Africanist Extraordinaire

&

Africa's Children--Let There Be Light...

The Mustard Seed

I

One planted a seed---'twas a little thing
To sow in the field of his Lord and King--
A grain of mustard. It grew and spread
Till it sheltered the weary toiler's head;
And within its branches sweet songsters rare
Sang hymns of praise, as they nested there
And he who had planted the tiny seed
Forgot his shame at the humble deed

II

And one gave his life---'twas a little thing,
But all he had to give his King.
The Master sent him where darkness dwelt,
Where the blind and lame to strange idols knelt
'Twas a lonely land; but he looked above
As he brought to the hopeless the message of Love
And many whose gropings had been in vain
To the Life of the Spirit were born again
And his life, poured out for a world in need,
Was multiplied like the mustard seed!

---Merrell Vories Hitotsuyanagi (1907)

PREFACE

Although I consider it more appropriate to append a formal preface to a scholarly text rather than to a novel, this is no ordinary novel, to me at least. There are two main reasons. The first is the subject matter of this novel, which though rendered in literary form, is of great moment in the history of Nigeria -- and, perhaps, the histories of other African states. Especially so is its relevance to the dynamics and problematical process of transforming the modern Nigerian *state*, born of the colonial crucibles, into the modern Nigerian *nation*. This is, of course a critical discourse because, for now, the most we can say with any degree of certainly is that Nigeria is a modern state made up of distinct nations or ethnic groups.

Can a modern Nigerian *nation* emerge out of the modern Nigerian *state*? Can a modern Nigerian nation be successfully created out of the great amalgam of nations or ethnic groups that compose the modern Nigerian state? Is a modern Nigerian *nation* already in the making, however incipiently? If it is, what are its discernable features? Should we look for those features in Nigeria's constitutional framework, in her electoral and political party system, or in a more equitable distribution of the "spoils of oil money"? Should we look for those features in the patterns and degree of social interaction and integration that exist between the constituent nations or ethnic groups that make up the modern Nigerian state?

Moreover, in what way (s) can one determine, take stock of and educate the multinational public of the modern Nigerian state about those features as well as the growth pains - the strains and stresses that come with that process of self-transformation?

One medium I have found to be of exceptional effectiveness -especially on a popular level is the *literary medium* - especially, the *story-telling* form of that medium. Story-telling is an ancient human tradition. It is a tradition that has great antiquity in African history and culture, albeit mostly of the oral form. A good story enthrals. It captures, first the reader's attention. Then, it animates the reader's imagination; and hopefully, the reader's fascination. A good story can entertain as well as educate. A good story can, itself, become an agent of change in the social and political dialectic, to be sure, for better or for worse.

Thus, at the turn of the last century, the Polish-born writer, Joseph Conrad, virtually put Africa out of business in the literary construction of the "modern" world, with the proverbial stroke of the pen. He achieved that singular feat with the publication of his famous book, *Heart of Darkness*. Conrad's book became the spectacle through which much of the western world views African humanity or the alleged lack thereof. Yet, towards the last quarter of the 20th century, another writer, this time an African, Chinua Achebe, all but rehabilitated Africans in the same business of the literary construction of the "modern" world, by virtue of the same metaphorical stroke of the pen. He authored his masterful novel - *Things Fall Apart*.

I have not written a novel or told a story anywhere as well crafted as Conrad's *Heart of Darkness* (thought I deplore its consummate denigration of Africans) nor Achebe's *Things Fall Apart*. I have, however, told a story - my own story- the best I can, with a view towards making a positive contribution to Nigeria's self-transformation from modern *statehood* to modern *nationhood*.

The second main reason why this novel is no ordinary novel to me, and thus deserves this rather wordy preface, is because it took me so long (twelve years to be exact) to complete. I put in so much of my mind and soul into it that I feel like it is almost a physical extension of me. The experience of writing this novel has also conjured in me a deep and abiding respect for the talent of great writers. For, take it from one who bears the battle scars of the great expedition of *creative* writing, that it is no fair for faint hearts!

6

What follows - *Black Mustard Seed*, is the result of threads of my experience growing up a Nigerian, and my hopes and aspirations for the great possibilities of that "paradise of stately palms," woven into the fabric of a literary work of fiction. If as few as only one Nigerian reads this novel and recognizes the features of her polity in it, is inspired by the its aspirations, and is entertained, or enamoured by what ever literary merit it may possess, then my work is done.

As one can well imagine, over the span of the twelve years that it took me to write this novel, I have had scores of people patiently listen to me read excerpts or whole sections of it -- in manuscript form. For their reactions I have hounded other equally generous people to read the entire manuscript for me. I thank each and every one of them from the bottom of my hear. Despite the premium of speech and time, some of these persons deserve special mention here. Ereomajuwa was one of the first people who knew I was writing a novel when during my service year in the National Youth Service Corp (NYSC) in Jos, Plateau State. I will never forget the encouragement and support she gave me during those nascent beginnings, when the realization of the goal of writing a novel seemed so remote, and perhaps, given the circumstances, even so unrealistic.

I thank my good friend, Daniel Okoli, who told me the first time he graciously endured the recitation of a part of the manuscript, that "this is great writing and it must see the light of day." That encouragement was very welcome, though I feared at the time that our friendship was getting in the way of his judgment of good writing. I also thank Ms. Vangie, a dear friend who encouraged me to finish the novel and make it available to the world because, as she so flatteringly put it, "it is the best thing I have read since *Things Fall Apart*." I Thank her for her generosity.

I thank also Ms Omakiche Ameh, who not only endured many occasions of the recitation of various sections of the manuscript but also helped me with some of the questions I had with respect to the Hausa language and culture. She had lived in the northern part of Nigeria for quite some time and speaks Hausa. I thank her for her assistance, encouragement and support.

I wish also to thank Chief Michael Ike, *Odenigbo Nnewi*, who took the time and trouble to take a copy of the first full draft of the manuscript all the way from Columbus, Ohio, to my publishers, the Fourth Dimension Publishers in Enugu. It was he who made the original contacts and arrangements between Fourth Dimension and me. The very positive comments of his beautiful and gracious wife, *Ebube Die*, about the novel are also highly cherished. She read the manuscript from cover to cover to her husband and me.

I would like to take his opportunity also to thank the Provost of Ohio Wesleyan University, Professor William Louthan, for all his moral and material support in making the publication of his novel possible.

I wish also to thank my wonderful parents, Honourable Justice A.N. and Lady M.C. Aniagolu, for giving me and the rest of my siblings a first -class education as well as a deep and abiding love for knowledge and the intellectual life. And for, as part of the same milieu, imbuing us with a love and respect for the power, function, and art of the written and spoken word. To all my siblings - Tony, Chika (Charles), Loretta, Mary-Anne, Jacinta, Uche, Chi-Chi, Kizito and Nwachukwu, and my sister-in-law, Ngozi - each wonderful in his/her own way, I am thankul for their support, love and affection.

I wish also to depress my deepest gratitude to my lovely and forbearing wife, Yvette, and to my two wonderful daughters, Asari and Nkiruka - my 'crown jewels', as I like to call them - for their unending love, support, and affection.

Finally. I thank my publishers – the Fourth Dimension Publishers, and especially their indefatigable Managing Director, Chief Victor Nwankwo, for the excellent work they have done in the publication of this novel. Having said so much and there remains so much more to be said, to God be the glory.

Emeka Aniagolu

ONE

Chike met Bisi at the medical school of the renowned University of Ibadan two harmattans ago. He remembers well how all the leaves turned brown and fell off the dry, skeleton-like branches of trees. The dry season in the tropical environs of Africa has a way of rendering unsolicited testimony. Stripped of his vegetational clothing, he stands naked for all to bear witness to his seasonal fragility.

This is *Ugulu* making his annual northwesterly sojourn and letting all living things in his path know it. *Ugulu* has to be male. Nothing feminine can leave such a trail of death. Natural forces referred to in the feminine gender are bringers of life, like *Ani*, the earth goddess of fertility, not death and barrenness like *Ugulu*. Just as heaven is the abode of God, so it is that the great Sahara is *Ugulu's* home. That great sea of sandy waste which is ironically a living testimony of how far *Ugulu* will go when his seasonal vexation turns into rage.

From the moment Chike set eyes on Bisi at the Medical Student's Association dinner, he knew he had to get to know her.

She is tall for a girl, about five feet ten inches, and has beautiful jet black hair, which she braids into beaded-cords that reach her shoulders and make clattering noises as she moves her head about. Her breasts are like two papaya fruits, ripe and ready. She has well-formed legs that attach to equally well-built hips that flute out in a gentle but firm swell. Her posterior gives the impression of the rotund firmness of an African earthenware pot. In Igboland, they would describe the shape of her posterior as resembling a pot known as *ite ona*.

Later, when Chike met Bisi's mother, he confirmed from whence Bisi inherited her nubile frame. Her mother's neck is slim and long and her skin black, with the smooth velveteen quality of a seal's. It glows with the sheen of polished ebonywood. He likes best Bisi's excellent set of white teeth and her full dark lips. Looking at Bisi, Chike thinks to himself that Onabrakpeya's heart must be eaten out by what the gods can do with their creative brushes on the canvas of nature.

Sitting across the dance hall, he mentally appraised his chances of scoring with Bisi. Summoning all his manly aplomb, he reminded himself that he was not so bad himself. He stands six foot one inch tall. Shoulders powerfully built like that of a veteran truck-pusher at *Ogbuete* market. His rather impressive shoulder muscles taper down to a narrow waist by way of a solidly hewn torso, which conjures up an image of a triangle turned downside up.

He takes particular pride in his bushy sideburns and mustache, incontrovertible evidence he thinks, of his virile manhood. He also takes great pains to trim the two with the precision that gives them a somewhat unreal appearance. He is one of the best students in his fifth-year medical class, has a government scholarship, and is Secretary of the Medical Students Association.

Because of his government scholarship, he has extra money to spare and can afford to own a car on campus. Assured that he meets the standard he got up, stretched himself to his full height, adjusted his jacket, fingered his bow-tie into a straight position, and crossed the hall to ask Bisi for a dance.

Bisi noticed a young man staring at her with that intense steady gaze that men tend to fix women when they are visibly interested. She dismissed the thought as part of her fevered imagination. He looks rather handsome and probably has all the girls falling at his feet, she thought to herself.

She notices him stand up, do his grooming act and start crossing the hall, heading in her general direction. Her heart began to beat faster. She fought for composure. As he came closer, her entire body tensed, he was coming to her after all.

Chike bent low, almost as though he was taking a bow on stage, flashed her the warmest smile he has and asked for a dance. As though in a trance, Bisi got up and they began slow-dancing to the baritone drawl of a Barry White tune. As the lights in the dance hall dimmed, Chike tried to kiss her full on the lips. She hesitated briefly, surprised at his boldness, then welcomed him with her own wet-lipped response. A tacit agreement had been sealed.

Ever since that fateful night at the Medical Students Association dinner, it was Chike and Bisi all over the campus. Their romance was unlike anything seen before at the university. They were like cattle and the egret. Wherever one was, the other was soon sure to be. Nobody could believe the change that had come over Chike. A certified, card-carrying Casanova, Chike, who had been written off by half the female population on campus as a lost cause, all of a sudden became a one-woman-man.

TWO

Both Chike and Bisi come from Wazobia. Chike is from the *Igbo* ethnic group of the eastern part of Wazobia, while Bisi is from the *Yoruba* ethnic group of the western part. Chike's parents moved to Lagos in Western Wazobia in the early 1960s. Then, life in Wazobia was good. The economy was stable, food plentiful and affordable. People harbored no fears for their personal safety when traveling from one end of the country to the other. Then, the country had an air of optimism about it. People got about their daily labors with the sustaining hope and assurance that tomorrow will be better than today.

It was not long, however, before ethnic or *tribal* politics, although lurking beneath the surface of the national life of Wazobia, broke out like hives all over the body politic of the country. Yet, before the rash of hives, in the brilliant sunlight of normalcy that was immediate post colonial Wazobia, hope tarried fleetingly, almost mockingly, wedged between the end of Anglian tyranny and the beginning of Wazobian folly.

Then, in that short-lived bedazzling sunlight of normalcy, Wazobia's port-city capital, Lagos, was a cosmopolitan hot bed of *highlife*. Even the popular music of the time came to be known for the spirit of the times, as *highlife*. People streamed in from all corners of the new nation. Awaiting them were the city lights of fantasy and faith, the neon promise of a slice of *modernity* and prosperity--a piece of what came to be much ballyhooed in Wazobia as *the national cake*. The City is the magnet. An electric stage prop of luminescent nights, humming factories, sleek automobiles, mind-numbing liquors, sex-on-tap, and the mother of them all, *the pursuit of money*.

The gold prospectors from the rural backwaters of Wazobia pour incessantly into The City--into Lagos, seduced by her bright lights and long nights. They pay no heed to the squalid shanty town tied around The City's cosmopolitan neck like a hangman's noose, threatening to choke the life out of her. Though it is The City's neck at risk of being choked to death, it is the lot of the gold prospectors from the rural backwaters of Wazobia to serve as the noose; and for all its grizzly task, the hangman's rope has no more life itself than the neck it breaks at the yank of the lever. Any wonder the now marooned gold prospectors in the great city of Lagos, whose hopeful fantasies had long been dashed into a huge pile of rubble by the gangantum demolition ironball of reality, coined the famous local colloqialism: 'to go *Lagos no hard, to return na 'im be the wahala.*'

It was upon the shifting ground from live-and-let-live prosperity and national confidence, to unapologetic ethnic or *tribal* chauvinism and national cynicism in Wazobia, that Chike and Bisi grew up. Unlike their parents and their parents before them, whose childhood memories were made up of fighting, serving, and again, fighting Anglians, theirs are made up of Wazobians serving and then, fighting each other.

Wazobia is an enormous African country. A number of estimates put her population at anywhere from eighty to one hundred and twenty million people. The country sprawls across three distinctive geographic zones: sahel, savannah grassland, and rain forest respectively, if one traverses it in a north-southerly direction. Vast areas of its territory are generously watered by the River Niger, its numerous tributaries branching out on a map like varicose veins showing through the unpigmented skin of the legs of an albino woman.

The Anglians, the colonial architects of the modern state of Wazobia, were responsible for putting that jig-saw puzzle together. One Anglian ex-colonial officer reflecting on this subject in his memoirs, which he gave the self-congratulatory title: *Footprints On The Sands of Time: A Personal Account of Anglian Exploits in The Dark Continent*, observed, that the reasons for that action were threefold: it made commerce for the Anglians easier by standardizing business and municipal laws; it unified administrative procedures--such as application of law and order and the civil-service bureaucracy; and, of course, it integrated the command structure of their colonial army and constabulary.

Had Wazobia simply been a zoo in which the zoo-keeper had of necessity to unilaterally decide how to organize the animals under his charge, it might have been understandable why consultation with the captive beasts would have been uncalled for and, at any rate, impossible. But, Wazobia was not a zoo. It was, rather, a territory filled with great African nations.

Nations with distinct political systems, cultures, religions, languages, and traditions. Nations that had dwelt in the same geographic vicinity for several millennia. Yet, Anglia behaved like a zookeeper. With little or no consultation, she mixed up those African nations like tossed salad contained in her colonial bowl, or more properly, like a large patchwork quilt that she made a poor seamstress of stitching together.

When at last, the Anglians made their rather ceremonious exit, the quilt they badly stitched together, began to come apart at the seams. The cracks on the shell of the tortoise, caused by its proverbial great fall from the heavenly abode of the gods, began to disintegrate on the impact of Anglian colonial departure, for no effective adhesive had been applied along the fracture lines to hold the shell together.

The over two hundred and fifty ethnic groups, large and small, in post-colonial Wazobia, boiled as though in a cauldron. The large ones sought to wield national power, the small ones wanted protection from the large ones as well as a piece of the action at the national level. Each was for self none for all. Less than a decade after the Anglians granted Wazobia her political independence, the family quarrel exploded into a full fledged blood feud.

For thirty grueling months the House of Wazobia tottered, divided against itself. The Anglians sat back in the warmth of their homes in their island stronghold, their fireplaces heated with timber from Wazobia; felled, cut into logs, loaded unto trucks and still later, unto steamers at port cities by the underpaid labor of the warring Wazobians, wringing their hands in sheer delight at the seeming folly of the so-called *Negro*.

The civil war that was fought in Wazobia was so fierce, so costly in human and material terms that scholars of African politics characterized it as the bloodiest in all of Africa south of the great Sahara. Millions died of hunger, malnutrition, disease, and actual combat. Some others died in prison cells on both sides, for real and imagined crimes against "the people"--- that amorphous, ambiguous, abstraction, under whose banner every conceivable inhumanity has been visited on people, and under whose edifying standard tyrants, democrats, and political bootleggers of all shades and stripes, have justified their keep!

Chike was quite young during that civil war, about ten years of age when it began, and about thirteen, when it came to as abrupt an end as it started. This is, of course, not quite true, for everybody knew that the departing Anglians set up the structure of Wazobia in such a manner as to self-destruct upon their departure. If they can not rule Wazobia and other parts of Africa directly, then they had to exercise remote control. Failing that, the whole *damn* thing could go to pot for all they cared.

Nothing quite provides the opportunity for such external control like internal disunity and disorganization. In the darkest hour of Wazobia's post-colonial history, the exploits of the Anglians appeared to be working like a charm.

Of all the things involved in Wazobia's fratricidal war, none left as lasting an impression on Chike's young mind as the sheer horror of that violent clash of wills. The horror was most eloquently expressed in the scale and tragedy of human suffering. The endless lines of famished refugees, migrating from one war-torn area of the breakaway republic's steadily shrinking realm to another. The horror and pain of gnawing hunger, starvation and grotesque malnutrition. The unimaginable agony visible in the vacant stares of helpless parents, as their young ones lie next to them, emaciated black rag-dolls of certain death.

Chike also recalls quite vividly the horror of mangled human body parts from the air raids. No. The bombing of civilian population centers--market places, schools, churches, hospitals, orphanages---by the Federal Air Force of Wazobia, was not mere propaganda by the *secessionists*. It was true. It was real. It happened.

After those terrifying air raids with the haunting supersonic sounds of jet fighters and bombers fade into the distant clouds, suggesting that the pilots may be taking a lunch break from their grizzly work as bringers of death; men and women of the Civil Defense and Red Cross, run helter-skelter, picking up dismembered body parts in wheelbarrows, to be sent unceremoniously to mass graves. The lucky ones die with their remains recognizably intact for a decent burial.

Hospital wards and their outpatient rooms overflow with the injured and the deceased. Doctors and nurses work round the clock in a zombie-like daze of fatigue trying to save a life here, a limb there.

At the end of all the horror of haunting supersonic jet sounds, acrid smells in the after-air of explosives and burning flesh, the macabre ritual of gathering body parts, overflowing hospital wards, wailing mothers and despondent fathers, the day after holds out only one sure promise: to bring yet another dreaded experience of violent death from the hell's angels of the sky.

How does a country exorcise this kind of horror from the minds of the victimized? Do you simply not talk about it and hope that it fades from conscious memory? Do you fabricate an alternative fable? Do you tell the children it never happened? That it was a lie—the figment of someone's imagination? Do you say to them that while it may have happened, it was not nearly as bad as some make it seem? Does quibbling over the magnitude of the horror outweigh the principle of inflicting the horror in the first place?

How does a country bury its dark past? How does a country purge its collective memory of the horror of its own willful savagery? Do you punish those who remember—who refuse to forget, as traitors of the hard won peace? Do you hire court historians to sing the obsequious praises of the victorious king, damning truth to kingdom come? Or do you assemble the nation's sages and let the truth they speak free the nation?

Chike had no ready answers to any of these daunting questions; however, there were two things he knew for sure would not go away: his long memory of the horror of that war and the fact that his people were back in Wazobia to stay, for better or for worse.

THREE

Although Chike is studying medicine, politics fascinates him. Everything for him revolves in one way or another on the pivot of politics. He finds every aspect of life inextricably interwoven with politics. Nothing, he, however, feels quite has the kind of intimate and peculiar connection with politics as religion. Its potential as a rallying force, its history, and certainly its inter-faith and inter-sectarian rivalries and conflicts. Each aspect of religion, breeds by its very nature, political consequences. He often finds it amusing whenever he hears people in Wazobia say that they are 'entering politics,' when, in fact, they are always in politics— living life. Perhaps what they really mean is that they intend to run for public office.

One of Chike's favorite pastimes is brain-storming the many contradictions that riddle the institutions and practice of religion and politics, especially regarding their interaction. Seemingly strange bedfellows, the former claiming to be of the divine and transcendent realm, and the latter, the earthly and temporal domain, they have a constant love affair with each other that would leave a merry-go-round dizzy.

Bisi has grown so used to listening to Chike's insufferable monologues about one aspect or the other of religion and the social and political life of Wazobia, that she feels she can recite them by heart. He almost always begins by saying in his acquired Americanism, something like, "My dear Bisi, they have this new thing up for sale and they want us to buy it."

Any one unaccustomed to Chike's manner of speaking, would honestly think that he is referring to a new commodity available at the downtown department stores. Invariably, his discourse would have something to do with the black man, the current political situation in the country, or his disagreement with some moral point or the other propounded by the Church. Both Chike and Bisi's parents are staunch Catholics and that may account for Chike's antipathy towards religion.

There is often this irrepressible rebel in him that seems hell-bent on bucking the religious establishment. His biggest

17

conflict is, of course, the same as with all his peers. He is not married to Bisi, but they have sexual intercourse and the Catholic Church does not mince words on its stance against pre or extra marital sex.

Chike was, therefore, caught in a bind between his natural physical desires and the moral canons of the religion to which he belongs. The two conflicting halves rage on in him like two great warring armies, each commanded by great generals bitterly opposed to one another and intent on winning not just the battle at hand, but the war over his soul.

Perhaps, the general of the rebel army is what his father and parish priest often refer to as *Satan*. Sometimes, it seems the conformity army gaines the upper hand and Chike is filled with guilt, swearing to himself that he will never again indulge in the perfidious ways of the flesh. On such occasions, Chike would be so moved by his feelings of remorse, that he desperately seeks out a priest craving his absolution in confession.

After the confession, Chike feels strangely relieved, much like a paranoia who has just had a very agreeable session with his therapist. No sooner has Chike turned the corner of the street on which the church is located, than he sees a pretty lady walking down the road wearing a very tight fitting pair of pants that accentuates her curves, or another adorning a beautifully embroidered loosely fitting African "see-through" *boubou*, with the shadowy outlines of her figure discerned through the veil like a perfect silhouette.

The effect is always the same. He momentarily imagines how nice it would be to make out with her. He would swear at himself for succumbing to his mortal weakness barely half an hour after he has just come out of the confessional.

FOUR

Chike considers Sundays to be the most interesting of all other days, not only because it holds a singular significance for Christians for whom it is an obligatory Sabbath, but also because of the general relapse in social and economic activities. There are fewer cars on the roads, fewer people milling around, few shops open; although the non-Christians do their utmost to make it appear like business as usual, which in all fairness to them it is. After all, Christians do not shut their stores on Fridays because Muslims are going to pray at mosques or on Saturdays because Jews are going to synagogues.

The Sunday relapse in activities is particularly striking because instead of the usual ubiquitous activities of other days, it is localized at various churches, with the faithful lobbying relentlessly the heavenly magisterium for the fairest hearing and consideration. Chike often imagines good old Almighty God up there overseeing the plethora of petitioning humanity and perhaps having a hearty chuckle.

He often thinks of Catholic high masses are especially theatrical affairs. Catholic high masses, until very recently, in the so called developing countries of Africa, were sung in Latin. In fact, so embedded in the psyche of African ex-colonials is the practice of Latin high masses, that a great many older Wazobian citizens, despite the obviously self-actualizing effects of indigenizing the Catholic liturgy, prefer masses sung in Latin.

This state of mind, Chike believes, is one of the clearest evidence that many Wazobian citizens are still caught up in the yoke of colonial values and laboring under the oppressive weight of a cultural inferiority complex which even the trappings of independence has not been able to erase.

It continues to amaze him that none of his pious Christian compatriots, ever stop to ask themselves the simple question, if Jesus Christ is the one whom Christians follow and he never spoke Latin, why would his followers need Latin as a medium to reach him? Nothing in biblical records or anywhere else for that matter, suggest that Jesus ever spoke Latin or conducted the last supper in Latin, which happens to be the very essence of the liturgy. And lest one forgets, the son of God made man never spoke English, Italian, Spanish, German, or French either!

During the Latin high masses that Chike would sometimes attend, it amuses him to no end how many devout church going ordinary Wazobians often mispronounce the words in the Latin songs, mouthing the phonetics rather than the correct words of the Latin songs. The 'Credo' is usually the funniest of the Latin songs. Not, of course, because there is anything funny about the song, but because of the way many of the people mispronounce the words.

Some would say something like "Credo nunum de o a," some others would say "Credo nunum de o o o," and yet others would say "Credo nunum de o oum," one is left definitely wondering which is which. Of course, the situation is quite understandable, as most of the Wazobian congregants cannot read and write. Those that manage with passable reading skills in English, and perhaps in their native languages, know next to nothing about Latin. Fortunately, the Almighty is more concerned with how genuine our hearts are rather than with a brilliant virtuoso performance.

Another phenomenon which tends to hold Chike's attention is what he describes as the Sunday dress competition. Every Sunday people go to church dressed in their 'Sunday bests.' This dress competition, as Chike calls it, reaches its peak during communion time. Well formed and beautifully dressed young girls and ladies, swinging their hips with practiced precision, heads held upright in regal fashion, wearing their well rehearsed holier-than-thou looks of pious innocence, walk down the aisle to receive communion.

One after the other they march up and down the aisle distracting Chike's attention from the solemnity of the reenactment of the biblical last supper. Also participating in this drama are the men, young and old. For the young men it is usually showing off either their height, well formed physiques, their nice suits or their excellently embroidered *agbadas*. The older men seem more preoccupied with how dignified and distinguished they appear.

At times like these when Chike attends mass on Sundays, he would sit listening to the priest's homily savoring every word of accusation and warning that invariably seem directed personally at him. On and on the priest would prattle about those who lie, those who are greedy, those unmarried people who indulge in fornication or those married persons who commit adultery and those who are of the habit of shirking their religious duties. He would admonish, cajole, and implore the congregation, being careful to remind them that if they do not change their evil ways, God will one day pay them back in their own coins.

Chike would sit in stoic silence listening to themes he had heard again and again over the years, feeling almost exorcised of his mortal imperfections by the very act of submitting himself to the mortification of listening to the preacher. In his more cynical moods, Chike would think to himself that the Pope ought to pass a canon law, Papal Bull or *whatever they call it*, to the effect that priests who are not gifted speakers should not preach homilies. They should simply stop at reading the gospel for the Sunday and quit babbling away unintelligible piffle that puts most of the congregation to sleep.

Jesus Christ, Chike would muse to himself, said that for someone to be saved he has to believe the word of God like a child: that is, with openness and innocence. He never said that his disciples should, therefore, preach to people as though they were children!

It always seems to Chike to last for an eternity when the priest starts plodding on in his seemingly endless monologue. Invariably, there would always be somebody sitting next to him on the over crowded pew who nods off, their head bobbing up and down in that rhythmic no-man's-land between sleep and half-awake. Chike would be livid with internalized rage.   His attention would become riveted towards when the theater will reach its grand finale.

At long, long last, when it appears the priest has grown tired of his own voice, he says,...."in the name of the father, the son and the holy spirit....", beginning to end Chike's ordeal. Miraculously, all his ebbing strength flows back into him. Revived from his stupor, Chike joins in the last rituals, making a big sign of the cross when the priest utters the magic words, "...go in the peace of the Lord, the mass is ended...", thanking God privately for saving him from the mind bending experience of the priest's monologue.

There is yet another moment when a personal miracle occurs for Chike in the course of the service and that is at the tail end of the mass, when the catchiest with the funny looking pair of plastic horn-rimmed glasses finishes his announcements in a sing-song intonation characteristic of the way western Wazobians tend to speak English.

Soon after the priest and his entourage take leave of the altar and the mass of humanity "trapped" in the church building for the one or two claustrophobic hours, begin to heave its way towards the exits, all the boredom that Chike was experiencing a short while ago, vanishes. For him the progress of the congregation towards the exits represent a definite movement towards freedom: to open sunshine, fresh air, innumerable flowers of all colors and shapes and to the beautiful African blue sky-- the true House of God. As he comes out of the Church building, a gush of fresh air hits him and he breathes in deep lungfuls of the sweet smelling air.

More often than not, Chike leaves the church after mass with more questions than answers. The turmoil in him caused by innumerable ambiguities are often counterbalanced by the sometimes strange sense of sublimation he feels after mass. He would often notice that people around him seem to experience what he describes as after-mass-euphoria.

Right after mass as people greet one another, they appear to have halos over their heads; smiling, pumping each other's hands enthusiastically, or patting some unfortunate youngster's head and commenting on how fast they are growing. They would all seem resolved to be better followers of Jesus Christ. Unfortunately, it is often short-lived, for the mundane humdrum of making a living in the modern urban soon consumes their energies and tries their morality to its elastic limits for the next six days, leaving only one day - the Sabbath day - for the sanguine drama in the name of God.

Chike, using the clinical imagination of a medical student thinks of the after-mass-euphoria as being the result of what he calls group therapy. The mass assists people in temporarily resolving their guilt complexes and rejuvenating their sense of meaning and purpose in life. It is an aphrodisiac, their 'Sunday, Sunday, Medicine.' The mass is the drug, the church the clinic and the priest, the M.D. It is a good deal for all concerned - the people and the priest, the doctor and the patient, each needing the other, each thriving on the other.

As the crowd surges out of the church, Chike sometimes stands in a corner observing people condescendingly dropping coins they can afford to loose into the aluminum bowls held out by the weather-beaten hands of crippled, blind and deaf beggars. Then, having confirmed to themselves and the whole world their charity of heart, they retire into the tinted comfort of their Mercedes Benzs, Volvos, Jaguars and the like.

The spectacle rouses the rebel army in him. For he knows that most of those people giving their pittance to the throng of beggars would violently oppose any government policy meant to increase their taxes in order to cater for those beggars and spare them their dignity. By now the rebel army is fully on the offensive and Chike is almost ready to bolt and run and just keep running, until somehow he is able to get away from the whole situation. He can feel the anger of the rebel army rising in him like nausea, threatening to choke him. The hypocrisy of the entire system makes him sick to his stomach.

FIVE

As soon as Chike returned home from Sunday mass he telephoned Bisi inviting her out to Tar-beach. Bisi asked him to give her a few minutes to cook up a story for her parents about where she is going and when she will be back. The 'few minutes' dragged on to a couple of hours and the wait began to annoy Chike, who is naturally impatient.

Why should there be so much pretension, shadow-boxing and downright dishonesty about something as perfectly natural as male-female relationships, Chike thought to himself. How is Bisi and himself annoying or sinning against God by indulging in their nature, of which the Almighty was himself (or was it herself) the sole architect? How is it that God, after creating man and woman to be anatomically different and attracted to each other, now turns around to punish them for being true to their nature?

Observing the immense variety of creatures in nature, it is clear that God, if he/she so desired, could have made human sexuality a hundred different ways or more, all of which would not have entailed the passion of sexual intercourse. After all, some other organisms in nature propagate asexually. Binary fission, he remembers his biology teacher in secondary school used to call it when he explains the asexual reproduction of amoebae to them.

Of course, Chike has no answers to these monumental questions, but that does not stop them from plaguing him. Nor does his ignorance make the burden of the conflict within him any easier. Besides, he is always careful not to become foolhardy about his radical views, as his friends describe them, for after all, he has no proof that his own position is ultimately the correct one either. His people have a saying that the tortoise once said that he had better learn to bear the burden of the shell on his back, for he may need to crawl into it some day.

As his thoughts wander, the telephone rings and Bisi's urgent but soft voice announces that she intends to meet him at the Tar-beach within the hour. A picture of her beautiful dark face momentarily appears in his mind and his melancholy

24

mood lifts, much like the morning sunshine lifts the twilight veil of early dawn.

SIX

Bisi had a hard time getting out of the house that Sunday. She was the last to get ready for church and had kept everybody waiting in the car and her father bellowing. She rushed out still tying her *onilegogoro*, muttering a breathless apology for the delay as she got into the automobile. Her father complained all the way to the church about the youth of today. He sermonized about their lackadaisia, immorality and general disrespect for everything.

Bisi kept a straight face, knowing that her father was indirectly referring to her as he always does when he undertakes one of his self-righteous, hard-hitting monologues against the youth of the world. She always makes sure on such occasions to rob his tantrum of any dignity by her total silence - waiting, as it were, for his rage to burn itself out.

Of recent, since her father got wind of her relationship with Chike, their normally fairly agreeable relationship has gone sour. He seems to find fault with everything she does. At times, he looks at her with such intensity as though he hopes to see right through into her decaying soul. At the slightest pretext, he flies into a rage, threatening to disown her if she does not watch herself. The main problem, they both know, is, of course, her relationship with Chike.

She tried to act as relaxed as possible over lunch, saying casually to her mother that she would be going over to a friend of hers and will probably be home late. She made sure to speak loud enough for her father to overhear. Bisi's mother is an easy going, soft spoken woman with few disagreements with life. She replied in the affirmative, only cautioning Bisi to be careful. Her father glared at her across the table. Bisi averted her eyes avoiding the drama of a contest of wills captured in eyes locked into each other.

He dropped his cutlery with a clatter on the china and said in a tone of restrained rage, "You are going where?"

"But Baba didn't you just hear me telling mama that I am going to see a friend of mine?", Bisi stammered.

"Just answer the question you insolent girl", he retorted, his voice rising.

"I am going to see a girlfriend of mine and we intend to go window shopping for most of the day."

Bisi's father paused for a few moments, probably hoping to score some dramatic effect, or studying Bisi's countenance in the hope of detecting the slightest facial expression suggestive of the falseness of her statement.

"Or are you going to see that...that...Igbo boy...whatever you call him?" he hurled at her.

Bisi kept quiet.

"I am asking you a question young woman", her father raged at her.

"I am not going to see Chike," Bisi lied, knowing that she could never tell him the truth. Her father belongs to a different world, a dying world. A world now nebulous and unreal to her. A dying world inhabited by Africans who were armed with the twin killer weapons of religious moral absolutism - no thanks to the white-kneed foreigners; and *tribalism*, as the colonialists taught everybody well to call it.

Having vented his spleen, Bisi's father appeared now ready to hold his peace. Nothing more was said about the subject for the rest of lunch. Bisi, mindful of the fact that she had told Chike that she would see him in an hour, hurried through her last pieces of *dodo*, picked up her purse and bade her parents good-bye. Her mother responded but, of course, her father ignored her.

No sooner had the front door slammed shut than an argument ensued between Bisi's parents. Each accused the other of not handling the matter properly. Bisi's father expressed his indignation at Bisi's mother for not doing enough to assist him in bringing up their daughter as an upright Catholic girl. She is too soft, too liberal. One day, he said to her, he fully expects that if Bisi brings home a man to the house, she would probably ask them which bedroom they would like to make use of.

Bisi's mother in her usual soft-spoken but hardly obsequious manner, told her husband that his problem is that he thinks that he has a monopoly on truth and that one day he will find out, perhaps the hard way, that there are many ways of killing a rat. Neither party gave in to the other, so true to the family tradition they let their differences go into temporary abeyance, only to be picked up another day - perhaps the next Sunday, after a particularly soul searching gospel or homily.

SEVEN

Bisi could hardly wait to see Chike. A mental image of his strong handsome face brings a satisfied smile effortlessly to her face.

"Taxzee, Tar-Beach," Bisi yelled at an approaching cab, in the unique pronunciation of taxi heard only in Wazobia.

The taxi driver paused momentarily in an impressive eye-hand-leg coordination of his gear shift and steering wheel, that would have left a tribe of monkeys green with envy. The reason for the acrobatics is simple. Cab drivers in Wazobia, and perhaps other parts of Africa as well, want to eat their cake and have it. Or rather, they want to be able to examine their cake for possible consumption before deciding to eat it or not. They want not to have to leave the road in the process of checking out a possible passenger. So they hang their heads window-low, scanning the grass verge like human raiders, asking waiting people for their destinations without actually leaving the road or stopping entirely.

As soon as one of the waiting people calling out their destinations to the slow-moving taxi-cabs mentions a place to which the cab driver is willing to go, what was a slow but nevertheless moving car, suddenly swings off the road without the least warning to cars following behind, exiting onto the shoulder of the road. Curses follow from the other motorists and the unrepentant taxi driver replies with his own insults.

The cab driver Bisi hailed down did a quick mental arithmetic as to his gain were he to run Bisi from Murulere to Tar-beach in the wealthy suburbs of Elizabeth Island. He decided that it will be worth his while if she pays the right price.

"3.00 naira last", the cabby yelled at her.

Bisi offered him two naira, and after a brief hesitation, the cab driver waved his dirty handkerchief at Bisi to get into the taxi. Bisi slipped into the front passenger seat and they sped off. After twenty minutes of hair raising driving, punctuated by a handful of near misses, they arrived at Tar-beach.

Bisi paid the taxi driver off and hurried as fast as she could manage through the reluctant sand to their usual meeting place - a raffia and bamboo gazebo built close to a clearing furnished by members of the *Aladura* church for their sea-side prayer meetings.

EIGHT

Chike was sitting on a pile of moist sand, starring vacantly into the open sea and watching the mighty waves go back and forth in an unbroken rhythm. There is God, Chike thought to himself. That fact being intuitively affirmed for him by the sheer immensity and power of nature, rather than by the flowery words of biblical stories.

The Igbo saying, "*Nka bu Chukwu anafu anya*--this is the God we can see," came to Chike's mind as most appropriate in describing the stupendous power of nature. Sitting there looking out into the Atlantic, its mighty waves making unending peaks and valleys, Chike sensed without doubt that mother nature is the home team in the base-ball game of life and sure to bat last. He lapsed into one of his spontaneous poetic moments. This time he tried his hand at one in his native language, Igbo.

> *Ndu bu onyiye.*
> *Ndu bu okwukwe.*
> *Ndu bu akwa anyi na kwa.*
> *Ndu bu ikuku anyi neku.*
> *Ndu bu ochi anyi na chi.*
> *Ndu bu ichiko alo.*
> *Ndu bu ndidi.*
> *Ndu dika akwukwo ofia,*
> *neso ebe nine.*
> *Ndu bu ebisie, ka awuo nu udo.*
> *Ndu bu isi.*

Bisi tapped him lightly on the shoulder and startled him. She teased him that he is so jumpy because he loves life too much. He got up and embraced her finishing up his welcome with a kiss. When they finally came up for air she pushed him away telling him to stop being naughty. Well, Chike thought to himself, it takes one naughty person to know another. He came at her again trying to wrap her in another bear hug, but Bisi eluded him and began to run. Chike took off after her.

They ran along the beach strip with the waves tickling their ankles. Chike, who was the stronger of the two and also in excellent physical condition, soon caught up with her. Bisi was panting with exhaustion and laughing in-between gulps of air, as Chike pulled her down to the sand, kissing and tickling her. After their playful frolic they sat next to each other looking out into the horizon, glad to have each other. Time dissolved but being stood still and in their togetherness the finitude of time became irrelevant to their being. It was only the reality of their material presence that mattered.

Bisi is naturally introverted. Because of this nature of hers, she has a penchant for introspection, which can easily be mistaken for day-dreaming. She would go into herself and contemplate for long stretches of time in almost morbid silence. Sitting next to Chike by the sea-side induced that mood of hers. She drifted into her own thoughts.

This time she was reliving the first time Chike made love to her. It was also her first time ever, for she was a virgin. In the course of their heated petting, Chike passed the point of no return, his faculties of reason withdrawing briefly to make way for the more persistent desire for carnal gratification. He forged ahead with memorable gallantry. Bisi can still remember vividly how his face shone with sweat and had a strange appearance of boyish excitement and urgency, as he struggled with her buttons, zipper and soon afterwards, her bra strap.

The rest is now history - their history. Her eyes filled with tears as she recalled her mixed feelings of joy and sorrow. Joy at the fact that she not only enjoyed the act, but also knew without a shadow of doubt that she loved him very deeply. Sorrow at having lost her virginity before becoming married, a thing she had prided herself with. Her chastity was something she had hoped would know unchaining only after a proper matrimonial union. All this had taken place nearly a year ago and now intercourse, which had been for her something in the domain of the unknown and wary, had become a compelling habit with this young man.

Chike, who was used to Bisi's day-dreaming as he calls it, left her uninterrupted in her thoughts, waiting for her to rejoin the real world. She smiled warmly at him, kissing him lightly on his rather broad nose.

"How are your parents doing?", Chike inquired from the blues.

"They are fine, why do you ask?", replied Bisi.

"Since when has it become a bad thing for someone to ask after a friend's parents?", Chike mused.

"Come on Chike stop playing games with me, I know you better than that. Now why were you asking after my parents?".

Chike paused a little trying to strike a contemplative pose. "Well, the reason I asked is that I am aware of the fact that you have been catching hell from your father, because we are going out together and I am concerned for you".

"But Chike, you've known for quite sometime now that he is dead against our relationship, why are you acting as though this is new and surprising information?"

"Lets just say that I have become increasingly concerned that I do not form a wedge between father and daughter. No one in their right mind would want that held over their heads."

A little boy hawking African *tie-dye* fabric came by announcing at the top of his voice the price of his wares as though he hoped to drown out the sound of the roaring waves with the sheer strength of his own voice. Horses for the hire, take person after person up and down the beach strip in a lazy almost forced canter, with their owners picking up their trail not too far behind.

"Chike, you know how our fathers are - stubborn and set in their ways. If there is another reason why you are bringing this conversation up why not say so, instead of hiding behind this tired old business of merely asking after my parents. Maybe you are getting second thoughts about our relationship, or maybe there is someone else in your life. Is that it?".

Bisi stared at him with a mixture of curiosity and guarded foreboding.

"Bisi, this has nothing to do with you and me as such. You know that I love you very much and would want nothing more than for us to get married and raise a family. And for your information, there is no other person in my life".

"The point is that I am really curious why your father is so against our relationship. Is it based on moral or *tribal* grounds?"

"I am not quite sure Chike, but I suspect that it might be a little of both," Bisi answered with furrowed brows suggesting deep reflection.

"Well, I would much rather prefer it if his objections are based on moral rather than on *tribal* grounds. At least, on moral grounds one can see how he might have problems with the issue of pre-marital cohabitation given the dictums of the Catholic Church. In that case, his objections would not be directed at me personally. It may well have been Okafor, Musa or Tunde! However, if his objections are based on *tribal* grounds, then I must say that I have nothing but the utmost contempt for them."

Although Bisi understands Chike's position and agrees with it, something about how he was voicing his disagreement put her on the defensive.

"Chike, you sound as though you have been living in Mars all this while. You know as well as anybody else that the problem of ethnocentrism or *tribalism*, call it what you may, has been an endemic part of our society since the Anglian colonialists sowed the seeds of discord among us and left them to germinate on the rich soil of our own devices. The problem is not unique to my parents".

"Try telling me next that your own parents are not opposed to our relationship, or that they are opposed to it on moral grounds alone, and I will show you the exact location of heaven from where I am sitting."

"Well, Bisi the truth is that I cannot make any such claims for my parents in good conscience. However, I honestly believe that the problem of *tribalism* is much worse with your people".

"Wait a....damn minute Chike", Bisi snapped, "What's this 'your people' business? I hope you realize that such statements smack of ethnocentrism....imagine....your people".

"Okay, Okay, I am sorry. I shouldn't have spoken those words. I apologize. Lets change the subject. Lets talk about the beautiful weather, the ocean, people around us, anything else but the issue staring our country in the face. Lets simply sweep our dirt under the rug and pretend that we have cleaned house."

They sat silently waiting for the awkward moment to somehow fade into oblivion. Their arguments always tends to follow the same pattern: disagreement, silence, momentary estrangement, make-up, intensified commitment and knowledge of each other.

A full five minutes went by as each peacock waited for the other to pull in its fanned out feathers of pride and take the initiative of suing for peace. After what seemed like an eternity, Bisi laid back on the sand, the sun caressing her face, legs, and upper thighs. Her skirt exposed her luscious thighs, as she placed both her arms behind her head to serve as a makeshift headrest.

Chike eyed her almost perfect frame. He never ceases to marvel at the dark, smooth excellence of her skin. It is flawless. Not a single blemish. Not the slightest trace of excess fat. Her breasts seem like mounds of black clay, holding out the promise of voluptuous warmth. How many times he has kissed those wonderful mounds. How many times he has rolled his tongue lazily over their turgid nipples, producing passionate sounds that drive him to exhilarating heights of ecstasy. He placed his left hand on her right thigh and began kneading it gently.

"I am sorry Bisi, I should not have uttered those words, please forgive me".

Even as he apologized, he cursed himself inwardly for the power women have over the will of men because of what they have between their legs. "Women can make a man weak," was how one of Chike's friends once put it. He recalled a poem he composed following an occasion he had been humbled by the powers of "Eve". "Hydra", he had called it:

Torn asunder amidst many goddesses,
each with her own beckoning, elusive appeal
of passions yet unexplored--a gossamer.

The goddesses vie relentlessly for my heart,
mind, and soul's loyalty. Yet, after the wine
tasting, and I crave a thirst-quenching
gulp or two, the oasis vaporizes like a
desert mirage.

Eros is their common abode within my mortal
being; a part of me that is perhaps sure to
lead to my final ruin.

34

To each new goddess I hasten my bountiful
tidings; my sand-stained forehead speaking
of many earth-kissed genuflections at
their altar's feet. There I lay prostrate,
forever muttering sweet-nothings into their
wax filled ears.

"It's all right Chike I accept your apology. I beg you to stop
taking out your frustrations with Wazobia or the rest of Africa
on me. I am just one individual who happens to love you very
dearly, not the political embodiment of Africa and all her
problems."

Her eyes were misty from a mixture of growing desire
from Chike's caresses and gathering tears. They lay on the
same spot for a long time fondling and kissing each other
affectionately and savoring the peace of their solitude. Bisi
glanced at her watch and exclaimed, saying facetiously that
she had better be on her way home before her father has her
for dinner. It was nearly 6:30 P.M. and dusk comes quickly in
the tropics. They got up, dusted sand off their clothes and
headed in the direction of Chike's car.

As they sped through the well paved streets of Elizabeth
Island, they passed the imposing building of the American
Embassy. With all the harassment Americans had been facing
in many parts of the world, the embassy had become fortified
much like a feudal manor rather than a diplomatic citadel.
When Chike saw the American flag fluttering in the gentle
breeze it reminded him of the summer he traveled to that
country on vacation. It had been quite a memorable trip.

He had gone to visit a cousin of his who lives in
Washington D.C. "Chocolate City" they call it, because it is
full of black people. He had jokingly wondered to himself
what they'd call Wazobia with a hundred million strong of
them if they thought Washington D.C. was chocolate! Perhaps
they will call it charcoal country!!

NINE

Chike also recalled the incident he dated an *onye ocha* girl--white girl, in Wazobia. She was vacationing in Wazobia from one of the Scandinavian countries, and was staying with an expatriate family, as they are referred to in Wazobia. He had met her at the Sports Club in an exclusive suburb of Enugu.

Every Saturday while he was in Enugu in the eastern part of Wazobia, he goes to play tennis at the Spots Club for a few hours. On several occasions, he noticed a beautiful young White *chic* playing tennis with an older looking White gentleman, whom at the time he assumed was her father. The girl always wore ultra micro-mini tennis skirts which show off a pair of well-formed legs that were quite tan from the intense African sun.

On each of those occasions, he always gets to use the tennis court right after them. The white girl and gentleman would leave the court chuckling between themselves, speaking a language that sounded like German and appearing to be having a wonderful time. But each time he meets them leaving the tennis court, she would say hello to him in a sweet, heavily accented broken English, and he would politely return the greeting, not imagining that there was anything more to it.

One day he came to the club to play tennis and there was the White *chic* loitering on the court as if she was hoping that someone would show up. Chike approached the court cautiously as he did not want to appear intrusive or to be misunderstood for wanting something else. He has enough experience with women in Wazobia to know that any time a man approaches a woman in this manner, the woman invariably jumps to the conclusion that the man has some ulterior motive in mind.

He stood by the side of the umpire's high chair and called out to her. She had bent over to tighten her shoe lace and her mini-skirt rode up her rear end, exposing a lacey white panty. Chike was not sure whether that was mere coincidence or a mating call.

36

"Hello, don't you have a partner to play with", Chike inquired.

She whirled around as if surprised to find that someone had in fact materialized.

"Oh, I was...eh...eh for to play with my Uncle. But he just called, say he much work in the office. You want to play, no?"

Of course I want to play tennis, Chike thought to himself, why the hell did I come all the way from my house dressed in tennis outfit with a racket.

"Yes," he replied in a very polite tone, "I would very much like to play. Do you have a preference for any particular side of the court?"

"No, any side okay. I play any side."

Chike suggested they toss a coin and she chose head and he tail. He let her flip the coin, and when the perfectly spherical piece of silver settled on the ground it was head. She picked the side to their left and proceeded into the court.

One thing led to another, and in no time at all, both of them became very good friends. She said her name is Greta.

He took her to many places that tourists from Europe and America never get to see in Wazobia as part of their inevitable package tours. He took her to his village once, and while they were walking around in the bushes, it started to storm. It rained so hard, coming down in torrential sheets, that they had to take shelter under a huge ebony tree to wait for the rain to abate. Going back to his grandmother's cottage in the rainstorm, could have been tricky because with the dark clouds, making one's way throw the dense tangle of branches, unseen tree stumps and thorn-bushes, would be dangerous. Greta was shivering from both her rain drenched clothes and fear. She felt a bit scared, caught in a torrential rain storm in an African tropical rain forest.

Chike sensed her uneasiness and pulled her closer to his body for reassurance. She melted into his arms as though she had been waiting all her life for that moment. Her large breasts rubbed against his chest. Chike needed no further ado. He planted his lips firmly on her mouth and they practically devoured each other. He felt out the zipper of her shorts and released her with great dexterity. They sank unto the earth and copulated in the eternal bosom of Mother Africa.

This incident soon became a routine. Every week or so they would drive from Enugu to his village, purchase a gallon of palm wine from the village square, and go to his grandmother's cottage, where she would already have a dish of *okoto* waiting for them.

Okoto, is a tasty traditional Igbo dish made of shredded cassava, mixed with just enough palm oil and potash to give it a yellowish color. Cray fish and chunky pieces of *mangala*, *okporoko* or smoked meat are added, along with *ukazu* and *nkpulu aghara*. To say that okoto is tasty is indeed quite an understatement - the dish is positively addictive! Chike had become hooked on the dish since he was a little boy, and has won many converts from among his friends from other parts of Wazobia. Greta was his latest convert and she too become a true believer.

After eating and drinking quite a bit of the frothing palm wine, they would take a walk to the forest. Greta was usually a bit tipsy, because palm wine is intoxicating. She would cling to his arm as they walked, as though she were afraid that he would suddenly disappear, and would let out silly outbursts of laughter at practically anything. The village children they pass on their way to the forest sometimes run along side them, giggling and pointing to Greta and saying "*oyibo, onye ocha torotoro.*" They meant no harm, of course, and Greta, too drunk to care anyway, usually waves back to them while she gives out her silly giggles.

Chike and Greta would time their walks to coincide with the gathering dusk, so that their lovemaking in the forest is provided with the cover of darkness. A combination of the excitement the setting affords and their concern for the sensibilities of a traditional African village dictated that. Once, however, Chike could have sworn that he saw a masquerade spying on them in the forest. The masked figure, barely discernible in the distance, stood perfectly still staring at them, or so Chike thought. When he tried to get a clearer view, it vanished. The incident left a question mark in his mind that has never been erased.

Always, Greta would barely wait till they were deep enough inside the forest before starting to tug at Chike's clothes, acting like an excited child hurriedly tearing through the wrappings of a gift to discover its contents as quickly as possible. Chike would let her undress him, because he knows she likes to do so. It gives her a false sense of being in control which she needs in order to feel that she is making the event happen. With the love dance in progress, however, he would get in the driver's seat. Sometimes, Greta would scream so loud from ecstasy that Chike would be sure that half the village would come running to the forest to rescue someone they imagine to be in distress.

As time passed, however, Chike grew as tired of Greta as she grew attached to him. She would call his home everyday. She wanted to be with him all the time. She loved him and "her Africa," as she would call it, and wanted to spend the rest of her life with him in Africa. The more Greta said these things to him, the more Chike felt like saying to her what his innermost thoughts were. He felt like telling her honestly that he had no intentions of spending the rest of his life with a White woman, and that moreover, he felt certain that she was in love with his member and not with his person.

As for Africa, he felt like telling Greta that he had yet to meet a White person who does not love Africa, but he could not say as much for their love of Africans. He could not, however, bring himself to hurt her. She is nice and kind-natured and he is a fair man. After the contract period of the expatriate family Greta was staying with in Wazobia ended, she returned to Europe.

TEN

Chike's mind drifted back to his Washington trip. He had been in Washington D.C. only three weeks going all over the very well planned city sight-seeing when a remarkable specter took place. The tour of the Washington Monuments, as Americans proudly refer to them, was most interesting. He saw the magnificent structures known as the Capitol Building, the White House, The Lincoln Memorial, the Obelisk opposite the Lincoln Memorial--ironically, an ancient Egyptian symbol of power, as well as other architectural marvels.

Not too long after, however, the bejeweled face of the city began to fall apart like the aftermath of the made-up face of an aging prostitute. The tell-tale wrinkles on the face and the pouches beneath the eyes from too many late nights and double brandies, began to show through the cosmetic facade. Her patrons come in all sizes, shapes, and shades. Night after night the seemingly endless stream of patrons haggle for her transient companionship. Africans, Asians, Europeans, Democrats,

Republicans, dictators, right wing death-sqaud leaders, and nationalist guerrilla fighters, all come to crave her indulgence. As always her policy with all of them is the same: she only counts the ceiling boards for the night for the highest bidder.

Chike began to notice an unusual amount of desolation, poverty and dereliction all around him. Only two streets or so from the White House, sprawls a ghetto in all its bomb-shattered glory--teeming with winos, pimps, prostitutes, drug-pushers, drug-addicts and crime, lots of crime. He began to notice that all was not well in this fabled city of chocolate and honey.

There may well be a lot of chocolate in this city, but it has the bitter after-taste of the cocoa seed. He also became acutely aware that most of those poor, wretched, ghetto-dwellers look an awful lot like himself. Not too long after this new dawn of awareness he found himself one afternoon at a nearby park composing a poem about America. "Americascape", he called it:

Veiled beneath the veneer of gold and glitter of
this American nation, lurks a demon. An untamed,
savage beast. The angry, ugly, raging monster of
hate borne deep in many a' hearts; the smoldering
frustration of dreams unfulfilled; the deepening
alienation of inner-city impersonality and suburban
narcissism.

Everywhere in this modern day "Rome", the foot
prints of this demon-beast can be seen by those
who care to look; who look and care to see; who
see and care to understand; and who care to
abide with the truth.

D.C. tells the summary story of America.
A glittering neon facade, pork-marked with the
blightful trade-mark of a ghetto here, a ghetto there.
City streets littered with human casualties of the
gold-rush; their arms, hearts and minds tattooed
with the tell-tale scares of too many battles lost.
The circus show goes on not minding, for what end no
one seems to know...or care.

Nothing struck him more on his short trip to the United
States, however, than the fact that they fly the American
national flag in churches. Was this not, after all, the country
that gave modern nation-states the constitutionally enshrined
doctrine of the separation of church and state? Or was the
symbol of their national flag permissible in their churches
because they feel, as they themselves often put it to foreigners,
that they live in "God's own country"?

Whatever the rationale, it came to Chike as a great culture
shock. He had, after all, been taught all his life that we are all
brothers and sisters in Christ--rich, poor, black, white or
brown and whether one is from London, Tokyo, New York or
Timbuktu! Yet, here clearly is a not so subtle attempt at
smuggling nationalism into the House of God.

Chike stopped in front of Bisi's front gate, kissed her
lightly on the cheek and as she shut the car door, he drove off
leaving a cloud of dust behind. Bisi went into the house met
by the routine shindig of the television sound in the
background, the chatter of brothers and sisters and her father
silently overseeing his household like the ultimate patriarch.

41

ELEVEN

Bisi's father, Mr. Akin Olatunji, comes from an old Lagos family, that was part of the royal family of that ancient city. Before the Anglians came, it was still known as Eko, and the reigning King at the time, was Oba Okosoko II, a fierce looking giant of a man.

Not long after the Anglians began mastering ways of enslaving machines instead of human beings, the enslavement of African men, women and children began to die a natural death. Just as the cultivation of cash crops in the so called New World awakened the appetite for slave labor, so too the use of machines for manufacturing awakened European demand for Africa's natural resources. Cocoa and palm oil, were two such natural resources that Europeans sought in great quantities from West Africa.

In Wazobia, cocoa grows plentifully in the Western part of the country, which is mainly populated by the Yoruba. In the eastern part, it is palm oil that dominates the produce trade, and that part of Wazobia is predominantly Igbo. Akin Olatunji's grand father, had been quick to realize the change in the economic scheme of things at the turn of century and had, therefore, set about purchasing large tracts of land, which at the time, went for give-away prices.

On those large pieces of land, he developed cocoa plantations that later turned into financial juggernauts. The family waxed strong financially, and although Akin Olatunji's grandfather was a polygamist with ten wives, his wealth was such that each and every member of his large polygamous family inherited sizable sums in their estates that has kept all members of the Olatunji family comfortably well off to the present day.

As a result of his considerable inherited wealth, Bisi's grandfather was able to send her father overseas to study to become a Chartered Accountant. It was while Bisi's father was a student in England that he met her mother, Fumilayo Adetoro, who was in Liverpool, England at the time, studying to become a Registered Nurse. She too comes from a prominent Yoruba family, with a long illustrious history in the old and sprawling city of Ibadan.

Theirs had been a textbook case of marrying right. They were both from prominent families; both of the same ethnic group and nationality. They were both Catholics and in England in search of the "golden fleece," as most Africans used to refer to the pursuit of higher education overseas in the old days. Finally, they were both quite ready to take the big plunge into married life.

Bisi and her two younger brothers were the offspring of their parents in the course of that sojourn in the United Kingdom. The other two children, would be born when they returned to Wazobia after a period of nearly ten years stay in England.

Whether during their stay in England or when they returned to Wazobia, Yoruba culture was always at the center of the life of Akin Olatunji's family. He is a dyed-in-the-wool Yoruba cultural nationalist. He relishes speaking Yoruba and hearing his fellow tribesmen and women speak it with voluminous abandon anywhere they happen to congregate. It kindles an enormous sense of pride and self affirmation in him.

Although all his children speak impeccable English, especially the first three who were born and lived in England for several years, he never speaks to any of them in anything other than Yoruba. He named each one of his children carefully, making sure to give them Yoruba names that bear rich philosophical meanings. His first child and daughter, whom in the secret of his heart was his favorite child, he gave the name *Olabisi*, which means "*joy is multiplied.*"

His second child and first son, he called *Adebayo*, meaning, "*he came in a joyful time.*" The third child and second son, he gave the name *Abegunde*, which means that the child was born during the *Egungun* festival. The last two children, both daughters, Mr. Olatunji gave the names *Olufunmilayo* and *Omolara*, meaning "*God gives me joy*," and "*born at the right time*," respectively.

Besides his Yoruba cultural nationalism, Akin Olatunji is also a devout Catholic. His own father almost became a priest, only dropping out of the Senior Seminary at Ibadan barely one year before he was to have been ordained. This helped to cement his devotion to Catholicism as a young man.

Owing to the fact that Lagos, the hometown of the Olatunji family is a coastal town, the people of that part of Wazobia came in contact with a motley lot of Anglian traders, explorers, missionaries and subsequently conquerors, earlier than those of the hinterlands of the country of Wazobia.

From the point of view of the advent of Christianity, this meant that Bisi's father was like the sixth generation of Catholics in the Olatunji family. The Catholic faith, therefore, becomes Bisi's father as easily as does his Yoruba culture.

As far as Akin Olatunji was concerned, he had carefully mapped out how the life of his immediate family would unfold before his watchful eyes and under the patriarchal guidance of his steady hand. His children were to be raised, firmly grounded in Yoruba culture and the Catholic faith. They would marry into equally well established Yoruba families like his own, and, the legacy would perpetuate itself.

He certainly expected that his beautiful and highly intelligent first daughter, Bisi, who was studying to be a doctor at the University of Ibadan, would take the lead and show a good example to the rest of the children. The last thing he expected from her, especially her of all his children, is this complication of wanting to marry...that...Igbo boy. It is bad enough that she is openly dating the young man and, in all probability, indulging in the ways of the flesh, but to talk of marrying the fellow.... He saw all his life's work seeming to come to naught before his very eyes.

He feared that if Bisi marries that...Igbo boy, for he could not bring himself to call Chike by his name, the Yoruba cultural identity of his daughter and his grandchildren, will be submerged under the weight of that of her Igbo husband.

What would the children be named? Would the young man be willing to let the children have Yoruba first names, second names or even Yoruba names at all? Which language will be the main one spoken in such a household? Would his grandchildren be able to return to the ancestral village of his people, to breath new life into age old Yoruba traditions and customs?

Would the children be able to return for the *Egungun* festival? Would they know of and take pride in the great pantheon of Yoruba gods---*Shango, Orisha, Ogun,* and others, that survived the distant travails of the journey of a thousand moons across the great salt water?

44

As far as he was concerned, there is often as much a struggle among human beings for physical survival as there is for cultural survival. For once a people make the transition from mere subsistence to the creation of civilization, the progeny of such a people assume the unavoidable burden of the eternal custodians of their civilization.

However, should the descendants of such a people to die, either a physical or cultural death, for the two in Akin Olatunji's mind are one and the same, there would be no one left to serve as the gatekeepers of such a people's civilization. He saw the prospect of his daughter marrying that Igbo boy, as being tantamount to cultural suicide and he was determined to avoid such a catastrophy.

TWELVE

T he cock crowed at dawn ushering in the crisp fragrance of an early Monday morning. The long, draining business week was about to start. Meanwhile, some Lagos workers were already well on their way to work, trying to beat the unprecedented "go-slow".

For those starting out a little later, the monster lay waiting for them--the snake-like back-up of traffic, crawling it's way at snail pace into Lagos Island--the hub of governmental and commercial activity.

Chike luckily did not have to deal with the traffic nightmare as he was on vacation. Usually, he would go to bed late either watching the late night show on television or playing jazz music. Invariably, he would wake up late at about 10:00 am. Leisurely, he would take a nice long shower, dress with his usual meticulous insistence on matching the right colors, sometimes right down to his underwear! He would then feast on a large breakfast. Chike would sometimes go to the state library to read up on some medical journals, or to the Lagos University Teaching Hospital to help with real life cases.

Besides these intermittent attempts of his at keeping intellectually engaged, Chike's main vacation pastime is spending time with Bisi. That Monday for instance, they had planned an outing to the picturesque Takwa Bay. Four boys and their girl friends. All of them were going to have a picnic with music and an outdoor game. It was planned to begin at about 12 noon and last until dusk.

Chike had just finished his breakfast at about 11:15 A.M., when the telephone rang. He thought it was one of his friends calling to find out if he was ready to go for the picnic.

Surprisingly, however, it turned out to be his father calling from his office. His gruff voice came through the line, heavy with its usual tone of unabashed self-confidence.

"Hello, Chike is that you?"

"Yes papa, its me. Is there anything wrong?"

"No, nothing is wrong, I just called to inform you and the rest of the family that we will be going to confession this evening. I just got an appointment with Father Balogun. It was so kind of him to make time for us at such short notice. So please let your mother and other members of the family know. The appointment is for 4 o clock."

Chike stood rooted to the spot, speechless. The phone started making a bleeping noise and he replaced the receiver in its cradle. There goes the picnic date, Chike thought to himself. Confession, at the beginning of the work week. Most people left those kinds of things for weekends, but not his father. Every day was perfectly fine for glorifying the Lord, his father would say.

Confession, Chike thought to himself, *whatthehell* was he going to say to the priest? Go over a prepared short-list of "possible sins" in his prayer book and recite them to the padre like a nursery rhyme? Or was he expected to tell the priest that he was sorry that he kissed Bisi. Or to put it in the language of the Church, lusted after her? He found the idea almost hysterical. He picked up the phone and dialed Osagie's number and it was Mohammed that answered the telephone. The rest of the gang had assembled at Osagie's house as planned. They were to go to Chike's house, pick him up and head for the Federal Royal Hotel, from where they would rent a boat to Takwa Bay.

The gang was casually sipping various alcoholic beverages and soft drinks, and making general conversation, when the telephone interrupted their chatter, and Mohammed, who was just coming out from the restroom situated towards the hallway where the house phone sits answered the phone.

"Hello, Chike how are you old fellow, we were just about to leave for your end. I hope that you are ready, because we have wasted enough time."

"Mohammed, I am sorry to tell you guys that I will not be able to make the picnic. My father has other plans."

"What do you mean you can't make it? Oh come on Chike, you are going to ruin the whole thing, what does your old man have in mind?"

"We have to go to confessions this evening at 4 o'clock and there is no way I can get out of it."

"Damn", Mohammed swore, "What is going to happen now? I guess we will just have to call off the picnic until some other time."

"I am really very sorry" Chike continued, "But its not my fault you know how these old folks can be."

Mohammed knew only too well. His own father is a fanatic Muslim, who believes that the only cure for all the world's ills, is to turn the whole world into an Islamic theocracy! Never mind the fact that not too long ago, two Islamic states were at each other's throat for eight torturous years.

Everybody knows that Mohammed's father is a religious zealot. His entire existence revolves around his religion. He would tell his Muslim friends, for those were the only friends he has---all others are business acquaintances as he puts it; that there are two types of creatures he can not stand: he can not stand a *kafir*, an infidel--a non-believer--meaning, of course, a non-Muslim; and, he also can not stand an atheist.

As far as Alhaji Futa Toro is concerned, for that is Mohammed's fathers' name, people who are not Muslims are a sorry lot. They not only lack true understanding, they are sufficiently misled as to call into question the very meaning of their lives. But at least those types suffer from the sound barrier of their own ignorance. They might be saved through conversion. But those other types of creatures, who claim not to believe in the existence of God at all, are not merely misled, but insane.

Allah can be seen everywhere, in everything. How then can some people have the temerity to open the flytraps they call their mouths to utter such sacrilegious nonsense? How can such people dare to poke their fingers into God's eye with such insult? Whenever he hears any one of those American and European trained Wazobian mad dogs, pontificate about so called theories of evolution, dialectical materialism, or some other tongue twisting *dogo turenchi*, he feels like smashing their heads like egg shells with a handy rock, and let their infected brains ooze out like puss from a leper's sores.

Alhaji Futa Toro, says his prayers five times everyday without fail, come hale or sunshine. He fasts with total dedication during the *Ramadan*, without as much as a drop of water touching his lips for the required period of the fast each day. Not a drop of alcohol touches his lips, nor is it bought, stored, or served in his household. Of course, he does not touch pork with a ten-foot pole.

"Don't worry Chike, we all know how they can be, Mohammed said. "I'll go tell the rest of the gang. By the way would you like to speak to Bisi?"

48

"Yes, Mohammed thank you."

"Sure, hold on a minute."

"Hello, Chike how are you doing?", inquired Bisi, her voice showing obvious disappointment at his inability to make the date. "Fine, thank you. I am sorry but I cannot come for the picnic," Chike stuttered.

"I know, Mohammed already told us, it's such a shame, after all the snacks we prepared and money spent. Anyway, I suppose that we can have a picnic some other time."

"But wait a minute, Bisi, why can't we have an impromptu party in place of the picnic after the confessions?" Chike asked.

Bisi thought that it was a good idea, but asked him to hold on while she finds out how the others feel about the idea. Everybody agreed with the idea and the time was set for 7:30 P.M. that evening. Bisi bid Chike good bye on the phone, cheering up considerably.

THIRTEEN

When Bisi came back to the living room from the adjoining hallway where the house telephone sits, hardly anybody took notice of her return, as the group was engrossed in a soul-searching argument over Euro-Christianity, Islam, and African unity and identity.

Mohammed is a self-styled social welfarist. He considers his greatest contribution to society to be that of an unyielding stance against pompous, self-righteous politicians, in or out of Khaki uniforms, who deceive the masses into an unreal sense of security, progress, and freedom. His line of argument in the discussion was, therefore, predictable: radical, contrary, and as he likes to put it himself, "progressive."

Speaking when it came his turn, Mohammed said with a goodly dose of cynicism, "the African is naturally susceptible to the mystery oriented ritual of organized religion. His background, coming out of the past of traditional African religions, is one of superstition, initiated by his continuous struggle with the natural elements. He never had a documented tradition of a God revelation; he made his gods, even though he had a concept of a supreme being. The main purpose of religion for him was to serve as a basis for his social ethics, and as explanations for the natural phenomena and cataclysms which seemed entirely outside his control."

"Oh come on Mohammed," Tunde cut in, "Are you not being a bit too hard on the African. Africans are just like any other people in the world. Religion satisfies a deep seated, perhaps even an innate spiritual need in all people. What the European missionaries who came to Africa called paganism, was nothing other than that common, primordial spirituality found among all humanity. The European missionaries, were merely agents of a larger European colonial advent, that used opposition to traditional African religious systems to undermine our political, social and psychic cohesion."

Tunde's girlfriend, Hadiza, raised her voice in spirited support of Tunde.

"I must say that I am inclined to agree with Tunde, although there are many other issues regarding the chauvinism of African men that I am at odds with him. I agree that all people must have their gods and goddesses, their heroes and heroines. Whenever you rob people of their own gods and

50

goddesses, their own heroes and heroines, their children will fill the social and psychic void created by that denial with the gods and goddesses, heroes and heroines of alien peoples."

"That is essentially what Africans have done in the event of European colonialism. In the place of our traditional gods, we have erected the graven images of alien gods---the gods of our conquerors. Having reclaimed our birthright of self-rule, is it not, perhaps time, for us to reclaim our collective soul as a people?"

Osagie raised another rather disturbing question.

"Is there a tension, a contradiction between Pan-Arabism and Pan-Africanism? And if there is, are there inherent difficulties associated with being a Muslim, since Islam is imbedded in Arabic culture and history, and being a Pan-Africanist? Is it not a requirement that a genuine Pan-Africanist divest himself of the hegemonic cultural trappings of alien peoples, especially those of our erstwhile colonizers?"

"What exactly do you mean," Mohammed demanded.

"Well, what I mean is that it may well be an unavoidable act of self-emancipation for the African to resist the process of continued cultural self-abnegation. Must he worship God in Arabic, Latin, Italian, English, German, or French? Must he sojourn to Mecca or Rome to get closer to God? Must he continue to pay homage to alien spiritual masters and citadels of power? Do we not require, as a necessary component of our emancipation, to have our very own African religious, cultural and political Reformation?"

"You know, Osagie," Mohammed said, "You may have a point here. Take myself, for example, I am from Kano. My parents are Hausa, with a family tree reaching back at least five centuries. Yet, my name is Mohammed. While I have the utmost respect for the Prophet Mohammed, and, therefore, can sympathize with why my parents gave me that name, being such devout Muslims, the fact remains that it is not Hausa, it is not African; it is Arabic."

"In fact, now that I think about it, I can say the same thing about that fellow who owns a mechanic's workshop on Independence Road, em...em..., Boniface. I always wondered how a good Igbo boy got a name like Boniface. And come to think of it, I have never seen any Germans, English, French, Italians, or Arabs naming themselves or their children Emeka, Tunde, Kwame, or Sipho."

"But what's in a name after all?" interjected Ngozi.

"If we are so concerned about African culture and identity, why don't we also abandon electricity, automobiles, telephones, airplanes, computers, etc. I get so tied of the selective Pan-Africanism of arm-chair ideologues like Osagie. It is as though they want to eat their cake and have it. Well, I am afraid that can't be."

"My dear Ngozi," Osagie replied, rather like a teacher patiently attempting to instruct their spirited but misguided pupil, "I am dreadfully sorry, but you have completely missed the point of my whole argument. But permit me to set you straight."

"Well excuse me, professor *Sabi-Sabi*, the floor is all yours," retorted Ngozi sarcastically.

"Many Third World peoples, especially Africans," continued Osagie, overlooking Ngozi's sarcasm, "have grossly misunderstood the difference between modernization and "westernization." While I think I have a fairly clear understanding of what modernization is, I am not entirely clear what many Africans mean when they talk of "westernization.""

"We know historically, that one of the major factors that helped the growth of knowledge in Europe, especially following the period of the Dark Ages, was the untold amount of knowledge that Europeans garnered from Africans, Native Americans, Asians and Arabs. Yet, nobody describes that process as European 'Africanization,' 'Chinesization,' 'Arabization,' and so forth.

"Why is it then, that when in a later age, non-European peoples borrow knowledge about modern developments in science and technology that occurred in Western Europe, it is dubbed "Westernization"? I think we must remain intellectually vigilant, in order to more properly sort out the wheat from the chaff."

Their philosophical banter went on for several hours. Each one making his or her point eloquently and with passionate conviction. After a while, the door bell rang and Chike made his entry. Bisi gave him a knowing smile, the kind that begins slowly at both corners of the mouth like some sort of a smirk and ends up exposing a great deal of enamel. Bisi jokingly warned the others that now that the king of argument has arrived, they had better begin preparing for the party or they would never be done with their argument before it is dawn. Everybody laughed as they got about rearranging the furniture in the living room in order to make room for dancing.

FOURTEEN

C hike's family came to St. Stephen's Cathedral for confessions being heard that evening by Reverend father Balogun, the parish priest and Reverend father Patrick Okoro, a priest who had just returned from Germany where he completed a doctoral degree in philosophy. He was spending a few days in Lagos with father Balogun, a friend from their senior seminary days, before continuing to his home diocese at Umuaka in Anambra state, where his bishop, His Lordship Rt. Reverend Cornelius Anakwenze, was eagerly awaiting his return.

A shortage of highly trained priests, as well as a general decline in the number of young men entering the priesthood, had created a high expectation for his return on the bishop's part. In fact, the Catholic church in Wazobia was in the process of conducting a major study into the causes of that decline in priestly vocation.

As it turned out, Bisi's father, who is also a member of the St. Stephen parish, had himself decided to go straight from his office to the cathedral as well, for the same confession that day. He had not had the time in between his highly crowded day to inform the rest of his family about it. His day had been filled with one board meeting after another, and although he was quite exhausted, he willed himself to go to the church anyway.

The confessionals set up for the two priests, who ironically come from different and often opposed ethnic groups, were placed about ten man-paces from each other on the lower step of the gold fenced area of the altar section of the church. The dual lines of people queued up to take their turns at the confessionals, looked like an assembly line of recalled human automobiles preparing to undergo inspection by the master mechanics of a soul mending factory. By an ironic, but nonetheless interesting twist of fate, Chike's father was on the queue that led to father Balogun's confessional, while Bisi's father was on the one which led to father Okoro's confessional.

Two parents, one Yoruba, the other Igbo. The former the father of a daughter, and the latter, that of a son, who were both in love with each other, but whom both fathers opposed their relationship merely because they happen to be born of different ethnic groups. What were these two patriarchs going to confess to these priests? Would they confess their *tribalism?* Their ethnic chauvinism? Would they ask the priest to forgive them for their ethnocentricism? Did they even define it in their minds as a wrong--a sin--at all? These thoughts filled Chike's mind as he watched the two men - his father and Bisi's father waiting patiently in line.

Chike's father, who was standing a few people ahead of Bisi's father on his queue, got his chance first. He reached the confessional and knelt down with great piety.

"Bless me father," he muttered to the Yoruba padre, "For I have sinned. My last confession was about three months ago."

He went through a number of venial sins--loosing his temper, failing to say his prayers at the appropriate times, using The Lord's name in vain, etc. Every time he raised his head to steal a glance at the priest, he saw the dead-pan look on the priest's face. A face whose main redeeming value is a pair of kind brown eyes. Father Balogun has four large gashes on each side of his cheeks. Gashes, which the uninitiated, save for their uniform pattern, would never have guessed were not inflicted as a vendetta by an arch enemy. Facial scarification, sometimes referred to as "tribal marks," is a tradition of some members of the Yoruba ethnic group.

Father Balogun has powerfully set jaws, a prognathous profile which gives him an appearance of unremitting determination. A combination of his facial scares and lionel jaws, would have given his face an arresting ferocity had the creative intervention of the pair of brown eyes not toned down the severity of the mask.

Having finished with his recitation of venial sins, Chike's father paused, awaiting the priest to give him absolution and set him free. The priest, in turn also paused, as though he was expecting more sins, especially in terms of their pernicious weight in gold. It was as though the priest were daring Chike's father, "Are you trying to suggest that these are the only bad things you have done in three whole months?"

Chike's father stayed his ground and after a while, the priest detailed his penance of six Hail Marys and three Our

Lord's Prayers. Chike's father got up gingerly from knees that were beginning to go to sleep from poor circulation.

When it came the turn of Bisi's father, he adjusted his white-lace *agbada* in the Wazobian style known as '*one thousand, five hundred*,' and approached the confessional with measured steps.

"Bless me father, for I have sinned," he mumbled.

"My last confession was about two months ago."

Bisi's father went on to recite his own short list of venial sins.

Father Okoro, is a young man of thirty five. He is tall and lanky, almost skinny. His face is a rather nondescript mold, whose only distinctive feature is a notably high forehead that shines with an oily sheen in the sunlight, like polished formica. When he grins, his lips reveal exceptionally bad dentition. Much of his crooked teeth having turned brown from chain-smoking. His breath, announces with every opening of his mouth, his bad habit. Bisi's father, who deeply detests smoking, had to endure father Okoro's foul nicotine breath during the confession. Had Chike been there to share the experience, he might have insisted that the nicotine fumes from father Okoro's mouth was already penance enough.

Father Okoro's career in the priesthood had gone on quite well. Through a combination of intelligence, wit, humility, hard work, and guile, father Okoro made it through the junior and senior seminaries with good grades, well-liked by his peers and superiors. He took good care during his final years in the senior seminary to ingratiate himself with the rector, his diocesan bishop, and some of the more prominent lay members of the diocese of Umuaka.

The political capital of goodwill and visibility, which he so carefully cultivated, proved to be invaluable assets when it came time for the powers that be in the diocese to pick the two young priests to be sent overseas, "for further studies," as the bishop had put it. That was how he came to be one of the two priests sent to Europe. He quietly determined to himself at the time to take the greatest advantage of the opportunity and did.

When Bisi's father finished, he paused, in an effort to non-verbally communicate to the Igbo padre that he was done with his recitation. Like Father Balogun, father Okoro hesitated briefly, as though to give Bisi's father time to recall to mind more venial or better still, mortal sins. Making the intuitive judgment that the elderly gentleman before him was done with his confession, father Okoro pronounced his penance of five Hail Marys and two Our Lord's Prayers.

Later on, after Chike had himself gone through with his confession, he was talking with his mother outside the church, telling her about what he called a bright new idea he had for the Church. Chike's mother who is quite familiar with Chike's indignation towards religion expected something in a sarcastic vein. Chike said that given the differences in the penance imposed on people at confessions for similar sins, it is clear that there is a need for some kind of 'quality control'.

"A manual ought to be written," Chike continued, "which standardizes the penance one receives from a priest with the type and severity of the sin confessed. This way, Catholics, the world over, can be sure that they are getting the correct dosage of medicine for their particular affliction. As it stands presently, the quantity and type of penance imposed for various categories of sins is entirely at the discretion of each priest. Consequently, two people, each having committed similar sins, for example, 'using the Lord's name in vain,' would receive very different weights of penance. One might be asked to say a whole rosary, while the other might just be let off on a penance of 'three Hail Marys'."

His mother told him in Igbo that he was a sick person, pointing her index finger to her head to dramatize her point.

FIFTEEN

Fighting sleep for about three hours, had left Bisi's father's eyes bloodshot, adding a fiercer appearance to his face. As soon as Bisi walked into the house at approximately 4:AM in the morning, she knew that her father had her where he wanted her all this while. In hot soup.

In traditional Yoruba fashion, Bisi went on her knees, crying, begging and extolling her father all at once.

"Ejo baba," she implored in between tear filled sobs.

Her father yelled at her, "stand up, you street woman. You have no respect for yourself and your family. Look at the time you are getting home, and you left the house since morning yesterday. Irresponsible thing."

"Baba, please let me explain", Bisi tried to interject.

"Shut up I said. You have nothing whatsoever to explain, your irresponsibility speaks for itself. A young girl like you out with a man until 4:AM in the morning, in a dangerous, corrupt and unpredictable city like Lagos. I will teach you a lesson you will never forget today".

Beating Bisi's reflexes, her father slapped her so hard that she fell down, screaming in pain. Bisi's screams of pain awoke her mother and the rest of the family. They all trooped out to the living room, only to find Bisi slumped on the livingroom floor. Still fuming with a curious mixture of rage and excitement, Bisi's father stalked off to his bedroom.

Bisi's mother helped Bisi unto her feet and supporting her, walked her to her bedroom. Bisi laid down on the bed as she continued giving out short bursts of muffled sobs. Her mother gently coaxed her to stop weeping and try to get some sleep. They will talk about it later on she had said to Bisi in her usual quiet and reassuring manner. After a while, in spite of herself, Bisi drifted off to sleep. Given the emotional and nerve racking experience she had just been through with her father Bisi had a nightmare. Or was it a daymare, for it was almost 7 o'clock in the morning by the time she fell into a deep sleep.

She was walking alone down a deserted street in the night. She could not quite tell what time it was. The street seemed unusually deserted. Not a soul was around except herself. She became scared and quickened her steps. As she quick-stepped along, she kept getting a weird feeling that someone or *something* was following her. The feeling worked its way up her spine, building in intensity like the tightening grip of a vice, and settled somewhere at the stem of her neck. It made the hairs on the back of her neck bristle like those of some feral beast with finely tuned instincts. The faster she walked, the closer "it" seemed to be getting to her. She dared not look behind her. In her dream it was during the rainy season and the rumbling thunder in the distance and intermittent flashes of lightening, added an eerie effect to the whole scene.

As she rounded the corner of the street, the street light threw a shadow by her side. "It" was the strangest thing she had ever seen. "It" did not seem fully human and yet "it" was not fully a monster. Besides, it was difficult to judge what "it" really was by the shadow alone and Bisi was determined not to look back. What she definitely noticed was the immense size of the...*whatever*.

Bisi could no longer contain her fear. She broke into a run, screaming or rather, trying to scream as no sound came out of her mouth. She screamed and screamed and yet no sound left her mouth. She could now hear the heavy breathing of the...*whatever*. "It" sounded like something between the nasal noises of a horse and the mating call of frogs. In short, "it" sounded most unearthly. She ran as fast as she could trying desperately to scream and almost fainting with fear. Just as it seemed that the....*whatever* could just about reach out and grab her, she fell into a big pit and instantly woke up, shaking and sweating.

SIXTEEN

Since Chike came back from the party at Osagie's there ensued a frosty chill in the house. It was as though his parents had declared the moral equivalent of a cold war on him. His father was as cold as an iceberg towards him. Not until then had Chike realized that silence could be so loud. That is to say, that it can have such an overpowering effect on your spirit. Benign neglect is what someone once called it. He was downcast and gloomy, and felt estranged from his parents.

Both his parents tried to wait up for him the day of the party until about 1:AM. By about 1:15 AM, Chike's father gave in to the overpowering lull of sleep and soon after, his mother followed suit. Chike came back that morning, tired and worried sick about his parents, because he knows that they do not like him staying out late.

He slipped in through the kitchen door, tip-toed across the living room into his bedroom which adjoins the parlor. As he switched on the bedroom light, there was his mother fast asleep on his bed. He almost burst out laughing. What on earth was he going to do with mother, he thought to himself. She is always too worried and would come up with the most unexpected moves in trying to make certain he was all right. Worrying for her children, she would always tell him, is both the burden and privilege of motherhood.

This act of sleeping on his bed assured her that she would know exactly when he gets in, since he would be unable to enter his bedroom or get into his bed without waking her. Chike decided to return the favour of his mother's game of wits. He decided to sleep on the bedroom floor, thinking that that way his mother's sleep would be uninterrupted. Just as he finished changing into his pajamas and pulled out two blankets from the closet to serve as makeshift bedding, his mother called his name in a gentle but firm voice.

"Chike, where have you been since yesterday?" At the sound of his mother's voice, Chike almost jumped out of his skin.

"Mama," he said in a slightly tremulous voice, "What are you doing awake at this time of the morning in my bedroom? Do you not think that yourself and Papa are overdoing this whole business of protection and concern for me? I am, after all, a grown man of almost twenty two years of age. Or is Papa's real concern the fact that I am with Bisi?"

By now, Chike's mother was sitting up on the edge of the bed, as fully alert as if she had been sleeping the whole day. "Now, you listen to me young man, where we come from, a child never outgrows his or her parents. For as long as you live, we will always be your parents and, therefore, deserving of your respect and honor until we breath our last and even then."

"As for over protection and concern, you wait until you have your own children, watch your wife slave through nine months of pregnancy, labor through childbirth, and the two of you spend the next twenty years of your lives raising those children, then you can talk to me about over protection and concern."

"Until then, Chike, I suggest you shut your big mouth, open your bug eyes as wide as you can and unclog your wax-filled ears, and hopefully, you might learn something before you are too old to learn anything new."

She got up from the bed, re-tied her wrapper, African style, and walked slowly towards the bedroom door. Just as she opened the door to make her exit, she turned half way around and addressed Chike again.

"And by the way, about the Yoruba girl that you have been going all over the place with, you better be careful before people begin to think that you are going to marry her. In fact, she might even begin to think as much herself. We have a long and illustrious lineage in this family and we wish to keep it that way."

Before Chike could say another word, his mother shut the door behind her with a gentle thud. Chike stood there, blanket in hand and mouth wide open, as much at a loss for words as he had been the day before when his father telephoned with the news about going to confession.

SEVENTEEN

Unlike Chike's mother, his father did not waste time trying to talk Chike out of marrying Bisi on his own. His observations of their comings and goings had convinced him that this was not a matter that he could tackle alone. He called a meeting of his *umunna*, in order for them to collectively trash out what he saw as Chike's intransigence. For among his people, no one owns them self. A person only lives because there are people who cared and care for them and because they themselves have people for whom they care as well. Only a vagabond lives by and for himself and Mazi Cornelius Obinna Nwafor is a far cry from one.

He contacted his uncles, and they came all the way from the town of Egbe, making the long journey to the big city of Lagos. There were five men of stature, not counting the venerable Eze Ozo Okeke, whom everybody calls *Eze Ozo Ojemba Ewe Ilo*---king among titled ones who travels hither and yonder without making enemies.

The other five uncles he invited were Ozo Okenihe, Ozo Obolo Dihe, Ozo Mba ana balu Agu, Ozo Nwa Oji na milu Oha and Ozo Osisi di mma na anu akulia. Each of these five uncles of his are accomplished men in their own right. They are all *Ozo* titled men and the names they bear are not their given names, but mantles of pride by which their peers show recognition and respect for their accomplishments and importance to the community.

Each of those names--those mantles of pride, embody a meaning that summarizes the value placed on each one of them by the community. *Okenihe*, for instance, means one who makes his bluff in the open. *Obolo Dihe*, the path or road that is broad and open. *Mba ana balu Agu*, the scolding given a lion only behind its back. *Nwa Oji na milu Oha*, the Kola nut seed that grows for the community. And *Osisi di mma na anu Akulia*, the tree that grows well on the soil in which it is planted.

Eze Ozo Ojemba Ewe Ilo, did not come by that title idly. He is a man who has lived for about eighty years, yet does not look a day older than fifty. He fought in World War II in different parts of the world. He even brought home a half-breed boy from Burma at the end of his tour of duty there during the second World War, whom he said a Burmese woman bore for him while he was fighting in that country. He had also fought in Egypt, India and parts of Europe.

Physically, he is what a great many people in Wazobia call a *man mountain*. Weighing in at about 240 pounds, with a stomach as flat as an ironing board, and standing at about six feet six inches tall, he is not a man to be easily missed in a crowd. All the hair on his head and his handle-bar mustache, has turned completely white, giving him an even more distinguished appearance. For an eighty year old man, Eze Ozo Ojemba ewe Ilo, does not have as much as slight stoop. He stands ramrod straight, seeming to defy his biological clock.

His vast experience and impressive physique, combine to cast him in the mold of a tower of strength in the eyes of people and thus, into one of the pillars of the Egbe community. If his people had a monarchical political system, like some of the other ethnic groups across the Niger to the west and across the Benue to the north, no doubt, Eze Ozo Ojemba Ewe Ilo would have been a king or, at the very least, a warrior Prince.

He had been personally responsible for several progressive developments among his people since his return from the Whiteman's great wars overseas. Upon his return from India, for instance, he insisted on the formation of what became known as the *Egbe Progressive Union*. That organization, saw to the establishment of an impressive list of things within a short period of twenty years. Within that twenty-year period, they built a small clinic, a primary and secondary school, a town-hall, as well as created a scholarship fund that sees to the education of at least a dozen brilliant students in primary or secondary schools each year.

In all those years, the village of Egbe realized every one of those projects without as much as a brass farthing from the government of Wazobia. Much of the credit for the civic-mindedness and leadership that went into the realization of those projects, undoubtedly belongs to Eze Ozo Ojemba Ewe Ilo.

Few men have the combination of physical size, strength, foresight, determined spirit and congeniality, found in the person of Eze Ozo Ojemba Ewe Ilo, which is why the people of Egbe added the word *Eze* to his *Ozo* title. *Eze*, means King. Thus, the prefix *Eze* before the *Ozo*, means king among *Ozo* titled men.

One community elder, commenting once on Eze Ozo Ojemba Ewe Ilo, mused that if it is true that The Maker breathes the life of his own image and likeness into each and everyone of us at the moment of our creation, then he must have taken quite a lung full before breathing in that of Eze Ozo Ojemba Ewe Ilo.

In fact, two yam planting seasons ago, the Council of Elders in Egbe met secretly, for it was the only way they could meet without including Eze Ozo Ojemba Ewe Ilo, a distinguished member of the self-same Council, in their deliberations about plans to invest him with the highest title of the land: the much revered *Akali Ozo*--one greater than an *Ozo*.

Only two other men in the long history of Egbe had ever been vested with that title. The first was the warrior-founder of the town of Egbe, Mazi Akaike. So great were his deeds in his time, that although he was not even an *Ozo* titled man, both the Council of Elders and all the people of Egbe unanimously elected to vest him with the venerable title of *Akali Ozo*.

The second was *Ozo* Obiora, who, following the first ever and unforgettable defeat of Egbe in one of her wars with Onitsha, offered himself up as sacrifice rather than have the army of the *Obi* of Onitsha sack the town of Egbe.

Fortunately for the town of Egbe, the victorious Obi of Onitsha accepted the offer and spared Egbe from what would have been certain destruction. *Ozo* Obiora requested two days and was granted them, to tie up loose ends in his household and make peace with his *chi*. The day before *Ozo* Obiora's public execution, the Council of Elders of Egbe convened in emergency session and knowing no other way of showing Egbe's gratitude to *Ozo* Obiora for his supreme sacrifice, bestowed upon him the title of *Akali Ozo*.

The next day at high noon in *Ama Egbe*--the town square, *Ozo* Obiora, his hands tied behind his back like a common criminal, was marched to a chopping block set up in the middle of the square. Looking as dignified as ever, his head held high, his *abuba ugo*--feather of pride--an ancient symbol of pride, stuck in his red cap, his well-polished ivory anklet--symbolizing his elevation to *Akali Ozo*, shinning against his black skin, his *efe isi agu*, worn luxuriantly over his white *akwette lappa;* reached the chopping block and gently knelt down beside it.

The men, women and children of Egbe present at the execution wept bitterly not only for *Akali Ozo* Obiora, but for their own weakness. For they all knew in their hearts that few among them had the courage to make such a sacrifice for members of their own families let alone for the town of Egbe. Few indeed, are those whose greatness of soul are ordained by the gods, for it appears as the way of heaven that heroes must die in order for people of the world to find moments of true human communion.

The commanding officer of the Obi's regiment got on top of a makeshift dais, from where all those gathered at the square could easily see him. He shouted an order for silence and a errie, haunting hush fell upon the square. With the same stoic, sublime, other-worldly self-possession, *Akali Ozo* Obiora bent over and placed his head and neck on the chopping block.

The commanding officer of the Obi's regiment barked another order and a hooded executioner emerged from among a phalanx of the Obi's warriors. In his right hand he held a large steel ax, its wide-span blade reflecting in the sunlight. The commanding officer barked yet another order and the hooded one brought his hideous tool down on the chopping block with a decisive thud.

EIGHTEEN

As soon as the six elders seated themselves in the living room of Mazi Nwafor's home, Chike's mother strode into the living room to greet the V.I.Ps. She may as well have been a young shy secondary school girl, given the way and manner she came out as though to meet people who had come for her hand in marriage. She was demurring and adolescent in her self-effacing manner towards her esteemed in-laws.

"Nnayi Nnonu, our father welcome," she uttered to each man, as she curtsied and extended her right hand for handshakes, holding it at the elbow with her left. In Igbo culture, this is an expression of deference and respect, when a woman is saluting a man old enough to be her father.

Each man replied by saying "ori aku Nwafor--the beneficiary of the wealth of Mazi Nwafor, I greet you too."

They extended additional compliments to Chike's mother, commenting on how healthy she was looking and on her enduring youthful beauty. Chike's mother hid her face in both her hands in feigned embarrassment, saying in response that it is to God that all thanks is due for his kindness and protection. She then excused herself, as she took leave of the elders to go prepare some amenities for them.

Soon after Chike's mother made her exit, Chike, who had been informed by his father several days earlier of the meeting that was now taking place, sauntered into the living room to greet his grand uncles. He greeted each man in much the same manner as his mother, except that he bowed instead of curtseying and his uncles took the liberty of patting him on the head, slapping him on the back and even squeezing his shoulder and arm muscles, as though to test the strength of his youthful body.

Each nodded approvingly, telling him that he has grown into a fine young warrior and that he was now ready to engage in combat for his people on the battle field of real life. Chike maintained a waxy smile on his face and a respectful demeanor through it all, wondering inwardly whether the allusion his uncles were making to his readiness to do combat "for his people," was an opening ploy to the main agenda item of the meeting, namely his intended marriage to Bisi.

The expression of pride and joy at the presence of his distinguished *umunna* was palpable on Chike's father's face, as he sat in the living room enjoying the banter of his uncles. The ease with which they hone proverbs into the fabric of their conversation, the dignified restraint and respect they extend one another, and the great care they take to circumvent the use of foul language in their speech, never ceases to amaze him. Yet, these were the very same people that an Anglian colonial District Officer in Wazobia once described as "a bunch of African savages with less decency than dogs."

Could that Anglian albino have been speaking of the same people he is now sitting in their midst, Chike's father thought to himself?

"It is funny how a sense of absolute power can so often blind its wielder of even the most obvious things around them," Chike's father muttered to himself, as he accepted the *okwa* containing kola nuts and *ose oji* from his wife, who handed the wooden bowl and its contents to her husband and disappeared once more.

"Ndichie," Mazi Nwafor said, getting to his feet with the *okwa* in his hands, "kola nut has come."

He made a gesture of holding out the bowl in front of him in much the same manner a Catholic priest does with the host during the communion period of the mass. Watching his father present the kola nut to their *umunna*, Chike remembered when he was much younger and Eze Ozo Ojemba Ewe Ilo explained to him the deeper meaning of the offering of the kola nut among the Igbo.

He explained that the breaking and eating of the kola nut is, indeed, a kind of Igbo traditional equivalent of the Catholic Holy Communion. He said that it serves as a symbol of communal sharing, as well as a symbol of peace and goodwill. It also acts as a medium for the remembrance of The Maker and the venerable ancestors. Finally, Eze Ozo Ojemba Ewe Ilo explained that it serves as a powerful civilizing force, for it helps to remind people of the things that bind them together, rather than those that divide them.

On yet another occasion at the feet of towering figure of Eze *Ozo* Ojemba Ewe Ilo, he had also explained to Chike what he called *omume ndi Ozo*--the code of conduct of Ozo

66

titled men. Eze *Ozo* Ojemba Ewe Ilo said that there were eight pillars that make up *omume ndi Ozo*. Chike remembers those eight pillars in his mind as though he had had that conversation with Eze *Ozo* Ojemba Ewe Ilo only yesterday. They went thus:

> *An Ozo's word is as good as gold. An ozo does not lie, steal or otherwise defile or demean himself, family or clan.*

> *An ozo is expected to be or to have been a brave warrior. For a man who has nothing for which he is prepared to die has nothing for which he is prepared to live.*

> *An ozo must be a successful and prosperous farmer. For*

> *a man who can not feed himself cannot fully own himself.*

> *An ozo is expected to have his domestic life in peaceable order. For a man whose household is in disarray is in no position to govern any one else.*

> *An ozo is expected to be well versed in the history, traditions, customs, sayings and proverbs of Igboland. For a man who does not know where he is coming from can*
> *not know where he is going.*

> *An ozo is expected to be able to give wise counsel; both to individuals and to the corporate entity of the village or the clan. For what use is a man's wisdom if it cannot be put to good use on behalf of the community.*

> *An ozo is expected to be even tempered--especially in public. For nothing can make up for a man's public loss of*
> *dignity and composure.*

> *An ozo is a custodian of his people's collective memory and identity. For without such custody,the living library of a people's way of life--their culture & history, dies.*

Regrettably, Eze *Ozo* Ojemba Ewe Ilo lamented, these days in many parts of Igboland, the noble tradition of the *Ozo* title is being bastardized by total nonentities purchasing the title for bags full of ill-gotten money and polluting the finest institution our forefathers had erected.

Chike's father spoke up and jarred Chike's mind back into the present proceedings.

"I will now hand over the kola nut to Eze Ozo Ojemba Ewe Ilo, to perform the *igo ofo*, for when I am with my children I am an elder, but when I am with my elders, I am a child," Chike's father said.

The six elders replied in unison, "Ise."

Chike's father handed over the okwa to Eze Ozo Ojemba Ewe Ilo and sat down.

Eze Ozo Ojemba Ewe Ilo, accepted the wooden bowl from Chike's father and cleared his throat.

"Umunna Nwafor, kwenu!"

The gathered men replied in unison, "ya."

"Obodo Egbe neene, kwenu!"

"Ya," came the reply again.

"Eh...our people say that he who brings kola brings life," Eze Ozo Ojemba Ewe Ilo, stated matter of factly.

"Ise," came the reply of his umunna.

"I am not going to worry about this kola nut that our brother has brought making its way in the proper geographic order among the people gathered here today, for we are all from the same place."

"Ise," came the reply again.

"Also," continued Eze Ozo Ojemba Ewe Ilo, "I need not worry about offending anybody here who might be my elder by not deferring to them to perform the *igo ofo*, for I am the oldest of all of you gathered here."

"Ise," replied the men.

"However, I must," Eze Ozo Ojemba Ewe Ilo added with a certain flourish, "in the time honored tradition of our people, return this kola nut to Mazi Cornelius Obinna Nwafor, by saying as we always say on occasions such as this, that the "kola nut that came from the king has returned to the king's house. The reason we have this custom is to pay tribute to the deeply held value among our people that every man is a king in his own house."

Eze Ozo Ojemba Ewe Ilo, handed the wooden bowl back to Chike's father. Chike's father accepted the wooden bowl, placed his right palm over the kola nut as though conveying blessings upon it, and handed the wooden bowl back to Eze Ozo Ojemba Ewe Ilo, asking that he do his household the honor of breaking the kola nut.

Eze Ozo Ojemba Ewe Ilo accepted the wooden bowl once more and went through an elaborate *igo ofo*, mentioning a long line of ancestors as he implored their guidance, prayers and intercession with Chukwu.

NINETEEN

After the *igo ofo* had been performed, the kola nuts eaten and wine imbibed, Chike's father got to his feet, clearing his throat as a respectful indirection to call the attention of the elders. They lent their ears to him. Respectfully, and with as little distraction as he could manage, Chike excused himself from the livingroom.

"The elders of my people, I greet you. Our people have a saying that if men urinate together, it produces a richer lather. I have called upon you today, the custodians of our traditions, the beacons of wisdom that guide our people through the stormy waters of life, to aid me with the problem of our son, Chike."

"It appears that he has learnt nothing from all his years on this earth, for though he is still too young to be an elder, he is old enough to shoulder the burdens of fatherhood. Yet, he insists on acting as though he is still suckling at his mother's breasts."

He paused to collect his thoughts, then resumed talking.

"He says that he wants to marry a Yoruba girl," Chike's father said with a heavy sigh, as though he was dropping the moral equivalent of a heavy bag of wet *akpu* on his *umunna*.

"Now, do not get me wrong, I have nothing against Yorubas. Why, some of my best friends are Yorubas. Our own parish priest, Reverend Father Balogun, is Yoruba. It is just that we are different peoples. Their ways are not our ways and ours are not theirs."

"Take, for instance, something as seemingly simple as eating. The Yorubas put their *fufu* and their soup in the same plate, instead of eating the right way, like we Igbos do, by putting soup in one plate and *fufu* in another. Moreover, they use entirely too much oil in their soup, which is why we call them *ofe mmanu*—oily soup."

"I do not, for instance, know how far these allegations may be true, but I hear that as a people, they are unclean and unreliable. Now, even if these allegations are merely rumors or only partially true, is this the kind of complication a right thinking young man puts himself into with his eyes wide open? It is almost as though *agwu*, has taken possession of him. This is why I called for your help."

Mazi Cornelius Obinna Nwafor, sat down. Ozo Okenihe, predictably, spoke first.

"You know that the right people to blame for this situation are the Anglian albinos---the colonial rulers, who forced us all into the confines of one country for their own convenience. If they had left us alone, each group in their own corner of the market place, the business of selling and buying would have gone on, however, each people would have known who was selling or buying what from whom and why."

"Instead, now, they have us all thrown together aimlessly with each other, leaving us to bump into one another, blinded by our own confusion. I suggest that we send Chike to Egbe, and insist that he stay there in the village for one full moon. I have no doubt that in the course of his stay in Egbe, he will strike up a relationship with one of the young maidens there, and all this worry about a Yoruba girl will soon be a thing of the past."

Ozo Okenihe sat down and Ozo Obolo Dihe stood up next.

This might sound to some of you as far fetched, nevertheless, I will mention it, lest it turns out to be the case and I have my conscience to wrestle with for the remainder of my natural life. It is my understanding that there is a place in Yorubaland called *Ijebu Ode*, where people go to obtain love potions and other strong medicines. The *dibias* in that part of Yorubaland are said to have especially potent powers. Is there not a possibility that the Yoruba girl has paid a visit to Ijebu Ode and obtained strong medicine for our son's love?"

"Since it takes fire to fight fire, I suggest that we dispatch a messenger to the great *dibias* of *AroChukwu*, to supply us with an equally powerful antidote. For our people say that one does not use the same thing that is used to clean the ears to clean the eyes."

He sat down and Ozo Mba ana balu Agu, got to his feet.

"It is true that our son Mazi Cornelius Obinna Nwafor, the father of Chike Nwafor, our great grandson, is a good Catholic. And I have no quarrel with that, even though I have no use for it myself. The traditional religion of our forefathers and mothers, is quite enough for me. The question must be

71

asked, however, "When last did Mazi Nwafor make offerings to the gods of Egbe in order to propitiate them? Does he imagine that our ancestral gods are any less jealous than that of the white man? If a man does not tender his offerings to the gods, whom should he blame when things go awry?"

Ozo Mba ana balu Agu, sat down.

Ozo Osisi di mma na anu akulia, stood up and cleared his throat.

"My esteemed *umunna*, I greet you. We have a saying in Igbo that if you see a toad running in broad daylight, be rest assured that something is chasing it. When you find distinguished and aged men such as us gathered here today, there should be no doubt in anybody's mind that something serious compels our meeting."

"This situation is very serious indeed. In all the years that I watched Chike growing up, nothing in his behavior alerted me to the possibility of this eventuality. He seemed such an intelligent, sensible boy. Not like some of the others that I have seen in my time, whose heads are full of 'book knowledge,' and no *ako nu uche*--common sense. And yet, now, here is this bombshell."

"My position is that Chike belongs to us, not to himself; just as surely as we all belong to him and to one another and not merely to our selves. We should simply call the young tendril and lay down the law for him. We should tell him that he cannot marry that Yoruba girl, and that is all there is to the matter. If he decides to go against the will of his esteemed *umunna*, then, perhaps, he can find himself another clan to which to belong! That way, we can arrest this looming calamity immediately. I have said my piece."

Ozo Osisi di mma na anu akulia, sat down.

Ozo Wa oji na milu oha, stood up. He took off his red cap, adjusted the *abuba ugo* stuck on the red cap, scratched his close-cropped grey hair, put the red cap back on, and performed the customary throat clearing to call his *umunna* to attention.

"My esteemed *umunna*, I salute you. Our people say that there is nothing that the eyes see and cry blood. No matter how sore the sight that human eyes behold, it is only tears that they can cry, not blood. Therefore, let us not act as though we are about to shed blood instead of tears because of the current situation before our eyes."

72

"We do not intend to loose Chike to strangers by forcing him into their midst as a result of our impatience or obstinacy. We also do not wish Chike to loose us, because he hears more beguiling tunes from a distant land. We should, therefore, stop all this talk of banishment or virtual imprisonment in the village and think of more creative ways to return our son to sanity."

"What if we search out a beautiful, well educated maiden from Egbe, and contract her to win Chike's heart and hand in marriage for us? We know that the young people of today lack the restraint of their forefathers. I harbor no fears whatsoever, that a little temptation from a dazzling beauty will, in no time at all, net our monkey in the trap; his greedy hands still sticky from the sweet banana he attempts to retrieve."

Ozo Wa oji na milu oha, sat down amidst the laughter of his fellows at the jocular ending of his talk.

Eze Ozo Ojemba Ewe Ilo, characteristically waited for everyone to speak before himself. He listened carefully to everyone and made mental notes of the strengths and weaknesses of each speaker's position. He stood up, his looming frame cutting an impressive figure. He played with his chalk-white handle-bar mustache, as he awaited the undivided attention of his fellows.

"Our esteemed *umunna*, I greet you. I have listened very attentively to each one of you. It is clear to me that we all want the same thing for our son, Chike. We all want the best for him. That is understandable, for we care deeply for him and do not wish to let down our glorious ancestors. For as our people say, a boy who has been handed live charcoal fire on a cold harmattan morning by a neighbor, does not want the wind to extinguish it before he reaches his mother's house."

"Yet, it seems to me that we must make a distinction between wanting the best for our son, Chike, and wanting what is best for him. For the two are not the same. In the first instance, we have a presumption of what is best for him. In the second instance, we make provision for the young man to decide what he feels is best for himself."

"Moreover, all of you seem to have completely lost sight of what ought to be the single most important element in this whole matter--*ifunanya*. Which one of you can honestly say that old age has so completely dried them up that they can no longer recall how wildly the flames of love burned in their hearts when they took their first bride?"

"We all know that *ifunanya* is an orphan child. It knows not father or mother, brother or sister, clan or nation. It tarries where it can and settles where it must. It pitches tent wherever it finds the open arms of welcome and solace. It is at such a place, wherever it turns out to be, that *ifunanya*—love, calls home."

"Although I have never told any of you the details of how I got my son in Burma, and you have all politely refrained from prying, I can tell you here and now that without the solace and comfort the mother of that boy provided me in that strange far off land, my spirit would not have survived the adversity I had to face there."

"My esteemed, *umunna*, all of you know what a proud Igbo man I am. All of you know that I love Igboland with every fiber in my body. All of you know that I would gladly give my life in a heart beat to defend our great culture and fatherland. Yet, If you ask me did I love that boy's mother? My answer would be YES! A thousand times yes! Where there days when I was young, that my throat was parched from thirst for the sweet nectar of her love? Yes! A thousand times yes."

"And yet, she was not even of our race, speak less of our ethnic group. I did not bring her back to Igboland with me, not because I did not love her, but because I had my sights firmly set upon the raising up of our people from the degradation and poverty that the Anglian colonialists had subjected us. For it has been ordained, that for some would be the task of laying the sturdy foundations for the erection of a great nation."

"I am not, of course, saying that there are no good reasons for healthy skepticism and caution. What I am saying is that we must keep that all important element of love in mind, for my own experience has taught me a singular lesson: *racial, ethnic and national boundaries have no place in the geography of the human heart.*"

"As for those of you who may harbor fears about how our culture will fare if Chike ties the knot with someone not of our ilk, let me assure you that while it is true that blood is thicker than water, it is equally true that culture is thicker than blood. Language, is the umbilical cord of a people's culture from one generation to another. If we raise the children that Chike and the Yoruba girl will have as Igbos, it will not matter that her blood flows in their veins."

"Let us, therefore, at least, give the young man a chance to address his esteemed *umunna* directly on the matter. That is all I have to say."

As Eze Ozo Ojemba Ewe Ilo sat down, a spirited chatter broke out among the gathered elders as they animatedly discussed the points he raised.

Chike's father got to his feet.

"My esteemed *umunna*, I salute you. I thank you for the *alo*--wisdom that you have all contributed to this matter today. It is not any wonder that our people say that one who has people, is more blessed than a one who has money. With all due respect to all of you, there is not one suggestion or statement that has been made here today that has not occurred to me at one point or another, except the last words spoken by our great father, Eze Ozo Ojemba ewe Ilo."

"That is not, of course, due to the fact your suggestions and statements are so simple minded that even I, a mere tendril to you all, had thought of them. Rather, it is the case, that if, as the saying goes, great minds think alike, then it must be equally true that even greater minds think unlike others."

"I was told that many years ago, when Eze Ozo Ojemba ewe Ilo returned from the Whiteman's great war overseas, his suggestion then that Egbe form a 'progressive union,' build a clinic and its own schools and establish a scholarship fund, met with a great deal of skepticism and resistance. There are even some among you today, I have been told, that had vehemently disagreed with him. Yet, today, it is clear before all our eyes that his suggestions showed great wisdom."

"Today, we are faced with another critical decision, and once again, Eze Ozo Ojemba ewe Ilo has taken a position different from the rest of you. Is the great Eze Ozo Ojemba ewe Ilo once more managing a better glimpse of the future from a higher perch or has his long years on earth taken their toll even on one such as he?"

"When I consider all that Eze Ozo Ojemba ewe Ilo has accomplished in his life time and the exemplary life that he has led, I am forced to say that his position deserves serious consideration. However, I will be being less than truthful, if I do not admit that there is, perhaps, as much skepticism in my mind towards his suggestion as might have been in each of your minds nearly a half century ago. Yet, I agree with Eze Ozo Ojemba ewe Ilo, that we should invite Chike to tell us what is going on in his head, and, perhaps, his heart. I thank you for you patience."

Chike's father sat down.

TWENTY

A short while later, Chike's father left the livingroom to fetch his son. When Chike heard the knock on his bedroom door, he knew instinctively that it was his father. He felt like a man on death row for whom the moment of truth had arrived, except that in this case, his father and his esteemed *umunna* are the executioners. He got up and opened the door.

"Yes, papa,?" Chike said, as though he did not know why his father was there.

"Come with me, Chike, our esteemed *umunna* has granted you audience so that you can explain to us directly, what is going on between yourself and that Yoruba girl."

"Very well, papa," Chike replied, "I will follow right behind you."

Chike returned to the livingroom with his father, their entrance largely ignored by their *umunna*, who were still engrossed in lively discussions over the earlier comments made by Eze Ozo Ojemba Ewe Ilo and Mazi Nwafor.

Mazi Nwafor returned to his seat, leaving Chike to sit on a large, multicolored ottoman, that his father acquired from Kano in northern Wazobia, during one of his trips to *ugwu a'usa*. After a short while, Chike's father cleared his throat loudly and the banter among his *umunna* simmered down until silence prevailed.

"Our esteemed *umunna*, I salute you. We have a saying in Igbo that there is no point searching for something you can find on the *uko ani*—floor of a house in the *uko enu*—the loft of the same house. It serves no useful purpose for us to carry on with our imaginative speculation, when we can find out what we wish to know directly from the horse's mouth. I have done as you instructed me. Here is our son, Chike."

Chike's father sat down.

Ozo Obolo Dihe asked Chike to stand up and address his esteemed *umunna*. Chike felt as though he was standing naked before a distinguished panel of generals at his court martial. Wizened faces, animated by pairs of intelligent marble eyes, starred back at him from all corners of the livingroom.

Knowing his grand uncles, Chike was fairly certain that they will be watching and listening for every minute detail in his presentation. Even before he gets to the substance of the matter at hand, they will watch to see if he slips up on procedural matters. Does he know how to properly greet his esteemed *umunna*? Can he handle the oratorical nuances of delicately balancing the use of proverbs, artfully massaging the extra-large, but well deserved egos of his custodial elders?

Can he persuade with skillfully embroidered oration, without loosing his composure and dignity? Without becoming bellicose and brash? These are not men to be trifled with. The slightest hint of insolence, quickly concludes for them a meeting such as this, long before the substance of the matter at hand is ever reached.

Chike, therefore, knew that he must choose his words with as much care as a skilled surgeon uses his scapel. He must locate the precise part of the anatomy he wishes to apply the blade and cut with swift accuracy. There is no margin for error. No room for the crude, butch-up job a blunt instrument can make. His esteemed *umunna* waited patiently for the young tendril before them to take his first tentative steps in a spirited effort to walk.

"My esteemed *umunna*," Chike began in a somewhat timid voice.

"It is only by your good graces that I stand before you today. Otherwise, what business does an *adanchi*--a pygmy, have in the midst of *gwodogwodos*--giants; or a bald *udene*--vulture, with a barber? After all, our people have a saying that if a young man who has not yet attained maturity, pretends to it by prematurely adorning the *ogodo* of his elders, when a strong wind comes, it will carry him away, *ogodo* and all. It is, therefore, by your kind permission alone, that I dare to open my mouth in front of an august gathering such as this."

His grand uncles nodded their heads in restrained agreement, indicating to Chike that however amateurish his performance, he is, at least, on the right path. Emboldened by that, he raised the ante a notch.

"Someone once said that the ancients are giants. But that we, the progeny of the ancients, are standing on the shoulders of our ancestral giants and, therefore, able to see farther than them."

Chike's father sat amongst his *umunna*, listening to his son talk, torn between pride at his son's undeniable eloquence and a little irritation at his effrontery. Chike pressed on.

"There is a very important reason our people believe in having many children. It is not, as some people suppose, because our menfolk can not seem to get enough of their wives' good thing. Or, as other equally ignorant outsiders have speculated, that they merely seek to fill their households with farm hands."

"Rather, they have children so that their offspring can be their eyes and ears into the future. So that their offspring can stand on their shoulders and see further than themselves."

"Given the accumulated wisdom in this room, it is hardly in my place to tell you that for any people to make progress in the world, there must be a symbiotic relationship between the elderly and the young in such a society. The young must listen to the elders, lest they forget their own history and customs. The elders must make room for the innovative dynamism of the young, lest they hold the nation hostage to the dead hand of the past."

"After all, our people say that anyone who thinks that his thumb is the only useful finger because it is big and sturdy, has never tried to scratch an itch in the inside of their ear."

By now, Chike's granduncles were showing unconcealed appreciation for his erudition, and Chike, not one to pass up an opportunity endeavored to press home his advantage.

"Has it ever occurred to any of you, why only a handful of Anglian albinos were able to rule over so many Africans during the colonial period?"

"That's an easy one, my young tendril," interjected Ozo Obolo Dihe.

"The Anglian albinos had guns and we did not. That allowed them to engage mostly in target practice rather than real war in Africa during the colonial period. Why, even an old woman, could have stayed in the ant holes* they make in the earth, and taken pot shots at any and all moving objects."

"It would have been quite another story had African warriors the opportunity to meet the Anglian albinos man-to-man. We would have taught the Anglian albinos a few home lessons from the pages of the book of the legendary *Amalinze*, the cat.

"I do not disagree with the point you have made, Ozo Obolo Dihe," Chike respectfully replied, "However, had Africans the benefit of unity beyond the narrow confines of their ethnolingual groupings, the Anglian albinos would have had a much taller order "pacifying" Africans, despite their guns and their ant holes."*

"So long as the African fights a two-pronged war; one against the intruding albinos and the other against himself, he is sure to loose. In such a scenario, the albinos will require very few guns indeed, for Africans will do much of their work for them."

"The point I am trying to make, my esteemed *umunna*, is that we Africans are not each other's enemies. We are, instead, allies. Allies in a war far greater than anyone of our individual groupings. We come from the same womb of Mother Africa. Our foes are the same; our destinies, forever, joined."

"How is it that within our own ethnic groupings, we realize the value and importance of marriage as a means of cementing blood and cordial relations between families, villages and clans. Yet, we do not see the same thing as able to cement blood and cordial relations between our various African nations and ethnic groupings?"

---

*Trench Warfare.

"The charge of your generation, my esteemed *umunna*, was to reclaim our land from the Anglian albinos and cleanse it of the polluting shame of our humiliation and the desecration of our glorious culture at their hands. One must admit, whatever exceptions are made, that your generation has given a good account of itself on that score."

"The charge of my generation is, I believe, to put to maximum use, the credits that your generation chalked up on our behalf. Our charge is not now to cover up the emperor's nakedness, but to dress him up in his finest robes."

"We can not properly achieve that end, however, without the aid of all of Africa's children. For as an Igbo saying states, the journey to a strange far off land undertaken by one person alone, is the journey of a dead man."

"It is because of all that I have said to you this evening, the great love in my heart for Bisi, the Yoruba girl, and my knowledge of her good and noble character, that I ask for the permission and blessing of my esteemed *umunna*. I thank you for hearing me out."

Chike took his seat.

After a few minutes of silence, Eze Ozo Ojemba ewe Ilo, asked Chike to leave the room for a few minutes in order that the gathered elders can *chiko alo*--put their heads together. Chike was further informed that he will be sent for as soon as the elders reach a verdict. Chike excused himself and left the room.

As soon as the door of the livingroom shut behind Chike, Eze Ozo Ojemba ewe Ilo, asked any one of the assembled elders who wished to express any objections with the granting of their permission and blessing on Chike to voice them now. No one spoke.

Eze Ozo Ojemba ewe Ilo, turned to Chike's father and asked him to go and fetch Chike, so that his *umunna* can cover him in the warm embrace of their approval.

TWENTY ONE

The feast marking the end of the *Ramadan* had just ended and people were gradually returning to their normal work schedules. The semi-arid environs of Kano with its jagged-edged streets and colorful market places seem like a surreal dust-bowl swirling with masses of people clad in mostly white *baban rigas* and brightly colored flowing *boubous*.

Blind beggars stroll around the streets of Kano, holding walking sticks in their right hands like mechanical extensions of their arms that helps them feel their way through the sightless void that engulfs them. A young boy or girl, usually the beggar's child, walks in front of the beggar, who places his left hand on the right shoulder of the young guide.

For some inexplicable reason, those blind beggars are almost always men. The young guide holds out an aluminium bowl whose paint coating has peeled at several places exposing rusting metal, as they periodically call out a refrain in Hausa to people from whom they solicit alms.

The beggars of the streets of Kano drift from place to place in that timeless city, dressed in their once-white, now dirty and tattered cotton robes. Their hand-woven, well-worn skull caps and cow hide sandals seem like costumes designed for clowns performing in a city-wide circus. The spectacle would have been hilarious were it not for the fact that it is a real-life human tragedy.

Those beggars are a poignant fixture in that time-honored city. The kind of fixture that bestows a defining personality to a place, without serving any other practical purpose. *The beggars of the streets of Kano*: It has a melancholy and almost poetic ring to it, one which any frequent visitor or resident of the city can easily detect in the sound of the beggar's voice or that of his guide, repeatedly chanting '*babi Allah.*'

Mosques are strewn around the ancient city of Kano like giant rubies glittering randomly in the sun. Reflections of the brilliant sunlight of the Western Sudan bounce off the characteristic gold-plated domes of the mosques, forcing squinting stares from naked eyes. Their tall, slender, tower-like minarets point to the heavens, ringed with one or two narrow balconies from where the *muezzin* calls the Muslim faithfuls to prayer.

On Fridays, the mosques of Kano and their immediate surroundings swarm with Muslim faithfuls, hurrying to and from prayer. This human herd of faithfuls is in stark contrast to the Christian herd of faithfuls that fill the streets of Kano on Sundays, similarly hurrying to and from their various churches. Both Christian and Muslim faithfuls seek absolution, exultation and ultimately, salvation. Each so different in form, yet so similar in essence.

One well-known Wazobian theologian contemplating this matter mused that although Christianity is the older brother of Islam, the two are siblings trying to establish separate identities for themselves.

The streets of Kano, like those of many of the other cities in Wazobia, are an unforgettable medley of sights, sounds and smells. Fulani herdsmen appear seemingly from nowhere, their herd of cattle saunter down the middle of major thoroughfares, rudely forcing man and machine off the road or to a standstill, as they commence their southerly journey in search of greener pastures. Frustrated automobile and motorcycle drivers toot their horns and shout at the inscrutable herdsmen to no avail, trying to get them and their cattle out of the way.

Nowhere is the mysterious, if not mystical, relationship between man and beast more apparent than in that between Fulani herdsmen and their cattle. The primordial capacity of man to subordinate members of the animal kingdom to his intellect and will; the capacity of man to command and condition the obedience of animals.

In the midst of a hundred or more rumbling herd of cattle, there are usually only two or three Fulani herdsmen in control. Through a combination of unique click sounds periodically called out to their cattle and the occasional cracking of the whips they otherwise carry across their shoulders, the two or three Fulani herdsmen expertly steer their herd of cattle through the cluttered streets of Kano, as though merely enacting the natural order of things.

Once in a while, a lone cow strays from the herd, prompting one of the Fulani herdsmen to sprint off after the renegade beast, coaxing and whipping the animal back to the rest of the herd. But how and why there is never a stampede of the herd of cattle, even in the midst of the cacophonous jangle of sounds in the street of Kano is, no doubt, part of the enigmatic bond between the herdsmen and their cattle.

Along the side streets of Kano, at T-junctions, on the shoulders of boulevards and at narrow alleys that lead to shadowy cul-de-sacs which reconnect major roads in a grid-like network that residents of the nondescript neighborhoods know like the backs of their hands, one intermittently finds earth-mounds alive with naked flames or smoldering red-hot charcoal. These are *suya spots*, at which thinly sliced chunks of choice beef marinated in a ginger and pepper peanut sauce, and spiked through with wooden spokes, keebab-style, and stuck in the earth-mounds, slowly roast in a ring around a fire.

Not too far from a suya spot, one finds what can only be described as *tea-stops*, where the Hausa come in an incessant flow to indulge their love for scalding hot tea and a locally brewed alcoholic beverage known as *burukutu*.

Without a doubt, the proprietors of those tea-stops have honed into a fine art the pouring of tea from aluminum kettles into tea cups or mugs. At every tea-stop, the dramatic art of deftly pouring tea goes on to the casual delight of regular patrons and the amazement of new comers. At a height of a foot or more from the tea cup or mug, the server pours the scalding liquid in a stream that resembles a waterfall, without as much as a noticeable drop falling on the table or on the watchful audience sitting around it. No sooner has the streaming hot liquid been poured into the tea cup than the server reverses the process, pouring the liquid from the tea cup or mug back into the kettle from no less an elevation. Back and forth the server goes, clearly trying to cool the scalding liquid, while at the same time entertaining and showing off to the customers. Many who can not afford the few kobos for the cups of tea stand around the tea-stops all the same, marveling at the skill of the tea servers.

Merchants heading to the local produce markets of Kano, cram so many goods into lorries that their wooden-frame carriers sag dangerously from years of overload and neglect. Goats, chickens, leather skins, vegetables of all kinds, large yam tubers, peanuts, palm and cocoa nut oils; and a thousand or more spices, fill up bamboo and raffia-palm baskets, cardboard boxes, cloth sacks, aluminum tins and the like, in transit to market places by human, animal or motorized vehicles of all shapes and sizes. As varied as these items are, so are the accompanying smells that emanate from them, treating human nostrils to an array of exotic aromas unimaginable in temperate climes. It is a scene that either exhilarates or exasperates its beholder. There is no middle ground and no neutral zone.

TWENTY TWO

Kano is Mohammed's birth place and residence. His father claims that his family has lived in Kano ever since the city was founded in the 10th or 11th century A.D. While no one in living memory can authenticate that claim by Mohammed's father, there is equally no one in living memory that can remember when the Futa Toro family has not lived in Kano.

A succession of Mohammed's great grandfathers and granduncles served as royal scribes; *mallams*; medicine men; and always, great cattle herdsmen. Mohammed's father is related to the ruling family of the Emir of Kano. In a monarchical system, there is no privilege more precious than blood-ties to the royal family. Besides guaranteeing you an irrevocable place of honor, power, and privilege in the social pecking order, it practically guarantees a place of leadership for you once you reach the right age.

Alhaji Futa Toro, is himself a haulage magnet. His company specializes in transporting longhorn cattle in twelve-ton trucks across the length and breadth of the federation of Wazobia. Every now and again, a lucrative contract falls into his lap from the breadfruit tree of his blood ties to a number of strategically placed members of the federal government of Wazobia.

A few blockheads, especially many of the *dogo turenche* speaking southern book worms, insist on characterizing such deals as "nepotism" and "bribery and corruption." As far as Alhaji Futa Toro is concerned, that is their business. It is in the very nature of things that someone standing close to or beneath a breadfruit tree will have a much better pick of its juicy fruits, than one standing much further afield. He happens to be one of those fortunate ones beneath the generous shade of the breadfruit tree. As for those other Wazobians who are less fortunate than himself, well, perhaps it is the will of Allah.

Alhaji Futa Toro's great hopes and plans for his son Mohammed, harken back to the circumstances of his birth. While it is true that the Koran permits a man to marry up to four wives—although it has never been made clear what it is about the magic number four, the Koran does not require of a man that he marry more than one wife.

Alhaji Futa Toro, had, in fact, not set out initially to marry four wives. That number crept up on him as he desperately sort to have a manchild. As though it were some kind of a curse, his first, second and third wives, each had four children all of whom turned out to be girls. It is not that he does not love and cherish his daughters, for he picked their mothers with great care and his daughters are exceptionally beautiful and very well mannered.

It is, however, a social fact of life that a man of his *timber and caliber*, as one of the late pioneer-politicians of Wazobia used to humorously refer to himself, needs a male heir to his family name. So, wearily, he sort out yet another bride--his fourth wife, and took his final stab at fate. He prayed and fasted fastidiously, begging Allah for his benevolent mercy and, alas, Allah showed his merciful hand and blessed him with a son, whom he gratefully named, Mohammed.

Interestingly enough, since his fourth wife gave birth to his son Mohammed, she has not been able to conceive again. But that was quite all right with Alhaji Futa Toro, for Allah had crowned his end-game with a sweet victory. He had decided long ago to dedicate his son, Mohammed, to the Prophet and to Allah. Perhaps, if Allah smiles on him long enough, his son, Mohammed, might grow up to be a great *Imam*, a great Koranic scholar, spreading light and understanding to millions of benighted people.

It, therefore, came as a big blow to Alhaji Futa Toro when his son refused to heed his counsel and insisted on going South, to the University of Ibadan, to study medicine. In his heart, his father knew that once Mohammed finds himself in the midst of their southern compatriots, his already nominal interest in religion would wane even further. But what was the choice? The modern world was already upon us all in a kind of forced marriage for better or for worse.

If one does not let Hausa children master the modern educational and technological systems and skills, there is the risk of their southern neighbors serving as the only technocrats of the nation. Even as Alhaji Futa Toro contemplated his son's decision, he knew there was hardly anywhere you can go in Kano or other parts of northern Wazobia in search of medical attention, automobile mechanics, electricians and the like, that you will not encounter a Southerner--especially, the *inya miri-* -the Igbos.

They are like technocratic locusts that descended on the North. Unless his people develop their own cadre of technocrats, capable of carrying the full weight of the technological demands of the modern world, they will remain caught between the rock of the services of the *bature*--the white man, and the hard place of the services of their southern compatriots. Based on that alone, Alhaji Futa Toro relented and allowed his son to enroll at the University of Ibadan.

TWENTY THREE

Mohammed always wanted to attend university in the southern part of Wazobia. The oldest and most illustrious institutions of higher learning in the country are in the South, along with some of the finest intellectuals in Africa and possibly, the world.

This is not to say that there are no reputable universities in northern Wazobia, or none with respectable age and history under their belts. There are at least two such premier institutions in the North. But even in those two universities, the ranks of their faculty are filled mostly with intellectual manpower from the South.

Mohammed had sense enough, however, to know that the situation was not due to genes. The reasons lay, instead, in historical and cultural accidents. One historical accident is the coming of Islam to northern Wazobia and the theocratic strictures it imposed on much of the culture of the North. A related cultural accident is the political and cultural implications of the traditional monarchical system of government in the North. The first historical accident made for suffocating orthodoxy and the second made for monarchical absolutism.

Mohammed especially admired the freedom of life in the South. The atmosphere of secular liberalism that pervades the everyday lives of people, permitting them to prosper as *individuals*. For Mohammed, southern Wazobia represents a living symbol of individual liberty and self-actualization. That was the main reason he chose to attend university there. To immerse himself in the modern intellectualism and bustling, *go-getter*, mercantile tempo of the southern life of Wazobia.

The one thing that might have made him stay back was the gorgeous Fulani girl he was dating at the Federal Government School in Kano. Her name is Fatumata and she is easily the most beautiful woman Mohammed had ever set eyes on. She is tall and slender, with angular features that make her look like a beautiful caucasian woman dipped in caramel syrup. She has thick long black hair that has the appearance of the wet mane of a lion.

The gods of Africa were generous with Fatumata's breasts and buttocks. She had, therefore, passed what Mohammed jokingly calls his *double b test* of femininity. For any woman to physically attract him, she must pass the double b test--the breast and buttocks test. If they fail the test, the relationship either automatically terminates or transmutes into a platonic one.

Fatumata's breasts are of goodly proportion. Their most striking feature, however, is not their prominence, but their firmness. They stand at admirable attention even when unaided by a bra. Whenever they make love, Fatumata's breasts manifest a curious unyielding, almost rubber-like quality, that announce their full intention to bounce right back to their standard position, no matter how much manhandling, so to speak, they receive.

Their relationship began to die a natural death, however, when it seemed Fatumata had no further ambitions after finishing secondary school in Kano other than getting married to a wealthy Alhaji. There was nothing Mohammed could say or do to dissuade her. She remained adamant in the view that the chances for professional advancement for a woman in northern Wazobia were limited and that she would be wiser to spend her time making babies and living in relative comfort, even as a second, third or fourth wife, than wasting time and energy working towards the acquisition of a university degree or degrees that she will not be able to utilize.

"What about moving to another part of the country after you finish your university training?" Mohammed asked Fatumata. She dismissed the idea as impractical.

"What about going South with me so that we can both attend university and live there where, surely, you would be able to grow and advance professionally?"

"No," Fatumata said flatly, "my father will never let me leave northern Wazobia to study in the South, even if I am supposed to go with you."

"What about the incalculable value of education for its own sake?", Mohammed pressed further.

"That," Fatumata said, "is merely a cherished myth; all education must serve practical ends. If the education fails to serve practical ends, it is not education at all."

At that point, Mohammed knew that no matter how beautiful Fatumata is, they are destined to walk different paths in life. With a heavy heart, he severed relations with her. He could not bring himself to exploit her friendship knowing that it would lead nowhere and he had no intentions of marrying a woman with only a high school education. He had long promised himself that he was embarked upon a journey to the mountain top - a journey to the educational apex. His children must have the benefit of a mother who shares the same burning desire for the highest educational attainment possible.

TWENTY FOUR

The first time Mohammed arrived at the University of Ibadan, he had to admit that he was tempted to catch the next available flight back to the familiar bucolic surroundings of the suburb of *Dogon Duse* in Kano. At the University of Ibadan, everybody seemed oddly foreign. He had, of course, heard Yoruba spoken on several occasions by a few of his Yoruba friends and in pockets of Yoruba communities scattered throughout the city of Kano. But never before, had he been so utterly submerged in the overpowering sea of that language.

Everybody he met and everywhere he went, Yoruba was spoken with a consuming persistence that seemed almost indignantly directed at the outsider--the person who can not speak the language. All the students he saw around the campus grounds appeared cock-sure of themselves, exuding airs of cosmopolitan confidence about them that only the well-heeled possess.

The women he saw on his first day at the University of Ibadan, were not the shy, retiring type. They walk confidently around the campus grounds, dressed in various provocative attires, showing no self-consciousness at the occasional lustful glances and catcalls from some of the male students. They wiggle their curvy frames about the place with what seemed to him careless abandon.

Mohammed could not help wondering how he would fit into this collage. Would the students accept him or would they see him as a breed apart? Would the girls be willing to go out on dates with him or would they treat him like an outcast? Would he be able to effectively compete academically with his classmates or would he fail to make the mark? These thoughts filled his mind as he wandered aimlessly around the beautiful grounds of the University of Ibadan.

TWENTY FIVE

One of the first people whose acquaintance Mohammed made at the University of Ibadan, was Chike. They met on the first day of their biochemistry class. They had ended up sitting next to each other on chairs bolted down to the floor of the auditorium-style classroom. They hit it off right away.

Chike is tall and powerfully built, with an expansive, ebullient personality, that immediately draws anyone that comes in contact with him into the spell of his charm. His up-beat personality and athletic frame conveys a sense of irrepressible energy that acts like an infectious stimulant to all those he encounters.

Mohammed, on the other hand, is in a number of ways the opposite of Chike. While he is also tall, in fact, easily as much as an inch or two taller than Chike, he does not have the impressive musculature or bone mass as does Chike. He has a reedy frame, lanky in an elegant, languid manner. His handsome clean-shaven face is highlighted by a rather aquiline nose, high cheek bones and shoe-polish-black, marble-smooth skin.

Personality wise, Mohammed is measured and taciturn. His calm, self-possessed, detached demeanor confers an aristocratic air that is often mistaken by people as stage-managed arrogance. Beneath that calm exterior, however, is a perpetual storm of thoughts, emotions, and nervous energy.

In the course of time, Mohammed and Chike discovered aspects of their personalities that were very similar. They both possess razor-sharp minds that accept no artificial boundaries to exploring the physical world and the world of ideas. They both have a streak in them of standing up for the underdog; of easily becoming enslaved by the cause of justice. Both Mohammed and Chike come from highly religious families. They are also both struggling to shake free the fetters of the respective orthodoxies into which they were born.

Both enjoy an occasional beer, a swig or two of brandy or some other hard liquor. Both men have a healthy appetite for the opposite sex. These shared traits and interests served as the glue that held their relationship together, allowing them to grow into very good friends. It was through Chike, that Mohammed met Tunde, Osagie, Bisi and Ngozi.

Mohammed, will never forget the effect meeting Ngozi for the first time had on him. He felt transfixed by her looks and mesmerized by her intellect. He is used to dealing with women in northern Wazobia who mostly had beauty and no brains. Or more accurately, who possess beauty and nothing -- in the form of knowledge -- in their brains. They are usually shy and retiring; barely seen and hardly ever heard. They feature in the background, like prized ornaments meant for the decoration of the parlor of civilized society, but lacking self-conscious animation.

He had to admit to himself that he had grown quite accustomed to that quiet corner northern society assigns its women. A corner from which he neither expects, nor frankly, brooks challenge, whether of an intellectual, verbal or social nature. But here now; now in the South, at the renowned University of Ibadan, he meets Ngozi, very much a woman -- an Igbo woman; who is a breathtaking combination of beauty and brains.

Everything about Ngozi captivates Mohammed. Ngozi is light-skinned, in that golden-brown hue found mostly among the Igbo of Wazobia and some other African peoples of the Southern veldt of the continent. Her light complexion is in stark contrast to his own jet-black sea-seal-smooth complexion. Although Ngozi is tall for a woman, about five feet ten inches, she manages barely to scale Mohammed's shoulders.

She has well formed, slightly bowed legs supporting ample hips that dovetail into a twenty-inch waist. In Mohammed's mind, there is no finer work of art than Ngozi in tight-fitting spandex leggings and a halter-top blouse that shows off her firm midriff and the cleavage of her pendulous breasts.

Even more striking to Mohammed about Ngozi is her mind. He simply can not get over her irrepressible intellect. Her flawless English, her fluency in French; and even more humbling, her facile ease with his own language, Hausa. To add to all this, she is a third-year medical student, with wide-ranging interest in and knowledge of current affairs.

In short, Ngozi embodied all the intellectual qualities and exuberance that Mohammed has over the years, assumed to be the exclusive preserve of men. Upon reflection several years later, Mohammed realized that the first day sof their meeting was the day he fell in love with her.

Twenty Six

Mohammed prayed and fasted for six days altogether. For the first three days, he prayed intensely, and for the last three, he fasted; imploring Allah for courage, resolve, clarity of mind and singularity of purpose. At the end of the sixth day, Mohammed was alone in his hostel room, a rare treat indeed for a space he shares with three other students. It was also a welcome coincidence with the end of his fast and the day he planned to write his father to break the news of his intended marriage to Ngozi.

Through the crittal windows of the east side of his hostel room, Mohammed could make out the small dark frame of a young Yoruba girl, dutifully hawking a tray-full of *amala* and *ewedu*. She had a plastic sheet covering the food from the inevitable dust constantly thrown up by the wheels of passing cars, especially the incessant taxi-cabs. Mohammed never ceases to marvel at the powerful immune system of the African.

On the west side window of the room, Mohammed can see university of Ibadan students hurrying back and forth to class, to their hostels, to the refectory, to the sports center, and the like. At a distance, they appear like ants in an anthill colony, scurrying back and forth like programmed robots on their way to execute precise tasks with mindless regularity and devotion. But that is from a distance only. Up close and in the mix of things, the complexity of individual wills, agendas, tensions, disciplinary interests, and criss-crossing connections of all kinds, takes on a whole new meaning.

The same west side window affords Mohammed a panoramic view of a whole quadrant of the expansive but unruly city of Ibadan. Five of Ibadan's seven hills are visible in the horizon from that window, their gentle undulating slopes rolling from one hill to the other. The lush green vegetation that covers the hillsides merge on their way down to the feet of the hills into savannah-like grass, and finally give way to the riotous scatterplot that is the city of Ibadan.

It must have been what inspired J.P. Clark's cryptically terse but powerfully descriptive poem, *Ibadan*. A poem that so enchanted Mohammed when he first came across it, that he immediately committed it to memory. As Mohammed was taking in the natural beauty of Ibadan and the equally chaotic splendor of her urban sprawl, the words of J.P. Clark's, *Ibadan*, rushed through his mind as rapidly as they are sparse:

> *Ibadan,*
> *running splash of gold and rust*
> *flung and scattered among seven hills*
> *like broken China in the sun.*

It was unusually cool for that time of the day. Normally, by noon time, the sun is already sitting on its high chair, punishing friend and foe alike with the intense radiance of its rays. Today, however, the sun is in retreat. Its rays shine through clouds that seem grayer than usual. The constant swirl of the standing fan in the far corner of Mohammed's room keeps the air cooler still.

In the quiet comfort of this cool retreat and on the third and last day of his fast, Mohammed collected his thoughts and wrote a momentous letter to his father. A letter that was destined to change his life forever.

Later that day, he will go down to the Ibadan Post Office located not too far from the university, to mail his fateful missive. It will reach his father by the time the school term comes to an end in three weeks, for in Wazobia mail moves at proverbial snail pace. It is the reason that in Wazobia, people ask only *if* the mail reached its destination, not *when*.

TWENTY SEVEN

Alhaji Futa Toro, had just returned from a meeting at the Emir's palace that evening. As he sat in his spacious livingroom, a place where he rarely entertains visitors; for here, his wives are free to come and go as they please, without their heads, faces and shapely frames covered from the lustful stares of other men.

Alhaji Futa Toro, customarily entertains his visitors and business partners in the outer room of his house. There, if any of his wives has reason to come, they will be properly covered from head to toe, guaranteeing that their natural wares are preserved for his eyes only. Also, in the outer room of his house, he puts on his formal and religious demeanor for his visitors, especially the *kafirs* with whom he does business.

There, he almost always dresses formally in a well-tailored, well-laundered, heavily starched and stiffly ironed *baban riga*. He would be sure to have his Koran and chaplet visibly displayed in front of his visitors. He would have a large jug of water on a stool next to him, *prima facie* evidence for his *kafir* visitors of their teetotaler Muslim host. They, can have their choice of sodas.

As a final act in Alhaji Futa Toro's staged drama for the benefit of the captive audience of his *kafir* visitors in the outer room of his house, he would speak nothing but Hausa, even though he understands and speaks flawless English. Usually, this is hardly ever a problem, for most of his southern business partners, especially the *inya miris*--the Igbos, oblige him by speaking to him in fluent Hausa.

This last act of linguistic chauvinism, is another way by which Alhaji Futa Toro tries to convey to his non-Hausa, non-Muslim, Southern business partners, his total unwillingness at cultural compromise. If they want to deal with him it will have to be on his own terms or not at all. And since speaking to him in Hausa or bringing along someone to act as an interpreter, suggests their willingness to meet him on his own terms, then, *shikina*--all is well.

This evening, however, he has no visitors and, instead of sitting in his outer room, he is lounging in a relaxed mood in his spacious livingroom. He had just been casually contemplating which of his wives it was her night for him to perform his manly duties, when the houseboy ambled into the livingroom and handed Alhaji Futa Toro a small pile of mail. On the top of that pile was Mohammed's letter to his father.

Alhaji Futa Toro was surprised to receive a letter from his son, Mohammed. Usually, Mohammed writes him exactly three times a term. First, to inform him that he has arrived safely at the University of Ibadan. Second, to request additional funds at about the middle of the term; and third, to thank him for sending him more money. This fourth letter is an odd ball. Has something bad happened? Allah forbid. Has Mohammed finally come to his senses and decided to return to the North to continue his education in the fold of his kith and kin and under the aegis of his Islamic faith? May Allah's mercy make it so!

Despite his curiosity, Alhaji Futa Toro, a man prideful of his self possession, finished the last morsels of his *tuwon masara*, which he was eating with *kuka* soup prepared for him by his fourth wife, Mohammed's mother. Right on cue, as Alhaji Futa Toro finished his meal, the houseboy emerged with a basin of water and a hand towel, hung over his left arm like an altar-boy in a Catholic mass, for his master to wash and wipe his hands.

Alhaji Futa Toro picked up the envelope containing Mohammed's letter, tore it open and fished out the missive. As he read the letter his hands trembled so badly and his heart raced so wildly, that he feared he might have a stroke.

Dear Alhaji,

I greet you in the name of Allah, the most beneficent andmost merciful. I trust that your health is good and   that business is going well.

Writing you this letter is surely one of the most difficult things I have ever done in my life. I have, in the manner that you taught all your children, prayed and fasted, asking Allah, the most beneficent and most merciful, for guidance and help, before deciding to embark upon the path about which I write you this letter.

I do not intend to be too wordy in this letter, as I plan to journey to Kano shortly to discuss the whole matter with you. For now, I wish only to relate to you my firm decision to marry an Igbo girl by the name Ngozi, that I met and fell in love with, here at the University of Ibadan. I know that this news will not come kindly to you.

But you have always told us that Allah has his own blueprint for each and everyone of his children and for the world as a whole. Perhaps, this is Allah's will for me.

Until I come to Kano, I greet you again with deepest respect in the name of Allah, the most beneficent and most merciful. A Sala maleku Salam.

Your Loving son,

Mohammed.

When he finished reading the letter, he gently put it down next to him, reclined on the couch and took a deep breath. The worst has indeed happened after all.

TWENTY EIGHT

The *Hausa* make up the third leg of Wazobia's major-ethnic triad, the other two being Igbo and Yoruba. Anyone hearing those three big siblings of Mother Wazobia quarrel and fight amongst themselves, would think that they are the only offspring she has. You would hardly guess that she has at least, three hundred and forty seven other ethnic-children! Yet, because those three siblings are bigger than Wazobia's other ethnic-children, their din is louder and more rancorous than all the others put together.

In the northern part of Wazobia, a little over five centuries ago, itinerant and intrepid Muslim Fulanis embarked upon the conquest of Hausaland using the banner of religion as their justifying ideology. Centuries later, the Hausa became so thoroughly Islamized, that the collective memory of Hausaland prior to the coming of Islam, faded into obscurity. Religious resistance gave way to ambivalence, which eventually succumbed to conversion and the overzealousness that is often its handmaiden. Hence, Alhaji Futa Toro's Islamic fanaticism.

Mohammed, made his way back to Kano from Ibadan for the term had come to a close at the university. Instead of taking a plane flight back to Kano as he normally does, he traveled instead by coach. A luxury coach service called, *Otito dili Olisa*--glory be to God, owned and operated nationwide by an Igbo transport magnet.

The coach, *Otito dili Olisa*, Mohammed was traveling back to Kano in was full to capacity, as it always is since it is easily the safest and most reliable means of public transportation in Wazobia. Wazobian Airlines is notoriously inefficient. It is hardly ever on time and its in-flight customer service is shoddy. Their fleet of planes are so poorly maintained that one high-ranking Wazobian official aptly described them as "flying coffins."

Wazobia has virtually no passenger train service. What remains of her railway system is the decaying carcass of rail lines laid during Anglian colonial rule--iron monuments to the forced labor of millions of Wazobian men and the determined will of Anglian colonial administrators and task masters, bent on making the colony pay her keep and turn a handsome profit for the 'Mother Country.'

The coach in which Muhammed is traveliong back to northern Wazobia, is a literal re-enactment of the biblical Tower of Babbles. Men, women, and children from every nook and corner of Wazobia are represented in that earth-bound voyager. Their mutually unintelligible languages clash cacophonously with each other in a kind of cultural war by linguistic means. Despite that initial appearance, it is really a phony war. A war not for God or gold, but a war for coherence. A war meant not so much to defeat one's enemies as it is merely to be heard above the deafening dissonance of noises--that is, languages of others that make no sense to you.

The long hours of driving from Ibadan to Kano provided Mohammed's mind ample time to wonder over a number of subjects. His mind wondered from Wazobia to Ngozi and himself and back again. The din of the multilingual passengers in the coach soothes Mohammed in a peculiar kind of way. It is familiar, even comforting background noise. The kind of reassuring background noise that greets a person who has been away for a while and returns to their childhood home. The kind of reassuring background noise that frames the composite picture of one's image of themselves.

It is also the kind of reassuring background noise that makes a child uneasy to leave their old school for a new one. In their old school, things while not perfect, are familiar--the noises, the faces, the physical structures, the smells, even the bullies, all have their settled places of residence in the cubbyholes of the child's mind; in the child's psyche.

There is a part of Mohammed--his psyche, in the cubbyholes of his mind, that can not separate *what he is, even who he is,* from the noises, faces, physical structures, mother tongues, cuisines and manners of Wazobia--the national equivalent of the child's old school, of one's childhood home.

Outside her borders, Mohammed knows that the victory of anyone of these Wazobians will be his too. So also will be their defeat. For few outsiders care to find out the grinding axes of members of a family if that family's name acquires a particular coat of paint. The members of such a family collectively labor, for better or for worse, under the weight of that reputation. For no finger succeeds where the hand fails.

Mohammed's wondering mind turned to Ngozi and himself. He began to think of the challenge that lay ahead of him--that of getting his stubborn and proud father to accept his choice of Ngozi as a wife.

Southern city after southern city faded behind them as the coach gained ground on Kano. Rich green foliage gradually gave way to savannah grassland and humidity ceded the atmosphere to aridity. All the while, Wazobia's Tower of Babbles on wheels--the *Otito dili Olisa* coach, buzzed like a beehive.

Even the little children, too young yet to understand or speak any of Wazobia's tongues, added their measure to the brew by periodically wailing for a morsel of some home-made treat or other, to be breast-fed or simply for maternal attention. Do those Wazobian children cry in their mother tongues or do they wail in the universal language of God-- their common humanity?

Seven long hours later, the coach made its way into the Kano Central Motor Park, another great meeting place of Wazobia's multitude of tongues. Mohammed disembarked the bus, walked over to the curb of the main road and hailed down a taxi cab. In no time at all, he was back to the quiet, familiar suburban environs of his father's mansion.

TWENTY NINE

The dry northwesterly winds from the Sahara that act as chaperon to the seasonal harmattan, ended about a month ago in Kano and in its place, the rains come in spurts as though unsure if the unwelcome visitor of the dry season has truly taken leave. The scanty rains nevertheless make the otherwise dry air more humid, letting the searing sun bake the oiled skins of people into musky balms of shear butter and sweat. As the day wears on, the heat of the sun subsides as it dips eastwards.

In the outer room of his home, Alhaji Futa Toro is sitting in a lotus position on a hand-woven rug made by Kano artisans, who have done the same thing from generation to generation, for as long as any living person in Kano can remember. Silently, Alhaji Futa Toro counts the prayer beads on his chaplet, as he recites his prayers for the fifth time that day. He makes a mental note to confront Mohammed on the issue of his intended marriage to that Igbo girl--that *inya miri* girl, that *kafir*, after he is done with his prayers.

Even as the thought intrudes his mind, his blood begins to boil. That is unacceptable. That is impossible. That cannot and must not be allowed to happen. It will be over his dead body that Mohammed will marry that *inya miri*, that *Kafir*. Even if they go ahead and get married over his dead body, he will surely come back from his grave to haunt them for the rest of their lives!

Again and again, Alhaji Futa Toro's head touches the rug as he bows to Allah in prayer, facing east in the direction of Mecca. Each time he completes a bow he stands all the way up, arms outstretched on both sides, with his palms open in supplication to Allah. A few minutes later, the whole process begins all over again.

His prayers complete, Alhaji Futa Toro, called out to his houseboy in his authoritative voice, "Zo nang"--come here. The nervous teenager, deathly afraid of his master, hastily answered the call.

"Go and find Mohammed, and tell him that his father wishes to speak to him."

"Yes, sir," the boy respectfully replied, and left the room.

Alhaji Futa Toro, remembers well as if it had been yesterday, how in the dying days of Anglian colonial rule in Wazobia, Southerners, especially Igbos and Yorubas, because they acquired degrees from Western universities and colleges, and became lawyers, doctors, engineers, professors, and the like, fancied themselves superior human beings to all Northerners--especially Hausas, including even those of his ilk.

He, who can recite the Holy Koran forwards and backwards by heart; he, whose family tree stretches back for seven unbroken centuries or more; he, whose family has been literate--able to fluently read and write Hausa and Arabic in the Arabic script for nearly as long as the city of Kano has been in existence; he, who annually makes the Hajj to the holy city of Mecca.

While he is aware of the great cultural traditions of the Igbos and the Yorubas: the elaborate New Yam festival, the plethora of theatrical masquerades and percussive course-line dances of the Igbos; and the equally elaborate theatrical ritual dances and incantations of the *Egungun* festival and pantheon of traditional gods of the Yorubas; He can never understand why they carry on as though the Hausas have no cultural traditions of comparable splendor.

If only he can take his southern compatriots to witness the sheer majesty of the *Grand Durbar*, a Hausa tradition, that celebrates with great fanfare, a thousand-year old equestrian culture. No word picture he paints, can properly describe for a listener the impressive scale of the spectacle of the *Grand Durbar*. Yet, if he had to make the feeble effort at such a portrait with the aid of the poor paint brush of words, he would describe the *Grand Durbar*, thus.

It takes place in an open field the size of, perhaps, two football stadiums put together. Massed on one end of the field is a great audience of people, eagerly awaiting the start of the event. Situated at the front row of the audience stand, is a dais covered with a large colorful canopy. This provides shade for the various Emirs of Hausaland and other V.I.Ps in attendance. At the other end of the field, is an assemblage of easily a thousand or more horsemen, mounted on their charges, patiently awaiting the bugle call.

When all is set, a turbaned trumpeter with his ample *baban riga* billowing in the wind and mounted on a steed that is itself draped in a colorfully embroidered cape, rips off the commanding tune. From the opposite end of the field, a thundering cavalry of horsemen galloping at breakneck speed, come charging directly at the massed audience. For a while, and certainly to the first-time spectator, it seems the charging cavalry is bound to stampede into the audience, causing mayhem. The air is electric. The thundering hooves of the horses, roll across the field with the reverberation of a thousand drum-majors playing the same tune all at once.

About twenty to thirty man paces from the front row of the massed audience, when it seems that no power on this earth can possibly stop the charging cavalry of horses, the trumpeter rips off another piercing command. All of a sudden, without warning, yet with uncanny precision, all thousand horses or more come to uniform attention! For a short while, a dust cloud, kicked up by the hooves of the gallant beasts, covers the field, enveloping the halted cavalry. Gradually, like a mirage emerging from a misty shroud, the halted cavalry comes into view, graciously accepting the deafening applause of the badly shaken but highly impressed audience.

Alhaji Futa Toro, a taciturn and methodical man, weighed carefully in his mind the best way to approach the matter of Mohammed's expressed interest in marrying that *inya miri* girl. Angry as he was at Mohammed, he did not think that venting his spleen will be very productive. Yet, he was not sure how well reason will work either; for he knows only too well how romantic love can becloud a man's judgment when one is in the thrall of its powerful grip. Moreover, he did not want to appear too conciliatory lest Mohammed thinks his resolve is not firm.

Perhaps he might begin by reminding Mohammed of their illustrious lineage and the distinctive privilege their religion bestows upon them. Then he will probe to see how much of the modern history of Wazobia Mohammed is aware of. After that, he will try to weave all those threads of thought into the single cloth of Mohammed's own responsibility to uphold and safeguard that legacy.

"Baba, you called for me?", Mohammed asked as he entered the outer room of his father's house.

"Yes, Mohammed, I called for you. Sit down."

Mohammed pulled over one of the several beautiful Kano leather ottomans scattered about the parlor of the outer room, and sat down. Alhaji Futa Toro who was chewing a piece of *gworo*, cleared his throat. He gently placed his Holy Koran, along with his chaplet curled up like a snake on top of the Koran, in a prominent place between Mohammed and himself, where the two of them can easily see the religious symbols. Mohammed eyed the Koran and the chaplet, as though they were talisman placed before him to ward off the evil spirits of *kafirs*. Out of the clear blue sky, or so it seemed to Mohammed, his father popped a rhetorical question at him.

"Mohammed," his father began.

"Yes, Baba," Mohammed respectfully answered.

"What is the color, taste and smell of time?"

Bewildered, Mohammed asked his father for clarification, as though he had not heard the question that he was just asked.

"Excuse me, Baba. Did you just ask me what the color, taste and smell of time is?"

"Yes, Mohammed, that was my question to you."

"But, Baba, time has no color, taste or smell? So I honestly don't know how to answer that question."

"Very well, Mohammed," Alhaji Futa Toro responded, "keep that thought in mind for now."

"Tell me Mohammed, what are the names and natures of the offspring of time?"

Mohammed was now even more perplexed. His normally unflappable, dead-pan face, was fully animated with furrows appearing on his forehead.

"Again, Baba, I don't know how to possibly answer this second question either, for time can not beget offspring."

Alhaji Futa Toro was feeling quite good that his tactic was working well, for he could tell that his son was genuinely puzzled. He leaned back on his chair a satisfied smile playing on his face.

"You are wrong on both counts, Mohammed. Time does have color, taste and smell. And time, my dear son, begets offsprings. The color of time is a people's *élan vital*. The creative force within the corporate organism of a people that enables them to bring forth necessary or desirable adaptations. It is the creative genius of a people."

"What about the taste and smell of time, Baba?," Mohammed uncharacteristically interjected.

"Patience young man, patience. The reason the eagle circles for as long as it does before carrying away its prey, is not for fear that its wings are not wide enough for the flight that will follow or that its talons are not strong enough for the needed grip. Its patience is meant solely for the most opportune moment of action."

"The taste of time is a people's culture. That veritable medley of a people's rituals, music, dances, foods, attires, folklores and folkways. The smell of time, Mohammed, is that dense aroma of self-knowledge that hangs in the air of the collective memory of a people of *who they are* and *who they must remain*, even in the face of the commingled air of the smells of other people's times."

"As for the names and natures of the offspring of time," Alhaji Futa Toro continued, now fully in his element, "I will tell you that too."

"Time begets the offsprings of a people's language, history and religion. All three are siblings and the eternal offsprings of time. Without the birth, growth and full development of those three siblings, the family that is a people atrophies and eventually dies."

"Therefore, my beloved son, Mohammed, how then do you think the time of our people is to be kept? Whom do you think are the keepers of our people's time? It is you and I, Mohammed, and every other Hausa man and woman. We are all the time keepers of our people."

Alhaji Futa Toro, reached into the deep pocket of his *baban riga*, fished out the remaining piece of his *gworo*, and unceremoniously tossed it into his mouth.

Mohammed has always admired his father's gift of garb. His ability to make words do his bidding. When he was growing up, his father would sometimes teach at the Islamic school at Kano, and Mohammed along with about fifty other youngsters, would sit at his feet, spellbound by his knowledge, wisdom and erudition.

Yet now, fifteen years later, his father's words had a strange emptiness about them. A hollowness that could not speak to Mohammed's new found knowledge of Wazobia, modern science and himself. He gazed upon his father. His tall slender frame, his dark handsome face with its high cheek bones and patrician nose, and he felt almost a sense of pity. He saw a glorious soldier who may never die, but who will slowly but surely fade away.

Yet, Mohammed is not used to challenging his father. Theirs is a relationship of absolute patriarchy. His father's wives are his God-sanctioned wards. His children, minions at the feet of a colossus, and the entirety of his father's household—his dominion, a fortress held together by his indomitable will and the indisputable license of his religious authority. In Mohammed's father's house, Allah's will is law; and Allah's will in the Futa Toro household is made manifest through the lesser god of his father. The buck stops with Allah by way of Alhaji Futa Toro.

Now, Mohammed, his son, his only son, his beloved son, is making ready to rebel against his authority, his will, the very ground upon which the foundation of his father's house rests.

Alhaji Futa Toro fixed his son with a steely gaze, as though daring him to go against his will in his very presence. Writing a trifling letter is one thing, standing before a man of such esteem as himself and uttering such nonsense is quite another. The pause stretched out long and thin like rubber band, until it became awkwardly taut. The pregnancy of that silence became so advanced that it had to give birth soon.

Will the birth-child of that expectant silence be born fully formed from the loins of the gods? Or will it be physically deformed, retarded, or stillborn? Worse yet, might that pregnant silence, despite its advanced stage, be aborted by want of courage on Mohammed's part? Mohammed broke the water of that pregnant silence with a throaty cough. Steeling himself to the task at hand he took the plunge.

If his father had a few rhetorical surprises for him, so does he for his father. As an Igbo saying he picked up from Ngozi goes, a lion can only give birth to its own kind.

"Baba," Mohammed ventured.

"Yes, my son," his father gently replied, hoping that the moment of his son's submission was nigh.

"What exactly does the term *inya miri* mean, where does it come from, and why is it supposed to be bad?"

Alhaji Futa Toro was caught unawares by Mohammed's question. First, he had not expected that Mohammed will have the audacity to engage in a verbal duel with him, given his upbringing of great deference and submission towards him, his father. Second, he had not anticipated this line of questioning.

He has always felt that allowing Mohammed to go to university in the South was a big mistake, now he knew for sure it was. *They* have completely corrupted him. Changed him from the quiet, respectable, God-fearing young man he raised, to a wild animal. Still, Alhaji Futa Toro, a seasoned gladiator in the marshal art of debating, understands well its first law of engagement: *never let your discomfort show through no matter how wildly the butterflies flap their wings in your stomach. Stay cool, calm and collected.*

"I am surprised, Mohammed, that you, of all people, who has elected to eat from the same plate as the Igbos, as well as with all the other southern *kafirs*, does not know what the term means, where it comes from and why it is used perjoratively."

Of course, Mohammed knows what the term connotes and its origins. He has had such conversations with Ngozi, *ad infinitum*. But he wanted to hear it from his the horse's mouth. To see how his father would wrap his mind around it. To see how he would deal with the prejudice that is the animus of that term, when he, Mohammed, relieves that purulent boil of its poisonous contents with the lance of logic and objective facts. It is a trap that he is shamelessly setting for his father to fall into.

Alhaji Futa Toro, continued.

"Since you claim ignorance over this matter, Mohammed, I will enlighten you. The term *inya miri*, is a Hausa corruption of the Igbo phrase *yem mmiri*, which means, *give me water.*"

Mohammed, who like his father has a razor-sharp mind, perceived even then, that he has already won a small but important victory. It was the first time he had ever heard his own father utter the words of any other language of Wazobia's ethnic-children, besides Hausa! In fact, as Mohammed listened to his father explain the meaning and origin of the term *inya miri,* he had a sneaky suspicion that Alhaji Futa Toro may very well know how to speak Igbo, or at the very least, understand quite a bit more of that language than he lets on! His father oblivious of the thoughts whirling around in Mohammed's mind, went on.

"When the Igbos first came to the North in trickles, then in droves, they naturally could not speak Hausa nor could the Hausa speak Igbo. When you look around the North today and right before Wazobia's Civil War, and you see Igbos everywhere thriving as great traders, and so forth, few remember that when they first came to Hausaland, many had virtually nothing."

"The Igbos who came to Kano, as well as all the other southern *kafirs*, lived in *Sabon Gari*--new town, outside the walled city of Kano. They will come into the walled city of Kano to transact their business, but would return to the *Sabon Gari*, at the end of business day. That way, it was hoped that the Northern Muslims and the Southern Christians, could conduct their business without stepping on each other's toes."

"While conducting business within the walled city of Kano, or as itinerant traders traveling from one Hausa town to another, whenever they get thirsty, the newly arrived Igbos would ask a Hausa person for water in Igbo--*yem mmiri*. Gradually, the Hausa, who are not only ethnically different from the Igbo but are also Muslims, while all the itinerant Igbo are either Christians or animists, began to use the corrupted version of that Igbo query for water, to pejoratively describe the whole group."

"Be that as it may, Mohammed," Alhaji Futa Toro continued, I do not wish to be distracted from the primary issues that I wish to deal with today by such trivial matters. I have read your letter and my answer is an unequivocal No! You can not marry that *inya miri* girl. So, put her out of your mind and get on with your studies. You are almost done with your studies anyway, and Allah has been merciful through it all. When you finish and return to Kano, we will go to Alhaji Sule Qaria's household to find you a bride among his beautiful daughters."

"But, Baba, I hardly know any of Alhaji Qaria's daughters and I am in love with the Igbo girl, Ngozi."

"You speak like a child instead of like a man. What nonsense are you talking about? All you need to know about Alhaji Qaria's daughters is that they are beautiful, and as such, whichever one of them you pick, will give you handsome sons and beautiful daughters; that they are well brought up, and so whichever one of them you pick, will a make good and obedient wife to you. That is all you need to know."

"Moreover, Mohammed, Alhaji Qaria's family is part of us. They are part of our Hausa folk. Part of our Islamic community. Part of the very fabric of our lives, of our people's time, of which I have spoken to you at length. Need I remind you, Mohammed, that we are good Muslims and that the woman you say you wish to marry is a *kafir*--a pagan."

"No, Baba, Ngozi is not a pagan. She is a Christian, and in Islam, Christians and Jews are recognized as *people of the book...*"

"Ah, Mohammed," Alhaji Futa Toro interrupted, waving his right hand dismissively at his son, "spare me the lecture. Or has your association with *inya miris* so emboldened you now that like the errant cub of the lioness, you presume to instruct your own mother on how to hunt?!"

"Whatever she is, she is not a Muslim, and that is the central point I wish to make. Our religion enjoins us to be good foot soldiers of the faith and, as such, we must not demur from our duty. Our admission into Allah's paradise in the hereafter depends on how good foot soldiers of the faith we have been here on earth. Do you hear me Mohammed. I want you in that paradise with me."

Alhaji Futa Toro paused, took a sip of water from the glass sitting on the side stool on which also sits the large jug of water that is almost a fixture in that room, and then, resumed talking.

"Even if one were to overlook the fact that that *inya miri* girl is not ethnically Hausa, how is one supposed to get around the fact that she is not Muslim? Is she willing to convert to Islam? Or has the madness that has taken hold of you become so debilitating that you, Mohammed, might be entertaining the idea of converting to Christianity?"

Mohammed readied his lance and took aim at the boil.

"But, Baba, our becoming Muslim was not a voluntary act. It was not the result of reaching a theological consensus between ourselves and our converters."

"It was, instead, Baba, as you, a great scholar, knows much better than I, the result of force. The result of conquest. A conversion that was not of the Biblical kind, of Paul's encounter with the voice of God on his way to Damascus. Rather, it was a conversion at the point of the sword."

Alhaji Futa Toro, an astute scholar of Hausa and Islamic history, knew that his son was right. But looking back on that past is too overwhelming and, at any rate, pointless. The dye has been cast. Hausas have become Islamized and the collective memory of their pre-Islamic traditional African culture, so hopelessly submerged in Islam that it is now a distant and blurred one. Its recovery or romanticization, is not worthy of the time and energy of a wise man such as himself.

"And what good, Mohammed, does it do a man caught in a rainstorm without a covering, to recount that the day before was as dry as desert dust?"

"But, Baba, you just got done telling me of the importance of keeping our people's time. Is that instance in our history not an integral part of our people's time? Must we not be sensitive to it in savoring the taste and smell of our people's time?"

"Moreover, Baba, young as I am, my education and experience, limited though they are, have firmly convinced me of two important principles. First, anyone willing to kill, maim, or otherwise, visit pain, hardship and injustice on innocent people, innocent men, women and children; children, not even old enough to understand the meaning of religion, let alone make a conscious choice of which to belong to, *does not and can not possibly know God.*"

"Second, Baba, for me, religious tolerance rather than religious chauvinism, is the true measure of faithfulness to God, to Allah. Everything else is politics masquerading as religion."

"Besides, Baba," Mohammed continued, growing more confident with every minute, "in every good Christian, there is a good Muslim, a good Jew, a good Hindu, Et. Cetera; in every good Christian, there is a good Jew, a good Muslim, a good Hindu, ET. Cetera; and in every good Jew, there is a good Christian, Muslim, Hindu, ET. Cetera. It is that goodness, Baba, found in any one or all of them, that unites their humanity and transcends the formalisms of their respective faiths."

Alhaji Futa Toro, a man quite unaccustomed to being at a loss for words, found himself curiously tongue tied and grudgingly pulled along by the sheer power of Mohammed's logic. He remained attentive, listening to his son speak with a man's voice.

"No, Baba, I do not intend to convert to Christianity, Judaism, Hinduism, or any other of the existing religions for that matter. I, however, fully intend to convert to an entirely new one: the religion of our *common humanity*. A common humanity that fuses all those religions into ONE. Baba, let all the contestants in the competition for our souls, bring their measures of virtue to the level playing field of justice and fair play and may the most righteous win. *Insha Allah.*"

Although Mohammed's father was impressed with his son's logic and choice of words, he was determined to give his point of view one last effort.

"And what happens, Mohammed, if and when you decide to take another bride--a second wife? Will that *inya miri* woman accept the situation or will she turn your household upside down, and, perhaps, leave you altogether?"

"Baba, polygamy is not a new and strange practice among Africans traditionally. It was not a case of traditional African culture trying to accommodate a Muslim practice in the form of polygamy. Rather, Baba, it was Islam accommodating a pre-existing practice. It is, therefore, important to remember that it is not a religious thing, *per se*."

"Moreover, Baba, while Islam permits a man to marry up to four wives, it does not *require* a Muslim man to marry more than one wife. It is ultimately a matter of individual choice and not an Islamic nor traditional African obligation. I think that I shall be quite content with one wife. However, should the contrary prove to be the case in the course of time, Ngozi and I will cross that bridge when we get to it."

"Baba," Mohammed continued, sensing that he has gained an upper hand, "what has becoming Muslims done *for* and *to* our traditional Hausa culture? Do we understand and appreciate our ancestors any better because of it? Do we take greater pride in our past on account of it? We take Arab names in place of our own in the name of Islam. We are not even allowed to pray to God, to talk to Allah, in our own mother tongue!"

"Baba, if the Prophet Mohammed, happened to have been an Arab, does that make God—Allah, also an Arab? Who has the authority to decide whether God—Allah, is monolingual, bilingual or multilingual? Baba, while it is true that water is necessary for the sustenance of life, is it not also true that one can drown in too much of it?"

Although Mohammed's father knew in his heart that what his son was saying is true, an inner fear and conditioning, compelled him to chastise his son.

"Better watch your mouth, young man, lest you blaspheme."

Knowing his father, Mohammed, felt it wise at this point to dress up the wound of the lanced boil with an appropriate passage from the Holy Koran. He reached into his shirt pocket, and retrieved his pocket-size Koran, opened up the dog-eared page where he had made a note of the passage, and quoted chapter 4 verse 135 of the Holy Koran to his father:

"Baba, is it not written in the Holy Koran, thus":

> *O you who believe stand out firmly for justice as*
> *witness to God, even as against yourselves or*
> *your parents or your kin and whether it be against*
> *rich or poor. For Allah can protect both. Follow*

not the lust of your hearts lest you swerve, and if
you distort justice verily Allah is well acquainted
with all that you do.

"That is all I have to say, Baba. Thank you for letting me speak. May Allah bless you."

Alhaji Futa Toro, knew at this point that his son's mind was made up and that there would be no turning back for him. He knew that Mohammed was going to marry that *inya miri* woman. Whatever *they* had done to him in the South, has worked well. Now, he must begin to orient his mind to that new reality, for it seems that he is destined to become more than merely business partners with the *inya miris*.

"Alright, Mohammed, if this is truly what you want; if that *inya...*Ngo..zi woman, is really whom you want to be your wife, then Allah be praised, *so be it*. Before the next *Ramadan*, we will make plans to go to her village to formally meet her family and ask for her hand in marriage. Leave me now, I need to be alone for a while."

"*Ranka dede,* Baba, may Allah bless you forever," Mohammed effused at his father, as he left the outer room of his father's house, feeling elated and triumphant.

THIRTY

The library was as quiet as anyone could hope to get in Lagos. The only noise is the steady humming of the central air-conditioning unit. But that is a meaningless sound. A background noise that is merely part of the audioscape. The quiet in the library is, otherwise, that of graveyard silence. People sit on wooden chairs, hunched over books and magazines, absorbed in their reading. Chike, although he loves reading, has a relatively short attention span. Whenever he studies, he needs several interludes in-between roughly two-hour blocks of time.

During one of his breaks, he noticed a young brown-skinned girl in a traditional outfit come into the reading room with an armful of books. He was struck by her fine features. She was of medium height and slender in build. In fact, so slender that ten pounds less and she might have been considered skinny. She had a good bone structure, a full head of hair and that inevitable ite-ona posterior. Her breasts seemed full without appearing droopy.

She finished her business at the circulation desk and disappeared into the book stacks. Chike was not consciously searching for her, but was rather aimlessly wandering through the book stacks. As he turned the corner of a stack to his left, he almost bumped into her.

"Excuse me", he muttered.

"That's all right", she replied, "I should also apologize to you; I really should have been looking where I was going."

"No, no, no, the fault was mine", Chike insisted. They stared at each other for an awkward moment, before Chike regained his presence of mind and said, "Oh, my name is Chike; what's yours?", extending his hand for a hand shake.

"Nice to meet you Chike, my name is Azuka." He had suspected that she was Igbo by her almost golden brown complexion, and now when he thought of it, her "george" wrapper.

Her eyes sparkled with obvious interest. She was a party waiting to happen. Chike, a past master at reading women, knew, at once, that this one was on the prowl, man-hunting. The question was not whether she was looking for a man - that much he was sure of - but whether he was going to take the bait.

He promised himself that he was going to be faithful to Bisi, and had done just that since they have been going out together for the last two-and-one-half years. He could not deny, however, that there were many days when the urge for another woman seemed almost unbearable. This had nothing to do with loving Bisi. He loves her very much, but men are such sexual vagrants that every so often they have to play the field, if for no other reason than to reassure themselves that they have not lost their hunting skills.

Besides, he often argued, there is nothing natural about sexual monogamy. It is a learned behavior, and like all things learned, some people learn it better than others; and even those who become good at it are bound to slip up every once in a while, exposing their essential nature.

As he stood there looking into the brown pools that are Azuka's eyes, he did something he had studiously avoided for the past two-and-a-half years. He asked her to go outside with him where they could talk freely. Azuka followed Chike to the Library garden at the rear of the building. The African sun was shining with its usual afternoon intensity and the variety of flowers in the garden made an indescribably beautiful tropical picture.

They reached one of the cement garden chairs and Chike sat down first. Azuka took some time readjusting her wrapper in the slow, deliberate manner so rich in sexual nuance that only African women can orchestrate. First they loosen the wrapper from the left-side hip where one end of the cloth is usually tucked in. Then they hold out the two top ends of the wrapper with both hands, as though they are inviting someone into a warm embrace. They then criss-cross the left end of the wrapper to the right side and the right end to the left side, wrapping the cloth much tighter to their bodies.

As Azuka completed this short drama, her *ite-ona* posterior became even more pronounced as the fabric gathered closer to her body. Chike, who prides himself at having what he calls a poetic appreciation for life, did not loose sight of that non-verbal communication.

Azuka sat down and fixed Chike with her large brown eyes, a smirk lingering at the corners of her mouth, as though she was suppressing a victorious smile. She always thinks men to be such weak creatures. They have the brawn and even sometimes the brains to go with it, but their lust is always their weak point. Any woman who understands the power that women have over men as a result of male lust would know that the ultimate rulers of the world are women, not men, as most people suppose. Men are so much like children. Any stranger can steal them away with an inviting piece of candy.

Chike stared back at her, not knowing exactly how to proceed and trying to guess at what was going on in her mind. He asked her the usual perfunctory questions. What school does she attend? What is her major? Which part of Igboland is she from? And in what part of Lagos she resides? She answered all the questions one after the other, unhurriedly. Something about this girl worried Chike, but he could not quite put his finger on it. She seemed too poised; too much like a cat slyly and sure-footedly making its way through a junkyard. Yet, he could not break loose from the spell cast by her eyes and her comely ease. He felt compelled by desire to explore this new mystery.

Her brown eyes shone in the sunlight against the background of a fragile-looking face marked by rather high cheek bones and full lips. If only Bisi was around, Chike thought to himself, he would not be bothering himself with this girl. But it had been nearly three months since he had been with Bisi and his loins were beginning to boil like the gas-laden molten lava in a volcano. Azuka threw him a knowing look with those liquid brown eyes of hers, but maintained her quiet effacing demeanor. It was at this point that Chike made one of the biggest mistakes of his life---he invited her out to a party a friend of his was having that night.

THIRTY ONE

From the Library, Chike went to Tar-beach Royal Hotel at Elizabeth Island for a short work out at their very modern gymnasium and for a dip in the swimming pool. In spite of the structural elegance of the Tar-beach Royal Hotel, its five-star pricetags for meals and lodging, and its incessant traffic of foreign visitors who all look like they just walked out of *Ebony* or *Essence* magazines, around the front gates of the hotel a persistent scene reminds one of the shocking contrast between the opulence offered by the magnificent hotel and the continuing poverty of many Wazobian citizens. That scene is the ever-swarming ranks of prostitutes, soliciting male customers for the opportunity to earn money by literally lying on their backs.

The scene never ceases to intrigue Chike. He marvels at the whole business of prostitution. At the audacity of women who fly in the face of, perhaps, the most private and hypocritical of human activities; literally, hawking their natural wares on street corners and in brothels, daring the world, since time immemorial, to stamp out that trade in basic human need, so to speak, by the sheer weight of its self-righteous indignation.

Chike also marvels at how the women engaged in the so called 'world's oldest profession,' manage to live with themselves. Aside from the physical wear and tear of being up many late nights and being with several men every night or so, there is the moral question posed by the lifestyle. There is also the sheer emotional abuse that such women experience, dealing with all manner of male customers who, with the payment of their almighty naira (or some other foreign currency), think they have the divine right to use, and often abuse, the bodies of the women in the pursuit of their sexual amusement and gratification.

It is also the case that in Wazobia prostitutes get little or no protection from the police. If anything, prostitutes probably require protection from the exploitation they receive at the hands of the Wazobia police. For Wazobia policemen exploit those women with an impunity that would boggle the minds of most decent, unsuspecting Wazobian citizens.

The policemen in the sprawling urban centers of Wazobia extort money and sex from whores on a routine basis. Women who engage in prostitution in Wazobia are, thus, the ultimate victims in a patriarchal world of sexual exploitation. They are exploited by their male customers who, through the exchange of money for the temporary use of their bodies, demand anonymous and unemotional sexual gratification. They are condemned by a society that considers them moral degenerates because of what they do for a living; and they are exploited by "the law" - once again, mostly men, uniformed men this time who, hiding behind the legal badge of "the law," impose a yoke of exploitation on the prostitutes unimaginable to ordinary Wazobians, since, of course, prostitution is illegal in high-minded Wazobia. Anywhere these women turn, the men manage to exploit them: physically, economically, morally and legally - they simply cannot seem to win.

As these thoughts about prostitution in Wazobia filled Chike's mind while he waited in a queue of cars in the nearly mile-long drive way of the hotel, he sees a handful of policemen hauling away a bunch of prostitutes from the premises of the Tar-beach Royal Hotel.

From the mouths of both the prostitutes and the policemen spew raw sewage in the name of words, as they trade insults and hard-biting street anecdotes. Prodded on by the truncheons of the policemen, the eight or nine handcuffed whores are marched towards a waiting Black Maria.

"James!," one of the whores yelled at the top of her voice at a youngish-looking constable standing not too far from her, "you know know me again because we dey for in front people now. When night come, you go begin won fuck. You tink say I know go remember who you be?"

Instead of ignoring the obviously angry and embarrassed woman in the time honored tradition of treating hysteria with dignified silence, in which case the small crowd that gathered to witness the spectacle might have dismissed the woman's insinuations as the sour grapes of a foul-mouthed whore, the policeman chose to reply in kind.

"Make you see this monkey. 'Xcept person be crase man, who go won fuck that your nyash wey don rotten finish?"

The crowd roared with laughter, clearly enjoying the gutter sniping.

"Na when i don rotten like *mangala* wey don spoil *kpata kpata*, you de like am well well," the angry whore hurled back at the constable just before they shoved her into the waiting Black Maria. The crowd roared with laughter again, entertained by the sordid exchange between the policeman and the whore.

THIRTY TWO

Chike picked up Azuka at exactly 8:00 PM. Unlike many African women who tend to treat time as though it is an afterthought of God's creation, she was ready to go. She wore a white silk dress that clung to her frame like wet cloth clinging to the folds of the wind when hung up on a clothesline to dry. It featured a low cleavage that shows off goodly portions of her breasts, and a back split to expose her body nearly down to the tail of her spine. The dress had a long slit up the front, allowing a preview of her smooth honey-brown thighs. Chike swallowed hard.

They drove to the party in near silence, broken occasionally by Chike's futile efforts at making small talk and by the inevitable but pointless tooting of horns by overtaking Lagos cabs. The Lagos marina glittered in quiet dignity as they drove by, masking the earlier pandemonium of the day.

Except during the arduous "go-slows" of the work days, when millions of cars snail-pace their way painfully from Surulere, Apapa and Ikeja, into Lagos island, driving in Lagos at night on week ends can actually be a pleasure. Eko bridge, a silent concrete monument to modern technology, lights up at night aided by the incandescence of a hundred electric bulbs or more, making it appear like a neon apparition. It looms over the stinking lagoon, bow-shaped as though countless fire flies were standing in an unbroken queue.

As they approached Olisa's place, they could here the muffled vibration of the stereo and see people milling around the front of the house, perhaps trying to catch a breath of fresh air. Parking was tight for this is Surulere, a place guaranteed to give any city planner a migraine. Houses are built too closely to one another, each house having a walled fence and a corrugated iron gate. People double-park on either side of the road. Trash bins spill their rotting guts in front of each one of those gates adding a disorderly accent to the street scene.

After about a half hour of searching, Chike managed to find a parking space almost a quarter of a mile from Olisa's place. He deftly squeezed his car in-between a trash bin and a car which seemed like it had been stationary for quite some time. Gallantly, he circled to the passenger side of the car, and opened the door for Azuka.

She swung her long honey-brown legs out first, flashing a length of thigh as the split played its part well, gaping open like the gills of a fish. He locked the door after her testing the handle once more to ensure that the lock was secure. They crossed the narrow street and headed for Olisa's house.

THIRTY THREE

They danced all night until their feet ached from the strain of standing and moving about for so long. The alcohol which had earlier acted as a stimulant now slowed everyone down as it depressed the activity of their central nervous systems. Chike and Azuka sat in the car, tired and soaked with sweat. The party room had been hot and stuffy from too many people and very little oxygen. The rest of the air was composed of nicotine gas from cigarette fumes.

Azuka rested her head on Chike's shoulder, staring at the star-studded sky. She felt strangely close to this man that she had known for only several days. Something about him seemed so solid, self-assured and stable. He reminded her of *Agu*, an animal that has the dual reputation of being probably the laziest animal in the world, while at the same time the most efficient hunting machine in all of nature. It would deceptively laze around under the shade of a tree, appearing nondescript and harmless, perpetually yawning even after many hours of sleep. But when the time is right, a transformation as intriguing as it is lethal occurs and Agu comes alive, leaving only the carcass of its victim as evidence of its earlier activity. Azuka, however, felt at that moment that she probably would not mind being devoured by this lion.

Chike snuggled closer to Azuka, embracing her in his strong arms. Although he was feeling quite exhausted from the party, his loin was beginning to respond. He kissed her gently on the neck as though she were breakable china. She encouraged him with a deep, throaty moan. Chike's hands became those of an orchestra conductor, directing her body to the heights of ecstasy. Passions rose in them like the fever of one with a bad case of malaria. Urgently, almost compulsively, driven by the consuming flames of passion, Chike freed himself of his clothing as Azuka did likewise. Within a few frenzied, explosive minutes, they spent themselves in an all-consuming, almost violent orgasm. Together they lay in the back seat of Chike's car savoring the post-coitus calm.

THIRTY FOUR

I t had been only about half an hour since Chike settled down in his office at the Lagos University Teaching Hospital, when the telephone rang. The *gring...gring...gring* sound of the phone shattered the silence of the office, startling Chike a bit. He stared at the plastic and metal contraption as though unsure of what to make of this rude mechanical intruder. At the third ringing, Chike picked up the receiver. It was unusual for anyone to call him that early in the morning - it was only about 9:00 A.M. Bisi, who would sometimes call at odd hours, was out of the country with her parents, vacationing in some part of Europe.

"Hello", Chike rasped into the static-filled line. There was a pregnant silence on the other end.

"Hello", he said again, this time a note of angry impatience creeping into his voice. There was a sigh and what appeared to be sobbing at the other end of the line.

"Who is this please and what do you want?", Chike said through clenched teeth.

"Hello, Chike this is Azuka", came the soft, reluctant answer.

Chike's heart began to race. "What on earth does she want from me?" Chike thought to himself. Nearly three months ago, after what must certainly have been the most intense two weeks of his life, during their mad, passionate encounter, he had explained to her that he had a fiancee and that they hoped to get married soon. He had assured her that he had thoroughly enjoyed their brief affair, but pointed out that they had to call it quits.

Holding the telephone receiver limply in his palm now, he could remember exactly the look of anguish on her face as he told her that they had to go their separate ways. She stared vacantly into space as though her mind had suddenly become blank. Tear drops tumbled effortlessly down the sculptured contours of her face and her lips trembled as she struggled to suppress fits of sobbing. "Why are you crying?", Chike remembers asking her. "Look, we both wanted to have some fun and we did. I did not ask you any questions and you did not ask me any, either. There were absolutely no strings attached. So I don't understand why you are putting on this melodrama."

"I love you Chike", Azuka muttered in between sobs. "I love you more than anything or anyone in this world and I want to spend the rest of my life with you."

"You what?", Chike almost screamed at her. "Azuka, what on earth are you talking about? If this is some kind of a sick joke, please stop it. You hardly know who I am and you are talking of loving me. Besides, you cannot just jump to the conclusion that because we made love, I am automatically obliged to be emotionally involved with you."

That had been a horrible day for Chike. He ranted and raved at Azuka for nearly three hours, pleading with her to get off his back. She sat there taking all the rage he vented on her with the inscrutable passivity of a statue of Bhudda. After each bout of rage, she would quietly reiterate her love for him, driving him to higher and higher levels of anger and despise. He had ended the day with her by warning her never to call him again and telling her he was not interested in seeing her any longer. Chike had stormed out of the room and hoped that he was done with her for good.

Now with the telephone receiver in his hand, he knew that some terrible event was about to unfold. He did not have too long to wait before the bad news was broken to him.

"Actually Chike, I had not meant to bother you again", Azuka said choosing her words deliberately, "But I had to speak to someone. I am pregnant. In fact, I am almost in my third month of pregnancy. I am sorry Chike, I thought that I was in my safe period and I had also thought that you were in love with me and, as such, we could get married".

Chike was holding the telephone receiver so tightly in his hands that he could easily have crushed the equipment. He froze like meat in a cold storage locker. His mind raced in various directions. Panic, anger, fear, self-loathing, then more anger. His manhood shrunk like a shriveled umbilical cord, hardly recognizable from the throbbing, turgid vitality that had heralded his earlier encounters with Azuka.

"You are three months what?", Chike snarled into the telephone.

"Are you out of your mind? First, you start off on

123

this ridiculous tangent of loving me more than anything else in the world, after barely two weeks of knowing me, then you let yourself get pregnant, and as if that were not bad enough, you let three months go by before letting me know!."

Azuka resumed her sobbing, mumbling unintelligible words in between sobs.

"What exactly did you have in mind for me?" Chike pressed on in total disregard for Azuka's crying.

"Did you hope that if you presented me with the *fait accompli* of your advanced pregnancy, I would be left with little choice but to marry you? Was that it Azuka?", Chike spat into the receiver with unconcealed disgust.

Muffled sobs emanated from the other end of the phone line, intermingled with static.

"Where are you calling from Azuka?", Chike demanded.

"I am calling from home", came Azuka's whispered reply. "Well, we need to talk. Can you meet me at the Island Club in half an hour?".

"Yes", Azuka stammered, "I will be there in thirty minutes". Chike dropped the phone and sat staring in utter dejection. The worst had indeed happened. Now, his earlier premonition about Azuka had been confirmed: the girl is trouble.

124

THIRTY FIVE

Belonging to the Island Club in Lagos is the ultimate status symbol in that steamy former capital city. Most of the professionals, successful business men and women, highly placed government officials, members of the international diplomatic corp and other expatriates in Wazobia either on business trips or as technical advisers, all meet at that veritable house of the rich and snobbish.

The children of this privileged class mill around the club grounds in droves, quipping interminably in accents of at least a dozen languages, but all striving to show-off their masterly grasp of the Queen's English. Here, race pales into obscurity and the size or perhaps the depth of your wallet marches to the forefront as the salient discriminating criterion.

The model and make of your car, the number of vacations to Europe or America your family can pull off every year, are the new badges of distinction that decide on which notch of the social ladder you belong. More subtle indicators of class that go completely over the heads of the uninitiated include the make of your sun-glasses, wrist watch, tennis shoes, T-shirt, shorts, and, of course, tennis racquet.

The Europeans among this motley crowd of multi-racial "haves", often appear overwhelmed by the indefatigable energy of their Wazobian hosts. The economic advantage they enjoyed in the old colonial days over the "natives", as was the fashion to call them at the time, have all but been broken, if not totally in economic terms, certainly in psychological terms. The well pampered children of wealthy Wazobians have no knowledge of, let alone respect for the old white self-serving bogey of superiority. They bubble tirelessly, ready to outdo any of their western peers. A clear case of the convert who has become more Catholic than the Pope.

The verdant parking lot of the club remains almost always filled with a vast array of slick metallic beauties. Every new make and model of car is sure to be found there, gleaming in the sunlight. The guards, for whom the task has been set of keeping the gates secure for the tranquillity of their lords temporal, sit around their posts listlessly chewing *oji-Igbo* or *gworo*, handing out and retrieving parking permits as cars come and go, forcing self-immolating grins in the hope of a tip. They must, it seems, remain content at heaven's gate.

Chike showed his family membership card at the entrance of the club and went straight to the lounge, a rather interesting quadrangular structure located right in the middle of the main club building. He chose a table in a remote corner of the room, which affords some privacy, but allows panoramic view of the lounge. Chike ordered gin and tonic with ice. He felt he needed a bit of alcohol in his system after the shocking news he had heard barely half an hour ago.

As the waiter took his order and hurried off to fetch his drink, Chike kept wondering what he should do about the terrible mess he was in. Should he just go ahead and marry Azuka and save everybody the pain and embarrassment? His father would be ecstatic. In fact, if he finds out about Azuka's pregnancy, he might try to force him to marry her. After all, she is all that he had wanted for him--Igbo, well educated, and from a good family, as he would have put it.

One cold fact, however, kept intruding itself. Chike did not love Azuka. He knew inside himself that he had no emotional feelings for Azuka and that marriage even between people who love each other dearly is difficult enough, let alone between those that do not share such mutual affection.

What they had was the passionate explosion of pent-up lust. It erupted like an active volcano, after which everything returned to a status quo ante. No, his heart belonged to Bisi and that was something he could hardly deny to himself or anybody else.

The only realistic option, he thought to himself, was for Azuka to have an abortion. He was still doing his residency, he had little or no money of his own to speak of, and he was surely not ready for the responsibility of fatherhood. But what if Azuka refused? The only thing she had on him now was her pregnancy. With her professed love for him, the chances that she would agree to an abortion were nearly nil.

But what about the morality of the act of abortion? The Catholic church, of which he is a member, clearly condemns abortion as a sin - a kind of infanticide, and Chike was not himself at all sure that they were wrong. After all, a life was in fact in the making. If it is to be believed that man is made in the likeness of God, then it would follow that a deliberate

126

destruction of any such life in the making would be tantamount to destroying a piece of *Godlikeness*.

Chike was tormented by a terrible feeling of guilt about the fact that he was so seriously entertaining such an option. He felt that it was proof positive of the evil nature that was buried deep in his being.

But the converse thought plagued his mind as well. What is moral or fair about bringing into being a person whose life chances were greatly reduced or nonexistent? How moral an act is it to bring into life a child whose parents have neither the means, knowledge, or parental commitment to give them a good and healthy family life? Although he could not honestly say that that scenario applied to his situation, he felt that it would be bad enough for the child that he neither loves the mother, nor is willing to be there for him or her, as his own father has been for him.

It is not, after all, as though an unborn child is like someone caught outside in the cold, knocking furiously on the front door to be let into the warmth of the house. Someone not born does not know that they are not born. They simply lack consciousness, and thus, any sense of self-awareness, awareness of the world or life as we know it. Chike picked up a napkin on the table and scribbled a quick prose which had entered his mind in the course of his reverie. He called it fittingly, 'Dilemma':

> Which path must one walk? The social
> game of name and fame, or the soulful
> peace of truth and virtue?

> Which master must one dutifully serve,
> the inner self or the outer self? Thy
> conscience or the cosmos?

> When does man truly come of age, in
> power and pride, or in peace and
> wisdom?

> Which intimates man most with being's
> awe, the dazzling incandescence of a
> sunlight day, or the shadowy twilight
> of the moon's night?

> Which truly fills man's eye with
> wonder, and swells thy head in ponder,
> the dry sandy expanse of the Sahara,
> or the vast frozen stillness of the

arctic snow plains?

The highest heights of the mountain tops,
or the gaping depth of the valleys below?
Which takes thy breath most, the splendor
of falling snow flakes, or the thundery
torrent of a tropical rain?

Which path to walk remains man's dilemma
....Yet this poor creature even in his
exit of life's journey of counterpoises,
is left with a final question -- that he
really is not sure if he wants to die or
or not!!

As Chike sat engrossed in his worried thoughts, the waiter returned with his drink. "Two naira fifty kobo, Sir", the waiter said in a practiced monotone. Chike handed him three naira and asked him to keep the change. The waiter's mood changed from that of colorless indifference to effusive gratitude.

THIRTY SIX

While Chike was waiting for Azuka to show up, he remembered an Igbo fable an uncle of his had once told him. Once upon a time, in a village there was a very old man who lived by himself. So aged was this man that he had difficulty doing things for himself. A young boy of kindly disposition would always stop by the old man's house on his way back from school to gather firewood for the old one. Each day he would do this and the old man grew to like this boy very much. One day, about roughly a week before the old man breathed his last, he decided that before he dies he was going to give this boy something of value to express his gratitude for his kindness. But the old man owned virtually nothing, so it was difficult for him to give the boy something of material value.

After much reflection, the old man felt that he knew just the right gift an old man like himself could give a young man who still had a whole life ahead of him. He would give him wisdom--the benefit of his many years on earth. That evening when the boy came by in his usual fashion to gather firewood for the old man, the old man was standing in front of his house dressed up with his walking stick in his hand as though he was about to go somewhere.

"Where are you going my father", the boy inquired.

"I am going to the edge of the world and I would like you to accompany me".

Since the old man had never made any such request of him before and the boy was most curious to see what the edge of the world looked like, he agreed to go with the old man.

For seven days and seven nights they journeyed, crossing many rivers and forests. When eventually they got to the edge of the world, the old man asked the boy to shut his eyes and hold open both his hands. The boy complied, his curiosity mounting. The old man picked up a handful of moist clay and put it in the boys left hand. Then he made a gesture in space with his hand as if he were "catching" a handful of air. This he "put" in the boy's right hand and asked him to cover both hands. He then asked the boy to open his eyes. The boy complied. The old man asked the boy to open his left palm and tell him what he finds in it. The boy complied.

"Yes", the old man said, "it is indeed clay. This represents your body, your physical self. You can mold it into whatever shape or form you so desire. If you choose to have the strong supple body of a warrior, you can make that happen, if, on the other hand, you choose to be a flabby, weak, indolent, and sickly man you can make that happen as well".

The old man then asked the boy to open his right palm and the boy complied.

"What do you see", the old man asked the boy.

"Nothing", replied the boy with a quizzed look on his face.

"Yes", replied the old man, "that openness represents the freedom of your spirit. Every man has a spirit with wings. He can soar like the eagle and reach any height he sets for himself. You must take your life into your own hands and make what you will of it."

Finally, the old man took the boy to the very precipice of the world and asked him to look long and hard into the pleonastic void and tell him what he sees. The boy looked long and hard and told the old man that he saw nothing.

"Are you absolutely sure that you cannot see anything", the old man asked the boy.

"Yes", replied the boy, "I am absolutely sure."

"Well, you see my son, it is those things that we cannot see that often really matter in life. But you are right that there is nothing in the horizon. So too is the case with life. Life is a blank slate on which you must write your own story. All life is nothing unless you think and make something of it. That is all my son."

THIRTY SEVEN

Azuka entered the quadrangular club room, dressed in a simple loose-fitting African caftan dress, that was fashionably designed to tie in two bows on the shoulders, with splits on the sides, perhaps for easier body movement. She had on a scarf on her head of the same material as her dress, tied in traditional style.

Chike could see her lithe body moving in a perfect left-right-left-right rhythm as her hips swung from side to side as she crossed the lounge to where he was sitting. She had a doubtlessly sexy body....but her mind....her reasoning....that was something else....Chike thought to himself.

As she got to the table, he stood up and came around the table to pull out the chair for her to sit down, his gentlemanly etiquette, being more the result of force of habit than genuine concern for her. She sat down stiffly, her face portraying a wooden impassivity. Chike returned to his seat and sat down heavily with a sigh. Sitting directly opposite Azuka, he noticed that her eyes were red and swollen from crying and this gave her usually narrow looking face a rather puffy appearance.

"Would you like something to drink", Chike asked her as a logical extension of his conditioned gentlemanly reflex.

"No thank you," Azuka replied, her eyes beginning to fill up with tears and her lips starting to tremble from an impending sob. "Why not have a shot of brandy or some other stiff drink, it will help your nerves?" Chike ventured.

"No, I'd rather not drink anything," Azuka replied in the same monotone.

At this point, Chike felt that the social preamble was over and the time had come to get down to business. He cleared his throat and took a swig of his gin and tonic.

"Azuka, I can hardly believe what you told me not too long ago over the telephone. What is this business of your being pregnant? Were you really serious, or were you playing some kind of cruel joke?"

Of course, inside himself Chike knew full well that she was dead serious, but somehow he wished for some higher power to miraculously turn the whole affair into a nightmare from which he was soon to awaken.

Azuka started sobbing softly.

"Chike, I already told you before that I am almost at the end of my first trimester of pregnancy. Why would I lie about a thing like this? Or does it mean that you no longer remember what you did that led to this situation?"

Azuka fixed her large brown eyes on him with a coldness that momentarily unnerved Chike. For a second, Chike could have sworn that he saw naked hate dancing in her eyes like little devils plotting the undoing of some unfortunate soul.

"When it was 'sweeting' you," Azuka pressed on, "you forgot that it is sperms that you carry in your testicles and not plain water. Now you act all surprised that nature has taken its course. Did you imagine that you are sterile, or that I am barren? What made you so cock-sure that the risk we took would amount to nothing? Or were you so enraptured in passion that you could not think straight? Tell me, Chike, I am all ears?"

In the brief period that Chike had come to know Azuka, he had never known her to be this vocal, combative and determined. Her anger and resentment were evident. She had gambled on the hope that her pregnancy would win him over. However, now that the strategy was not working, her fangs were out, ready to draw blood.

"First of all, Azuka, I would never have had sex with you if I had the slightest idea that you were not using any kind of contraception. The very fact that you are a woman, and as such, the one that directly bears the burden of pregnancy and the pain of childbirth, behooves you to be more responsible about getting pregnant."

"Oh, I see," Azuka cut in, "because I am a woman, does that excuse you, the man, from your own responsibility in getting me pregnant?"

"No, it does not," Chike quickly responded. "However, I think that given the biological realities of the disproportionate burden that a woman bears in the process, she should be the wiser for it."

"What if I simply picked up and faded into the sunset, abdicating my own responsibility as the man, whom, as you put it, got you pregnant? What then? Where does that leave you, the woman, who remains heavy with child? Tell me, Azuka, I am all ears."

"Anyway," Azuka interjected, "all this is water over the dam. The deed has already been done. I am already pregnant and you are not about to fade into the sunset. Therefore, I think that the more pertinent question is, what are we going to do about our situation?"

"Did I just hear you say 'our situation'? Am I pregnant?," Chike asked rhetorically, rubbing both his hands on his surf board flat stomach as he spoke. "I believe it is more like 'what are we going to do about your situation?' I need to make something perfectly clear to you right away. I am deeply in love with Bisi and we are engaged to be married. I made that clear to you right from the onset, and nothing has or will change in that regard."

Chike's last comments hit Azuka like a mailed fist. She sat silently for about five minutes, attempting to digest the harsh reality of the fact that Chike does not love her and is not going to marry her, regardless of the fact that she is carrying his child. She nevertheless made one last valiant effort at changing Chike's mind by employing the use of some diplomatic arm twisting.

"Well, let me make one thing clear to you right away, Chike, I have every intention of having this baby, with or without you. I do not intend to have an abortion, so don't even entertain that as an option in your mind."

Azuka studiously watched Chike's facial expression to see if her ruse was paying off. To her dismay, Chike stood his ground, totally unmoved by her scare tactics. They argued back and forth, each putting forward one eloquent argument after the other for their respective positions: Chike, that she have an abortion; Azuka, that she carry the pregnancy to term.

By the time their painful encounter came to an end, it was almost dusk and the club was about to close for the day. Chike reiterated his position with brutal emphasis, even as he got up to leave.

"Azuka, I tell you one last time. I have a good friend, Dr. Okoronkwo, who is a gynecologist. He can take care of this problem with no difficulty at all. If you agree to have him take care of it, perhaps you and I can revisit this whole business of a relationship. But if you refuse to have him take care of it, you can be sure that you are very much on your own."

Azuka knew that if she agreed to have an abortion, that would be the last she would ever see Chike again. She was not stupid enough to believe that if she went along with him, he would actually reconsider having a relationship with her, let alone marrying her. She got up slowly and accepted the piece of paper that Chike handed her, containing Dr. Okoronkwo's clinic address.

THIRTY EIGHT

Chike's appetite almost completely disappeared. His normally forceful personality became a shadow of its former self. His mind was in perpetual turmoil. He had nightmares that left him drained the next day and days that left him too worried to sleep peacefully come night time.

The one question that kept haunting him was, what if something happens to Azuka during the abortion? What if she is permanently deformed, unable to bear children or even more troubling, what if the worst were to happen and she dies? He had heard enough horror stories about girls who tried having abortions and ended up bleeding to death or dying as a result of one infection or another. Although he was studying to be a medical doctor, his area of specialization was not gynecology, and worse still his training made him even more aware of some of the potential dangers.

Chike's fears haunted him right up to the time the abortion was finally scheduled. The night prior to the day the abortion was to be performed, Chike suffered a terrible nightmare. He dreamt that something horrible had happened. Although he could not quite remember the specific details of the tragedy, he had gone completely out of his mind and had to be committed to an asylum.

The asylum Chike was sent to in his dream was the one located at Uwani in Enugu. It lies next to the old highly reputable high school called College of Emmanuel's Consecration, or simply C.E.C. The school had been established many years ago by Irish missionaries bent on the Christianization of that part of Wazobia. Its barbed wire precincts had produced over the years an enviable alumni in all works of life spread across the vast country of Wazobia and beyond.

Ironically, opposite this exemplary educational monument, lay the asylum. A hideously stolid brick and mortar configuration that bears a look about it as solemn and eerie as the scenes that take place within its confines. Behind the curious enough bedfellows of the nut house and the highbrow secondary school, lies a huge thickly vegetated gorge, that gapes open wide enough to perhaps be called a valley.

At the bottom of this valley-gorge runs a small freshwater creek, which for many years served as the sole source of water for the residents of the community built on the edge of the valley-gorge, known generally as *Ugwu Aaron*--Aaron's Hill. At dawn, this vegetation-rich valley-gorge turns into a spontaneous orchestra of insects, birds and a thousand other nondescript creatures as Mother Nature rouses her mysterious companions from their countless nocturnal habitats.

As Chike lay in his hospital room in his dream, streaks of daylight streamed in, waking him from his drug-induced sleep from the previous night. His eye lids fluttered open, quickly narrowing into slits as his eyes adjusted to the shock of the daylight.

Yesterday had been one of his most violent days since he arrived at the asylum. After biting one of the hospital attendants, strong arms bore him down as he frothed and foamed in the mouth like a rabid dog, gurgling and shrieking unearthly sounds. The strong arms were those of the hospital attendants struggling desperately to force him into a straight jacket. Somehow, even though they were four able-bodied men, uncanny, almost superhuman strength issued from Chike's body, giving the attendants a very hard time.

Chike's eyes had that vacant, crazed look that one so often sees in the eyes of a goat being slaughtered as the final gasps of life leaves its body. Chike's mind floated about in his head like a detached fetus in the amniotic fluid of a womb. He was utterly confused about himself.

His mind-self stood dispassionately aside from his body-self and his body-self seemed to linger with no apparent connection to his being-self. Who he is, his essence and his existence, both of which he grasped little of anymore, had parted ways in his mind, leaving him a hydra-headed freak. Chike kept on struggling, although his physical protestations were no longer as prodigious as was earlier the case.

As his wild thrashing began to subside, one of the attendants produced a hypodermic syringe full of a powerful sedative. Timing Chike's struggle-pause, struggle-pause rhythm, he sank the needle into an exposed bicep and emptied the contents of the syringe. Many balls of light exploded in Chike's head. Bluish, yellowish, greenish balls of light flared, grew in size and exploded into a shimmering nova of other rainbow colors. His mind melted before him like ice-cream placed on the hearth of a fireplace. No, it was more like a piece of plastic thrown into a furnace - it crumpled, liquefied and melted into a dripping sog, discolored and unrecognizably disfigured.

His legs became rubber and came loose underneath him. They seemed like two uncoordinated extensions with minds of their own. Each leg went its merry way. His left leg simply would not budge. He could not even wiggle his toes. They lay there numb and limp, dead weights. His right leg twitched as though possessed by an epileptic fit. Something must be wrong, Chike vaguely remembered thinking in his soporific delusion.

His head throbbed from a steady ache that would not go away. It felt like it was being stampeded by a herd of African elephants. He tried to command both his hands to hold his head, but, naturally, trapped in the straight jacket, they were oblivious to his urging. They lay there, lifeless clay forms. Chike burst into tears, sobbing with the helplessness of a child being punished by a totally dominant adult.

As he nursed his headache, a chasm opened up in his mind's eye. From the edge of the chasm, he peered precariously into the bottomless abyss and could see fumes emanating from it like dust haze hanging over a valley on a cold harmattan morning. As Chike tried to get a better view of the chasm, he tripped, lost his balance and plunged into the void. He tried to scream, but nothing came out. Once more he fell into another deep, drug induced slumber.

THIRTY NINE

Chike awoke from his nightmare, soaked with sweat. He was also quite certain that something had gone wrong. He could not call the clinic where Azuka was because it was too early in the morning, and he could hardly drive there as well for the same reason. His anxiety was feeding on itself and driving him half out of his mind, or what was left of it. Little devils danced in gleeful mockery in his imagination. Their horned foreheads, hoofed feet, and arrowhead-tipped tails completed the medieval picture of their unholy appearance in his mind.

To drag himself out of his muddy thoughts, he lapsed into his poetic mood. But the lines that were occurring to him were neither strictly poetry nor prose, meandering one into the other, and back again. A jumbled philosophical journey of a worried mind groping for a lifeboat in a raging ocean storm. He reached out for a note pad on the bedside stool and wrote down these thoughts anyway:

> For what this waiting game life? Why
> does a flower blossom only to wither
> away sometime?
>
> Why do we have to be born so dainty
> and fresh, only to grow old, sickly,
> and die?
>
> Why is it that the sun rises every
> dawning day, only to set at dusk?
> Pray tell, for what this endless
> cycle?
>
> Why is it we have pleasure and
> happiness, only to be soon accompanied
> by pain and sorrow?
>
> OBODO-AMANKWO -- ancient oracle of my
> ancestors, open my eyes that I might
> see, my ears that I might hear, my mind
> that I might understand, my heart that
> I might have faith and love; reveal to
> me through some divine spectacle the
> purpose of life's being.
>
> I scream a howling rage of sorrow, so

deep within nothing can quite fathom.
Its resounding echoes beckons the
emptiness of life. Its scowling
wretchedness wrapped in life's
cyclical finitude.

Why must one grow into adulthood only
to be exposed to its trials of weary
helplessness, naked inhumanity, and
endless worries -- for what this waiting
game, life?

Pain, Oh pain, life's closest companion.
The curse of the gods on all humanity.
The wrath of nature on all living
creatures found within her ever moving
bowels. Pleasure's eternal opponent.
Able captain of the ship of sorrow.
Victorious conqueror of intermissions of
pleasure and happiness; what is your
purpose in life?

Still those moments of joy in life
persist. Verily, verily, life is an
eternal mystery. Embodying deeper
mystery than that which holds all the
heavenly bodies sway; greater mystery than
that which signals the seasons change;
greater mystery still than that which has bred
such wondrous variation in nature--Oh
for what this waiting game, life?

FORTY

Meanwhile at the clinic, Azuka had been put on drips, according to the doctor, to make her womb dilate. For much of the day, she bore the discomfort of the needles in her veins and the torment of her conscience. Her mind went round in circles. Why would Chike not simply marry her? Was she not good enough for him? After all, she is bearing his child. They both appeared to have really cared for each other when they had their intense frolic.

Why are men so selfish and insensitive, Azuka thought to herself? All Chike seems concerned with is his convenience and his freedom. Yes, freedom to move on to new pastures, to covert and corrupt innocent and unsuspecting young girls; get them in trouble like she is, and expect them to just do what is most convenient for him.

As her thoughts traveled, so did her emotions. They went from blaming herself, to blaming Chike, to blaming her parents, and to blaming "society." Finally, her thoughts and emotions made their way to the inevitable issue of the morality of abortion.

Azuka struggled with the issue for almost an hour, asking herself serious questions about the pros and cons of the issue.

What right, she queried herself, did she have to bring a life into the world that would not have a father there for it? To bring into the world, a child that might not have the economic opportunity for a healthy development as an individual?

What could possibly be moral about such an act - condemning a human being to a lifetime sentence of unnecessary hardship under the bogus pretension of a reverence for life. But then she struggled with the converse. What right did she have to terminate the coming into being of a life which no one can foretell what it might turn out to be?

There are, after all, enough rags-to-riches stories in the world to fill a several libraries. What if this child turns out to be Africa's next great leader? What if..., what if.... what if.... The questions flooded her mind, but the answers were nowhere to be found.

The more she thought about the issue, however, the wearier she became about going through with the abortion. Eventually, by about six in the evening, when dusk was beginning to set in and the nurses were taking their evening shift, Azuka decided she would not go through with the abortion, come what may. Steeling herself, she pulled out the needles one after the other from her arms, drawing a stream of blood every time each needle made its exit from her veins. She made her way gingerly to the wardrobe, where she put on her street clothes.

Tiptoeing out of her room and down the stairs, she let herself out of the clinic building. Her heart was throbbing almost uncontrollably. Two thoughts preoccupied her mind: What is she going to do about having the baby?, and what will Chike do to her when he finds out what she has done?

FORTY ONE

Azuka hailed down a taxi cab. "Where?," asked the cab driver in that inevitable tone of impatience that every one who has ever taken a cab in Wazobia is familiar with.

Cab drivers the world over have a remarkably similar range of attitudes towards passengers. They are either very talkative, jacks-of-all-trades-and-masters-of-none kind of fellows, or they tend to be very withdrawn and sullen. In whichever case, they invariably act towards the passenger like they are doing them a favor, as though they are providing the ride free of charge.

Without answering the cab driver, Azuka opened the rear door and let herself into the car.

"Sister, where you de go?," the cab driver inquired again, expressing a rare patience which he reserves only for pretty young women like Azuka. Only they are allowed in his unwritten code of conduct to take certain liberties.

"Just drive around for a while please, while I make up my mind where I should go."

"Dat one na your own palaver sister, my own be make you pay me my money. Me, afit take you go Jericho if na de ting you want. But sister make I ask you, how person like you go call taxzee when you know know where you won go? Children of nowadays, na wa for una."

He deftly slipped the cab back unto the busy road, and began heading in the general direction of Lagos mainland.

Azuka was trying desperately to decide where on earth she should go. She knew that her parent's home was completely out of the question. Her father, especially, would probably carry out her execution personally. At any rate, he would never allow her to stay in his house through her pregnancy. She could not think of any friends that she could go to stay in their homes. She would be faced with the same problem as with her parents, assuming that they themselves were willing to help.

She toyed with the idea of going straight to Chike's parents and spilling the beans, but she decided against it for the simple reason that she is aware that if Chike were seriously bent on not marrying her, not even his parents, in the final analysis, can force him to do so. What, after all, can they do, tie a rope around his neck like *efi*, and drag him to the altar? Besides, she thought to herself, what kind of a life would it be to live with a man whom you know full well does not love you and does not want to be married to you?

It was at this point that the thought occurred to her that she could go to her aunt Nneka. Yes, aunt Nneka would surely help her. She was one of the kindest human beings Azuka had ever known. Aunt Nneka's deep humanity arose partly out of her own life experiences. Life had not been very kind to her. She was married, divorced, re-married and divorced, with six children altogether from her first and second marriages to show for it. She would understand like nobody else.

"Driver," Azuka called from the back seat of the cab, "please take me to Surulere number 41 Onitsha street off Oguneye Road."

"Sister," the cab driver replied, "I go charge you from here go Surulere, plus including de one weh you done dey drive up and down dis place. Not when I tell you de money weh you go pay, you go begin de make wahala for me."

He swung his car unto the freeway from the service road, and sped off to Surulere.

142

FORTY TWO

The sun seemed to stand still in the horizon. Its orange glow filtering through the blue sky and the white clouds looking like puffs of cotton wool suspended in space. Yet, Chike knew that this image of seeming motionlessness is an optic illusion.

Still dreary and depressed from his dream and hounded by his worries about Azuka, Chike thought that perhaps even life itself, with all its teeming animation, may well be an illusion. An appearance which deceives the human eye with the illusion of permanence, meaning, and purpose. Perhaps, all that is real is the appearance, the illusion itself.

He drew himself out of his reverie with a shudder and made haste to go to the clinic where Azuka was in order to check on her condition. He walked to the junction of the major road in his neighborhood, where people usually pick up taxi cabs. In a short while, a taxi came by and Chike told the cab driver that he was going to Ikeja. The taxi driver pulled over and Chike got into the car. When he reached the clinic, the nurse in charge of the ward in which Azuka was admitted was almost hysterical. She had been searching for Azuka all night long. She could not explain what had happened. Had somebody kidnapped her? Had her boyfriend come earlier on in the day and forced her to leave with him? Or had they both changed their minds about going through with the abortion and decided simply to leave?

All night long, she dashed around the clinic asking other nurses and ward attendants if they had seen Azuka. She knew, of course, that if anything goes wrong, she would be held responsible as the staff nurse in charge of the ward at night. Their head nurse, a woman with whom she had no love lost, would undoubtedly use the incident as a convenient excuse to nail her for incompetence, as though there was anything she could have done to have avoided the present situation. After all, she thought to herself, already mentally rehearsing her defense, she discovered the present situation yesterday evening when she came to the clinic to take over from the nurses that had been on the day shift.

As soon as she put away her personal effects into her locker, she made a beeline for Azuka's room, only to find that she was nowhere to be found. She checked the bathroom, the lounge area and the veranda, but there was still no trace of Azuka. She then went back to Azuka's room, only to realize that in her anxiety and haste, she had failed to take notice of the half-full plastic drip bag hanging on it's stand with the needle on the end of the flow-tube dangling freely. It was then that she began to seriously panic.

When she saw Azuka's boyfriend, Chike, walking into the ward, she practically crashed into him. She peppered him with questions. For a moment, Chike was totally bemused. It was only gradually that he began to make sense of what the young nurse was saying. An incredible sense of panic enveloped him.

"What has Azuka gone and done now,?" he thought to himself.

Once more, his deep mistrust of her judgment, her reasoning, as he puts it, gnawed at him.

"Where, for Godsake, could she possibly have gone to," Chike thought to himself.

His immediate conclusion was that she must have escaped with the objective of carrying the pregnancy to term.

"Women," Chike thought to himself, "they can be such impractical creatures...such a pain in the....No wonder his people have a saying that a woman can be like a bee perched on a man's scrotum. One does not quite know what to do with it. If you let the bee stay on the scrotum, it may sting you. If you try to smack the bee, you may do damage to the old testicles."

"Well," Chike managed at last to say to the nurse who was still standing literally in his face wild eyed, "I think I better go and start looking for her. Please let Dr. Okoronkwo know as soon as he gets in what the situation is. And be sure to tell him that he should mail the bill to me. I will pay for everything."

Chike walked out of the clinic in a daze. He had not the slightest idea where to begin looking for Azuka. The familiar myriad emotions of fear, rage and disgust, began to haunt him in succession. He kept asking himself why one should have to go through so much trouble for such momentary pleasure? It all seemed grotesquely out of proportion - the pleasure matched against the pain, it was altogether too high a price to pay.

He crossed the road to a kiosk where snacks and cold drinks are sold. He ordered a cold bottle of Coke-a-Cola and some 'roasted chicken parts,' as the sign hanging over the glass-sided container which held the pieces of chicken read. In the 95- degree heat and 100% humidity of Lagos, the cold drink felt refreshing beyond words.

FORTY THREE

Aunt Nneka was busy washing *onugbu* leaves, which she was going to use to make bitter-leaf soup. She is the second child of her parents, Mr. and Mrs Obi. Everybody in their village agrees that Nneka Obi was the most beautiful girl in the village when she was a young teenager. She grew tall, pretty, and well built, and her father especially, looked forward with pride to when a suitor would come laden with gifts, to ask for the hand of his queen as he often called her. As time went by, many suitors did come, many Nneka rejected, many her father rejected, until Dr. Ikechukwu came along.

"Doc," as everybody calls him, studied Civil Engineering in the United States. He earned his doctoral degree in a university in the northwestern part of the United States. Earlier, he had graduated *suma cum laude* as an undergraduate in a university in the South, before going to the northwest to pursue his graduate studies. Throughout his graduate education, he maintained a nearly 4.0 cumulative grade point average. As far as he was concerned, this outstanding academic achievement of his confirmed beyond doubt that he is God's gift to humanity in general and particularly to women, for whom he imagined he represents the ultimate eligible bachelor.

While in the United States, "Doc" steadfastly resisted the temptation of marrying a "foreign" woman, as he refers to them. Of course, totally out of the question for him was marriage to any woman who is not black. However, an additional stricture which attended his definition of "foreign" women was that it included every woman except Igbo women. Worse still, the definition included women of all of Igboland except women from his village. He had well-worn uncomplimentary stereotypes for women of every Igbo sub-group other than those from his village.

The Onitsha-Igbo women, he would say, cannot stay in a man's house - ascribing to them a congenital unfaithfulness that militates against family life. The Imo-Igbo women, he would say, "has an excessive love of money." Even if a man were lucky enough to find one that does not love money too much, he will grow gray hairs early in his life from footing the bill for the education of every single member of her immediate and extended family. A kind of never-ending dowry.

The only good women were women from his village. They alone qualify to enter the race to compete for the trophy of his hand in marriage. Consequently, although "Doc" spent nearly fifteen years in the United States and had many relationships with her "foreign" women, he kept his solemn oath to marry none of them.

A nutrition and exercise fanatic, "Doc" kept himself trim and fit through all those years in America - the 'land of the fat and happy', as he would sometimes jokingly refer to the United States. When he finally returned to Wazobia, he looked every bit the most eligible bachelor. Fairly well-to-do, solid educational credentials to boot and the proud owner of a brand new Mercedes Benz, a major status symbol in Wazobia.

The girls in Wazobia swarmed around him like flies in a local abattoir, each hoping to be the lucky one to bear the title of Mrs. Ikechukwu. True to style, "Doc" wined, dined, and then made each female pilgrim pay due homage to the altar of his phallic god, without committing himself to any of Wazobia's "foreign" women, who had the singular misfortune of not hailing from his village.

It was during this period that "Doc" went home to his village one Christmas and met Nneka Obi. He was completely smitten by her beauty. Her tall elegant frame. Her long slender torso that carries a pair of marvelous "boobs," as "Doc" refers to them in his acquired Americanism. Her backside, which flutes out prominently without the hint of excessive protuberance. It moves around under her clothes with a rhythmic precision that suggests healthy muscular tone.

Her face is, by far, her greatest asset. A beautiful set of perfect white teeth greets her every smile. She has lips that are perhaps uncharacteristically thin for an Igbo, but which are boldly defined even in their thinness. Sort of like two lines drawn with the aid of a magic marker that contains very dark legible ink.

Her hair is a thick black mass of woven snake-like patterns piled up on her dome. Her legs, slightly bowed, perfectly molded cylinders. Her skin color is of a light-brown hue. All in all, she could go anywhere in the world and several heads would undoubtedly turn in her direction if she strolled by.

"Doc" went after Nneka Obi like a hungry lion. He was determined that she would be the prize-chosen mother of his children. Here at last were all his dreams realized: an Igbo girl from his village, a stunning beauty from a good family. What

146

more can a man ask for? His hunt for Nneka, however, was by no means an easy one. In addition to her physical beauty, Nneka was arrogant, self-assured, and possessed of a mind entirely her own. Biding his time, "Doc" decided to tread softly.

He forced himself to exercise far more patience than he is of the habit of enduring for womensake. He forced himself to observe his manners strictly, to follow meticulously the social graces of opening car and restaurant doors for Nneka, holding chairs for her to sit in and buying her an incessant flow of well-timed gifts.

Complementing this hot pursuit of Nneka was "Doc's" strategy for winning her father over. He fed the old man's pocket and ego. His pocket he lined with money. His ego he fed with flattery. He fed Mr. Obi's delusion that Nneka is not just a beautiful woman, but the most beautiful woman in the world--that she is a queen. He constantly gave the old man the impression that he is captivated by his wisdom and intelligence. Mr. Obi, a thorough-going sop, soaked up "Doc's" gambit like a floor mop.

Contrary to the impression "Doc" was giving to Mr. Obi, he actually thought of Nneka's father as a self-indulgent, pompous, self-opinionated old goat that was living out the last dreary days of his life in the village with nothing better to do than dote on his daughter. But his daughter, Nneka, was exquisite and he, "Doc," wanted her desperately.

Eventually, "Doc" got his wish. Nneka became his wife and they had four children, one right after the other. But as the saying goes, 'be careful what you wish for, it might come true'- this marriage, seemingly made in heaven, began a turn for the worse after their last child.

For some inexplicable reason, Nneka started to gain enormous amounts of weight. Her breasts, hips and buttocks ballooned. She began to take on the appearance of a bowl of pounded yam, to which are attached celluloid stumps called legs and hefty arms that seem like bags filled with melting duck-fat hanging end-to-end on horizontal poles. She became lazy and shiftless. Her appetite increased dramatically, as though rising to the occasion of supplying the expanding blimp with the extra nutrients required to maintain its new elephantine proportions. It was not too long before "Doc" bolted from the marriage and Wazobia, returning to the United States and its "foreign" women.

FORTY FOUR

Aunt Nneka is a woman full of life. Her buxom figure adds a wholesomeness to her appearance that is only outdone by the perfect symmetry of the bone structure of her face. She was certainly blessed by the Maker with a deceptively youthful appearance, for she is about forty five years of age, but could easily pass for twenty five, although she has definitely grown quite fat.

As a result of her life experiences, she had become somewhat of a religious fanatic. She has a most consuming religious faith, which is anchored to her unshakable belief that God has a special place in his heart for her. She is possessed of a faith in God that might embarrass even the Pontiff in Rome. Constantly, she tells her friends and relatives that God watches over her, sometimes quoting from one of the numerous biblical passages she often reads that the Lord, ..."is her shepherd and lays her down to rest in green pastures..."

One good thing that her faith does for her, however, is that it makes it possible for her to take philosophically the many hard knocks that life has dealt her. If she did not have such stout faith, it is quite possible that she might have died out of sheer despair. Whenever something goes wrong in her life, she tells herself that things could have been worse, or that the misfortune she is experiencing is, in fact, a blessing in disguise. On other occasions, she convinces herself that the misfortune is penance that God is sending her in order that she might atone for her past sins.

One example of such misfortune in her life was most certainly her second marriage. It had been, to put it mildly, an unmitigated disaster. She had been remarried for less than two years when her husband's attitude towards her changed from heartwarming affection to burning despise. So scathing was this despise that even thinking of it six years after their divorce still makes her shudder.

Her second husband beat her every once in awhile, and on almost every occasion, for the most trivial reasons. On one occasion, for instance, he claimed that there was too much pepper in his soup. The next day, he complained of exactly the opposite: there was supposedly too little pepper in his bitter-leaf soup.

In reality, he was simply a near-retard bent on compensating for what he lacked in civility and intelligence with brute force. He made love to her like she was a woman of easy virtue that he had bought for a bargain price in the red-light district of Lagos. He topped off all this with a seemingly incessant barrage of unprintable insults, designed to batter down the wall of her self esteem.

Eventually, the situation got so bad that he began threatening to kill her. It was at this point that she decided that the time had come for her to make her exit. His periodic brutality she might have endured; his philandering she chucked up to the insufferable sexual nature of men; but his homicidal threats were simply more than she could take.

When the nightmare finally ended, Aunt Nneka went to her local parish priest and had him offer *Novena* masses for her, telling herself in her usual fashion, that this was probably a blessing in disguise, and that things could have been a lot worse.

FORTY FIVE

Aunt Nneka had become quite heart-broken from her failed second marriage, which in all fairness to her, had been no fault of hers. Yet, Wazobian society, steeped as it is in its split personality of traditionalism and modernity, treated her as though she is a failure because she is a divorcee. In fact, at some point a rumor started to go round from Godknowswhere, that she was some kind of a witch that had the habit of jinxing her men when she got fed up with them.

Heavy-hearted and quite forlorn, aunt Nneka decided to go and stay in the village for a while to let things cool off. There, she knew at least that her many relatives, in their usual manner, would show her unconditional love and understanding. Moreover, she knew that in the village she would meet her paternal uncle, a man she loves and adores so completely that she sometimes wished that he had been her biological father.

Two days after she got back to the village, she went to see her uncle. After their greetings and warm embrace, she poured her heart out to him, sobbing uncontrollably. He listened in rapt attention, seeming to store away every word she uttered into the inner recesses of his mind. She remembered the wizened look on her uncle's face. Oily waxen creases furrowed on his forehead, giving him the distinguished appearance of a deep thinker. After listening to her for what seemed like an eternity, her uncle took her right hand gently, clasping it between his two rough palms.

Staring at her for about a minute, words began to issue from his mouth in a soft gentle stream that sounded to aunt Nneka like sweet melodious notes of aged wisdom.

"My daughter," he said, his voice wavering ever so slightly, "it is important that you realize that a human being who has been raised by loving parents, and who have themselves become a loving parent, forfeits the right to lose hope. By becoming a parent, you have made a pact with Chukwu and the ancestors, that you will do all that is within your power to make the future a better one for those whom you have brought into this world."

"My child, always bear in mind that you give up your right to despair and faithless inaction the moment fate extends to you the privilege and responsibility of parenthood. Go back to the city my daughter, do that which must be done right for the young ones to grow strong and sensible, just as you have grown, and smell the roses whenever and wherever you can. Remember the great wisdom of our people, when they say that time is man's greatest challenge. Time he does not have, time he does not know what to do with, and time he must have to do what he must, while he can. Try my lovely daughter to use yours wisely."

With that piece of advise, her uncle got up, gave her a long hug, kissed her on the forehead, and retired into his bedroom. He was no longer a young man, and, therefore, tires easily. Two days after their heart-to-heart chat, aunt Nneka's uncle died. His household woke up the morning of that fateful day, only to discover that he had died quietly in his sleep. Once again, it appeared that life had no place of mercy in its heart for aunt Nneka. First, it had been her ruined second marriage; now, it was death stealing away her most beloved uncle just when she felt she needed his presence more than ever before.

FORTY SIX

"Nene," aunt Nneka yelled at her house maid, "bring your lazy self here immediately."

The poor wretch nervously ambled in from the adjacent room, where she had been looking for a bottle of palm oil for aunt Nneka, with both her hands on her head as though she had grown quite tired of waiting hand and foot on aunt Nneka.

"Where is the palm oil I asked you to bring nearly half an hour ago? Nene, you are the laziest girl I have ever met." Actually, Nene was anything but lazy. Her daily work schedule would have strained even the most diligent adult worker, let alone a twelve-year-old girl. Every morning without fail, she was up at six a.m.. She would sweep the house, boil hot water for 'madam's bath,' as she most times refers to aunt Nneka, and then, cook breakfast. Aunt Nneka in the meantime would still be snoring soundly, only to awaken at about eight o'clock, barking one order or another at Nene, or complaining that she had failed to execute some chore at all, or not done another well enough.

"Madam, I could not find the bottle of palm oil, I was still looking for it when you called me," Nene managed to stammer.

"What do you mean you could not find the bottle of palm oil, did the bottle grow legs and walk away? Or have you gone and sold my palm oil to someone? Come on, go back into that store and bring me that bottle of palm oil immediately before I beat some sense into your head."

Nene beat a quick retreat. The last thing she wanted was one of those knuckle blows that aunt Nneka sometimes deals her on the head. They are so painful that they usually give her an instant headache.

Azuka got out of the cab in front of aunt Nneka's house. She asked the cab driver to wait a few minutes, while she goes into the house to get some money to pay him off. The cab driver immediately begins protesting about how she is wasting his time and how time is money or some such worn out cliche'.

"Ah, sister make you do quick quick ooh. I know de get moni for *garri* from carrying woman up and down like 'driver-madam.' Ah, no be so ooh. Make you try do quick," the cab driver called after her as she made her way to her aunt's front door.

Azuka did not even bother to dignify the cab driver's innuendo with a reply. Azuka knocked firmly on aunt Nneka's front door.

"Onye?," came aunt Nneka's strong voice.

"Aunt Nneka, it is Azuka Nkemdilim, may I come in?"

"Onye," aunt Nneka called out again a little louder, apparently not hearing Azuka the first time.

"Aunt Nneka, it is Azuka may I come in?!!," Azuka practically shouted.

"Oh, Azuka, my wonderful daughter, give me one second I am coming to open the door right away."

As soon as the door swung open they both flew into each other's arms.

"Azuka," aunt Nneka crooned in undisguised joy, "let me look at you," she continued sumptuously, pushing Azuka away from her to arms length and looking at her from head to toe and back to the head.

"You look quite well. You have grown into a very beautiful young woman. Do you realize how long it has been since I saw you last. It has been at least four years and yet we live in the same city. I think you simply decided to throw away your aunt Nneka." The cabby blew his horn.

FORTY SEVEN

zuka woke up during the first night of her stay at aunt Nneka's place with streaks of pain shooting through her body. She felt the pains come and go at regular intervals. She knew at once that the pains were the dreaded "contractions. By about 4 A.M. in the morning, the fetus aborted with a swiftness that belied her earlier agony. She was filled with a great sense of loss and anguish.

Azuka felt like she had now lost everything. First it was Chike, whom she soon discovered was not hers to keep, and now, it is the pregnancy, the only living testimony of their shared passion. Tears flowed freely down Azuka's face. She sobbed steadily, wishing that somehow a miracle would turn everything into merely a bad dream from which she would soon awaken.

Azuka decided in her dark grief that she will never marry in her life time, and that never again will she give herself so freely to any man. She thought to herself that even if and when she decides to do so, her heart will never be in it.

Men, she thought to herself, do not understand the meaning of true affection. All they want is bestial gratification of their carnal desires. Whenever they are in heat, much like the proverbial *mkpi*, they will lie through their teeth, feign love, admiration and dedication, anything it takes to get the poor unsuspecting women to indulge them. No sooner are they sated, than they start discovering all the reasons in the world why the woman is not quite the right person or why the relationship simply would not work.

The part of the whole affair that had Azuka totally mystified, is why, again and again, women fall for the same ruse, almost as if they are in some kind of an absurdist drama written by Mother Nature, in which the male is forever destined to lie and the female forever destined to believe.

Azuka crawled back into bed shivering slightly as she was becoming a little feverish. Aunt Nneka, who had been awakened by the sound of the creaking hinges on the bedroom and bathroom doors, and the water from the faucet, had hidden behind her slightly ajar bedroom door, when she realized that it was Azuka. She saw Azuka walk into the bathroom with a bundle of soiled sheets. She, of course, knew what had happened, since the night before, she had mixed into Azuka's bowl of bitter-leaf soup an ancient African herb which was used many centuries ago for these kind of contingencies.

She felt sorry for her little niece, for she knew from personal experience, how alone a woman can feel at moments like these. She felt certain, however, that she had done what was best for Azuka. The last thing she needs is the life long responsibility of a child, and the equally life long social stigma that would surely come with having a bastard child.

Azuka got up in the morning feeling slightly nauseous. Her fever had got worse during the night, leaving her with a high temperature. Her aunt appeared at her bedroom door a few minutes later like a fairy godmother. She opened the door with a contrived flourish meant to cheer Azuka up. Aunt Nneka was carrying a locally made tray in her hands. The tray is made of bamboo and woven raffia and contained a plate full of *akara*, a steaming bowl of *akamu* and two neatly peeled oranges. She knew that this was Azuka's favorite breakfast food from when she was a little girl in Enugu.

Outside the front yard, one could overhear the chickens already busy with their endless search for edibles in every nook and cranny of the yard, *kokoroko-ing* to one another as they go about their business. The neighbor's mangy dog darts about the yard, yelping and barking, as he always does in the mornings, as though declaring for all the world, his sheer joy at having survived yet another day. The little children from homes of aunt Nneka's neighbors gather under the umbrella-like breadfruit tree, which occupies the center of aunt Nneka's front yard, romping around the sand on naked bums.

"Azuka, I hope you slept well?" aunt Nneka asked pleasantly, pretending not to know what had transpired the night before.

"No, aunt Nneka," Azuka replied, "I am actually feeling rather feverish."

"What might be the problem?" aunt Nneka pursued, keeping up her pretense of ignorance.

"Aunt Nneka, let me be honest with you," Azuka volunteered, sitting herself up on the headboard of the bed. "I think I may have lost the baby. I may have had a miscarriage. Yesterday, in the night, I woke up and found..."

Aunt Nneka, who had reached the side of the bed, put down the tray on the bedside stool and gently placed her index finger on Azuka's lips, indicating that she need not say any more. Both women just held each other in an embrace. Words were not needed. Indeed, the feeling expressed by their spontaneous embrace was so powerful that words may have got in the way of that pure, exquisite communion of kindred spirits.

FORTY EIGHT

Chike's father, Mazi Cornelius Obinna Nwafor, is a man possessed of two powerful forces: Igbo traditional culture and a deep Christian faith. His parents, had themselves been strong traditionalists and raised him in like manner. They meticulously schooled their children in the ethics, etiquette, arts, crafts and pantheon of lesser gods in Igbo culture that served the supreme *CHUKWU*: such as *Ani*, *Agbala*, *Ifejioku* and *Amadioha*. They also taught them about the four great Igbo market days: *Nkwo*, *Eke*, *Orie* and *Afor*.

Later in their lives, however, when the white missionaries, whom everybody thought at the time were people who had come from a far off little-known country of albinos, arrived, they eventually became converted to the Christian religion. It was as a result of their new found faith, that they gave the name 'Cornelius' to Chike's father, whom everybody had always known by his Igbo name *Obinna*---which means, 'father's heart.'

For some reason, during the catechism and Bible knowledge classes that father McMahoney held every Saturday and Sunday at the small church he built at their village, they fell in love with the name *Cornelius*, and decided to give that name to their son Obinna as his "Christian name," when he went through the Christian ritual of 'baptism.'

From fervent traditionalists, Chike's parents became fervent Christians---Catholics to be exact, and proceeded to impose a code of conduct on their household that could only have been bested by that of Mendicant monks.

Chike's father was made to attend "morning mass" every day, as well as attend the regular sabbath mass every Sunday. He was made to attend catechism and Bible knowledge classes regularly and punctually. He served as an altar-boy for many years, helping father McMahoney with household chores as well. Yet, his parents never really gave up their cultural traditions. They merely rearranged things in order to better accommodate the new visitor of Christianity into the livingroom of their being.

Chike's grandfather used to look forward to the masquerade and *Abiansi* seasons with the same expectant relish as he did Christmas, Easter and other major Christian feast days. There were few times when Chike's grandfather felt happier than during the *Abiansi* festival - an annual festival held in their village in honor, it would almost appear, of the sheer rhythmic power of African percussion.

The *Abiansi* festival is, truly, a sight to behold. It involves about a thousand men, each with a drum about the height of a boy of ten years old; encircling women, young and old, and teenagers, all dancing to a steady, synchronized drum-beat!

At the center of the swirling bodies of women, children and teenagers, is a group of about thirty to forty men, drumming to the same tune as the outer circle of about a thousand men. This inner circle of men is known as the *obi igba*---the heart of the drum.

The men that make up the *obi igba*, are among the best drummers on the face of the earth. Their proficiency at beating the drums is known far and wide; and the uncanny strength in their arms - the stuff of which legends are made. They belong to the prestigious drum cult known as *Odenigbo* - that which is heard of and talked about throughout Igbo land.

The task of the *Obi Igba* is straightforward, though daunting: the heart of the drum must never cease beating, lest the body, the *Abiansi* festival itself, die a premature death.

The individual men who are part of the outer circle of drummers can periodically drop out from the circle of drummers to quench their thirst, flirt a little with some of the maidens under the shadowy glow of the moonlit night, or rest their tired palms and arms from pounding on the drums, but those of the inner circle, the heart of the drum—the *Obi Igba*, must continue the drumming, neither moving or talking to anyone, until it is dawn.

Once in a while, however, someone would bring an *ogbo* half-way full of frothing white palm wine or plain water, and pour the contents of the cup down the opened up mouth of an inner-circle drummer. In the course of all that, however, the drummer would not have missed a single beat.

The story is still told of how in the old days an inner-circle drummer who broke the sound of his drumming brought such shame and disgrace to his family that even members of his own family, joining in the taunting, urged him to take a piece of rope, hurry to the nearest forest and hang himself. It is still rumored that the man took their advise.

The reverberation of the simultaneous drumming of so many men is something quite indescribable to someone who has never witnessed the spectacle. Because the town of *Egbe* is snuggled in a valley that is surrounded picturesquely by four other towns, perched respectively on four hills that enclose the valley-town of Egbe, during the *Abiansi* festival, one can see a heavy trail of dust cloud rising steadily to the heavens from the dancing feet of Egbe, as though they are sending a smoke signal to the gods and the ancestors with their rhythmic offerings on earth.

On the Christian side of the equation, Chike's grandfather equally loved and looked forward to the Christian feast days, especially Christmas. He always made sure that out of his savings, he bought a gift for each member of his family. For his first wife, and since his conversion to Christianity - his only wife remaining from what had been a total of six wives - he always bought a length of expensive *akwette* cloth.

Without fail, the whole family would attend the midnight mass on Christmas, as the first Christian act commemorating the birth of "our lord Jesus Christ," as father McMahoney always puts it. After mass, the festivities begin not only in the Nwafor household, but all over their town as it does throughout the rest of the Christian world. Wonderfully spicy dishes of all kinds are prepared after mass and visitors come from far and near in an unceasing flow, with everyone saying to everyone else they meet, "*appy kris'mass.*"

Masquerades of all sizes and shapes run around the town, chasing people hither and yonder, performing sundry dances and acrobatic feats, to entertain endless crowds on every street corner of the town.

And so, it was in the midst of this cultural dualism that Chike's father, Cornelius Obinna Nwafor, grew up. From father to son and from father to son, the family tradition of juxta-positioning Euro-Christianity with African culture was handed down, Chike being the latest generation of the Nwafors to be laundered through that process.

Part of the cultural tradition that came down to Chike was also, unfortunately, the ethnic chauvinism or "tribalism," that marred relations between the three biggest ethnic groups in Wazobia: the Igbo, Hausa and Yoruba. Of course, the fault was not exclusively that of any one of the three groups. They all shared in the blame to one degree or another, although one can point to strong evidence that the fires of *tribalism* had been largely started and stoked by unpigmented outsiders.

Even so, that is hardly a good excuse. It is, after all, only a mad man whose insanity has sent him wandering aimlessly around the town in total nakedness, that cannot recognize a member of his own family. The albinos who set Africans at each other's throats, even as they cooperate among themselves, should never be blamed more than the Africans who let them get away with it.

FORTY NINE

It is a crystal clear day. The sun is shinning brightly and the clouds are an ethereal combination of immaculate white and azure blue puffs in the sky. The noise of traffic, car horns and jostling people, gives the city of Lagos its unmistakable stamp of identity.

In the quiet and verdant suburb of Ikoyi, the well-to-do have managed to carve out for themselves a luxurious sanctuary in the midst of an otherwise insufferably noisy and filthy city. The passport into that manicured retreat is money - ill gotten, or hard earned. Everybody in Lagos and the other parts of Wazobia understand well the rules of the game. The game is to get rich, however you can, and stay rich, however you can.

The poor bellyache about the mismanagement of the country by its ruling elite and the greed of rich merchants, politicians and "ten-percenters," only because of their poverty and powerlessness. Theirs is not a case of higher morality, but sour grapes. The moment any one of the poor get a chance at the lifestyles of the rich, they take to it like fish to water, not looking back for as much as a second to help any of the fellows they leave behind as a result of their new found wealth.

The rich, on the other hand, understand that membership in their exclusive club comes at a price. The price of conscience and compassion. Once you become a member of the exclusive club of the rich, there can no longer be any gray areas. You are either for or against the members of your club. You are either a champion of your club interests or a traitor. There are no in-betweens.

In order to be a good champion of your club, you must cut all ties of conscience and compassion with the poor - the non-members of the club. A heavy sense of guilt is too burdensome a weight to carry on a hike to the top. It weighs you down, making the climb that much more difficult, if not impossible. To become a traitor, on the other hand, all you need do is empathize with the plight of the poor or worse still, become an advocate for the non-members of the exclusive club of the rich.

The reason for this clear-cut division is not at all complicated. Rich people are rich because they can stay rich. Staying rich requires keeping your wealth, not giving it away either through personal charity or government taxation. Anybody who advocates giving away that wealth threatens the rich, because they threaten their riches.

There is no doubt as to which side of that great divide Bisi's father belongs. His house sprawls on a forty-acre piece of land in Ikoyi. The lawns and gardens are meticulously tended by a gardener, who comes every morning by bus from the rat-infested shanty town of *Ikoloise*, across the westward delta of the Lagos lagoon. Bisi's father also has a driver, a steward, a chef and a nurse-maid, all of whom, except for the nurse-maid (who lives with the Olatunji family) commute every day to and from the same hell hole as the gardener.

Relaxing on the veranda on top of the car porch of his castle-like house, Mr. Olatunji was deep in thought about his predicament regarding Bisi's threatened marriage to...."that Igbo boy." Even as he thought of what to do about the situation, he had a strong premonition that his efforts at trying to reign in his daughter, to make her change her mind about marrying that...Igbo boy, were going to be in vain.

In his heart of hearts, he knows that his daughter, Bisi, is very much like him. Like him, she is strong willed, determined and risk-prone. In fact, he has always sensed that of all his children, although Bisi is a girl, it is she that is the chip off the old block. He would have loved nothing more than to hand over the running of his business to her when he retires, if she had been a boy.

Unfortunately, she is a girl. And although she is just as competent and intelligent as the best of any of the boys, the fact remains that being a girl, she will one day marry into another family, take on the name of her husband's family and, once she produces offspring, become part of the fabric of her husband's people. It is due to that reason, that it is sometimes said in traditional circles that raising female children is like one spending countless hours cracking palm kernels for others to eat.

Yet, he has also known several women who do not fit that mold. Whose sense of family and themselves is so strong that nothing is able to severe the ties that bind them to their roots. His own mother is a shining example of such a woman.

There is nothing his father could have said or done, to have made her turn her back on her own family, and he never tried. She stubbornly insisted on serving the two masters of her husband's family and her own equally, and did so with admirable success. Such women, however, are few and far between. They sprout, here and there, like African violets in the midst of large weed-covered fields.

Mr. Olatunji nevertheless determined to give the situation his best effort. He planned to approach the matter with different strategies. First, he would have Bisi's mother try to talk some sense into Bisi by applying her soft touch. If that fails, he will come down with the sledgehammer of his rage and threat of disinheritance. If that fails, he will summon a meeting of their extended family as a last ditch effort to call Bisi to order. He hopes and prays that Bisi will relent under the pressure of that strategy of graduated pressure.

FIFTY

When Bisi returned from the Lagos University Teaching Hospital that evening, she could sense something was amiss. Her father walked up and down the house in a very measured manner, and her normally agreeable mother seemed aloof. Her brothers and sisters had all gone to visit their aunt, Mrs. Funke Adebisi, who lives clear across on the other end of the city of Lagos, in a newly constructed housing estate in Badagry.

Judging from the time she returned from the Teaching Hospital, which was about 9:30 PM, she guessed that her brothers and sisters were most likely going to be spending the night at their aunt's place. By 10:30 PM, there was still no sign of her siblings, by which time Bisi reached the conclusion that they would be sleeping over at their aunt's.

In her usual quiet manner, Bisi's mother slipped into her daughter's bedroom as gently as only a house cat might have managed and sat down towards the end of Bisi's bed, which occupies most of the central section of her bedroom. Bisi was lying on the bed with a massive textbook on human anatomy balanced on her stomach, her trunk supported by the headboard of the bed at almost a right angle to the rest of her body.

When she heard the bedroom door open, she raised her eyes above the rim of the text book, thinking that possibly her siblings had returned from their aunt's and were about to invade the quiet of her immaculately kept room with their unending palaver. To her surprise, it was her mother, who very rarely comes to her room, except, of course, when something goes wrong in her daughter's life and she feels the need to step in with her maternal support. It was also an unusual time of the night for her to pay Bisi a visit in her room. The wall clock in Bisi's room was barely a few minutes away from striking mid-night, and Bisi's mother is an early sleeper.

The rarity of her mother's visits to her bedroom and the lateness of the hour raised Bisi's suspicion that something was definitely in the offing. She put aside the textbook as her

164

mother made herself comfortable at the foot of the bed and braced herself for the purpose of her mother's visit.

"Ekale ma," Bisi said, greeting her mother in a soft, controlled voice.

Her mother returned her greeting, in a tone of voice devoid of the characteristic softness in her usual manner of speech. Cutting to the quick, Bisi's mother went straight to the point.

"Bisi," she said in a grim voice, "your father and I are not very happy with you. You are no longer a child; therefore, I will speak to you in plain language. We are terribly worried about what is going on between yourself and that....Igbo boy.

"At first, I thought it best to ignore it, hoping that after a while the excitement and euphoria that comes with those kinds of novel experiences will wear off and you would return to your senses. However, that has not been the case. In fact, things have gone from bad to worse. You carry on with that young man as though he has already claimed your hand in marriage."

"Have you any idea what this whole thing is doing to your father? It has sent his blood pressure through the roof and well near broken his heart. After all the faith we reposed in you all these years - and this is how you choose to pay us back."

"As for myself, I cannot tell you how many nights I have laid awake, crying my eyes out because of this terrible situation you have put yourself into. However, I thank God that all is not lost yet. There is still time to rescue the situation. I strongly urge you to stop your relationship with that....Igbo boy immediately, find yourself a nice Yoruba boy from a respectable family like the one you come from and get on with your life. That is why I have come to talk to you tonight."

Bisi was stunned. Nothing had prepared her for her mother's bluntness about the subject of Chike and herself. Her mother did not even pretend to any subtlety about the matter, as she bore into Bisi like a Temple toggle harpoon might have an unfortunate whale. The unvarnished manner in which her mother dealt with the matter also confirmed for Bisi the deep-rooted nature of the problem of ethnocentrism in Wazobia. Her mother, who can hardly hurt a fly, was now poised at the foot of her bed like a seasoned warrior. Bisi sensed immediately that the metaphorical hour hand of the clock was

165

about to strike midnight. It is either she takes the bull by the horns, or she will loose the battle, altering forever her destiny and that of Chike.

She pulled herself further up on the head board of the bed. "Mama," Bisi ventured in a very measured voice, "in all the years I have lived and grown up in this house, I cannot remember a day that I refused to do anything that you asked me to do. Whether house work, running errands, assisting with the care of my siblings or anything else. But for the first time Mama, I am going to say no to you.

"I love Chike, and it does not matter to me that he is from a different ethnic group. You once told me Mama, that even among the Yorubas there are major issues of prejudice and mutual suspicion. The *Lagosians* view those from the hinterlands, such as the *Ijebus* and *Ibadans*, as beneath them. And everybody dumps on the *Ijebus*. So it seems that there is no end to the cycle of prejudice and social alienation among people, unless some high-minded people seize the initiative of breaking that vicious cycle of ignorance, prejudice and hate.

"At least," Bisi's mother cut in, "all the Yoruba sub-groups that you speak of are members of the same ethnic family. They all speak Yoruba, lay claim to the same ancestral womb, and are covered by the fabric of the same cultural cloth. But in your case, you want to force us to take a total stranger into our midst. A man who knows and cares nothing about our culture. What will become of you if, after several years along with a few children, he abandons you and seeks out a new bride among his kith and kin? What then? Who will you turn to then, if not the very same people you are now acting as though they do not matter!"

"With all due respect to you Mama, I believe that if I marry Chike and have children with him, our children and I will be part of his kith and kin. Anyway, Mama, Chike is not that kind of a person. You nurse those fears in total ignorance of the man. Moreover, have you not heard what they say about the Igbos - they never abandon their children, especially if there are male children involved."

"Olabisi," her mother said, calling out her full name in a slow deliberate tone, as she placed a soft moist palm on her daughter's exposed right foot, "I have never abandoned you before on any issue. But I must tell you that if you insist on this course of action, you will be very much on your own."

"Do not expect me to come to your rescue when things get hot. It is always better to suffer with dignity within the confines of one's family compound than to become the laughing stock of the entire village! If you tell me that you are not going to reconsider your stance, then I shall have the unpleasant task of informing your father of your position. It would be left to him to take it from there."

Bisi's mother got up from the bed and paused a few moments, hoping for her daughter's recantation. It never came. Visibly crestfallen, she took a few steps backward before turning around and letting herself out of Bisi's bedroom.

For a long time, Bisi sat silently going over what had just transpired between herself and her mother. She, of course, loves her mother beyond words and the last thing she wants is anything that will bring her parents heartache and disgrace. Yet, she knows deep in her heart that she is doing the right thing. She knows that when they get to know Chike as well as she does, they too will grow to love and respect him. However, she is well aware of the fact that it is not going to be an easy fight, especially with her father.

From underneath her pillow, Bisi retrieved her worn Book of Psalms and began reading silently to herself, finally falling into a deep and dreamless sleep.

FIFTY ONE

B isi's father had just returned from a hard day's work at the office and was settling down to a large dinner of *amala* and beef stew with freshly boiled chopped *okra*, when his normally quiet and retiring wife pensively told him that there was an important matter she had to discuss with him.

"Did someone die?" Bisi's father inquired in a slightly sarcastic tone.

"No," replied Bisi's mother.

"Did an unfortunate accident occur?" continued Bisi's father along the same rhetorical line of questioning.

"No," replied Bisi's mother, her voice beginning to show some irritation.

"If some one did not die and there has not been a bad accident, can you kindly tell me why whatever it is you wish to tell me cannot wait for a man to swallow a few morsels of food in his own home at the end of a hard day's job?"

Trying to match her husband's sarcastic wit with her own, Bisi's mother replied with a rhetorical answer that was equally laden with sarcasm.

"Is this a law court? No," she said, answering her own question."Am I talking to a madman? Perhaps," she said, answering her own rhetorical question again.

She got up from the dinning room table and, slowly and dramatically retying her wrapper, said to her husband, "Perhaps when you are done eating your food and your more civilized temperament has been restored, we can talk about your daughter's predicament."

She walked away from the dinning room with a swagger reminiscent of her youthful beauty. Her husband stole a glance at her ample but well-shaped backside, swallowing hard on a large ball of *ewedu*.

After his meal, which Bisi's father washed down with a mortuary-cold bottle of Star beer, he grabbed the newspaper and retired to the master bedroom, where he knew his wife would soon join him, if for no other reason than to needle him a bit more for his earlier rudeness.

A part of him earnestly hoped that she would arrive soon, either for the ribbing or for whatever it is she said she wants to talk to him about regarding Bisi. For he knows that after about an hour or so, he will be soundly asleep, due, largely, to his system trying to digest the mound of carbohydrate he just consumed.

Predictably, about fifteen minutes after Bisi's father settled into bed, casually glancing through the newspaper, his wife swept into the bedroom, still visibly smarting from the earlier encounter with her husband.

"I had the discussion you wanted me to have with Bisi, and it was an exercise in futility. The girl is dead set on marrying that Igbo boy. And let me tell you something as a woman and a mother: I looked long and hard into that child's eyes, and it is my feeling that nothing is going to change her mind. I, therefore, advise you to start working on your "plan B," if you have one."

"What do you mean your talk with Bisi was an exercise in futility? Are you trying to tell me that your own child, your own daughter, has grown wings right under your very nose without your knowing it? Does it mean that she is now the one running this household? May the spirit of *Oduduwa* be my witness, I will break her neck with my own hands before allowing her to bring disgrace to my esteemed family name."

Bisi's mother interrupted her husband's tirade, cautioning him not to approach the matter inflexibly.

"I am still not persuaded that your approach is the best one. The more upset you get about the whole matter, the more combative you make Bisi. I suggest that we both try using love and affection to win back her loyalty and obedience."

Her husband glared at her as though he detested the very ground on which she walks.

"It is that same idiotic advise that you have been giving all this while that got us into this mess in the first place! You remember when I was trying to nip this whole nonsense in the bud, and you kept telling me about your so-called 'many ways of killing a rat.' Now, pray tell, what method do you recommend to solve the problem after, as you yourself has just told me, the horse has already left the barn? I do not, repeat, *do not*, want to hear any more of your advise."

He turned on his right side, his back to his wife, who was standing towards the end of the huge king-size bed, in the direction of the bedroom door. Bisi's mother, livid with rage from her husband's outburst, stormed out of the room slamming the bedroom door.

FIFTY TWO

The moment Bisi's mother left the room, Bisi's father returned to his former position on his back. He felt his heart palpitating dangerously. It was as though he was on the very edge of a heart attack. His blood pressure shot up like an ignited fire cracker, adding to the distress of his racing heart.

Should he simply disown her and be done with the matter once and for all? In his heart, however, he knew that disownment is one of those legal fictions introduced into African society by the Anglian colonial authorities; for everyone knows that blood is thicker than water—and ink, for that matter. No legal document, however impeccably worded, can alter the organic link a parent has with their own blood and flesh.

What should he do? What did he possibly do wrong to deserve this calamity? His mind went to his good friend Dr. Kola Ogbomoso, a man from another solid Yoruba family like his own. Everything went with textbook precision in his case. His daughter qualified as a Lawyer, took and passed the Wazobia Bar Exam, and soon after, fell in love and married a well-cut Yoruba medical doctor, who had studied neurosurgery somewhere in Scotland. That was the same thing he wanted for his daughter, not this complication of an Igbo...fellow.

He decided that first he was going to have a talk with Bisi alone. Then he would invite her mother and only if that fails, would he call a meeting of the Olatunji family.

All night long, Bisi's father tossed and turned. He could not get a wink of sleep. His mind was preoccupied with what to do about what he knows deep inside him is his daughter's impending marriage to that ...Igbo boy. How should he approach the matter? What could he possibly say or do to dissuade her from her present course of action?

There is, of course, an enlightened part of him that knows that the boy's ethnicity does not and should not matter. That it is, as the great African American Civil Rights leader, Martin Luther King Jr., once eloquently put it, 'the content of his character' that ought to matter. Yet, another part of him, a more native part of his being, recoils at the prospect. That part of him wants to rush to the gates of the empire and push back all invading barbarians; a part of him that feels like a member of an infantry, responding to the clarion call of the sacred duty of defending the integrity of the fatherland.

What course of action would his great grandfather have prescribed? A man who bore with breast-beating pride the glorious title of *Kakanfo* of Eko. Would he have advised erring on the side of reason or nation? But for which "nation" should he, the great grandson of that great patriarch and warrior err today? Yorubaland or Wazobia? The old ancestral nation or the new modern one, within the confines of which Yorubas, Igbos, Hausas and countless others now find themselves?

He contemplated briefly going to talk to the parish priest, Rev. Father Balogun, about the matter, but dismissed the idea almost as quickly. While it is true that Father Balogun is a fellow tribesman, there are two drawbacks to talking to him about a matter such as this. First, his religious calling is bound to make his advice somewhat unrealistic. He would most likely quote some Biblical passage about what the Cannaanites, Israelites or some other supposed group did in far off Palestine a thousand years ago or more. That would serve no practical purpose for resolving the matter at hand.

Second, although Father Balogun is Yoruba like himself, he is Ijebu. And everybody knows that all that an Ijebu man can think of is money and witchcraft. It is, indeed, a wonder that Father Balogun was able to become a priest at all - a vocation that requires, among other things, the taking of the vow of poverty.

Bisi's father resolved to take up the matter with his daughter the next day as soon as he returns from work. He tried to get a few winks of sleep in the few hours left before dawn.

FIFTY THREE

The following day, Bisi's father returned home from work much earlier than usual. He ate a light meal of *Jelof* rice and stewed chicken. Refraining from his customary bottle of beer, he drank instead a glass of cold water.

Rather than retiring to his bedroom after his meal, he tarried awhile in the livingroom, and then went into his study, a large room situated at the west wing of the mansion. Towards one of the end walls of the study is a huge mahogany office desk, with an expensive looking black leather swivel chair behind it.

Carefully arranged on the mahogany table are the usual assortment of office supplies: a stapler, rolodex, clear tape, a brass dish full of paper clips, a plastic silo-shaped holder containing a variety of pens and pencils like a quiver of arrows, an appointment calendar and a book-size diary. A white rotary telephone sits on the right hand side of the table next to a compact answering machine that emits a steady low hum.

Two feet or so in front of the office desk are three black leather seats, arranged as though they are meant to serve as a mini livingroom. One seat is a loveseat, another a "lazyboy", and the third, a rocking chair. In the middle of the three seats is a beautiful Persian rug that Bisi's father had ordered directly from Baghdad. The patterns on the rug resemble stylized mosques complete with domes, minarets and archways.

The walls to the left and right sides of the study are covered with books that run wall-to-wall and floor-to-roof. Books of every imaginable genre. Bisi's father is an avid reader, devouring scores of books on practically every subject each week.

It is, therefore, into his study that Bisi's father comes whenever he has serious intellectual work to do, important business to transact with someone at home, a private discussion to hold or simply to reflect in tranquil solitude. That is, perhaps, why he calls his study his sanctuary. It is in this sanctuary that he planned to have his crucial talk with Bisi.

FIFTY FOUR

Bisi's father sent for his daughter. Bisi was almost done with her supper, when the butler told her that her father wanted to speak to her in his study.

All the Olatunji children know what it means when you are summoned to the study. In fact, Bisi and her siblings have a standing joke that the dining room during meals constitutes the court of first instance in the Olatunji household; the livingroom, the High Court; the master bedroom, the Court of Appeal; and the study, the Supreme Court.

Bisi knew exactly why her father wanted to speak to her. She hurried through the last spoonfuls of *Jelof* rice and washed it down with a half glass of Canada Dry Gingerale. She rose and walked slowly towards the study. The moment of truth had arrived.

Bisi knocked gently on the door of her father's study and his booming voice rang out, "Yes, who is it?"

At the sound of his voice, Bisi's heart began to pound and her mouth dried up. She replied in a quavering voice, "Baba, it is Bisi."

"Come in, and shut the door behind you," came her father's stern reply.

Bisi entered the study, momentarily intimidated by the monastic austerity of the retreat. Her father was sitting on the black leather swivel chair behind the huge mahogany office desk, looking every bit the presiding judge, especially as he was dressed in his perfectly pressed, stiffly starched, immaculate white *danchiki*.

"Ekale, Baba," Bisi greeted her father, as she curtsied modestly.

"Sit down, Bisi," her father said, by-passing the customary niceties of greetings and small talk, "We have a very important matter to discuss today, and the sooner we get to it the better."

Bisi sat down, waiting for her father to initiate discussions on the matter they both knew was at issue.

"Bisi, her father began matter-of-factly, "I am sure that you know very well why I have called you into my study to talk to you. Your mother tells me that she spoke to you the other day

174

about your continuing association with that...that Igbo boy. It appears that you are adamant about continuing with the association. I even heard her say something to the effect that you are thinking of marrying him."

"Bisi, you are my beloved daughter, and while I may not always outwardly show it, inside my heart my love for you shines brighter than the North Star. When a child has the twin blessings of his or her parents' love and experience to draw from, there can be no greater gift. Parents love provide reassurance and healing, while their experience serves as a lodestone that assists the child in charting a way through life's trials and tribulations."

"A wise child makes good use of such blessings and does not overlook them. Now, I am sure that you are aware that your mother and I can never lead you astray. You will, therefore, do well to heed our advice. It is not a wise course that you are presently following, continuing your association with that...Igbo boy. You must end your association with him immediately and stop all this nonsense talk of marrying him."

"There is so much at stake, Bisi. There is the family name to think of, and our beloved culture. I have even seriously considered handing over the family business to you when I retire. But, how can all this be preserved for the family and the Yoruba nation if you tie your destiny to that of a total stranger?"

"Are you going to start learning to speak Igbo in your old age? And if you do not learn to speak their language, how do you propose to make conversation and bond with them as in-laws? A people's language is the key to the soul of their nation. Without knowledge of it, a person remains, forever, locked out from the collective spirit of a people."

"And what do you propose to call your children in such a union? Will they have Yoruba or Igbo names? Which would take first place and which would take second place? What if your Igbo husband refuses to have his children by you bear Yoruba names at all? Where does that leave your own people's culture? Life already has enough worries for all of us, without our going out of our way to look for additional burdens to place upon our shoulders."

"I need not tell you that this whole thing has caused your mother and I much grief. However, I am sure that we can put all of it behind us and start afresh. Finish your medical training and we will all put our heads together to find you a fine Yoruba gentleman for a husband."

Inwardly, Bisi prayed for courage and the right words. She remembered one of her social studies professors once say that words deserve to be treated with utmost respect. For not only do they provide us with one of the most efficient means of conveying our thoughts and feelings, but they also serve as symbolic tools with which we craft images of reality in the minds of others. Those images can be either exquisite or rough hewn.

Where she found the courage and the words to express herself in the way and manner she did that evening in her father's study, she will never know. Somehow, from somewhere, the words came in bountiful harvest.

"Baba, first let me humbly thank you for calling me into your presence to talk to me. I am very grateful that you have given me this opportunity to explain things to you. I am, Baba, and will always be, your child. But I am no longer a child. And I would hope and pray that being your child does not mean that you will forever look upon me as a child.

"As your child, Baba, I believe I have tried to be very responsible. I do not smoke or drink. I do not sleep around and I have done quite well in school. I help with household chores and I am extremely respectful of you and mama."

At this point, her father cut in.

"That is why, Bisi, I was extremely surprised when this problem arose. It seems so much out of character; for, indeed, you have been an exemplary child."

"No, Baba," Bisi boldly interjected, "That is why when this situation arose, you should have given me more credit than you did. That is why, Baba, you should have reposed far greater confidence and trust in my judgment than you have. That is why, Baba, you should have realized that a child that has been that good may have good reason for the direction they have chosen."

"Baba, you are a very well-educated man, and you are a good Christian. I find it impossible to believe that there is no room in such a cultivated mind to properly accommodate reason. Nor, frankly, am I willing to accept the idea that there is no place in your heart, with room to spare, for love and compassion."

"Chike has given you no cause - no reason - to be prejudiced against him. As I am sure you are well aware, the accident of his birth is no reason at all. Baba, I did not plan to fall in love with an Igbo man...or any other man, for that matter. It simply happened, like some cosmic force that drew me ineluctably to itself."

Before her father could fully digest the torrent of words that poured from her mouth, Bisi walked around the mahogany table and knelt down beside her father. She placed her soft hands on her father's left hand that was resting on one of the arms of the black leather swivel chair and resumed her impassioned plea for understanding.

Bisi's father had not expected this degree of boldness and eloquence from Bisi. More especially, he had not expected this dramatic move on her part of coming to kneel down next to him to plead with him in this manner.

Bisi seemed unstoppable. She begged for her father's understanding, leveled one elegant argument after another, and tried to emotionally wear her father's resistance down.

"You have nothing to fear, Baba," Bisi continued. "Chike and I intend to find a happy medium between our two cultures."

"Although, as the man of the house, Chike will surely be the head of our household, he will only be the first among equals. And yes, Baba, I intend to learn how to speak Igbo. But also, Chike intends to learn how to speak Yoruba. In fact, Baba, Chike already knows how to speak quite a bit of Yoruba; enough, I believe, to really surprise you if you hear him.

"I implore you, Baba. Please allow us the opportunity to give birth to a new Wazobia. A Wazobia capable of taking full advantage of her vast God-given human and natural resources."

Knowing that her father is one who loves the intellectual life, Bisi ended her plea with a quotation from a famous Wazobian philosopher.

When Bisi finished, she was in tears. She and her father held each other in a heartfelt embrace. Her father knew then that whatever lies ahead, he at least has, a daughter who understands well the place of dignity and pride in the social scheme of things. He also knew that whomever she marries, wherever she goes, he will never lose her.

Bisi, on the other hand, knew that she had won the greatest battle of her life. Chike and her now have the way cleared for them to beat a path to the heavens.

FIFTY FIVE

Once again, Chike's father contacted his *umunna*, the six distinguished gentlemen who had come to his house to help him deal with Chike's alleged intransigence. But this time, he wanted them to accompany him on the *Ibu Mmanya*, the traditional "wine carrying" ceremony to Bisi's family in order to formally consummate their marriage.

Marriage among Africans is not a simple matter between two individuals "in love", who can independently enter into a marital contract and then ride off into the sunset. A marriage is never of two individuals, but of two families or even two clans. That is why, among the Igbos, no one goes by themselves to ask for a woman's hand in marriage. Those who "own" you will not let you do such a thing, nor will those who "own" the girl whose hand you seek in marriage give their consent, without the request coming from a properly constituted delegation of the suitor's family members.

This practice serves as a kind of social insurance policy. It underscores for the two parties directly involved the seriousness of their undertaking. It provides for the involvement of responsible eye witnesses on both sides of the families. It allows time for both families to check each other out. It provides a context in which elders, on both sides of the families, share their wisdom on the associated problems of married life with the young people about to embark upon that journey.

Finally, it provides a forum for settlement of the "bride price", something a great many people have mistaken for the buying of a wife. The *ibu mmanya* is, actually, the last stage of a drawn-out process that is collectively called *ije okwu nwayi* - the journey to speak for a wife.

The process begins with *iku aka nu uzo* - knocking on the door. This entails essentially, coming to "whisper" your intentions to the family of the girl that you seek to marry. A few drinks accompany this first visit, but you need only come with one or two of your family members, perhaps as few as the young man and an uncle of his.

The second process entails coming back to feel out the sentiments of the girl's family to your proposition. This is called *ibata nu uno* - coming into the house. This second process involves a greater number of the suitor's family members, though nowhere as many as during the last stage of the *ibu mmanya*. This second stage is accompanied by a greater quantity of drinks and, perhaps, some foodstuffs and domestic animals as gifts.

In the interim between the *iku aka nu uzo* and the *ibata nu uno*, the family of the girl undertakes serious investigative work on the family of the suitor. The background of the suitor's family is gone over with a fine tooth comb.

Are there any blemishes on the suitor's family's immediate or distant past? Has, for example, any member of the suitor's family ever committed an *nso ani*-an abomination, in the collective memory of the community? Is the family tainted by the stigma of *Osu*? Has there been a history of thievery or cheating in the family? Is there a history of mental illness in the family? Does the family seem to have the vicious cycle of *Ogbanje* with their offspring? Are there problems of impotence among the menfolk of that family? Do the menfolk of that family have a strong work ethic or are they lazy and indolent?

All these bits and pieces of information are gathered through inquiries from many quarters, much like assembling a jig saw puzzle, until a coherent picture of the place of the suitor's family in the social scheme of things in the community stands out in bold relief.

Chike's family had already gone through the *iku aka nu uzo* and the *ibata nu uno*, for although Bisi's family is not Igbo, there are analogous traditions among the Yoruba with regards to marriage. They had thus arrived at the final stage of the process, the *ibu mmanya*.

This time, Chike's father's *umunna*, the six distinguished gentlemen, brought their wives and several other close and distant relatives with them. A fifty-person bus was hired to accommodate additional members of the extended family, kegs of palm wine, *okoto*, pieces of *akwette* cloth, a variety of ornaments and a dance troupe of ten women from Egbe.

The women sang throughout the five-hour journey from the village of Egbe to the city of Lagos. Their melodious voices accompanied by the intermittent chakara...chakara...chakara sound of the *Ishaka* - calabash gourds covered with beaded nets that make rattling noises when they are beaten upon with open palms, clenched fists or hit against the thigh. As is traditional in most of Africa, the women used the familiar *call and response*, with a lead singer telling a story that is punctuated at regular intervals by the chorus and instrumentation of the other members of the musical group.

FIFTY SIX

Almost every aspect of the traditional wine-carrying ceremony of the Igbo are similar to that of the Yoruba, and as such, during the initial phase of the ceremony, things went fairly smoothly. The exchange of traditional gifts, the flowery speeches by relatives and prospective in-laws, libations poured to the ancestors, and so on.

Even the usually palaver-filled Igbo custom of the breaking and distributing of the kola nut, did not go too badly. The Olatunji family wisely let their Igbo suitors take the lead on that matter, perhaps knowing that time will come to exact their own cultural pound of flesh.

The time arrived none too soon, when they reached the part of the ceremony of the Yoruba marriage custom known as *Idobale*. A custom that requires of the suitor to prostrate fully before his prospective father and mother in-law.

Bisi's uncle, her father's eldest brother, got to his feet and cleared his throat. After a while, silence prevailed.

"Our esteemed prospective in-laws, I greet you all in the name of the Olatunji family. We know that you have come a long way to Yorubaland for a bride, and we respect the love and determination that motivated that sojourn. Yet, as we are all witnesses today, you have come from a land rich in customs and traditions to a land equally rich in customs and traditions."

"As such, we have reached the point in this traditional marriage ceremony at which in our own tradition, the young man who seeks the hand of our daughter in marriage, must *dobale*--fully prostrate, before the father and mother of the bride-to-be. Thank you."

Bisi's uncle sat down, amidst the animated chatter of their surprised and ruffled Igbo visitors.

For the Yoruba, the custom of *idobale* as part and parcel of their traditional marriage ceremony, is a very significant act. It is a symbolic way by which a prospective son in-law shows respect, honor and humility towards the parents of his bride-to-be.

181

A suitor who refuses to *dobale*, will not only have disrespected, dishonored and disgraced the family of his bride-to-be, he would have sent a powerful message of much greater problems that loom in the horizon. For if a prospective son in-law is unwilling to perform such a symbolic act of respect, honor and humility at the high point of his grasp for his coveted prize, when then will he be so disposed?

That Yoruba custom of *idobale*, however, is as familiar to the Yoruba as it is alien to the Igbo. For as the Igbos say, where one thing stands, another thing will stand next to it. It appeared from the looks on people's faces, that no one prepared Chike's *umunna* for that not-so-minor detail of traditional marriage ceremony in Yorubaland.

The mortification felt by the members of Chike's *umunna*, was palpable. This was for them an unacceptable act of humiliation. They of the Igbo, who hold the belief that 'every man is a king in his own house;' who eschew kings and queens in their political system; who go so far as to assert that a person is in constant negotiation with their *chi*---their personal god, their very fate. A negotiation in which it is said that if a person is stubborn and hardworking enough, they can alter the course of their fate, change the very mind of their *chi*. How then can they accept to prostrate before other human beings, mere mortals like themselves?

Moreover, they have *Ozo* titled men in their midst. Some of the most respected titled men in the whole of Egbe. How can they subject those venerable men to the humiliation of having that kind of travesty enacted in their presence? It would be nothing short of sacrilege, an *nso ani*.

The *Ozo* titled men of Chike's *umunna* huddled together to ponder this unexpected development. *Ozo* Okenihe could hardly contain himself. His nostrils flared intermittently as he hyperventilated from rage.

"*Chineke*," he exclaimed to his peers, "let us leave this place at once. This is a terrible insult on Ozo titled men. If it were in the old days, I will be sure to leave this place with the head of at least one of these jokers. They would have remembered the day *Ozo* titled men were insulted in their village."

Ozo Obolo Di Ihe, chimed in.

"Do these people have no shame? Do they have no pride?," he hissed through clenched teeth.

"How can they make grown men do this kind of thing in public? In full view of women, children and strangers?"

Ozo Wa Orji Na Milu Oha, lowered his voice to a virtual whisper.

"I have always suspected that more than just the blinders of prejudice separate us from these people. Now I know what it is. Why would anyone want to have another human being prostrate before them just because they have come in search of a bride? As far as I am concerned, it is a twisted custom. A custom unbecoming of a nation of free and proud men."

Ozo Osisi Di Mma Na Ani Akulia, spoke with a great sense of urgency.

"We must decide quickly who among us will explain as clearly and as diplomatically as possible to our hosts that what they ask of us is not possible, especially in the presence of *Ozo* titled men. They must be made to understand."

Eze Ozo Ojemba Ewe Ilo, in his usual manner, weighed matters carefully. He decided that it will be a good idea to sample Chike's opinion before they proceed with whatever cause of action they choose to follow.

"I think we should speak briefly to Chike about this situation before deciding on what to do. It is, afterall, for the traditional wine carrying of his bride-to-be that we are here."

Eze Ozo Ojemba Ewe Ilo, beckoned to Chike to come over to where his esteemed *umunna* were huddled. Chike knew, of course, why he was being summoned. He had not expected this development himself either. And he was not sure that he can go through with the *idobale* himself. It is, indeed, a difficult proposition for an Igbo man. Every instinct in him rebels against the idea. Every fiber in his body militates against that kind of gross obeisance.

Chike reached the caucus of his esteemed *umunna*, and squatted next to his father. Eze Ozo Ojemba Ewe Ilo put the matter to him bluntly.

"Well, my son, Chike, you have heard what our prospective in-laws have asked of us. They say that this act of prostration---*ido..ba..ba..le*, they call it; is an integral part of their traditional wine carrying. There are, however, two stumbling blocks here. First, we are Igbos and we bow to only Chukwu, and not to mere mortals."

"Second, even if somehow, we were able to accomodate their wish, we have the additional complication that there are

Ozo titled men in our midst. In the light of those two stumbling blocks, compromise over the matter is completely out of the question."

Chike was stomped by the situation. Knowing his esteemed *umunna* as well as he does, he was fairly certain that they will not budge. For the first time since he began the traditional process of winning Bisi's hand in marriage, he found himself sharing the repugnance of his *umunna* towards a cultural practice of another of Wazobia's ethnic groups.

He was not sure that he can bring himself to prostrate before these people, and is in agreement with his esteemed *umunna* that they should not be subjected to the humiliation of witnessing such a spectacle.

"My fathers," Chike managed, rather meekly, "I must confess that I do not know what to say at this point. I had no idea that they have this kind of custom or I would never have let such an important detail escape the prior consideration of my esteemed *umunna*, especially knowing that there are *Ozo* titled men among you. I am as surprised as you all are and just as equally befuddled as to what to do."

Ozo Okenihe jumped in, still chaffing at the bits.

"Chike, you are right that this their *idobale* business comes to us all as a great and unwelcome surprise. But you are wrong in suggesting that we are befuddled. We need only make it clear to them that their *idobale* custom cannot take place in our presence. It is you that may be befuddled, my son. For as the one in search of their daughter's hand in marriage, you will still have to find a way around this Gideon knot."

"So," Ozo Osisi Di mma na Ani Akulia interjected, coming to Chike's aid, "are you suggesting that we throw Chike to the pride of hungry lions after having come this far with him?"

"I am suggesting no such thing," Ozo Okenihe flung back at Ozo Osisi Di mma na Ani Akulia, clearly irritated. "I am merely laying out the situation for what it is."

"Eh, perhaps if we explain the situation carefully to our hosts, they may be made to understand where we are coming from," Eze Ozo Ojemba Ewe Ilo, gently added.

Other members of Chike's *umunna*, nodded their heads vigorously in support of that suggestion.

Eze Ozo Ojemba Ewe Ilo asked Chike to go and tell Bisi's uncle, the one that made the announcement about the *idobale* custom, that he would like to have a word with him. A few minutes later, Chike returned to the caucus of his *umunna* in the company of Bisi's uncle, Mr. Babatunde Olatunji.

Tunde, as he is fondly called by everyone, was dressed in an off-white *agbada* made of the expensive and popular *woyosi* lace material. His is a fairly tall man of about six feet two inches. Although his does not have a massive frame to go with his height, his lithe gait gives the hint of a powerful body. He sports a full beard that buries most of the lower half of his face in its lush abundance, and he carries himself with the kind of dignified bearing that bespeaks excellent breeding and economic security.

As Chike and Tunde Olatunji reach the caucus of Chike's *umunna*, Eze Ozo Ojemba Ewe Ilo stood up, towering over both men. He shook hands with Tunde Olatunji, steering him by the shoulder to a corner where the two of them can enjoy some privacy.

"Eh, Mr. Olatunji Senior, my name is Eze Ozo Ojemba Ewe Ilo. I am one of Chike's granduncles. It seems to me that we have somewhat of a problem here."

Tunde's forehead furrowed in curiosity.

"A problem? What might the problem be?," he asked, puzzled.

"Well, it has to do with this *ido...ba...le* custom of yours. You see, we are Igbos and, therefore, not accustomed to this kind of display of obeisance to another human being. It is simply not part of our culture or part of our very make up as a people."

"No, no, no, Eze Ozo," Tunde hastened, "you completely misunderstand. *Idobale* is merely a symbolic gesture of respect, honor and humility on the part of a prospective son in-law towards his prospective father and mother in-law. It has absolutely nothing whatsoever to do with submission of one human being to another."

"That may well be so, Mr. Olatunji Senior," Eze Ozo Ojemba Ewe Ilo rejoined, "but the eyes with which a lion whose main food is meat sees a lone antelope, are not the same eyes with which a cow whose main food is grass, sees the same antelope."

"Moreover," Eze Ozo Ojemba Ewe Ilo pressed on, "we have an additional problem here as well. There are *Ozo* titled men in our midst. That kind of public display can not be undertaken by a son of theirs in their presence and in the company of strangers. Where we come from, it would be an *nso ani*---a sacrilege, a desecration of the honored *Ozo* title they bear."

Tunde Olatunji was perplexed. The matter seems straight forward enough, why are these *kobokobo* people making a bigger issue of it than it is or *ought* to be? A part of him felt like simply telling Eze Ozo...*whatever the hell the rest of his name is*...to go fly a kite and take the rest of his brothers with him! But, of course, he said no such thing. It is the hallmark of the Yoruba to lick hot soup from the edges of the bowl.

"In that case, Eze Ozo..., perhaps I should go and consult with the rest of the Olatunji family, for if your son, Chike, will not perform the *idobale*, then, I am afraid, we may have reached an impasse here."

"Very well," Eze Ozo Ojemba Ewe Ilo replied, "go and put your heads together. We will wait to hear whatever solution your family comes up with, so long as it takes into full account our stance."

Tunde Olatunji returned to the fold of his family members with the news of this development. There was consternation among the gathered menfolk of the Olatunji family.

"What exactly do they say is the problem they have with the *idobale*?," Bisi's father asked his elder brother, Tunde.

"They say that it is a practice that is deeply abhorrent to their culture and their constitution as a people. They claim further, that it is equally impossible, based on the time-honored tenets of their culture, for such an act of humiliation--as they perceive it, to take place in the presence of their *Ozo* titled men."

Talking now in low, measured tones, Tunde Olatunji vented some of his frustration over the matter at hand and his overall disapproval of the idea of Bisi marrying an Igbo man.

"This is precisely the problem I have with these Igbo people. They tend to be unduly strident and dogged over issues that a little diplomatic finesse can easily straighten out. Now, are we to believe that if their son, Chike, who seeks the hand of our daughter in marriage, performs the purely symbolic act of *idobale*, it will suddenly turn them into slaves or what?"

"Personally," Tunde continued, "if they are unwilling to let their son perform the *idobale*, let them go back where they came from. It might actually turn out to be a blessing in disguise."

Bisi's father, a much cooler head than his elder brother, sat silently trying to digest the situation. He knows that *idobale* is an age-old marriage custom of the Yoruba. If it does not take place at this ceremony, no Yoruba man or woman present at that gathering or who gets wind of what transpired, will consider a marriage as having been consummated at all! A way must be found to bridge the yawning gulf between the two peoples.

Further away, in a chalet located behind the row of tent-like tarpaulin canopies erected to shade the large number of visitors to the home of the Olatunji family, Bisi, in company of her mother, aunts and neices, was waiting, resplendantly attired in rich traditional Yoruba *asoke*. There, she will remain until the "bride price" is settled. After that, she will be called upon to take a cupful of palm wine to the man she has chosen to be her husband and sip wine from the same vessel in full view of everyone present.

Suddenly, Funke, one of Bisi's young nieces, burst into the chalet and excitedly dropped the bombshell.

"Auntie Bisi, auntie Bisi," she managed to blurt out between gulps of air, "your Igbo suitors say they will not *dobale!*"

A cold shiver ran down Bisi's spine. What is the meaning of this now? What will happen to the rest of the ceremony if this glitch is not resolved? Is Chike party to this refusal? These and other questions crowded her mind and, after a while, it all seemed too much and she broke down in tears.

Seeing her daughter cry brought back memories for Mrs. Olatunji of all that Bisi has been through to ensure that this day becomes a reality. Her courageous stance against her parent's preferences; her unalloyed loyalty and deep love for Chike; the joy that glows on her face at the mere thought of life together with Chike. And now, now, at the very dawn of a new day, *they* want to spoil it all for her. To disgrace her daughter and the whole Olatunji family in front of all these people. To break her daughter's heart as though her feelings count for nothing on the scale of the outsized egos of septuagenarians at the dusk of their lives, even as their children are at the dawn of theirs. She will be damned if she is going to stand by and let that happen!

187

Her maternal instincts for protecting her young was now in full bloom. Like a mother hen, Bisi's mother turned from a harmless chicken minding its own business while busily picking edibles on the grounds of the neighborhood, to a combative bird of prey. Her feathers fanned out like the ears of the great African elephant. Her eyes flashing like flames, searching for who will dare make the first move towards her chicks!

She walked up to Bisi and cuddled her in her arms, gently reassuring her that all will be well. Then, she called Bisi's niece, Funke, the self-appointed bearer of bad news.

"Funke."

"Yes, Ma," answered Funke.

"Go over to where our Igbo suitors are sitting in the livingroom of the main house, and tell Chike, that I wish to have a word with him right away. Go now, hurry."

"Yes, Ma," Funke replied, as she took off from the chalet as quickly as she had burst into it a few minutes earlier.

The tone in her mother's voice and the fire in her eyes had Bisi worried. What does she want to say to Chike? As upset as she is, her heart might get in the way of her head, making things far worse than they already are!

"Mama," Bisi gently asked her mother, "why are you sending for Chike? Might it not be better to let Baba and his brothers handle this matter?"

"Be quiet, child," her mother snapped at her, "there are some things that only a mother can and must do. You will just have to trust that I have your best interest at heart."

Although Bisi momentarily remembered her father's favorite saying that, "the road to hell is paved with good intentions," she held her peace as well as her breath.

Funke reached the caucus of Chike's *umunna* and approached Chike. Wisely, she went up to him and whispered into his ears instead of openly announcing her message. Chike got up, excused himself and followed Funke to the chalet.

As Chike entered the chalet, he saw Bisi crying in her mother's arms. Instinctively, he went over to her and held her hand, anxiously asking her what was wrong.

"Bisi, what it the matter? Why are you crying?"

"What is the matter, you ask her," Bisi's mother interjected, "do you not know what is holding up this wine carrying ceremony, Chike? Is this how you intend to look after my daughter in your house and among your people? As soon as the first rainstorm comes, you run for shelter among your kith and kin, leaving her out to get drenched in the rainstorm. Tell me young man, is it?"

"Today is supposed to be one of the happiest days of her life. A day that she has looked forward to for a long time. A day for which she has endured all manner of trials to see come to fruition. And now, just like that, you and your granduncles want to ruin it all. And you stand there and sheepishly ask her what the matter is?"

"But...em...but, Mrs. Olatunji," Chike stammered, "you do not understand. I can not just override my granduncles, my *umunna*. These men are *Ozo* titled men, the pillars of our community."

"No, Chike, I understand one thing only too well. I understand that you have no backbone. I understand that you are not man enough to stand up for what you want and believe in. Not man enough to look after my daughter as your wife. That when the chips are down, really down, you will cut loose and run. You will pull anchor and sail off into the sunset. Oh yes, I understand, I fully understand."

Chike was both embarrassed and surprised at Mrs. Olatunji's combativeness. In fact, for all the while he has known Bisi's mother, he has never seen her like this. It was as if she were an entirely different person. Even then, Bisi's mother was not quite done with Chike. She let go of Bisi and stood virtually in Chike's face.

"Chike Nwafor, tell me to my face, tell me right here and now, that you are going to let Bisi go, that you are going to let everything both of you have struggled for all this while amount to nothing, for the simple reason that you will not perform the purely symbolic act of *idobale*. Tell me to my face."

Chike stood in front of Bisi's mother, rooted to the spot. He felt caught between two great demanding gods: the god of cultural and filial loyalty and the god of the heart. What was he supposed to do? Follow the god of cultural and filial loyalty and risk the wrath of the god of the heart or vice versa? Finally, he could only manage a lame answer.

"I do not know what to do, Mrs. Olatunji, I honestly don't."

"That is exactly what I thought you would say. Go. Go back to your granduncles with your tail neatly tucked in behind your hind legs. Go and snuggle in the warm safety of their feet. Just be sure to piss on one of the nearby trees before you leave, to mark the fact that you once passed through these parts."

As Chike was slowly heading towards the exit of the chalet, Bisi began to sob all over again. *Something* in her anguished cry stopped Chike in his tracks. By now, he was almost at the front door of the chalet when that *something* made him change his mind. He whirled around and called out to Bisi's mother, "I will do it, I will do the *idobale*! But that does not solve the problem of my granduncles. They are *Ozo* titled men and do not bend easily."

"Good for you young man. Good for you," Bisi's mother crooned joyfully, "you leave your granduncles to me."

FIFTY SEVEN

Mrs. Olatunji is an example of a woman whose physical beauty deceives its beholder of the strength of character that lies within her person like tempered steel in a velvet glove. Her supple, feline body, her regal carriage, her easy smile, her gentle retirement; all combine to give the false impression of weakness, of fragility. They give the false impression of a *damsel in distress*, that needs rescuing by a chivalrous knight in shinning armor.

In reality, physically beautiful and feminine though she is, Bisi's mother is very resilient. Since she qualified as an RN, she has never taken ill except for an occasional cold or headache. This is despite the fact that she is constantly around sick and dying people.

Moreover, Mrs. Olatunji has a punishing work schedule as an RN. A work schedule that would try the endurance of any man. Yet, she has held up remarkably well, looking much younger than her forty five years of age. More importantly, perhaps, Bisi's mother is a woman very much in touch with herself--emotionally and spiritually. A self-possessed woman, completely at home with her feminine and intellectual being.

She adjusted her *onilegogoro*, retied her wrapper more tightly around her waist and hips, pulled herself up to her full height and gathering all her female aplomb, made her fateful move.

"Chike," Bisi's mother said with a straight face, "take me to your granduncles."

"Excuse me, Mrs. Olatunji, did you just say that I should take you to my granduncles?"

"I know that you are not deaf, Chike. Yes, that was what I just said. Now, take me to them we do not have much time left."

"But...but...Mrs. Olatunji, what are you going to say to them? How are you going to say what you plan to say to them? These men are wordsmiths. They treat the art of speaking as though they are producing of an exquisite work of art. I am not sure that this is such a good idea."

191

"What I am going to say to them and how, Chike, is for me to know and for you to find out. Now, take me to them, unless I will have no choice but to go over there by myself."

Chike and Bisi's mother walked towards the livingroom of the main house of the Olatunji family home, with Chike in the lead. As they entered the livingroom, Chike could see his granduncles huddled in the corner, no doubt still mauling over the same issue.

On the opposite side of the livingroom, the menfolk of the Olatunji family; Bisi's father, uncles and granduncles were gathered, discussing possible courses of action in the light of the current situation.

Chike and Mrs. Olatunji stepped into the livingroom and began making their way towards the caucus of Chike's *umunna* through the unoccupied middle area of the livingroom. All eyes fell upon them even as a dense silence enveloped the livingroom. As they made their way through the fixated stares and the silence, the short distance from the entrance door of the livingroom to the caucus of Chike's *umunna*, seemed like a journey of a thousand miles.

Bisi's mother knew exactly what must be going through her husband's mind and those of her brothers in-law as well as the rest of the gathered menfolk of the Olatunji family. They must be thinking that she has lost her mind. Unfortunately for them, the distance between them was such that they could not speak to her or try to restrain her without making a scene.

They consider matters of this sort to be the exclusive preserve of the menfolk, and are, therefore, probably thinking that she is overstepping her traditionally allotted boundary, and they would be right. Except that once in a while, mothers like herself, who have raised both male and female children, need to remind their children, their *manchildren* especially, how to behave themselves! It is precisely that which she intends to do with Chike's granduncles.

Exasperated by the situation and what he fears is going to be the disastrous outcome of *whateveritis* his wife is about to do, Bisi's father swore under his breath, calling on *Oduduwa*, to come to their rescue.

When Chike and Bisi's mother reached the caucus of his *umunna*, Chike quickly introduced Bisi's mother and explained that she wants to have a word with his *umunna* about the *idobale* debacle. The *Ozo* titled men of Chike's *umunna* regarded Mrs. Olatunji with a mixture of curiousity and mild amusement. Predictably, *Ozo* Okenihe, broke the silence. Without directly addressing Bisi's mother, *Ozo* Okenihe spoke rhetorically but to her hearing.

"What does a woman want to say to us about the matter at hand? What can a woman possibly have to say to us about this matter? As if the problem of prostrating before other human beings is not bad enough, it appears the menfolk of the Yoruba do not have balls enough to come and speak face-to-face with us. They send their women to do the work meant for men."

"How things have changed," *Ozo* Okenihe bemoaned, shaking his head, "I can still remember when the closest a woman could approach an *Ozo* titled man in such a brazen manner, was either underneath him in the heat of passion as one of his wives or gently playing the *uboh* or the *ekwe* in his *Obi*, to help along his digestion after a large meal."

"Or could it be," *Ozo* Okenihe continued sarcastically, "that they do not consider our petition of sufficient weight as to warrant one of their esteemed elders coming to parley with us?"

Before any of the other *Ozo* titled men could add to *Ozo* Okenihe's comments, Bisi's mother spoke up.

"Respected elders, let me say to you right away, that I am not an emissary of the Olatunji family. I am merely acting on my own. As a matter of fact, the menfolk of the Olatunji family are probably as puzzled as to what I am doing here in your midst as they are offended by it. I am merely here in my capacity as the mother of the bride-to-be."

"I have heard about the clash between your Igbo culture and our *idobale* custom."

"In that case," interrupted *Ozo* Obolo Di Ihe, "you have heard well. Did you also hear that even if we were to agree to let our son, Chike, do your *idobale* custom, there are *Ozo* titled men among Chike's *umunna* and, therefore, such a sore sight cannot take place in their presence? Did you hear that as well?"

"Yes, I did," Bisi's mother respectfully answered.

"Well, if you did, why are you here to talk to us about a matter of which you already know the boundaries of the possible and the impossible?"

"Well, respected elder," Bisi's mother responded, "we have already removed at least one of those two obstacles."

"You have," "You have," the rest of Chike's granduncles excitedly chimed in, "how exactly was that achieved?"

They swarmed around her like killer bees ready to sting at the slighted provocation. Bisi's mother stood her ground.

"Chike has agreed to do the *idobale?*"

"What?," "When?," "Why?." As they peppered her with questions from all sides, one of Chike's granduncles called him out to verify what they just heard. He confirmed it. Sighs, popping of thumbs and middle fingers, head shaking, and *tufiakwas*, broke out among the caucus of Chike's *umunna*. They were in a state of disbelief and disappointment. Once again, Chike has gone against the grain of tradition. Once again, he has forced them into a rear guard action.

Eze *Ozo* Ojemba Ewe Ilo, sensing that things were reaching a critical point stepped in.

"Well, Mrs. Olatunji, the information you have just provided us addresses only one of the two obstacles that we have before us today. How do you propose to remove the second one?"

"Thank you for that question respected elder, but before I get to that second obstacle, there are a few questions I wish to ask all of you: what does Igbo culture recommend as a course of action for a mother trying to rescue her daughter's dignity and future happiness?"

"What does Igbo culture recommend for rescuing the happiness of a wonderful young couple, deeply in love with one another and committed to a future together as husband and wife?"

"Noble as your culture evidently is, does it prescribe that the legitimate concern of such a mother for her daughter and for the young couple, be set aside and trammeled under the feet of the very men who purport to love them most?"

An awkward silence greeted her question. But Eze Ozo Ojemba Ewe Ilo, was not yet prepared to yield the initiative to Mrs. Olatunji although he was becoming impressed by her courage and candor. He posed a question to her.

"Mrs. Olatunji, your point is well taken. As a matter of fact, it is because we appreciate the maternal instinct that compels your transgression on behalf of your daughter, that these *Ozo* tilted men you see here have not let loose their indignation like iron balls fired from Dane guns. For patience with upstarts is not one of their strong points."

"Yet, as moving as your philosophical questions are, they fail to provide a concrete solution to the second obstacle of *Ozo* titled men being present in our midst."

Bisi's mother, a highly perceptive woman, already could sense from his bearing, eloquence and air of authority, that this mountain of a man, Eze Ozo Ojemba Ewe Ilo, if not the formal head of the group, is, at the very least, the first among equals. Moreover, *something* in his eyes, *something* in the deep, resonating cadence of his voice, intuitively made her sense his warmth, his empathy, his deep-seated humanity. She focused her energy on him although she spoke in plural terms and loud enough for the others to hear. She correctly surmised that if she succeeds in winning Eze Ozo Ojemba Ewe Ilo over, the others will follow.

"Respected elders," Bisi's mother ventured, "if the problem is simply that a custom like *idobale* can not take place in the presence of your *Ozo* titled men, can we not resolve that technicality by the *Ozo* titled men graciously agreeing to remove themselves from our midst for a short while?"

She paused, hoping that she is making progress with these wizened patriarch's of Chike's family. The consequences of failure are too grave to contemplate.

"That way, we kill two birds with a stone. The *idobale* custom would not have taken place in the presence of the *Ozo* titled men, avoiding violation of their traditional honor and dignity. At the same time, the *idobale* custom would have been performed by my daughter's suitor, Chike, clearing the way for the rest of the traditional wine carrying ceremony to go forth as well as giving our own Yoruba custom place of pride in the proceedings."

Eze Ozo Ojemba Ewe Ilo, saw immediately the power of Mrs. Olatunji's suggestion. It lay in its simplicity. His admiration for this beautiful, stubborn, Yoruba woman, rose several notches. Any wonder his people say that men build great empires but women build great bridges between them.

The *Ozo* titled men of Chike's *umunna* murmured amongst themselves for a while longer. Finally, speaking for the rest of the group, Eze Ozo Ojemba Ewe Ilo, turned to Bisi's mother, who was anxiously awaiting their verdict and said, "We think that your solution is a good and practical one.

Since our son, Chike, has agreed to do your *idobale* custom, the *Ozo* titled men have agreed to go along with your suggestion. We will stroll for a short distance outside the compound of the Olatunji family, and wait until the *idobale* custom has been performed. After that, we shall return for the rest of the wine carrying ceremony."

Bisi's mother was overjoyed and relieved. She thanked them profusely, curtseying slightly in the Yoruba traditional fashion known as *ikunle* meant for greeting elders and returned to where the menfolk of the Olatunji family were themselves anxiously wondering what was going on. She had killed a big elephant right in front of everyone and felt very good about it.

Before they strolled out from the compound, one of the *Ozo* titled men of Chike's *umunna,* pulled out a three-feet long *oji* and raising it up in the manner of a javelin, thrust it into the ground of the Olatunji family compound. The metal pendants on the *oji* arranged in layered cascades on its stem, continued making jangling noises from the force of the thrust, even as the *Ozo* titled men took brief leave of the gathering.

FIFTY EIGHT

D ramatic as the episode of the *idobale* custom was in the course of that traditional wine carrying ceremony, incredibly, yet another high point will be reached. That was when they reached the point of deciding on the "bride price" for Bisi's betrothal to Chike.

When they reached that point, Bisi's father did something that left a deep and lasting impression on Chike's father and the rest of his *umunna*. It was an act that Chike's father would later admit was worthy of an *Ozo*--a man whose life is predicated entirely on courage and honor.

Bisi's father asked one of his several house servants, who was standing at a respectful distance from the guests in the large living room of the home of the Olatunji family, to go and fetch him the largest basin he can find in the house. When the young man returned, he had in his hands a rather outlandish container. Mr. Olatunji asked him to place the basin between himself and his daughter's suitors. Then he got on his feet and cleared his throat.

"Respected elders, our mothers and sisters, and all the young tendrils in our midst, I greet you all once again. I have not much to say for now, except to ask that you have somebody, perhaps the young man asking for our daughter's hand in marriage, go outside and fill this basin with all the stone pebbles he can find. When he returns, I will finish what I have to say." He sat down.

The men of Chike's family, his father and his *umunna*, huddled among themselves, talking in low tones, puzzling over the meaning of Mr. Olatunji's request. Bemused, they reached the polite decision to oblige Bisi's father under the assumption that the request was, perhaps, yet another kind of custom among the Yoruba people.

Eze Ozo Ojemba Ewe Ilo motioned to Chike to pick up the basin and do Bisi's father's bidding. An awkward silence settled in between the delegates of the two families in the living room of the Olatunji home, even as some of them tried to interject a few ice breakers by talking about Wazobian politics and the continuing inflationary prices of consumer goods in the country.

Half an hour later, Chike returned to the living room, doubled over by the dead weight of the basin that was now filled with stone pebbles. He placed the basin in the middle of the living room, as though in a buffer zone between the two contending families. He returned to his seat, his chest still heaving from the effort.

Bisi's father rose to his feet again.

"Our elders, mothers and sisters, and all the young tendrils among us, I salute you all once more. I can see that your thirsty son has made the trip to the river to fetch the water he seems to need to quench his thirst. However, my esteemed friends, I have one more request to make of you. I would like your son to count all the stone pebbles in the basin before our very eyes. How ever many of those stone pebbles he finds there to be, is how much "bride price" I want for my daughter, Bisi."

Mr. Olatunji sat down, a smirk lingering on the corners of his mouth. A subdued babble broke out among the Nwafor *umunna*, the elders obviously astonished at this new request, and not a trifle irritated. Eze Ozo Ojemba Ewe Ilo rose to his feet, his impressive frame dominating the living room.

"Eh, Mazi Olatunji, with all due respect, permit me to say that this second request of yours seems quite a bit unreasonable to us. Assuming it were possible to count all the stone pebbles in that basin, there is not enough time between now and when the moon gives the sun a chance to get some rest, for our son to count them all. And it is not our custom for titled men - *Ozos*, to sleep overnight at the abode of strangers whom it is not yet clear whether we are to make war or peace with."

Eze Ozo Ojemba Ewe Ilo returned to his seat.

"Moreover," said Ozo Obolo Dihe, getting to his feet, "How much is each stone pebble worth in real money? Is each stone pebble worth one naira, ten naira or ten thousand naira? We do not know, and it seems to me that that is a vital piece of information we need to know before proceeding with any counting of the pebbles."

Chike's father rose to his feet.

"Elders, members of my *umunna*, Mazi Olatunji and his family, I salute you all. We are aware that the binding together of two families in marriage is no small matter, and, therefore, great care must be taken. Our people say that raising a young woman to the point where she is safely ensconced in her husband's house is like running a long distance race over rough terrain with rare ostrich eggs in your hunting bag. You are never in the clear until those eggs have been safely put away in their proper place in the *uko* of your home, without cracks appearing on their shells. Therefore, there is hardly anyone in this room who does not appreciate Mazi Olatunji's legitimate concerns."

He paused a few moments, as if waiting for the weight of the point he just made to sink in.

"But it would seem to us that we have been through two stages of this process already, the *Iku aka nu uzo* - knocking on the door, and the *Ibata nu uno* - coming into the house. And now, we are at the final stage of the whole process, the *Ibu Mmanya*--the 'wine carrying' - the consummation of the process. It seems to me that if Mazi Olatunji knew all along that he was going to present us with this impossible hurdle at the tail end of the process, it would have been far more considerate, not to speak of honorable, for him to have saved us all the trouble and expense that we have been through."

He sat down heavily, his disappointment palpable. Ozo Osisi Di Mma Na Ani Akulia rose to his feet, supporting his slightly overweight body with his ornately carved walking stick, cleared his throat and began speaking ever so slowly.

"Elders, sons and daughters of our fathers, Mazi Olatunji and his family, I greet you all. We have a story in Igbo land, that once upon a time, the mouth, the ear and the head were planning to execute a project. It was a great and important project, one likely to bring them fame and fortune if they do it right. But the ear complained that he could not understand what the head was thinking, the head complained that the ear is not paying attention, and the ear and the head complained that the mouth is speaking in garbled tones. The mouth retorted that the ear is loosing his sense of hearing and that the head is dense. Yet, they are all part of the same body and would all benefit if the body to which they all belong, prospers. What must they do to stop talking at cross purposes?"

"It seems to me," Ozo Osisi Di Mma Na Ani Akulia continued, "That the best course of action is for the mouth and the ear to hold their peace, and let the wellspring of the thought, the head, set the record straight. We invite you, Mazi Olatunji, to set the record straight for us."

He sat down to the spirited affirmation of his fellows, who called him various praise names to indicate their appreciation of his erudition. Bisi's father rose to his feet again, speaking in a much more deliberate manner.

"Elders, sons and daughters of our fathers, and the young tendrils among us, the second request I made of your son is not a custom of the Yoruba people as some of you might suppose. It was a gimmick I contrived to make a point at this august gathering. The point I wish to make is that my daughter is invaluable to me, her mother and all the other members of our family. No amount of money you give us today, tomorrow or the day after tomorrow, can ever suffice to compensate us for her."

He paused, surveying the audience as though he were delivering a lecture in a classroom.

"I do not wish to be given a single kobo. As you can all see, my family and I are of comfortable means. All I ask of your son and your family is to look after my daughter and the children she will bear for you and us. If I find her hungry, I will hold your son and your family responsible. If I find her naked, unkempt or sad, I will ask your son and your family for an explanation. Otherwise, they have my blessings. That is all I have to say."

A thunderous applause broke out in the livingroom. When it died down, Eze Ozo Ojemba Ewe Ilo, though impressed with Mr. Olatunji's dramatic gimmick and oration, was not about to let the occasion end solely on the high note of Mr. Olatunji's diplomatic maneuver. There were, after all, six *Ozo* titled men in that room. Men whose next most important preoccupation besides farming, valor and honour, is wordsmithing.

He rose to his feet and stretched himself out to his full height, cleared his throat and slowly adjusted his *Konkosa* in the 'one thousand five hundred' style. Suddenly, without warning, he thrust his clenched fist into the air and exploded in a booming voice.

"*Umunna* Nwafor kwenu."

"Yaa," came the reply.

"*Igbo* Kwenu," Eze Ozo Ojemba Ewe Ilo boomed again.

"Yaa," came the reply.

"*Umunna* Mazi Olatunji Kwenu," Eze Ozo Ojemba Ewe Ilo shouted again.

"Yaa," replied members of the Olatunji family, a bit tentative in their own affirmation, for this is an Igbo custom.

"Wazobia Kwezuonu," Eze Ozo Ojemba Ewe Ilo bellowed again.

The entire audience exploded in a tremendous "Yaa"!!!

"Mazi Olatunji, you have spoken eloquently and we have heard you well. Your mouth is good and so are our ears. Now, I wish for you to hear us well too. We are a proud and hardworking people. We ask nothing of anyone except respect and that which is our just due. The reason no one is able to ride the back of any man from whence we come, is because all of them are standing erect. You can not ride the back of a man whose back is not bent over. Our honour is, therefore, everything to us."

He paused momentarily, seeming to glare at Bisi's father as he waited for his moments of pause to have their full dramatic effect.

"All these women you see here," Eze Ozo Ojemba Ewe Ilo said, waving his hand in the direction of the Egbe women, "are either our sisters or the mothers of some of the young tendrils you see among us here. None of them are, nor have they ever been, hungry, naked or unkempt. We look after our women and our women look after us. We will do no less for your daughter and we expect no less from her."

"As for the happiness of our women or anybody else's for that matter, we leave that up to them and their *Chi*. For as we say in Igboland, it is the burden of the person who refuses to smile because the one has problems, to explain how his fellows whose problems are even greater than his own, manage smiles with every morning's dawn."

Eze Ozo Ojemba Ewe Ilo paused, adjusted his *Konkosa*, and resumed his talk.

"Eh, Mazi Olatunji and his esteemed family, permit me to ask a rhetorical question that our people use in the form of an allegory to illustrate the essence of human communion."

"If there is a full moon, is there any one in the vicinity in whose compound it does not shine?"

"The answer to that question is no. When there is a full moon, its glows in everyone's compound."

"Yet, if this is the case, as it most certainly is, why then do people still go to the village square when there is a full moon though all are equal beneficiaries of its incandescence?"

"The answer to that question is that the essence of our humanity lies in associating together. Therefore, whenever an opportunity presents itself for us to get together, because it is the very core of our humanity, we take to it like fish to water."

"The reason we have come all this way to Yorubaland for a bride is not because there is a shortage of young maidens in Igboland. We know also, that the reason your daughter accepted the proposition of our son is not because there are no young men among your people. There is a drum beat, a tune, that only their two hearts understand its accompanying dance steps. That is why we are here today. The son of my father has finished what he has to say."

Eze Ozo Ojemba Ewe Ilo sat down with a flourish as his fellow *Ozos* peppered him with congratulatory praise names. Bisi was called out, and in customary fashion, given an *ogbo* of palm wine and asked to identify the man she has accepted to be her husband by offering him the cup of palm wine. Bashfully, Bisi walked slowly over to Chike, got on one of her knees and offered him the cup of palm wine. Chike got to his feet and accepted the drink. They both embraced each other to the thunderous applause of the audience.

The women dance troupe from Egbe began to sing and dance in the course of much eating and drinking, after which a Yoruba solo drummer performed, stringing together ancient words into ageless stories in the language of the intricate percussive rhythms of the "talking drum".

FIFTY NINE

For days Ngozi mauled over in her mind how best to broach the subject of Mohammed to her parents. For the past two years, she had successfully concealed her relationship with Mohammed from her family. During the long vacation, even her conservative father once cautiously asked her why she never seems interested in going out with her friends. She replied, lied, that she had more important things to do with her time than while it away at frivolous parties.

That reply, naturally pleased her father much. For he felt that Ngozi has turned out exactly as he had hoped: intelligent, single-minded, focused and ambitious. Little did he know that her apparent lack of interest in socializing with her friends was due to her painful longing for Mohammed rather than her superior moral or intellectual inclination.

Two weeks before the term closed for the long vacation at the University of Ibadan, Ngozi decided that since her friend Chike is also Igbo and is dating Bisi, a Yoruba girl whom everybody on campus knows he intends to marry, he is a good person to solicit advise from regarding her own situation.

At the end of their morbid anatomy class that Friday, Ngozi cornered Chike in the hallway of Independence Hall where they have their labs, and asked if she could have a few words with him.

"Chike, I need to talk to you about something very important."

"Sure, Ngozi, what do you want to talk about," Chike responded, putting down the stack of hefty medical texts in his arms on the floor. He wondered whether Ngozi was pregnant, and if so, why she had chosen him to confide in.

"Well, Chike, the problem has to do with my relationship with Mohammed."

"What about your relationship with Mohammed?," Chike pursued, a worried look appearing on his face, "don't tell me that both of you have broken up, please don't tell me that."

"No, no, no. Its nothing of the sort. It is just that the relationship has gotten serious enough that we plan to get

203

married as soon as we graduate next year. But I have no idea how to tell my parents about the situation. They do not even know that Mohammed exists, let alone my going so far as to get married to him. I have been worried sick for the last couple of weeks."

"What do you suggest I do, Chike? After all, you are the local expert on inter-*tribal* affairs," Ngozi jokingly added trying to reclaim some self-possession with the anecdote.

"Well, Ngozi, it is hard to say how best you should approach the matter, because, unfortunately, such matters are somewhat more difficult for a woman than for a man."

"How so, Chike?," Ngozi asked, her hand at akimbo on one of her shapely hips.

"You should know that as well, Ngozi, you are a big girl now. When a woman gets married she is claimed by the man she is married to rather than the other way around. She assumes the name of her husband's family."

"In a patrilineal system such as we have in Wazobia, her children come from her husband's village or town and not her own. This, of course, has profound social, cultural as well as psychological implications for the children. The predominant language the children will speak is that of their father. Their ethnic identity---their social and cultural stamp, is that of their father."

"But that just doesn't seem fair to the woman," Ngozi replied, "I hear that among a certain Ghanaian ethnic group---the Asante, I believe, they have a matrilineal system..."

"What *is*, Ngozi, is not necessarily what *ought* or *ought not to be*. And *what ought* or *ought not to be*, is certainly not *what is*. I am dealing here with *what is* and not *what ought* or *ought not to be*."

"In my humble opinion though, there are good reasons why our forefathers and foremothers instituted those traditions. I do not share the belief, like many seem to do nowadays, that those traditions were put in place merely to be mean to women or to simply buttress the power of men."

"Our forefathers and foremothers had a good understanding of the strengths and weaknesses of men and women, and tried to craft traditional roles that took them into account. But this is not the time nor the place to get into a philosophical discussion over that issue."

"Getting back to the matter at hand, Ngozi, the reality is that telling your parents about Mohammed and your intentions to marry him is unavoidable. What we ought to be thinking of is how best to do so and how to deal with their reaction when they are apprised of the situation."

"Let me tell you the story of my experience with my own parents, perhaps there may be some lessons in it for you. It is not a short story by any means, so I think we had better find somewhere to sit down."

They went and sat down on one of the benches lined up along the opposite walls of the hallway. Chike told his story in colorful detail. When he finished, Ngozi reclined on the bench and sighed heavily.

"*Odiegwu!*, Chike, that was quite an experience. Going by your theory, you are a man and still had it that bad, imagine what will happen to me!"

"To make matters worse Chike, I am the *ada* of the family--the first daughter as well as the first child of my family. My parents are bound to feel that they are loosing their prized jewel, and that I am setting a bad example for my siblings. So what can I do in the circumstances, Chike?"

"Well, my dear Ngozi, the first thing to bear in mind is that there is ultimately no way of avoiding the burdens of being a pioneer in any endeavor. Those burdens come with the territory. We are pioneers in the great endeavor of putting our country's ugly past behind us, and there is no escaping the burdens that will come with that task."

"Second, Ngozi, my own experience with this inter-*tribal* business has taught me beyond reasonable doubt that while the mothers--the women, share the prejudices, stereotypes and reservations of the fathers--the men, they remain the soft underbelly of the crocodile's tough hide. That soft underbelly is the best way to burrow into the beast's bowel."

"I am convinced that women are basically *universalists*, while men are basically *territorialists--nationalists.* At the end of the day, a woman is capable of and open to loving and living with a man from anywhere on earth, so long as that man is willing and able to protect her, provide for her material needs and wants, and shower her with affection, attention, and good lovemaking."

"However, since women mostly live under the political and economic power of men, they tend to go along with the territorialism--the nationalism, of men. Still, it is not their essential nature. It is the reason, I believe, that for most women, when push comes to shove, love for a man almost always overrides loyalty to nation or *tribe*. But for men, loyalty to nation or *tribe* usually overrides love for a woman."

"The women, are the key to reigning in the stubborn and egotistical territorialism of the men. Only the women, can ultimately call a truce in the pissing contest of the men."

"My advise to you then is to go through the soft underbelly of your mother to check the stubborn prejudice of your father. It is a strategy that I am fairly certain based on my experience, will work."

"One other thing, Ngozi. What you are doing, what you are about to do, is of indispensable value to our pioneering cause--of indispensable value to Wazobia's future as a united and virile nation. You must therefore persevere in your efforts. For as we say in Igbo, one should never shy away from a just and necessary war because a few comrades will perish on the battle field."

Ngozi thanked Chike for his time and advise, gave him a big hug and left more determined than ever to face the looming storm of her parents' wrath.

SIXTY

The Imo River flows for about two hundred miles through lush tropical vegetation meandering round small hills and flowing through shallow valleys that periodically narrow into goose-necks, turning the great volumes of water coursing through their yawning divides into natural hydro-dams. At the end of the river's epic journey, it miraculously drains into a basin whose mouth, permanently open like a doorless trap, empties into the shimmering Atlantic.

This fresh-water river has been the very source of life for all the Igbo communities located on or close to its banks. It quenches their thirst, waters their farmlands, gives them abundant fish and washes their bodies and their apparels. The Imo River is quite literally, their life source.

For thousands of years, the people of Isiobodo and their neighbors, lived in near-perfect harmony with the River. It takes care of them and they take care of it. They give it respect, treat it with the care it deserves, perhaps, even with awe. So integral to their livelihood is the Imo River, that they ascribe to it the power of a goddess--the River goddess; for they understand correctly, that it has the power of life and death over them.

Once in a while, however, despite their care and respect for the River goddess, despite the awe and reverence they accord her, she looses her temper and becomes unruly. She swells up until she overflows her banks for miles on either side, ruining farmlands and threatening homes in nearby villages. When this happens, people from the surrounding villages bring offerings to appease the River goddess in the hope of restoring her even temper. Fortunately, her tantrums are few and far between.

When Ngozi was a little girl, herself and other little children in Isiobodo, would often run along the banks of the Imo River, singing the lively refrain of a song that kids sing to the River goddess to affirm their honesty:

ego papa,
singily wata

ego mama,
singily wata
if na me steal money,
singily wata,
Disi wata carry me,
singily wata.

Under the provisioning care of the Imo River, the people of Isiobodo, Ngozi's village, grew strong, wealthy, robust, independent and proud. Like all the other Igbo communities spread out from the swampy reaches of the Oil Rivers in the southwest to the Udi hills in the northeast, poverty was largely unknown. Landlessness was non-existent, and begging, completely anathema.

The first time members of these Igbo communities came in contact with a culture in which there were landless peasants-- people living completely at the sufferance and benevolent will of others; a culture in which there existed what one might call, *professional beggars,* men and children who do nothing else for a living except beg for alms; was when they came in contact with the Hausa in colonial Wazobia.

The reaction of the Igbos to the culture shock of that revelation was revulsion and disdain. They felt that people who indulged in that kind of begging had no shame, no dignity, no pride. That people who indulged in that kind of solicitation for alms were lazy and improvident. That they lacked ambition, industry and the fire of creativity in the pits of their bellies.

Something else came with the culture shock of that revelation. The Igbos are deeply republican whereas the Hausas are raised on the sap of absolutist monarchy. For the Hausas, the word of their king is law. For the Igbos, every man is a king, especially in his own house. Every person is considered an autonomous individual though connected to the community through a gamut of familial ties and obligations.

Looking north of Wazobia, the Igbos saw blind, uncritical followership and obedience towards arrogant, self-serving, absolute monarchs. Looking south, the Hausas saw individualism verging on anarchy. Individualism that appears to lack anchor to the timeless certitude of perpetual rulers. Like all such things, however, for the Igbo and for the Hausa, the truth lay somewhere in between, even if neither side knew it yet.

SIXTY ONE

Ngozi Chidimma comes from a typical Igbo family in the village of Isiobodo. Hers was not a wealthy family but a respected one. Her life is firmly balanced on five pillars: *Chukwu*--God, *umunna* and *umunne*--family, *omenani*--tradition, *igba mboh*--hardwork, and *imuta akwukwo*--education.

Ngozi's father came originally from a poor family, but slowly and dutifully, he worked his way up to a senior civil service position over a period of about thirty years. When he saved enough money to build his own house and take a bride, Ngozi's father, Mazi Chidimma, married a girl from a neighboring village. Soon, they were blessed with four children, two girls and two boys. The girls came first giving Mazi Chidimma no small cause for concern. For already, the rumor mills were beginning to churn that the lion is bringing forth pussy cats instead of cubs.

Mazi Chidimma's girls turned out to be especially good looking and bright. However, that did not stay the tongues of the rumor mongers. They spun yard-length yarns meant to ruffle Mazi Chidimma's feathers.

"Fine," went one such yarn, "so the Chidimma girls are bright and beautiful, but who will break kola nut and pour libations in that household when their father is not home?"

Or as yet another pique went, "we know of those among us who never have to scratch their heads in worry about the safety of their sons in time of war."

Not long after, Mazi Chidimma and his wife were blessed with two boys.

SIXTY TWO

Ngozi made *oha* soup that evening because she knows that is her mother's favorite soup. She prepared the soup, as they say, with the thoroughness and care of one who washed their hands well.

Earlier that day, Ngozi had gone to *Afia Uwa*--the world's market, Isiobodo's bustlng main market, to buy fresh *oha* and choice chunks of *mangala* fish for the soup. She also bought a small quantity of *ogili*, a strong smelling ingredient used to give various kinds of soup a unique and irresistible flavour.

When Ngozi returned from *Afia Uwa* by mid-day, she quickly busied herself with preparing the *oha* soup and a little later, pounding the yam fufu with which the soup will be eaten.

In the evening when Ngozi's mother returned from her *Otu Omu* meeting and perceived the mouth-watering aroma of the *oha* soup, she jokingly commented to Ngozi that the soup smells so good she can *hear it*!

When they finished their meal and Ngozi cleared the table of dishes and tumblers, they removed to the parlor where they lounged and made small talk over myriad issues. Heeding Chike's advise about the soft underbellies of crocodiles, Ngozi probed for the most opportune moment to bring up the issue of Mohammed. In her mind, she grappled with how best to phrase her words. Finally, she decided to make her move diplomatically.

"Nne"--mother, Ngozi began cautiously, "I bet that when yourself and Nnayi--Papa were young, when you both first met, you must have been madly in love with each other?"

"Ah, Ngozi, stop torturing an old woman with memories of the *egwu owa*--moonlight games, of her youth."

"Oh, yes indeed, your father and I were madly in love with each other when we were young and first met," Ngozi's mother continued, completely oblivious of the fact that she was being ensnared by her daughter.

"Your father and I were so in love with each other that it mattered little to us that we did not come from the same village."

"As you well know, you father is from Isiobodo and I am from Isiukwuano, a full day's journey from here on foot."

"The two villages have been in perpetual competition with each other. To this day, nobody knows what they are competing over. The competition between the two villages, one might say, has become a tradition in itself, with no objective reasons needed to keep it alive."

"There were many relatives on both sides, who did not want your father and I to get married precisely because of that age old senseless competition between our two villages."

"Our hearts knew better however, and your father and I stuck to our guns. Now, look at us. All the naysayers have been silenced by the benevolence of Chukwu and the ancestors. Let those who refuse to concede that the world belongs to God continue fooling themselves that their preferences have anything to do with the fortune's of *umu Chukwu*--the children of God. It is indeed true what they say that *man proposes and God disposes*."

All the while as her mother was telling her story, Ngozi felt like shouting out loud, "that is precisely my present condition, precisely the sentiments of Mohammed and I; perhaps your own experience, mother, will make you more empathetic towards my predicament"; but she held her peace.

At the end of her mother's love story, tears flowed freely down Ngozi's face. At first her mother could not tell that Ngozi was crying, for her face was turned downwards as though she were looking for something on the floor. Moreover, Ngozi was not sobbing, she was not making any audible sounds that could suggest that she is crying. The tears just flowed freely down her face.

What clued her mother to her crying was the involuntary sniffling that comes with profusely tearing eyes as mucus builds up in the nostrils.

"Adaeze"--the first daughter of a king, Ngozi's mother called her, "what is the matter?"

Instinctively, Ngozi's mother came over to the love seat on which Ngozi was sitting and put her arms around her daughter.

"Ngozi, what is wrong? You can tell me whatever it is, I am your mother and I love you more than anything in this world."

"Are you pregnant?," Ngozi's mother queried guardedly.

"Mba"--no, Ngozi gently replied, tears still streaming down her face.

"Is something wrong with your school work?," Ngozi's mother pursued.

"Mba," Ngozi replied.

"Did you take what does not belong to you?," Ngozi's mother continued.

"Mba," Ngozi replied in monotone.

"Then what on earth could be making you so sad as to cry in this way?"

"Nne," Ngozi began, raising her head up for the first time since she began crying, "I am in love with someone."

"You are a silly girl. Is that why you are crying? Being in love is a thing of joy not a thing of sorrow. It is not as if you are under age and one is worried that you are reaching for fruits on tree branches that are outside your grasp. You are a grown woman and it is expected that now is the time for you to start feathering your nest."

"Nne, like you and papa, my man and I are both madly in love with each other and little else matters to us."

"But that is as it should be my dear daughter. Who likes to begin a good meal with cold food? The food should be hot and steaming with its aromatic vapors filling the nostrils and beckoning to the stomach to hasten to the dinner table."

"There is something more, Nne," Ngozi said.

"What more is there? Or rather, what more could there possibly be? Does the man have two heads? Does he have a horn on his forehead? Is he a highway robber? Is he not well educated? Does he not have a good job or good prospects for one? Is he an *osu*? Is he an *anyali*--an albino? What is the something more, Ngozi?"

"Nne, he is not from Isiobodo," Ngozi said. Her mother laughed out loud and said, "Ngozi, you are not only silly you are absurd. Lest you have not noticed, most of the world is not from Isiobodo, although your father's people proud and arrogant as they are, like to think otherwise. Your own mother is not from Isiobodo. That is hardly an issue of great moment."

For a second Ngozi's spirits lifted. Perhaps the task is going to be a lot easier than she had imagined, especially with her mother. Perhaps Chike's prescription is exactly the right medicine.

"Which part of Igboland is he from?," Ngozi's mother casually asked her, taking completely for granted that the man in question is an Igbo man.

Ngozi swallowed hard. She had started her celebration way too soon.

"Nne, he is not from Igboland."

"I beg your pardon," Ngozi's mother said, the tone of her voice discernibly changing.

"He is not from Igboland," Ngozi repeated, her face turned downwards once again.

"What do you mean he is not from Igboland?," her mother continued, her voice developing a shrill edge to it.

"Exactly what I said, Nne, he is not from Igboland."

"Is he from Wazobia?," her mother queried cautiously.

"Yes," Ngozi replied.

"Which part of Wazobia is he from?," Ngozi's mother asked, her demeanor becoming clearly hostile.

Ngozi remained silent.

"Ngozi Chidimma, I asked you a question. Which part of Wazobia is he from?"

The moment of truth had arrived. That moment in life when time and action conflate into the same space of being.

"He is a Hausa man," Ngozi blurted out.

"He is a what..?," Ngozi's mother shouted hysterically.

"You mean to tell me, Ngozi Chidimma, that you are in love with *onye 'ausa?*"

"Yes, Nne, and we intend to get married next year."

"You plan to marry an *'ausa man*? Ngozi, what has come over you? Have you lost your mind?"

A sorrowful lament could be heard piercing the quiet of Isiobodo's early dusk as Ngozi's mother, with both her hands on her head, cried over the news of her daughter's intended marriage to *onye 'ausa*.

What possible misdeed did members of her family commit to deserve this misfortune from the gods? What is to become of their illustrious lineage? The mere thought of her intelligent, beautiful, well-behaved daughter, Ngozi; her *ada*, the crown-jewel of the family, becoming the wife of an *onye 'ausa*, makes her shudder with goose bumps swelling up all over her body.

How can she become in-laws with *ndi 'ausa*? Will some of her in-laws be among those blind, leprous beggars who go from city to city shamelessly begging for alms from total strangers? Or will some of her in-laws be among those filthy cattle herders, who drift from place to place like homeless vagabonds tied to their flea-ridden cattle?

And what is their family supposed to do with the memory of Wazobia's pogroms and Civil War? That memory is like a fart that has been held for too long in the gut. When it is finally let out, it produces a fetid, sickening odor. A putrid smell that will send everyone in the company in which it is released, scurrying for cover with their hands over their noses. Where are they supposed to let out the fart of that memory that distends their stomachs with its poisonous gas, if they are to remain in the midst of their erstwhile antagonists as in-laws?

Ngozi has killed her soul. She has put a knife in her heart and cut it to shreds. Of all the men she could have chosen, it had to be an *onye 'ausa*! Yet, even as she wailed about the present situation, Ngozi's mother knew only too well that she would not have been anymore sanguine had Ngozi brought home a Yoruba man. For among her people, the Yoruba are no more welcome than the Hausa.

What if Ngozi had brought home a man from one of the numerous 'minority' ethnic groups in Wazobia? That might well be more tolerable so far as such a man understands that his people's culture will remain a quaint appendage to that of the great Igbo nation. In truth, nothing short of Ngozi marrying an Igbo man would have been good enough.

Ngozi's mother remembers a number of years ago when the first set of National Youth Corpers arrived in Isiobodo to teach at St. Patrick's High School. The news traveled fast across the village and beyond, that among those Youth Corpers was an *'ausa man* who is going to teach mathematics at the high school. Nobody in Isiobodo believed the rumor. It was thought ludicrous that an *'ausa man* was sufficiently well read to teach mathematics at a high school. The only ones most people in the village knew were beggars and cattle herdsmen. A number of others were soldiers and the vast majority seemed to wallow in the amorphous realm of Koranic schools and in the role of *mallams* in the North, busily taking in each other's laundry in an area of knowledge no one else understands or cares about.

Yet, the rumor turned out to be true. That Youth Corper was real. The school term began and students enrolled in his math class with extreme reluctance and skepticism. Ever so gradually, however, the attitude of the students changed from skepticism to surprise, and finally, to grudging respect. That Youth Corper almost single-handedly overturned the prevailing stereotype of the lack of intelligence of *ndi 'ausa* in that Igbo village, before someone announced with evident relief that that Youth Corper was not Hausa after all, but Nupe.

"No wonder," went the huge sigh of relief throughout the village. Many swore that *something* about that Youth Corper always made them suspect that he was not a *real 'ausa man*. Ngozi's mother was one of those who claimed that she could tell that that Youth Corper was not really Hausa. Yet, often enough, all Wazobians from the northern part of the country are lumped together as *ndi ugwu*---people of the hill. Here, however, was the loophole everybody was perhaps, sub-consciously, hoping for in order to restore the mental equilibrium of their stereotype of the *'ausa man*.

Eventually, Ngozi's mother managed to calm herself down. She decided that as soon as her husband returns from his meeting, she will convey to him the terrible news Ngozi has just shared with her. It promises to be a long night indeed.

SIXTY THREE

Having retired from Wazobia's *olu oyibo*--Civil Service, after thirty some odd years of uninterrupted work, Mazi Chidimma occupies himself with the activities of the various religious and civic organizations in Isiobodo to which he belongs. He often makes the comment to people who ask him what he does with his time now that he is retired, that he retired from Wazobia's Civil Service not from life!

Mazi Chidimma is Secretary of the Catholic Laymen's Council (C.L.C.) of Isiobodo, which organizes fundraisings of various kinds for their parish and coordinates people from Isiobodo and other neighboring villages and towns interested in making the annual pilgrimages to Rome and the Holy City of Jerusalem.

He is also Vice President of the Isiobodo Progressive Union (I.P.U.). The I.P.U., acts like a virtual parallel government to the official Local Government Authority (L.G.A.) which Isiobodo is under. The main difference between the two, the I.P.U. and the L.G.A., lies in the fact that the I.P.U. is a dynamic and effective *government 'of the people, by the people and for the people.'*

The L.G.A., on the other hand, is a foreigner in their midst. It is the heavy hand of the government of Wazobia pretending to take up residence in their community as a friendly and dependable neighbor when, in fact, it is nothing more than an alien tax collector and a reminder to the people of where the big stick lies in wait.

The people of Isiobodo dutifully pay their taxes or what some people jokingly refer to as their *protection money* to extortionist gangsters, and pay no further attention to the shenanigans of the L.G.A. For all other matters of importance to their well-being as a community, they turn their full attention to the I.P.U. and with good reason.

Mazi Chidimma returned to his house at about 7:30 P.M. In his usual manner, he parked his Peugeot 505 in the car porch located at the front entrance of the house. Clad in traditional blood-red *efe isi agu*, *akwette* lappa, a pair of leather sandals, a red cap with an *abuba ugo*--feather of pride, stuck in it, and clutching his ornately carved walking stick, he went into the house and sat down in the livingroom.

As usual, his wife, Ifeoma, brought him a glass of freshly tapped *ngwo*--a sweat-tasting variety of palm wine from the raffia palm that is less alcoholic than *nkwu enu*--palm wine, common in these parts of Igboland on the southwestern side of the great Imo River. However, there was *something* unusual in her demeanor. Her scarf was carelessly tied and at a crazy angle on her head. Her hair appeared unruly and her *akwa ntukwasi*--her lappa, hung loosely around her waist.

Moreover, Ifeoma was moving about like an automaton. More importantly, she failed to greet Mazi Chidimma in her usual spirited and warm manner. When it comes to Mazi Chidimma's *uye*--wife, he knows instinctively when *something* is weighing heavily on her mind. She becomes sulky and withdrawn. She will never shirk her household duties, not even if his manhood calls for her attention. Yet, she will get about those duties like a robot without her heart or soul being in what she is doing.

The human spirit is the soul of our lives. Without the spirit, the *human being* becomes no more than an animal--a *human doing,* as someone once put it so well, that gets about life's chores without the ability to fit the *doing* into a larger purposive meaning.

"Mama Ngozi, is something wrong?," Mazi Chidimma asked his wife as she was about to leave the livingroom.

As soon as Ngozi's father asked her that question, she began to cry all over again. Her crying alarmed Mazi Chidimma, for he feared that someone may have died in the course of his absence that day.

"What is the matter *ori akum*--the beneficiary of my wealth?"

"Did anyone die while I was gone?"

"*Mba*--No, nna Ngozi, everybody is well," Ngozi's mother managed between her sobbing.

"If everybody is well, nne Ngozi, why then are you weeping as though someone has died?"

"Is death the only bad thing that can happen in a household?," Ngozi's mother replied.

"It may not be the only bad thing that can happen in a household, but it is certainly the only thing that I know of that we can do absolutely nothing about once it happens."

"Now, Ifeoma, wipe your tears and tell me what is eating you so."

"Mazi Chidimma, someone may as well have died in this household for a terrible calamity has befallen us."

"For Godsake woman," Ngozi's father snapped his growing impatience evident in the tone of his voice, "what is the matter?"

"I had a conversation earlier this evening with Ngozi and she informed me that she is in love with an *'ausa man* to whom she is already engaged and plans to get married to next year."

"What did you just say?," Ngozi's father asked in a tone of voice full of cold dread. Ngozi's mother repeated herself.

Suddenly, without warning, Ngozi's father sprang to his feet yelling at the top of his voice, *"Mmuo liemu*--may the spirits devour me, that whore will leave my household before she brings disgrace to it. I want that girl out of this house tonight!"

He began making his way towards Ngozi's room. Ngozi, over hearing her father began putting a few of her personal effects in her overnight case, getting ready to leave as soon as he asks her to do so. There was commotion throughout the Chidimma household. Ngozi's mother was crying, begging her husband to show Ngozi some mercy as well as hanging unto one of his arms and trying to restrain him from going to Ngozi's room. Ngozi's siblings, alerted by their father's fury, trooped into the livingroom.

Mazi Chidimma broke free of his wife's grip and swiftly made his way to Ngozi's room. He opened her bedroom door with such force that it crashed into the closet to its side as it swung open. Ngozi was standing at the far corner of her bedroom clutching her overnight case, fearing that in her father's mad rage he might do physical harm to her.

Her father stood by the side of the door and yelled in a frightfully loud voice, "get out of my house immediately, I do not want to set eyes on you ever again! You are a disgrace to your family, your village and your tribe. Get out now!!"

Ngozi slinked past her father at the door, tears streaming down her face. As soon as Ngozi got past the door, her mother, sobbing uncontrollably, pulled her into an embrace.

"Ngozi, why don't you just apologize to your father and I and we will forget that this ever happened? What has come over you Ngozi? Look at me. Look at us. Look at what you are doing to this family, to your family!"

Ngozi starred blankly at her mother, tears streaming steadily down her face. After a few minutes, Ngozi's mother let go of her and sorrowfully said, "It is pointless, she is not the same person we used to know."

SIXTY FOUR

Ngozi made her way to her aunt's house situated about a mile away from her father's house. Her father's eldest sister, Chinyere Chidimma, whom everybody, especially the young tendrils in the family like Ngozi, call *Ada Ukwu*--big first daughter, is undoubtedly the grand matriarch of the Chidimma family.

Ada Ukwu's matriarchy is unmistakable in the manner in which she insists on the meticulous observance of traditional customs, protocols and etiquette in conducting all aspects of their family affairs. Though Ngozi's father, in the official scheme of things in the Igbo patriarchal traditional system, is the head of the family being *di okpala*--the first male child, Ada Ukwu is, in a manner of speaking, the queen mother of the family.

Over the years, especially following the death of their parents, Ada Ukwu perfected the art of persuasion. The art, one of her younger siblings once jokingly commented, of diplomatic arm-twisting. Her strategy is as simple as it is effective. The essence of the strategy lies in holding out the promise of relief from some personal debt you owe her--and there are many debts owed Ada Ukwu, even as she squeezes concessions out of you over a totally different matter. As soon as she achieves her objective, she modifies whatever offer she may have made to you regarding the debt you owe her in the light of her strengthened hand.

Some people think of her as ruthless, others as a political genius. As for herself, she states matter-of-factly that life is a wrestling match in which the contestants grapple for a good grip--the grip that will ensure that their challenger's back makes contact with the ground. No wrestler in the thick of a match for their life, pauses to contemplate the nicety of which body part they are taking into their grip. They leave that fine point to the referee--if there is one, and perhaps, the arm-chair wrestlers that are the spectating audience.

"*Kpoi, kpoi, kpoi,*" echoed Ngozi's voice through Ada Ukwu's house.

"Onye--who is it?," Ada Ukwu demanded.

"Ada Ukwu, greetings to you, it is Ngozi Chidimma."

"Ah, my darling niece, hold on I will be at the door in a minute."

Ada Ukwu opened the front door and embraced Ngozi.

"What brings you here this late at night? Do you realize that it is almost 9 P.M.?

"What do you have in your hand Ngozi? It is as though you are going away on a short trip," Ada Ukwu queried Ngozi pointing to her overnight case.

"Ada Ukwu, my father kicked me out of his house," Ngozi said pointedly as she began to sob, "and I fear that the worst is yet to come. I fear that he might disown me as well."

"Come into the house Ngozi," Ada Ukwu said, gently closing the front door behind her.

With her arm draped over Ngozi's shoulder, Ada Ukwu stirred Ngozi to a couch in the livingroom and they both sat down.

"Ngozi what did you do to make your father kick you out of his house? You of all people. The apple of his eye. Are you pregnant?"

"No, Ada Ukwu."

"Did you take something that does not belong to you?"

"No, Ada Ukwu, never."

"Were you insubordinate to your father or your mother?"

"Not really," Ngozi replied."

"Not really? What do you mean by not really," Ada Ukwu probed.

"I suppose it depends on the way you look at it."

"How do you mean it depends on the way you look at it, a spade by any other name is a spade."

"Well, I announced to them the man of my choice as a husband and they did not approve of it."

"Ngozi, your parents are not mad people who do things for no reason or at least for reasons that no reasonable person can comprehend. What were their reason or reasons for disapproving of your choice of a husband?"

Ngozi wiped away tears from her eyes with the handkerchief Ada Ukwu handed her and cleared her throat.

"He is a Hausa man."

Ada Ukwu froze.

"He is a...what? My child what madness has possessed you? Now that you have told me what the problem is, I am no longer sure that I blame your father for what he has done. Ngozi, do you have any idea how serious a matter this is?"

"Yes, Ada Ukwu, I realize that it is a very serious matter, but I am at the cross-roads of my heart and my people. Can it really be that I must choose between the two? Why must I be called upon to choose between the two?"

"Ngozi," Ada Ukwu began in a slow gentle voice, "it is your personal interest and the integrity of the family name that your parents seek to protect. They do not want to see you suffer and they do not want to see the good name of the family carefully built up over so long a time, destroyed in one fell swoop. Can you understand that?"

"Yes, Ada Ukwu, I can understand where they are coming from. However, surprisingly no one has asked me yet anything about the man in question, not even his name! Once they hear that he is a Hausa man, their minds lock up like the jaws of a crocodile clasped tightly around its prey. Everything else becomes irrelevant."

"Can you really blame them for that? Consider the fact that no one marry's anyone by themselves. You and your family become immersed in your in-laws for better or for worse. For our people have a saying that the problem with *ike* efi--the butt of a cow, is not merely that it is ugly or that it belongs to the cow, but rather the flies that come with it."

Ada Ukwu, fearing that Ngozi may be making a rash judgment swept up by youthful infatuation, decided to tell Ngozi an old Igbo fable used to clear such cobwebs from the heads of young maidens.

"Ngozi, let me share with you an instructive folktale of our people. Once upon a time, it is told, there lived a young woman. She was so beautiful that everybody including her own parents called her *Apu na awu*--one too precious to be let out in the sun."

"Suitors came from far and near seeking *Apu na awu's* hand in marriage. One after the other, she rejected them for one reason or another. She complained that they were too short, too tall, too fat or too thin. No one among her people--either from her village or from neighboring villages--was good enough."

"Finally, one day, there came along a handsome gentleman from a totally different group of people from her own. *Apu na awu* fell desperately in love with that gentleman. So enamored

222

did she become with that gentleman that *Apu na awu* threw all caution to the wind."

"In her eagerness to get married to that gentleman, she refused to follow the time-honored betrothal customs of her people--not even the fact-finding usually undertaken between the *knocking on the door* and the *coming into the house.*"

"Her parents cautioned her that she knew little or nothing about the gentleman, that *ifunaya*--love is important but no substitute for *ako na uche*--common sense. For a person who loves the warmth of the fireplace in the cold night of harmattan, does not then throw themselves into its naked flames."

"*Apu na awu* dismissed her parents as old fashioned and prudish. Eventually, *Apu na awu's* enthusiasm and persistence wore her parents down and they reluctantly gave their blessings to a hurriedly arranged marriage ceremony."

"After the marriage ceremony, *Apu na awu* and her husband set out for their new home. On their way, her husband stopped at someone's house and excused himself for short while. When he returned, he had no cloths or shoes on. 'What happened to your cloths and shoes?,' *Apu na awu* asked her husband."

"Oh, I am sorry," her husband replied, "but I borrowed those cloths and shoes for the marriage ceremony and had to return them."

"They continued on their journey, but now *Apu na awu's* curiosity was awakened. A short while later, they came upon another of his friend's house. They stopped and once again her husband excused himself for awhile. This time when he returned, or rather, rolled back on the trunk of his body, for he had no hands or legs; he had borrowed those too and had to return them."

"As it turned out, the man owned nothing, not even himself--his own body. Needless to say, *Apu na awu* ran all the way back to her parent's home not turning back for even a moment."

"The morale of the story, Ngozi, is that a young woman must be careful who she gets mixed up with, especially when it comes to something as serious as marriage, for as they say, all that glitters is not gold."

"However, my darling Ngozi, it is perhaps appropriate for me to let you tell your own story, for nothing relieves a heavy heart quite like a willing ear. *Who* exactly is this man and how did you get mixed up with him?"

For the first time since the saga of her revelation to her family began, someone asked her to tell them *who* Mohammed is rather than merely *what* he is, for there are great differences between the two. There is a reason no one ever asks of animals *who is that cat?, who is that dog? or who is that horse?* For the *who* refers to *human beings* whose totality of essence in being is at once immanent and transcendent of matter, time and space.

Ngozi felt as though she were a courier carrying important news with the potential of changing the entire course of a battle--perhaps even bringing it to complete cessation, but nobody wants to hear it! Ada Ukwu's invitation to Ngozi to tell her about Mohammed was like the opening of the floodgates of a dam. Ngozi spoke non-stop for a solid hour.

She talked of how she met Mohammed through Chike at the University of Ibadan, of how intelligent and open minded he is and of how he is a champion of the cause of justice. Ada Ukwu let her speak without interruption, for she was listening with the keen ears of a grand matriarch with wide-ranging experience.

As Ada Ukwu often puts it herself, she wants to do more than just hear a person's story, she wants to *feel it.* To feel the person's story in the pit of her stomach. Then, like food that one has just eaten, give it time to digest and then, let her *spirit* speak to the matter.

Moreover, Ada Ukwu, has an uncanny instinct for assessing the mettle of people--for assessing their *philosophical* depth, that is as keen as a dog's sense of smell.

Upon meeting someone, once they open their mouth to opine over an issue or to respond to a question that requires no less than a full sentence to answer, Ada Ukwu is at once able to place the individual on his or her appropriate philosophical weight class.

Employing the weight classification in boxing as metaphor, Ada Ukwu automatically places the person in their proper weight class: *feather, bantam, light, middle* or *heavy* weight divisions. In her experience, most people tend to fall between bantam and middle weights. Every once in a while, however, one runs into those who fall into the polar extremes of feather or heavy weights. Even more rarely, one runs into those at the outer extremities of those polar opposites--the true *freaks* of nature. In such instances, normal human scale, standard human proportions become shattered and completely new yardsticks must be sought.

"Well, Ngozi," Ada Ukwu said when Ngozi finished telling her about Mohammed, "our first task is to mend fences between you and your parents. No matter what happens, that which binds you to them must never be broken."

"Next to Chukwu, your father and mother are the source of your life. You and the children you will bear and their children and their children's children and so on and so forth, are your parent's claim to immortality. A tree not properly anchored to its roots and nourished from the soil in which it has roots, sooner or later dies. And a tree that lacks leafy branches that indicate its vitality, is soon marked for the felling."

"For now, however, you need to get some sleep. We shall continue our discussions tomorrow. I shall give this matter a great deal of thought tonight. Go now my precious one, *kachifo*--good night."

Ngozi bid Ada Ukwu good night too and retired into one of the spare bedrooms. She fell into a deep sleep almost immediately.

SIXTY FIVE

Mazi Chidimma paced back and forth in the livingroom in a confused rage like a caged panther. Over and over again he asked himself the same questions to no avail: how could this happen? Why did this happen? Where did Ngozi's mother and himself go wrong in raising Ngozi? How could she possibly do this?

After awhile, he could not take it any longer. He picked up his walking stick, fished out his flashlight from the glove compartment of the Peugeot, and headed for *Ama Isiobodo*-- the village square, on foot.

Although it was now quite dark Mazi Chidimma knew that at Ama Isiobodo, under the huge Iroko tree at the center of the village square, which everybody calls *Osisi Obodo*--the town's tree, there will still be a number of men, some of whom will be his blood relatives. There, the men will be drinking palm wine in the shadowy glow of *mpanakas*-- traditional lamps, and trading all manner of stories until the wee hours of the morning.

In their company, he can unburden himself and dull his senses with cupfuls of frothing *nkwu enu*--the sour-tasting and more alcoholic variety of palm wine.

On the unlit narrow dust-road to Ama Isiobodo, the pitch blackness of the night is so complete that one can *feel it* pressing in on you, literally compressing your mental sense of space. Enveloped in that pitch blackness, everything becomes part of a dense blackhole. Every now and again, Mazi Chidimma switches on his powerful flashlight and its light beam slices a path through the black void, illuminating a two feet circumference on the dust-road or wherever else it is pointed, but leaving intact the darkness outside that light patch of luminous vision.

Enveloped in that pitch blackness on the narrow dust-road to Ama Isiobodo, every once in awhile one sees in the distance what appears to be a string of lights suspended in mid-air. The naked flames dance in mid-air, their rhythmic movements choreographed by the gentle breeze that threatens but does not extinguish them.

Those dancing flames are *mpanakas* held up by people on their way back from Afia Uwa or the Imo River. When they get close enough, their faces become visible in the faint glow of their lamps. Invariably, greetings are politely exchanged between the passersby and before long, the solid void of blackness and its accompanying quiet return.

SIXTY SIX

Mazi Chidimma reached Ama Isiobodo, walked over to osisi obodo and took a seat among his fellows even as they exchanged greetings and showered him with praise names. He had hardly sat down when he was offered some *okpa*--steamed bean cake made from a rare specie of beans of the same name and a frothing *mpu efi*--cow horn, of palm wine.

Among the men sitting under osisi obodo was Mazi Nnayelugo, a comedian with a well-deserved reputation for a sharp wit. There was also Mazi Tobeolisa, whom everybody humorously calls *nwa fada*--the priest's child, because of his zealous commitment to the Catholic faith and its local parish mission in Isiobodo. There was also Mazi Akwa Akwulu, the village sop, whose love and tolerance for alcohol is so legendary that it earned him the sobriquet *akpa ngwu*--a kind of insect of the bee family that perpetually hovers around and feasts on palm wine.

Mazi Nnayelugo was in the middle of one of his side-splitters while the men were merrily quaffing their palm wine.

"When the white missionaries first came to Igboland, the story goes that one Sunday in the course of a homily, the priest said that on the Last Day Jesus Christ will come again to judge the living and the dead."

"At the end of the church service a precocious old woman, whom everybody in Isiobodo calls Old Bones, went up to the white priest and said, "'my son, during the homily you said that Jesus will come again.""

"Yes, grandma, that was what I said."

"Now, why would he want to come again has he forgotten what they did to him the first time he came?," Old Bones questioned the white priest.

The gathered men roared with laughter at Mazi Nnayelugo's anecdote.

"Oh," Mazi Nnayelugo said, "but there is more."

"More?," joyfully asked Mazi Akwa Akwulu.

"Yes, more" replied Mazi Nnayelugo.

"The white priest answered Old Bones by saying, "but grandma, no word of God will come to pass unfulfilled. It has been written in the scriptures that our Lord Jesus Christ will come again on the Last Day in all his glory, to judge the living and the dead!"

"Then Old Bones asked the priest," "but my son, all jokes aside, if Jesus Christ were your own blood brother, from the same womb as yourself, would you advice him to come again in the light of what happened before?"

The gathered men cracked up with laughter.

"As if that were not enough," Mazi Nnayelugo continued, "during the following Sunday school class the white missionary was holding, a statement he made as part of the 'catechism' he was teaching the Christian converts of Isiobodo, caught Old Bone's attention."

"In fact, as soon as the white missionary saw Old Bones shuffle into the hall-like room he uses for Sunday school, he knew that he was in for more disconcerting questions that Sunday."

"Old Bones surprisingly contained herself for most of the class until one comment made by the white missionary stuck in her craw. The white missionary said that Christians are enjoined to 'love thy neighbor as thy self.'"

"Old Bones raised her walking stick up in the air to call the priest's attention. Reluctantly, the white missionary acknowledged Old Bones, asking her what the matter is."

"My son," Old Bones began in her usual dispassionate and logical manner, "does that entreaty that a Christian love their neighbor as themselves apply across the board or can it be applied selectively?"

"No, grandma, it applies across the board. There should be no discrimination in our application of that fundamental Christian principle," the white missionary replied."

"If that is the case," Old Bones continued, "who in their right mind would want that *anu ofia*--wild animal of the forest, *odi ndu onwu ka mma*--the living person for whom death is better, who roams *Ama Isiobodo* totally naked with his manhood dangling about for all to see, to love them like himself?"

"The entire Sunday school class erupted in laughter and the white missionary secretly prayed in his heart for God to somehow remove the thorn in his flesh that is Old Bones."

The men gathered under osisi obodo broke into paroxysms of laughter. The only one among them who was not amused was Tobeolisa. He thought the jokes irreverent, almost blasphemous. The rest of his fellows dismissed his sensitivity as a case of a man who violently throws himself to the ground in grief at the funeral of a total stranger whose own family members have long since accepted their loss!

Mazi Tobeolisa in his humorless Christian devotion, accused his fellows of enjoying Mazi Nnayelugo's irreverent jokes because they lack *grace*; the *grace* of God in their souls. Mazi Nnayelugo far from being apologetic responded with more sardonic wit.

"If you and your fellow Christian faithfuls have so much *grace*, what accounts for your flat feet during the *ite egwu emume ji ofu*--the dance of the New Yam Festival?"

The other men roared with laughter at Mazi Nnayelugo's witty twist of Mazi Tobeolisa's point, infuriating him even more.

It was Mazi Akwa Akwulu of all people, the reputed *akpa ngwu*, who took notice of Mazi Chidimma's melancholy and changed the topic of discussion. His state of pickled alcoholism had apparently not robbed him of a keen sense of perception.

"Mazi Chidimma," Mazi Akwa Akulu began as he wiped away palm wine froth from his lips with the back of his hand, "although we appreciate your company, I must say that it is very unlike you to lounge under osisi obodo this late at night."

"We know that while the lion has eyes that can see at night, it prefers to hunt in daylight. If one were to find the lion hunting at night and sleeping through the day, those familiar with the ways of the big cat would sense that something has gone awry."

"What brings you to our midst tonight, Mazi Chidimma? Perhaps your *ori aku* refuses to loosen her *lappa* at your behest? Or, perhaps, you had a moonlight rendezvous and need us as alibi?"

"Save your creative imagination for more useful ends, Mazi Akwa Akwulu. While you are right that something weighs heavily on my mind, it has nothing to do with libidinous pursuits. Besides, I am the son of my father and if I choose to hawk my manhood around town, I will not do so like a thief lurking around in the shadows. I will pick my choice of fruit from among the offerings and relish it in full view of all and sundry."

The gathered men peppered Mazi Chidimma with praise names, locking arms with clenched fists in a show of solidarity.

"Well, what is it that is weighing so heavily on you, Mazi Chidimma, perhaps we can lend a helping hand and lessen the burden of the load," Mazi Obiagu offered.

"None of you here can begin to guess at the nature of my burden."

"What's the point guessing at all when you are right here in the flesh and clearly in need of support," Mazi Tobeolisa said.

"My daughter, Ngozi, the *ada* of the family, announced to her mother and I earlier on this evening that she intends to marry *onye 'ausa!*," Mazi Chidimma stated with a heavy sigh.

A great babble of *Chinekes, Tufiakwas,* Godforbids, invocation of Igbo gods and goddesses, as well as a few unprintable epiteths, broke out among the gathered men. When the babble simmered down and it seemed the gathered men had absorbed the shock of the initial blast of the explosive news, they began to discuss the matter in a more orderly but no less incendiary manner.

"This is the worst news I have heard this year since the untimely death of the twenty-year old *di okpala*--first son, of Mazi Ikejiuwa. Such a promising young man in the prime of his youth. Out of nowhere, a reckless driver of a car tearing down the terrible exit road that leads from the highway to the Four Villages Junction, lost control of his vehicle and drove straight into Mazi Ikejiuwa's son, who was waiting on the side of the road for a taxi to take him from the Junction to the highway."

"The young man died instantly and so did all the passengers in the car except the errant driver. The people around who witnessed the whole incident were so angry with the driver for causing such carnage due to his irresponsible driving, that they dragged him out of the wreckage and clubbed him to death."

"Now, I am being presented with yet another kind of fatality with this news of our illustrious daughter, Ngozi and an *'ausa man.*"

Mazi Nnayelugo, who considers no subject too sacred to be poked fun at, tried unsuccessfully to lighten the mood.

"Is it true what I hear that *'ausa men* are uncircumcised? That the heads of their manhood are hidden from sunshine and fresh air by useless pieces of foreskin?"

"Enough, Mazi Nnayelugo, Mazi Obiagu quickly cut in, "this is not a joking matter."

Seizing the moment, Mazi Tobeolisa said triumphantly,"Oh, so now you realize that there are somethings better not subjected to trivial humor. Why are you not all holding your sides in laughter? I was under the impression that among you all is fair game for ridicule and laughter."

"All right, Mazi Tobeolisa, count this as one day you caught us red-handed in the act of eating our own words. Now, clap for yourself and let us get on with more important matters," Mazi Akwa Akwulu responded as he chugged yet another *mpi efi* of palm wine.

"As far as Wazobia's Civil War is concerned, I have always said," Mazi Obiagu solemnized, "that we fought for patrimony and honor, and were right to have done so. For which self-respecting people would allow their own kith and kin to be hounded out and slaughtered like *anu ofia*--wild animals of the forest, and do nothing about it? As our people say, it is only a tree who is told that it will be cut down and remains standing in the same place."

"That war, however, reversed our fortunes greatly in this land that our people helped incomparably to free from Anglian rule. Was it not after all, one of our illustrious sons who was the most eloquent spokesman against Anglian colonialism? Was it not the same illustrious son of ours, who has rightly become the illustrious son of all of Wazobia, that used his superb penmanship to effectively challenge the Anglian colonialists and to awaken the slumbering giant that is Africa? So good was he that those who say that the pen is mightier than the sword began to say that perhaps the pen is another kind of sword!"

"Then, which *'ausa man* dared think of himself the intellectual or social equal of the Igbo man? All they had to buoy themselves was the chauvinism of their acquired Muslim religion towards so called *kafirs*--non-believers."

"As a result of the War, however, the proverbial older man has had to wait for the younger man to grow up--to catch up with him in physical size and manly thirst for maidens. Now, it is hard to tell them apart. In fact, sometimes people mistake the younger man for the elder brother of the older man. The consequence is that the younger man no longer knows nor respects the boundaries between himself and the older man."

"You are absolutely correct, Mazi Obiagu," said Mazi Ngala, speaking for the first time that night, "but even more troubling is this. Had it not been for that War, which well-bred Igbo woman would have agreed to intimacy with *nwoke onye 'ausa*--a Hausa man, let alone consider marrying one!?"

"Yet, now, a girl as well brought up and well-educated as our daughter Ngozi, feels no shame--actually feels proud announcing to her parents that she is in love with and plans to marry one of them. What else will we encounter in our sojourn on this earth?"

"By the way, Mazi Chidimma, who exactly is the *'ausa man* in question?," Mazi Akwa Akwulu asked.

It was only then that it occurred to Ngozi's father that he knows absolutely nothing about the man in question, not even his name! He had been too blinded by rage and his own prejudice to have bothered to find out anything more about him.

Mazi Chidimma would not outwardly show his sudden realization of his own blinding prejudice. He wears his prejudice like a mask--a grotesque looking woodwork that covers the human face behind it from recognition either by itself or by others.

"I don't know the man's name nor do I care to know. It is quite enough for me that he is an 'ausa man. If a man smells excrement nearby does he need to know whose waste it is in order to know that he does not want to step in it?"

"I know exactly what you mean, Mazi Chidimma. After all, what sort of person accustomed to dinning in style on an exquisitely laid table, voluntarily decides to go and eat on the bare floor?"

"We have not spent all these years working so hard, building this country of ours, educating our children at home and abroad, only to end up tying the knot with never-do-wells! God forbid!," Mazi Obiagu, echoed.

"How did things get to this point in the first place anyway?," Mazi Akwa Akwulu asked.

"I was under the impression that Ngozi is attending the University of Ibadan in Western Wazobia--which is in Yorubaland. How did an 'ausa man get into the picture at all? If anything, one would have expected that she might have got mixed up with a Yoruba man; but an 'ausa man at the University of Ibadan, that just does not make any sense."

"What do you mean it just doesn't make any sense?," Mazi Tobeolisa queried.

"Is there a law in this country that 'ausa men -- fellow citizens of Wazobia, can not attend university wherever they choose to in this country?" Are there no Igbos and Yorubas in universities in the North?"

"Of course there is no law barring citizens of Wazobia from attending any school they wish to in the country. There is also no law in this country enacted to make certain that children suckle only their own mother's breasts," Mazi Chikelu interjected.

"Children naturally prefer to suckle the breasts of their own mothers even if they are in a room full of other women."

"Now, if a child in such a room were to crawl or walk over to a woman other than their natural mother, clamber unto her laps and settle into suckling that woman's breasts, neither the child nor the woman would have broken any laws, nor will they be prosecuted. Yet, we would all be quite intrigued by such a phenomenon."

"While I have a good sense of what you are getting at," Mazi Tobeolisa proffered, "I think your analogy is a bit too fanciful. It is not as though institutions of higher learning in this country or anywhere else for that matter, are to the students that attend them as nursing mothers are to their birth children."

"You sound as though 'ausas have never attended universities outside northern Wazobia before. Surely, out of their numbers common sense dictates that at least some of them would have chosen to attend universities outside the North."

Ngozi's father brought up another point.

"Are we not jumping to the hasty conclusion that the 'ausa man in question is at the University of Ibadan or even at a

234

university at all? Are we not assuming that he is even educated?"

"What if he is a cattle herder? Suppose he is a much older man, perhaps even one of those lascivious, wealthy, gworo-chewing, semi-illiterate Alhajis, seeking to make Ngozi his fourth wife? Have you thought of that possibility?"

"Well, what of the converse possibility? What if the 'ausa man in question is well-bred and well educated? Will that make any difference in your stance against Ngozi marrying the man," Mazi Tobeolisa asked.

"That is a very hypothetical question. For one thing, the probability that he is well-bred and well educated is very low indeed. For another, one does not begin to teach a right-handed man how to use his left hand in his old age. I am used to seeing 'ausas in a certain light and thinking of them in a particular vein. It will be hard for me, at this late stage of my life, to change my mind."

"I hope you realize Mazi Chidimma, that that is not a very Christian attitude," Mazi Tobeolisa pursued.

"As a Christian, you are called upon to extend charity and fairness to everyone without exception. That was how Jesus Christ lived his life and expects us to live ours."

"Well," Mazi Nnayelugo cut in, "see where that kind of attitude got Jesus Christ among his own people! Perhaps he should have tempered his charity and fairness with a healthy dose of *ako na uche*--common sense."

"Moreover," Mazi Nnayelugo went on, "'ausas are not Christians and as such, those rules do not apply to them; and even if they do, the saying goes that charity begins at home."

"That is where you are wrong, Mazi Nnayelugo," Mazi Tobeolisa replied, "that Christian injunction of charity and fairness applies to everybody whether or not they are Christians; and if I might add, the problem with the kind of charity you advocate is not so much its beginning at home but its ending there as well!"

"Let me be sure that I understand properly what Mazi Tobeolisa is getting at. Is he suggesting that in the name of Christianity Mazi Chidimma should hand over one of the brightest plumes from our colorful crown of feathers to an 'ausa man?"

"Personally," Mazi Ngala interjected, "I think it best to leave Jesus Christ out of this matter. After all, from the stories of him the white missionary tells in his Sunday school classes, Jesus Christ never took a wife in the course of his own life even though by the time he was killed he was a grown man of thirty three years of age. What can he possibly know about the business of marriage and the raising of children?"

"There again, Mazi Ngala, you are as wrong on that point as Mazi Nnayelugo is on the point of where charity begins and ends. Jesus Christ is the son of God made man, the *alpha* and the *omega*--the beginning and the end, there is nothing he does not know and can not do if he chooses to do so."

Mazi Chikelu shifted the discussion in another direction.

"Something else that we should consider is the possibility that that 'ausa man might be the first man our daughter Ngozi, has known. We all know that nothing makes a virgin quite as giddy as the intoxicating effects of first love. Perhaps, that is partly what we are up against here?"

"Assuming that what you suggest is right," Ngozi's father pursued, "what can be done to break the spell cast by such a situation?"

"Mazi Chidimma, for both men and women, the best cure for the loss of one good thing is the swift replacement of it with another good thing. For as our people say, good things never run out in this world," Mazi Nnayelugo volunteered.

"If you forbid the relationship between Ngozi and that 'ausa man and quickly present Ngozi with a good Igbo man to fill the void, Ngozi, like any other normal person, will become attached to the new good thing. For as our people say, when two kegs of good palm wine meet each other, they try to out-foam one another."

"There is a philosophical and moral conundrum here that we are all trying to side step," Mazi Tobeolisa stated, still bent on pursuing a Christian hard line.

"Why is a good 'ausa man, assuming we can establish him to be one, not good enough for a good Igbo woman? Or put another way, why is a good Igbo man better for Ngozi than a good 'ausa man?"

"With all due respect Mazi Tobeolisa, that is a silly question to ask," Mazi Obiagu flatly stated.

"One is an Igbo man and the other an 'ausa man. Which child does not say that his mother's soup tastes better than any other? Moreover as the saying goes, the devil you know is better than the one you don't."

"Yet, it does not explain away the philosophical and moral tension that lies at the heart of our thinking on that matter," Mazi Tobeolisa persisted.

"If both men are by their very nature *good* what difference does their ethnicity make? Or is the problem the fact that what makes them *good* or *bad* in our eyes is the ethnic group to which they belong and not their *goodness* or *badness* in and of themselves? Is a *bad* Igbo man, for instance, preferable to a *good* 'ausa man? Would any man present here prefer their daughter to marry an Igbo scoundrel rather than an 'ausa saint?"

"Moreover," Mazi Tobeolisa continued, "has it not been said often enough that we are a very generous people. That our heart is bigger than our hurt; our hope stronger than our hate?"

An awkward silence greeted Mazi Tobeolisa's last rhetorical questions, for he was tugging vigorously at their masks, threatening to rip them away from the faces of the gathered men.

Mazi Chidimma, like the other men gathered under the majestic osisi obodo, desperately held onto his mask--his public facade of implacable obstinacy. Yet, how was he to hide from his own head and heart? Mazi Tobeolisa had sown a seed of thought in the fertile soil of his mind.

As the gathered men under osisi obodo haggled jocularly over who should get the yeasty dregs of palm wine at the bottom of the keg, shafts of twilight filtered through the lifting black curtain of night, signaling the coming of early dawn.

The men gathered their personal effects--hats, leather hunting bags, walking sticks, flashlights, *mpi efis* and so on, greeted each other and began making their way to their respective hamlets and homes.

On the pathways and on the main narrow dust-road that leads to and from Afia Uwa, Ama Isiobodo and the Imo River, early birds with their large baskets of market wares or earthenware pots balanced expertly on their heads, were already on their way to Afia Uwa and the Imo River. The inevitable *mpanakas* dance to the gentle twilight breeze of Isiobodo's early dawn.

SIXTY SEVEN

Ada Ukwu woke up early and prepared a light breakfast of fried *ogede*--plantains and boiled *akwa ogazi*--patridge eggs, for herself and Ngozi. She had not slept much as she turned the matter of Mohammed over and over in her mind.

By dawn, she had reached the decision to support Ngozi and help her win her parents over. Ngozi is a good girl. A sensible, careful young woman. She is not the type to be carried away merely by the good looks of a man or his sweet tongue. Ada Ukwu's instincts were to give Ngozi the benefit of the doubt, to pin her hopes on Ngozi's record of common sense and intelligence.

In her usual manner, Ada Ukwu began to map out a war plan for how she will deal with the Ngozi's parents.

After they had eaten breakfast, Ada Ukwu asked Ngozi to go to Afia Uwa and tell her mother that she would like to see her when the market closes at sunset. In the pecking order of the Chidimma family, when Ada Ukwu summons any of her sisters in-law it is expected and wise of the one to heed the summons *post haste*.

"When you see your mother at Afia Uwa, greet her as cordially and as respectfully as you normally do. Ask after her health and the rest of the family. Make no mention of the matter in dispute."

"Yes, Ada Ukwu."

"When your mother gets here at sunset, make yourself scarce. Go and visit some of your relatives or stroll down to Ama Isiobodo. Preoccupy yourself with something that will keep you away from here until I am done talking with her. Do you understand me, Ngozi?"

"Yes, I do, Ada Ukwu, but what should I do after that?"

"Come back here, collect your belongings and return to your parent's house."

"Return to my parent's house!?," Ngozi virtually screamed, "isn't that a bit too soon, Ada Ukwu?"

"Collect yourself my dear child, remember it is I, Ada Ukwu of the Chidimma clan that you are dealing with. The great queen mother whose fart alone can put out cooking fires in any woman's kitchen. The great queen mother who has been known to turn roaring lions into harmless pussy cats. Do exactly as I tell you and everything will be fine."

Ngozi thanked Ada Ukwu, took a bath and set out for Afia Uwa.

SIXTY EIGHT

Ngozi reached Afia Uwa a few hours before sunset. Although some people were beginning to close their stores, others who do not own stores were gathering up their wares on their tables, mats and cotton cloths spread out on the sand floor; still others stay open until the gathering dusk begins to make it impossible to see without the aid of flashlights and *mpanakas*. Those ones are the congenital traders. Those with the itch to sell in their blood. They hold out to the last minute for the possibility of an eleventh-hour sale. Ngozi's mother is one of those natural-born traders. Her store remains open until virtually every other store in Afia Uwa closes its doors to business.

Ngozi's mother was sitting on a high stool in front of the service desk of her store when Ngozi stepped into the store. She was surprised to see Ngozi, though glad to find her looking well rested and properly groomed.

"Mama, *Kedu kidi?*--how are you?," Ngozi gently asked her mother with a genial smile on her face.

"Ngozi, *adamma* Chidimma--beautiful first daughter of Chidimma, I am well. How are you?," her mother replied, as she got off the high stool and gave her daughter a hug.

"I am well, mama," Ngozi replied, "how is Papa and my siblings?"

"Oh, Ngozi, it has only been one night since you have been gone from the house. Everybody is well. Where are you staying, anyway?"

"I am staying at Ada Ukwu's place. As a matter of fact, she is the one who sent me here. She asked me to tell you that she wants to see you at her place after Afia Uwa closes at sunset today."

"I actually had a number of errands to run right after Afia Uwa closes this evening. However, when Ada Ukwu calls everyone listens. Some claim that when she calls, even the birds pay attention. Go and tell her that I will be at her place as soon as Afia Uwa closes."

Ngozi hugged her mother once more and left the market.

SIXTY NINE

By the time Ngozi's mother reached Ada Ukwu's house from Afia Uwa, she had to light an *mpanaka*. Nightfall had set in and Egbe's narrow dust-road was becoming deserted. During the hour long trek from Afia Uwa to Ada Ukwu's house, Ngozi's mother wondered what point of view Ada Ukwu will take on Ngozi's matter, since she was certain that is the reason she sent for her.

Ada Ukwu is as unpredictable as she is tough. Sometimes, her moves are entirely dictated by pragmatism and at other times, by sublime idealism. This is a hard one to call, for Ada Ukwu is a staunch traditionalist and not one easily swayed by emotional frippery. She reached Ada Ukwu's front door and announced herself. The door was soon answered by the matriarch herself. Greetings and bear hugs followed, amenities of *fanta* and *kpof-kpof* were served Ngozi's mother, before they settled down to the reason Ada Ukwu sent for her.

"Ifeoma Chidimma, where are you from?, Ada Ukwu asked matter-of-factly.

"That is a strange question coming from you, Ada Ukwu. Of course you know where I am from."

"I know where you are from, Ifeoma, but I want to hear it from your own mouth."

"Well, Ada Ukwu, if you insist, I am from Isiukwuano."

"Ah, that's what I thought. Do you recall how your husband's brothers and uncles felt about his marrying you?"

"Yes, I do. They were opposed to it."

"That's exactly correct. They were very much opposed to it. Does your memory serve you well as to the reason they were so against his marrying you? Were you not from a good family? Were you not a well-bred and beautiful Igbo woman? Had you not gone as far as the Teachers Training College in your formal education? Why then were they so opposed to their brother marrying you?"

"They opposed it, as you well know Ada Ukwu, because I am from a different village."

"Exactly, Ifeoma, they were opposed to it because you happen to come from a different village. A neighboring village with whom Isiobodo has a long-running, ridiculous competition. Is that not so, Ifeoma?"

"Yes, Ada Ukwu, it is so."

"Does your memory serve you well as to who came to your spirited defense--the person who came to your rescue?; the person who insisted, against all odds, that the horse of reason be put before the cart of prejudice? For as our people say, a person who forgets when and where they got caught in a rainstorm, is unlikely to remember who sheltered them from the same rainstorm."

"My memory serves me well, Ada Ukwu, it was you."

"Does your memory also serve you well with respect to what happened when your first two children turned out to be girls?"

"Ah, yes, Ada Ukwu, I remember that harrowing period like it were yesterday. My brothers in-law, my husband's uncles and other relatives; worst of all, even many of the women of Isiobodo, who should have known better, joined in the rumor mongering and cruel snickering."

"Good, Ifeoma, I am glad that you have such a vivid recollection of what happened then. In that case, I trust that you remember who came to your aid as well. The one who stood up to the family and the women of Isiobodo and told them to go and clean their mouths of shit like *Shinay*--the proverbial village dog!"

"I remember that it was you, Ada Ukwu, and my gratitude knows no bounds. In fact, I remember that at one *Otu Omu* meeting, when I raised my voice in objection to a point made by one women, she sarcastically responded to me by saying that those who have not produced warriors have no business fanning the ambers of war."

"You stood up with fire in your eyes and said in response to that woman, that anyone who praises the fruits of a young tree more than the young tree itself is feebleminded. For they ought to know that like a deep-water well, there is much more where those fruits came from."

"In that case, Ifeoma, since your memory serves you as well as it apparently does, how can you be so devoid of compassion and understanding for your own daughter's predicament? Need I tell you, Ifeoma, that a mother's bosom is a child's last refuge? Our people say that whatever kind of food one prefers, water is universally needed to cook all types

242

of food. A mother is to a child as water is to food. It is the reason our people give their female children the name, *Nneka-*-mother is greater."

"Similarly, it is the same reason our people say that if a person finds their mother being held on the ground, they don't wait to find out why. They first try to free her before inquiring after what precipitated the situation. It is expected that a mother will do likewise for her child."

"With all due respect, Ada Ukwu, as our people say, excessive indulgence is always sweeter when the footing of the bill comes from someone else's pocket. It is easy for you to advocate my understanding and compassion over this terrible situation, because, after all, it is my own daughter involved and not yours."

Ada Ukwu took a deep breath and hissed out her response slowly like a venomous snake.

"Ifeoma Chidimma, I trust that you have not lost your mind or that you are not merely trifling with me. Your children are my children. Ngozi is my daughter too. All my siblings children are mine too. I am scandalized that you would even make this kind of statement. I sincerely hope that you are not loosing your mind!"

"Chineke," Ada Ukwu exclaimed, making a popping sound with her thumb and middle finger as she spoke, "no wonder our people say that sometimes it is good for a strong wind to come along and lift the feathers that cover the butt of a chicken so that we can all see how it really looks!"

In a tone of manifest contrition, Ngozi's mother said to Ada Ukwu, "I apologize for what I just said, Ada Ukwu, I did not mean to offend you. I know that my children are yours too and that you will do for them as you would do for your own natural children. I was merely trying to convey to you the depth of our chagrin over the situation her father and I find ourselves in."

"Be that as it may, Ifeoma, that is no excuse for you to allow your tongue and your head to go their separate ways. I accept your apology on the condition that you never utter such words to me again."

"I promise on the graves of all my ancestors," Ifeoma replied, "If I ever utter such words again, may the Imo River goddess take me down to the bottom of her abode."

243

"Now, Ifeoma, I want you to listen carefully to what I have to say. When you get home tonight, I want you to be Ngozi's shield from her father's wrath. I have asked her to return home tonight. Let no harm come to her. Tell your husband that you are merely doing the bidding of the gods--especially, *Ani,* the earth goddess of fertility. Tell him that you did not give birth to your children only to see them destroyed in your lifetime. Then tell him that Ada Ukwu wishes to speak with him tomorrow after his men's meeting ends at noon."

"Tell him that if he lays a hand on my daughter--Ngozi, or even as much as raises his voice at her before I have had a chance to speak with him, both of us will force our legs into his trousers. Mention also, that I am in one of my bad moods, he will know what that means."

SEVENTY

By the time Ngozi returned to her father's house that night, her mother had already come back from Ada Ukwu's place. Her mother prepared a delicious dish of *ugba* for her and put away a bottle of *Fanta* in the refrigerator to chill, so that Ngozi can wash the *ugba* down with the refreshing beverage.

As soon as Ngozi's mother heard her daughter's bedroom door open, she hurried over to the room and embraced Ngozi tightly. Mother and daughter broke into tears as they remained in each other's arms. Ada Ukwu's words kept ringing in Ngozi's mother's ears over and over again: *a mother's bosom is a child's last refuge.*

What powerful words. How true those words, Ngozi's mother thought to herself, as she felt the deep emotional release her embrace--her unconditional love and affection, was providing Ngozi. How could she have been so short-sighted, so bereft of understanding and compassion, as Ada Ukwu had pointed out earlier on? She began whispering into Ngozi's ears.

"My beloved daughter, I am sorry I turned my back on you the way I did. I was so shocked by the news you broke to me that I could not think of anything else. Perhaps also, there was a part of me that knew that your father would react very badly to the news, and I was probably readying myself for the inevitability of that impending storm."

"Now, thankfully, your big aunt, Ada Ukwu, in her usual manner, has restored my sense of perspective. Come, I have prepared some *ugba* for you, when you are done eating we will sit down and think through how best to approach your father. At any rate, before you get to speak to your father, Ada Ukwu would have done a number on him, for she asked that he come to her house tomorrow afternoon. I am quite sure that by the time Ada Ukwu is finished with your father, he will be a lot more agreeable."

Mother and daughter headed into the kitchen and sat down to a tasty meal of *ugba*.

SEVENTY ONE

Mazi Chidimma knew instinctively what Ada Ukwu was going to use to try to get him to accept the calamity brought upon his household by his beloved daughter, Ngozi. It is the long-held secret of his that is only known to Ada Ukwu and himself.

Many years ago, as a young man he had just joined the Federal Civil Service of Wazobia and was posted to a remote place in Northern Wazobia called *Medobi*. He was young, unattached, care-free, strong, ambitious and full of a lustful thirst for life. He was one of the few well-educated 'native' civil servants around then, for this was in the 1920s, when Wazobia was still very much a colony of Anglia, and whitemen where the ones who made up the managerial echelons of Wazobia's Federal Civil Service. 'Natives,' if they were lucky, occupied the lower rungs of the ladder of Wazobia's Civil Service at the time. They were the clerks, messengers, interpreters, stenographers, drivers and the like.

The situation of things at the time, turned the handfull of 'native' civil service administrators in Wazobia, especially in northern Wazobia, where they were fewer still, into local celebrities. Thinking back now, Mazi Chidimma had to admit to himself that those were heady days indeed.

One Friday, after work, Mazi Chidimma retired to a local bar and eatery run by an Igbo woman whose bottom is so big that many joked that she walks well ahead of her backside. At that tarvan, 'native' workers and civil servants congregate on weekends to let off steam after a long, tedious work week; to have a few drinks, perhaps more than a few drinks, before heading to the local cinema to watch the inevitable 'Indian films.' The more cultivated among them endure the interminable arguments among the cinema audience over which of the characters in the movie is "the actor."

A youngish-looking, beautiful Hausa-Fulani woman was working in the tarvan that evening as a waitress. Mazi Chidimma could not recall ever seeing her there before. Somehow, amidst the bawdy din of drinking and drunken men; amidst the hustle and bustle of moving bodies and the chatter of loosened tongues from alcohol, their eyes met. Let those who say that such magic moments are found only in fairy tales, speak for themselves. For this was no fairy tale--this magic moment for him and the northern maiden.

When finally she made her way to his table to take his order of Star Beer and *isi ewu*, the words came as though part of his order, as he shamelessly asked for a rendezvous later that night with her.

"Wen you de close work?," Mazi Chidimma asked her eagerly in pidgin English, his heart pounding in his chest.

She answered without flinching or shifting her stare away from his face, "Ten o'clock."

"I go wait for you for taxi outside, wen ten o'clock knack. Make you no disappoint me ooh!," Mazi Chidimma responded.

It was more than a magic moment, it was a strange, almost out-of-body experience. Why did their eyes meet in that instant? Why did their eyes speak such deep, intimate mysteries to each other? How did her spirit know to answer the call of his own? Why him among so many men? So many choices? Let those who say that such magic moments are found only in fairy tales speak for themselves.

Ten o'clock came and Mazi Chidimma waited in a rented taxi cab at a corner street a few yards away from the tarvan. There, in the cab, on the corner of the street, he waited like a spy in a game of international espionage, for the northern maiden whose name he still did not know, but whose eyes and smile held the keys to this strange fateful drama.

Minutes ticked by in Mazi Chidimma's mind like hours. When the minute-hand in his time-piece hit a quarter past ten, he gave up hope and felt foolish for having believed. He was about to ask the taxi driver to take him home when hope struck again.

She emerged from the front entrance of the tarvan. He could see the dim reflection of her beautiful face under the street light, her languid frame discerned through her *lappa* and fitted blouse. His heart resumed its frantic pace.

She paused on the corner of the street, as though checking to see if her date had come. By now the minute-hand was close to the half-hour. Does she not realize that she is almost a half-hour late or was she merely being a typical African woman when it comes to keeping time?, Mazi Chidimma thought to himself.

He let her tarry a while longer, for he was not entirely sure that someone else may not be in the picture. Duels over women are not his cup of tea, no matter how good-looking the woman may be. For his people have a saying that tomorrow has the power to produce a prettier woman than the most beautiful woman you see today!

She began to walk away from the tarvan and from where Mazi Chidimma lay in wait, as though she had reached the conclusion that her date did not or would not show up. At that point, Mazi Chidimma asked the cab driver to drive slowly along side her and as close to the curb as he can manage. He wound down his window and called out to her, "abi dis na your ten o'clock?"

She stopped suddenly, whirled round and flashed him an unforgettable smile. The cab driver stopped the car and Mazi Chidimma opened the door of the cab to let the northern maiden into the cab. As things would later turn out he let her into much more than just the taxi cab; he let her into his life permanently. Nine months later, a baby boy was born of which only Ada Ukwu knows in the whole Chidimma clan in Isiobodo.

Mazi Chidimma ran away from the situation. He lacked the courage to face the situation squarely and deal with its natural consequences. He could not face the shock and disappointment of his people--his *umunna*. He who had done so well. One of the few who had made it into *olu oyibo*--the whiteman's Civil Service; he whom everybody in Isiobodo expects to take high titles in the course of time. He turned his life savings up to that point over to the northern maiden to buy her silence and his freedom.

How was he going to say to his *umunna* that he sired a bastard son with this total non-entity of a Hausa-Fulani woman? His *umunna* will also find it hard to forgive him for letting others claim the plume of a young warrior who has their blood flowing in his veins. They will rightly charge that the young man has been allowed to know nothing of Igbo culture and tradition; that he will see his own blood relatives through the jaundiced eyes of others; perhaps, even think of them as strangers with whom to someday quarrel over where the boundaries of their ancestral patrimony rightfully begins and ends.

Yet, as his people say, if the mouth keeps quiet for too long about what the ear hears, it is the heart that bears the brunt of that silence. He just had to tell someone and he did. He told Ada Ukwu, and while she was very supportive of him at the time, she has held that information over his head all these years like the proverbial *ibi*--hernia, that only a man's wife knows he carries beneath his manhood.

SEVENTY TWO

As soon as Mazi Chidimma sat down in his sister's parlor, Ada Ukwu began to speak without pretentious preambles.

"Broda, I will make it plain to you. Our daughter Ngozi, is a grown woman and has found a man with whom she is in love and wishes to marry. We need to respect her feelings and her choice. I see no problem with that."

"Ada Ukwu," Mazi Chidimma began slowly, "Are you really comfortable with the prospect of Ngozi marrying an 'ausa man? Are you comfortable with having them as *ndi ogo*--in-laws? You who is the matriarch of the Chidimma family, whose responsibility it is to keep the brood together. Why are you so willing to let this chick stray away so easily?"

"Broda, listen to me. Ngozi is not straying away. She is a very sensible young woman and I believe her when she says that she is truly in love with the young man, Mohammed, and that he is of excellent breeding."

"Oh, is his name Mohammed,? I see. I wonder what they will name their children--our grandchildren? Are you and the rest of the Chidimma clan, ready for nieces and nephews with Arab names who will be forever facing east?"

"Broda, you sound as though it is only Muslims who face east. Do we Christians not face east as well? After all, Jesus Christ does not come from Isiobodo! He comes from Nazareth and the holiest land of Christians is Jerusalem, which is in the same Middle East as Mecca and Medina!"

"Moreover, Broda," Ada Ukwu continued, "even if it is to Rome that we Christians face—in the West, it is still not to Isiobodo that we turn when we pray as Christians. Therefore, let us not hold that against Muslims as though we are entirely free of the same shackles."

Ngozi's father changed his approach and tried to pull on the dusty cords of Wazobia's memorable fratricide.

"What is more, Ada Ukwu, what do we say to our new found in-laws about Wazobia's Civil War in which so many of our kinsmen and women shed their blood? Do we say that while they starved and killed us for daring to claim our patrimony; that while we raised our voices in order that our ancestral land not become our mass grave amidst a callous and indifferent world; that our defeat has washed away our woes? That our defeat has paid their debt to the many souls of the faithfully departed. That our defeat has soothed the spirits of compatriots angrily roaming the land. Is that what we will say to our grandchildren and our newly found in-laws, Ada Ukwu?"

Ada Ukwu tried the tactic of invoking the nostalgic memory of their father's words to steer her brother in the direction she wants him to go.

"Broda, need I remind you of the cautionary words of *Nnayi* Chidimma? As you well know, he was fond of saying to all his children and others: 'There is no point trying to squeeze out drops of hope from the stone of despair. Faith cannot be taught, it must ensue as the birth-child of endurance; it is a piper's call from the Great Beyond that awakens in the souls of the anointed, a dutiful answer to serve at the pleasure of the gods and the wayward ways of fate! Give yourself up to the battle, for victory always belongs to The Owner of the world. For what aid can be extended *mkpi*--the he-goat, if it cannot stand its own foul smell?'"

"Is this your answer, Ada Ukwu, to the practical problem we face with Ngozi marrying an 'ausa man? You surprise me, Ada Ukwu. If this is all you can come up with, I do not think it is worth my time."

Ngozi's father sat up on the edge of the seat as if he were making ready to leave. Ada Ukwu sensed that she was loosing the initiative and decided to throw in her last card. Her timing, as always, was perfect.

"Broda, I will tell. I swear on the graves of both our parents, I will tell. I will tell the whole of Isiobodo about your 'ausa woman and the bastard son she bore for you. I will make sure that they all know that you have denied and kept it a secret all these years, if you do not show Ngozi some understanding and support."

"Oh, Ada Ukwu," Mazi Chidimma responded, "you have really outdone yourself this time. You have managed to combine shameless breech of trust with blackmail."

"Go ahead, tell it to the whole of Isiobodo. Climb to the top of *ugwu akpulu aku*--the hill of the lone nut tree, and shout it out to all the villages of Isikwuano, Obododike and

251

Aniumueze to hear, it would still not make me give my blessing to something I know will not augur well for this family."

"Broda," Ada Ukwu replied, "I suggest you think it over very carefully. What will happen to the *Ozo* title you were hoping to take if this information gets out? For the last few years, everybody has assumed that you will soon join the exalted ranks of the *Ozo* titled men of Isiobodo. Some have even resorted to calling you at public meetings, *eze ama na ege chi*--the king-to-be everyone knows is soon to be coronated."

"Do you imagine that the *Ozo* titled men of Isiobodo will entertain the idea of your joining their revered circles with that kind of scandal hanging around your neck like the dead chicken used to mark the village thief? I rather doubt it myself."

Mazi Chidimma knew that Ada Ukwu is right. If the *Ozo* titled men of Isiobodo get to know about his bastard son by an 'ausa woman; an 'ausa woman at that, his chances of ever becoming one of them in Isiobodo will quickly slip into oblivion. Even if they forgive the fact that he sired a child with a total nonentity, they are unlikely to forgive the dishonorable manner in which he hid the fact from his *umunna* and turned his back on the child--a manchild at that. They will say that he of all people should have known better that their blood is too precious to be left behind no matter the womb in which it is conceived.

Mazi Chidimma reclined in the seat a beaten man. In a slow, tired voice that bespoke his defeat, he said to his elder sister, marveling at her resilience and resourcefulness even as he spoke, "Ada Ukwu, what would you like me to do...?"

SEVENTY THREE

Ngozi walked listlessly into the livingroom, her eyes carefully averted from her father. She was not looking forward to the conversation with him. Despite her mother's reassurances that Ada Ukwu would have softened him up, she was of the mind that it is going to be an intractable encounter. She was wearing a simple cotton frock, made of African print material known as *abada*. The simple dress and her lack of facial make-up, allowed her natural good looks to show through in a wholesome way, devoid of the contrived clutter of trinkets and a caked face.

Ngozi went and sat as far away from her father as she could manage. Her father's eyes followed her into the livingroom as she walked to the furthest sofa from where he was sitting in his large mahogany rocking chair. For the first time in all the years he carefully and dutifully raised Ngozi, he could see that she was now a *woman,* not merely his *daughter.* He could see that nature had been generous with her. Her tall, slender firm frame. Her regal neck and perfectly symmetrical face. Her flawless, tawny skin and her excellent figure. This is his beloved *daughter,* his *abuba ugo*—his plume of pride. But this is also a *woman* in her own right!

Ada Ukwu was right in recounting the famous words of their father. It is indeed the anointed harkening to the piper's call from the Great Beyond...who give themselves up to the battle...who give themselves up to the dictates of the gods and the wayward ways of fate! He could see now that as her biological father, he was only her earthly guide, her privileged mentor, her *foster* parent. In the end, *all* children, all *our* children, belong to their God-parent, The Owner of the World. We, the *foster* parents, the earthly guides, are privileged only to partake of their making and in their raising; to partake in their *fostering.* When our work is done, they return to their true owner—-their God-parent, The Owner of The World.

'What aid can be extended the he-goat that cannot stand its own foul smell?,' their father would always end his famous entreaty with. Why beat one's head against the unyielding wall of the fated order of things...give yourself up to the battle...'

Yet, Mazi Chidimma thought to himself, did not the Nazarene ask his Father repeatedly to remove the cross he was about to bear on behalf of man's intransigence, despite its apparent preordination? He will make his offerings to the gods, so that when judgment is passed, when things go awry, the blame will be with the spirits of The Great Beyond and not himself. He will take his last, and hopefully, best shot at dissuading his daughter from marrying that 'ausa man.

"Ngozi," Mazi Chidimma began slowly, "I am sorry that I lost my temper with you the other day when I first heard the news of...As you well know, our people say that a father is usually the last one to get used to the *womanhood* of his daughter."

"But why is that so, papa, did not such a father marry someone else's daughter?," Ngozi queried gently.

"I do not purport to have all the answers to life's myriad problems, Ngozi, but I suspect that the reason lies in the fact that being a man himself, a father is well aware of what his own kind is capable of."

"The truth is that women generally fear physical harm from men not from their fellow women, and men equally fear physical harm from other men and not from women. Have you ever seen a women who is afraid to go outdoors for fear that another woman might mug her? Or a man afraid of leaving his own abode for the same reason?"

"No. Both men and women have men to fear for their physical safety in human society. So, when a father hears that another man is about to claim his daughter's hand in marriage, his first thoughts are about her physical safety and well-being. He instinctively worries whether she is about to fall into the hands of a *human being* or a beast!"

An awkward silence began to build between them. Ngozi was not sure what to say next or even if she should say anything more. Her father wondered himself what to say next. He felt like a man in a wrestling match thrashing about for a good grip. Yet, he knew that the silence must not be allowed to develop a life of its own. He broke the silence unceremoniously.

"Ngozi, I know that you imagine that you are in love with that 'ausa man, however, I can assure you that it is mere infatuation. An infatuation that will pass with time. Like they say, when there is a sea storm and waves rise up like great walls, it appears as though the whole world is submerging. Yet, even the worst storm is always followed by a calm. This too shall pass my dear daughter."

"But, papa," Ngozi responded, I am not infatuated. I am in love with Mohammed. I did not just meet him yesterday, papa. We have been friends at the university for a couple of years now. I have known him long enough to distinguish between being in love and being infatuated with him."

Her father resumed speaking as though she had said nothing.

"I don't want to contemplate the consequences of what you are about to do. How are we supposed to hold our heads up in this community if you place this burden on our family's shoulders?"

"But, papa," Ngozi ventured again, "I am not asking anybody to marry Mohammed with me. I am the one who is going to be married to him and I will be the one to worry about the problems that come with that decision."

"This shows how little experience and common sense you have, Ngozi. How do you expect to prosper in a marriage if the members of your own family desert you? Do you imagine that you can live as though you were hacked out of a tree trunk, without *umunna* and *umunne*?"

"How long do you imagine your husband's respect for you will last once he realizes that you stand alone without the emboldening support of your immediate and extended family? Trust me, Ngozi, it will not be for long. You will be like someone standing naked in full view of everyone in the middle of *Afia Uwa*."

Ngozi felt that the time had come for her to press her father more directly for the exact nature of his concerns, although she knows the cultural basis of his prejudice.

"Papa," Ngozi said to her father, "how can you be worried about someone you do not even know?"

"Ngozi, perhaps that is precisely why I am worried. If I knew the young man, I would be in a much better position to determine what kind of man we are about to play house with."

"But papa, you are bothered by the very fact that he is Hausa and not Igbo, is that not so?"

"In all honesty, Ngozi, I am. I feel that the cultural gulf between our people and theirs is too great. I feel that our different religions constitute another big divide between us and them. And I would be the first to admit to you that the bile of the Civil War that was fought between our people and the rest of Wazobia, still leaves a bad taste in my mouth."

"But papa, Mohammed was not even born during that Civil War! Do you think it is fair to visit the sins of the fathers on the children? What if there was something bad you did in the past, would you like it if someone were to hold it against me?"

Mazi Chidimma's heart skipped a beat. Had someone let the cat out of the bag? Had Ngozi got to know about his northern impropriety? Was that what she was broaching by this line of questioning? He held his breathe even as he probed her face intensely for tell tale signs.

Perhaps it was in the look in her eyes, perhaps it was in her *body language*. Perhaps the clue lay in her countenance, but somehow, intuitively, he realized that it was merely a coincidence and that his own paranoia was getting the better of him. He relaxed and assumed a more self-possessed posture.

"Yes, Ngozi, you are right. I would not want anyone to visit my sins on my children. It would not be fair to the children to be penalized for their father's sins. But one could reverse the question and ask, if children are entitled to inherit the assets of their father, why should they not be willing to inherit his liabilities?"

"I know that you can't be serious papa, when you say that. A person should only be held liable for what they have done themselves, and not what someone else may have done, even if they are related by blood. That is what justice and fair play is or *ought* to be all about."

Mazi Chidimma knew that his daughter is right. It is the way of his people to only fight just wars and to never pick a fight with someone who has done nothing wrong to them. For they believe that that kind of injustice acts like a boomerang, coming back at a later date to haunt the perpetrator.

"No papa, this that you presently fear is the very stuff of which the future is made. Only those whose reaches are well beyond the confines of their homesteads will have the necessary tentacles to cope with the complexities of tomorrow's world."

Ngozi's father was trying to make full sense of what Ngozi was getting at, when she expounded further on her point.

"Papa, would you want your grandchildren to camp at the borders of that brave new world or would you rather see them completely at home at the heart of that budding cosmopolis?"

"Papa, those who fear change so much that they fail to make necessary changes, die. They become *'worn out limps on the chain of animated matter.'* On the other hand, those who change for change sake, who fail to carefully assess why the change they accept is necessary, plunge like blind fools into an abyss that a little caution might have spared them."

"Papa, we should be neither dinosaurs, incapable of adaptation, and hence, destined for extinction; nor fools who rush in where angels fear to thread! There is a middle ground between the two. A point at which necessary caution and necessary change have a happy medium. That is where we should be. That is where I believe I am, papa."

Mazi Chidimma thought silently for a long while, then he said to his daughter with a tone of finality in his voice.

"Ngozi, the best I can do for you is to make a deal with you that will be devoid of any promises. I will let your 'ausa suitor and his family members come to Isiobodo to negotiate for your hand in marriage."

"However, if he and his family members fail to meet the mark, either in terms of their deportment or their behavior; or in terms of their ability to scale the philosophical high bar that our *Ozo* titled men and elders set for them, then all bets are off. For our people say that a wise person should use their tongue to count their teeth."

Her father felt certain that Ngozi's 'ausa suitor will lack the refinement and personality necessary to make a favorable impression or failing that, will surely trip over one stumbling block or another that his wily *umunna* will place before them when they come to Isiobodo; and then, the matter would resolve itself by way of the self-evidence of their failure.

Ngozi smiled inwardly. This is a deal she can live with, for she is supremely confident that Mohammed will meet the mark. For her present situation with her father is like a person trying to describe a beauty queen to someone who has never set eyes on her. The most descriptive words conjured, fall like hurled stones that expend the force of their thrust well short of their intended target. The person requires the compelling force of their own eye witness to propel them to true appreciation and understanding.

"I accept the deal papa. All I ask in return is that in fulfilling the terms of the deal, you give Mohammed and his family members a fair chance at succeeding."

"Very well, Ngozi, the deal is done. For your own sake and for the sake of the family, I hope and pray that your *chi* is not only alive and well, but awake!"

Mazi Chidimma got up from his rocking chair, hugged his daughter briefly and retired into his bedroom to meditate and offer prayers to The Owner of the World.

As her father left the livingroom, Ngozi's mind went back like *de javu,* to when she was about to leave for the University of Ibadan, nearly six years ago. Her father had finished having a long talk with her, and just as he was about to take leave of the livingroom in exactly the same manner as he did today, he uttered words to her that never left her mind. He said, "my darling daughter, go to that big school, garner all the knowledge and information you possibly can, the pen is the Whiteman's hoe!"

SEVENTY FOUR

The news spread like wildfire throughout the village of Isiobodo. Virtually the whole village turned up at the compound of the Chidimma family. Everybody had heard that *ndi 'ausa*, where coming to ask for Ngozi's hand in marriage. It was such an unusual occurrence, so outside the realm of the normal, that many did not believe it and came to the compound of the Chidimma family for the sole purpose of determining the veracity of the rumor.

The large compound of the Chidimma family filled with people as though arriving at a stadium for a cup final. Mini buses carrying hired dancers and masquerades from several neighboring villages arrived, one after another, disgorging drummers, flutists, gong players, masquerades, as well as male and female dancers attired in colorful costumes.

First came the *Atilogwu* dancers, then the *Oji Onu* masquerade dancers. A short while later, the *nkwa umu amogho* arrived. The atmosphere in the Chidimma compound was alive with music and the pulsating energy of so many people gathering in one place.

Ngozi's family, left no stone unturned in making sure that their prospective in-laws get a powerful dose of the richness of their culture. That their prospective in-laws never forget the day they came to *ani Igbo*. For the truth is, as one of Ngozi's granduncles said at the family meeting called to plan for this day, that we can not measure the true mettle of a man merely by the length of his shadow at high noon. We need to come up close, to get a good feel of the substance of the man. Their prospective in-laws have gone beyond merely viewing the shadow cast by their presence in the gathering dusk, but seek now to come up close to feel their true mettle.

Mountains of yam fufu were pounded. Four types of soup- -*egusi, okra, ogbono and onugbu*, were prepared in order to make the yam fufu's journey to the stomach a smooth and enjoyable one. *Okoto, ugba, ngwo-ngwo, pepper-soup, Jelof rice,* et. cetera, were prepared. Countless kegs of palm wine, cartons of various brands of beer, Champaign and spirits, were stacked up to the ceiling of the storage room, like a war chest soon to be unleashed on invaders.

SEVENTY FIVE

lhaji Futa Toro has been to southern Wazobia several times, specifically, one should say, to Lagos, the port town that the Anglian colonialists turned into the main capital city of Wazobia during their rule. But he has never been to the eastern part of Wazobia, to Igboland.

In the capital city of Lagos, he finds the heat bearable since his own up-country gets extremely hot. But it is the humidity, the moisture-laden air that sits on one like the vaporous steam of a sauna, that he can not stand. Yet, since Wazobia's seat of government was there in Lagos for years and the economic heart that pumps life-giving blood into the arteries of the country lay in that city, he went there periodically stoically bearing its oppressive humidity as well as frenetic pace.

Igboland, however, is a complete mystery to him. He hoped, even as he prepared to sojourn there with his son, Mohammed, that it is not as oppressively humid as Lagos.

Of what he had come to know of Igbos in Hausaland, they are a proud, hardworking, intelligent and boisterous lot, who tenaciously hang unto their traditional culture. Although he has never admitted it to any one, and probably never will, a part of him has great admiration for them. Their pride, industry, adventurous nature and brilliance. He personally knows some of them who came to Hausaland with nothing and within the short space of a few years, thoroughly mastered the Hausa language and became millionaires by the sweat of their brows and their thrift.

Alhaji Futa Toro remembered a popular joke among Northern and Western Wazobians, about the unquenchable thirst for commerce that *inya miris*--Igbos, have. The joke goes that if you hear that an *inya miri*--an Igbo person, is dead, do not believe it even if you see his or her body lying in state. Wait until you have administered the ultimate litmus test. Slowly wave a crisp banknote back and forth over the nostril of the one presumed dead. If they fail to awaken, then and only then, can you conclude that they are truly dead!.

Alhaji Futa Toro is, however, aware that it is a joke as unkind as it is untrue. For it is merely a way by which the rest of non-Igbo Wazobia psychologically protects itself from the unrelenting and, for many, inexplicable tidal wave of Igbo commercial energy.

Alhaji Futa Toro is also much impressed by the gallantry and heroism Igbos displayed during Wazobia's Civil War and the way they recovered from that terrible devastation which took place in their own backyard. Now, they are to become his in-laws. He had already done battle with the triple-headed monster of his prejudice, indignation and religious chauvinism. Now, he was at peace with himself. The kind of peace that comes from resolution. He has resolved the menace of the three-headed monster by giving the situation up to the will of Allah.

When the day arrived for their trip to Igboland, Alhaji Futa Toro was determined to make a big impression on his prospective in-laws. He decided to take as his personal gift to Ngozi's father, a richly embroidered hand-woven *baban riga*, made by the best tailor in all of Kano. For Ngozi's mother, he took with him an equally richly embroidered *buba* as well as an assessory set of earrings, a bracelet and a necklace made of pure Asante gold.

For the Chidimma family as a whole, Alhaji Futa Toro took with him a white Arabian thoroughbred, twenty long-horn cattle, a box full of *gworo* and a hundred bales of Kano-cloth. All these items were carefully loaded unto one of his twelve-ton lorries, while he rode ahead of the gift-laden lorry in his chauffeur-driven Mercedes Benz with his son, Mohammed. Kano faded quickly behind the convoy as they sped their way southward to the rain forest region of Wazobia.

The drive was smooth enough from Kano to just beyond the River Benue. From thereon, open savanna grassland gave way to more deciduous foliage. Pot-holes began to appear with greater frequency on the highway, and densely populated villages and towns, appeared on either side of the highway at shorter intervals.

Three hours of high-speed driving, with a few stops at gas stations or what is better known in Wazobia as petrol stations, they entered the quaint university town of Nsukka. Once again, they stopped to fill up on gas or petrol, and wending their way through the narrow streets of Nsukka, resumed their high speed chase of the Imo River goddess.

Alhaji Futa Toro's convoy reached the city of Enugu. It was his first time coming to that Igbo citadel. He had, of course, heard of it, seen film clips of it on television and met dozens of Igbos from that city.

During the Civil War, Enugu, like other major Igbo cities such as Onitsa, Aba, Owerri, Umuahia, and so on, held a magical place in Alhaji Futa Toro's imagination. To him, they were exotic sounding places that needed to be *'liberated'* by Federal troops, and so often mentioned in the Federal Government radio broadcasts.

Those broadcasts always ended with the slogan, *'to keep Wazobia one is a task that must be accomplished.'* Everyone, including himself, knew the slogan was part and parcel of a propaganda campaign by the Federal Government of Wazobia meant to give the war a moral character and political justification. Yet, everyone, including himself, welcomed the propaganda campaign; because everyone on the Federal side of that war needed and thrived on the delusion the propaganda provided.

Now that the war has ended for over thirty years, now that the dust has settled, now that *the task of keeping Wazobia one has been accomplished,* Alhaji Futa Toro realizes the powerful impact systematic repetition of lies can have on the human mind. Over and over again, the same cobbled falsehoods are uttered, the same justifications trotted out, the same cast of characters vilified; until gradually, imperceptibly, minds privy to naked truth begin to dress themselves up in borrowed robes! Minds that were witnesses to the unfolding saga of a national tragedy, begin to yield to the plastic re-molding of reality.

Yet, that re-molding of reality is only made possible because the propagandist and the populace share an unspoken pact: *provide the home-spun yarns and 'we, the people,' will gladly adorn them.*

Alhjai Futa Toro did not have time to tarry in Enugu though he would have loved to acquaint himself with the city. Once again, they filled the tanks of the car and the lorry with gas, or is it petrol?, and got back unto the highway for their last stretch of coal-tar driving, before they exit unto the erosion-destroyed, pot-hole full, road access to the village of Isiobodo.

SEVENTY SIX

The nine-mile drive from the highway exit to the junction that splits into four narrow dust-roads leading respectively to Isiobodo, Isiukwuano, Obododike and Aniumueze, was slow due to poor road conditions. At several points on the exit road, Alhaji Futa Toro's convoy had to slow to a crawl as they made their way through trench-like pot-holes and treacherous gullies formed by erosion that has eaten away at the edges of the two-lane road along with its thin layer of coal tar. It made for very hazardous driving.

From the Four-Villages Junction, as it is known, however, the narrow dust-road that leads directly to Isiobodo, though untarred, had a smooth even surface, having been recently graded at the end of *udumili*--the rainy season, as a result of the self-help efforts of the indefatigable I.P.U.

Alhaji Futa Toro was especially struck by the neatness of Isiobodo as they passed the main market--Afia Uwa, and soon afterwards, reached the village square--Ama Isiobodo. The market place and the village square were neatly swept. The regular patterns made by *aziza*--broom, on the sand covered grounds of the market place and the village square were still clearly visible. Alhaji Futa Toro noticed the same kind of broom patterns in the front yards of homes flanking the narrow dust-road on both sides.

Something else struck Alhaji Futa Toro and Mohammed. In this Igbo village far removed from the big cities, large beautiful mansions and villas seem to pop out from nowhere. They can be seen in the leafy shades of clusters of giant trees at the end of gated drive ways from the main narrow dust-road of the village.

Alhaji Futa Toro had heard it said that Igbo traders and professionals having learnt a bitter lesson following the Civil War over the *'abandoned property'* fiasco, stopped investing in landed property--especially family homes, outside Igboland. Now he could see clearly where those investments were being redirected.

The convoy stopped briefly to ask for directions to Ngozi's family compound. Instead of trying to explain to the visitors the intricate twists and turns to the Chidimma compound, one of the young men standing on the corner of the narrow dust-road offered to ride along to guide them to their destination.

SEVENTY SEVEN

Mazi Chidimma was filled with anxiety as the expected time of arrival of Mohammed and his father drew nearer. He had invited the six men he talked and drank with under osisi obodo at Ama Isiobodo, to join him as part of his negotiating team. They had all gladly agreed to come, especially Mazi Nnayelugo, who was eagerly looking forward to using his sharp wit to puncture holes in the armors of the visitors.

As he contemplated the impending situation, Mazi Chidimma's mind could not stray far from the stereotypes of *ndi 'ausa* that he has harboured in his mind for much of his life. He kept expecting to be embarrassed in front of all of Isiobodo by the appearance of his prospective in-laws. Even worse, he imagined, will be his mortification when they open their mouths. For all he knows, the boy's father may have little or no teeth left in his mouth and might be suffering from one form of blindness or another.

Worse yet, when the conversations begin, will it be conducted in Hausa, Igbo or English? He felt reasonably certain that they don't speak Igbo and that their English is poor. To guard against complications that might arise from lack of communication, he had taken the precaution of asking one of his relatives--Mazi Akajiaku--the hand in possession of wealth, who specializes in long-distance trade to and from, *ugwu 'ausa*--Hausaland, and speaks flawless Hausa, to serve as interpreter for both sides.

As he returned to the livingroom from the backyard where he had gone to check on the drinks and other matters, he saw a Mercedes Benz car pulling up his drive way, followed by a twelve-ton lorry that was taking up half the length of his drive way. The moment of truth had arrived.

SEVENTY EIGHT

Mazi Chidimma paused in his livingroom, unsure whether to go outside and meet Mohammed and his father or wait for them to make their way into the house. He decided to wait. From where he was sitting in the livingroom, he could see what was going on in his front yard.

He could see a uniformed chauffeur, smartly get out of the driver's seat of the metallic blue Mercedes Benz, half-way circle the car and open the door at the "owner's corner." A tall, lanky, handsome gentleman, resplendent in a white agbada, embroidered with a rich tapestry of black threading on the front and back sections, emerged from the car. An equally tall, lanky, younger-looking gentleman, dressed in a sky-blue agbada elaborately embroidered with white threading, emerged.

Mazi Chidimma surmised that the younger-looking gentleman is Mohammed and the older gentleman, his father. A small crowd of people gathered around the visitors, gawking at them as though they are alien beings. The two men paused seemingly unsure whether to wait for someone to meet them outside the house or to proceed indoors. After a short while, they proceeded into the house.

Mazi Chidimma was impressed by their deportment. These are no cattle herdsmen. They have the bearing of nobility. Yet, he must not jump to hasty conclusions. Their princely dressing and noble carriage could be mere camouflage; disguises that might soon come off the moment they open their mouths. For as his people say, all lizards lay on their stomachs, therefore, it hard to tell which one of them has a stomach ache.

The two men ascended the staircase on the front porch of the house and stepped into Mazi Chidimma's household. Mazi Chidimma, flanked by his relatives, a selection of *Ozo* titled men, his drinking circle of friends and a number of other elders, waited for the precise moment before making any move. That moment arrived none too soon when Alhaji Futa Toro and his son, Mohammed, walked into the livingroom of Mazi Chidimma's home. Ngozi's father and his fellows rose to their feet in a respectful welcome of Mohammed and his father. The curtains of a momentous drama had just been raised.

Mazi Chidimma's relative, Mazi Akajiaku--the hand in possession of wealth; stepped forward to act as interpreter for introductions and the exchange of greetings. Mazi Chidimma and Alhaji Futa Toro approached each other like prize fighters and grasped each other in a firm handshake.

Mazi Akajiaku turned to Mazi Chidimma and said to him in Igbo, "Onye nka bu Alhaji Futa Toro, nna okolobia, Mohammed, nacho inu Ngozi"--"This is Alhaji Futa Toro, the father of the young man, Mohammed, seeking Ngozi's hand in marriage."

"Nno--welcome, Alhaji," Ngozi's father starchily offered.

Mazi Akajiaku, turned to Alhaji Futa Toro and said to him in Hausa, "Alhaji ga Mazi Chidimma--Alhaji, this is Mazi Chidimma, Ngozi's father."

"Sannu--hello, Mazi," Mohammed's father gently replied.

One by one, the same introductions and greetings were repeated between Alhaji Futa Toro, his son and *Ozo* titled men, elders, relatives and others gathered in the Chidimma livingroom.

When all were sitted, *orji*--kola nut, was brought for the Igbo traditional welcoming ceremony of the breaking of the kola nut. One whole kola nut was handed to Alhaji Futa Toro to take home with him as is normally done for a man of substance; the rest of the kola nuts in the serving dish were broken for the consumption of the gathered company.

Ozo Okechukwu, the oldest and most respected of the elders in Mazi Chidimma's clan, was handed the kola nuts to perform the *igo ofo* that always accompanies the breaking of the kola nut.

Ozo Okechukwu rose to his feet, adjusted his red cap and the *abuba ugo* stuck on it and loudly cleared his throat. His call for attention sparred briefly with persisting chatter before the former gave in to the latter. Mazi Akajiaku was close at hand to make sense of the sounds of one of Wazobia's tongues in the ears her visiting sons accustomed to the different sounds of another of her numerous tongues.

As is always the case on occasions such as this, without warning, *Ozo* Okechukwu, took a few short steps towards the august visitors and thrust his clenched fist into the air, bellowing at the end of the theater.

"Cha!, cha!, cha!, Isiobodo kwenu!"

The gathered members of Mazi Chidimma's clan responded in a thunderous, "Ya!!"

"Cha!!, cha!!, cha!!, Igbo kwenu!!," *Ozo* Okechukwu demanded again in a booming voice, his clenched fist still in the air as though preparing to throw a punch at someone.

"Yaa!!!," came the explosive reply.

"Cha!!!, cha!!!, cha!!!, 'ausa kwenu!!," *Ozo* Okechukwu demanded once more. The gathered members of Mazi Chidimma's clan politely joined in replying "Ya!!," in order to give the greatly out numbered visitors a representative voice in their midst. For it is a saying and given name among their people that *Obiageli*--the visitor should partake of the feast.

One last time, *Ozo* Okechukwu bellowed, "Cha!!!, cha!!!, cha!!!, Wazobia kwenu!!!"

One last time, the gathered members of the clan thundered their collective affirmation, "Yaaah!!!"

"Eh, the people of Isiobodo, I greet you. So also the visitors in our midst, for whose purpose we are gathered here. Fortunately, we have among us the person of Mazi Akajiaku, who speaks the language of our visitors well and can, therefore, translate what we say to them and what they say to us. I say this because the *igo ofo* must be done in our language--Igbo, for our ancestors do not understand any other tongue."

The gathered members of Mazi Chidimma's clan chuckled heartily, generously offering *Ozo* Okechukwu various praise names.

Having said this, *Ozo* Okechukwu, burrowed deep into the entrails of the Igbo language like a cancer worm. He wove threads of proverbs into cloth-lengths of philosophy; tied sayings into tight bundles of wisdom; scaled terraced contours of supplication, hope and vision. At the end of his *tour de force*, he offered an entreaty pregnant with meaning: he said to his fellows that however much their curiosity compels them, they must wait for the visitors to go first; for their people say that it is the person whose bowel is moving that should be first in line to relieve himself.

One of Mazi Chidimma's paternal uncles, *Ozo* Madubuike, a good friend of *Ozo* Okechukwu, got up to speak on behalf of Mazi Chidimma's father, whose rightful place it should have been to spearhead these marital negotiations, were he still alive and well.

Not as loquacious a person as *Ozo* Okechukwu, *Ozo* Madubuike, is known as a man short on words but long on action. As he would often say himself, nothing tries his patience like situations in which 'the benediction is longer than the mass.' In keeping with the value he places on brevity, *Ozo* Madubuike, went for the jogular.

"My esteemed *umunna*, the great people of Isiobodo, our esteemed visitors, I greet you all. Our people say that if the mouth keeps quiet for too long about what it hears from the ear, it is the heart that bears the brunt of the safekeeping of that secret."

"Moreover, our people say that one should not swallow what they know to be a poisonous potion out of shame. I do not intend to bite my tongue instead of speaking the truth out of politeness to our visitors. The purpose of your visit to Isiobodo may be understandable and noble, but procedurally, it is badly flawed."

"In the tradition of our people, technically, we do not yet know the reason that you are here. If it were in the old days, when Isiobodo was Isiobodo, we would politely break kola nut with you, share a sumptuous meal and palm wine with you, and quietly disperse as though nothing else were at stake. For you have not followed properly the procedures of the *Ibu mmaya*--the traditional wine carrying ceremony. You did not *knock on the door, whisper in our ears,* and then, if all goes well, *come into the house.*"

"Consequently, we have not had time to carefully check out your family background, as is customarily done, in order to be sure what kind of people we are getting in bed with."

"As it turns out, things are no longer the way they used to be in the old days. Needless to say that the mere fact that you are sitting where you are, and from as far away and as different a group of people from us as you are, is all the proof anyone needs that things are no longer what they used to be in the old days."

"In accordance with our traditions and customs, it would not be at all out of place for us to politely listen to you about the reason for your sojourn here and then, send you home in order for us to ponder what you have told us. But you have come a long way on a noble mission, and however ignorant of our *omenani*--traditions and customs--you may be, we are a fair and compassionate people."

"Unless any of the other *Ozo* titled men or elders in our midst have anything else to add to what I have said so far, I will ask that our visitors begin by telling us why they are here."

Ozo Madubuike sat down even as he was showered with praise names.

SEVENTY NINE

Alhaji Futa Toro panned the audience in Mazi Chidimma's livingroom. For the first time in all his years of dealing with Igbos in the North, he could see a totally different side of them; he could feel the robust pulse of their *folk*. In the North, they come to his house where he has home-court advantage.

There, at his place in the North, they are usually few in number. One or two, perhaps, no more than three. Their concerns are narrowly focused on business—on making the deal. There, they are consciously deferential and self-effacing, even indulgent of his egocentric aloofness and autocratic pretensions. There, they are like, they themselves might have said in one of their innumerable proverbs, a chicken that stands on one leg in unfamiliar surroundings, gingerly putting down its other foot only after becoming used to the place.

Here at Isiobodo, on their own home turf, it is a different matter altogether. These are no mere traders. These are no *Shylocks*, whose only interest is the proverbial *'pound of flesh and nothing more.'* This is a full-blown nation--a cultural universe unto itself. Alhaji Futa Toro could see the nobles among them--the legendary *Ozo* titled men, that he himself had read about in one of the Anglian colonial reports on the various *tribes* of the lower Niger. Like the report alluded, he could sense their self-possession, their preoccupation with dignity and honour. These are not a people whom it has been claimed the waving of banknotes across their nostrils can awaken from a coma or bring back from the dead.

Alhaji Futa Toro, turned to Mazi Akajiaku and told him in Hausa to tell Mazi Chidimma's clansmen, that his son Mohammed will speak first and that later, he would have a few words to say on the matter at hand.

Mazi Akajiaku translated and a murmur swept through the audience. How can a father step aside for his son to be the spokesman on a mission as important as this? The jarring sounds of the clash of cultures, many felt, were already beginning to make jangling noises in their ears.

Mohammed got to his feet to address the august gathering. He remembered the advise Ngozi gave him regarding when and if this moment arrives. She told him to come off as humble as possible, to sound deferential and in awe of the elders, especially the *Ozo* titled men. She advised him to take as much poetic license as he can muster, for her people, especially the *Ozo* titled men, never tire of oratorical extravagance.

She said that it will be an all out war of words and wits. A symbolic battleground in which the live ammunition of words are used to subdue opponents. A war of proverbs and sayings in mortal combat with each other. A war of oratorical excellence in which the victorious army will have to put to use an impressive arsenal of *logos* and *pathos*, in order to gain the upper hand. The one good thing about that war, however, is that the loosing side--if at all there is one--will live to tell the tale of how and why they yielded ground.

"Esteemed *Ozo* titled men, elders, Mazi Chidimma's family and friends, I greet you all. I am indeed honored to be in your midst today. I am especially privileged to be able to speak to so esteemed an audience as this."

"Even if it once was, the purpose of my sojourn to Isiobodo is no longer a secret, for as my people claim the cow once said, it is pointless to try to hide his horns from onlookers, because they stick out on both sides of his head for all to see."

"Let me begin immediately by allaying your concerns. I do not speak for my father, I speak for myself. My father has asked me to speak first not because where we come from, the tail wags the dog--that is, that a son takes the rightful place of his father; but rather because he wishes to keep his powder dry, to save the big gun for last. For as an Igbo saying, which I am sure you are all familiar with, goes 'when sleep becomes sweet, we begin to snore.'"

Ripples of laughter broke out in the audience in response to Mohammed's timely use of that Igbo proverb, as well as mutterings of surprise at his familiarity with the proverb. It is much like the surprise one might feel if someone you presume to be a total stranger tells you where you keep your snuff box in your own house. Mohammed continued.

"Moreover, my father asked me to speak first so that this august gathering can hear first hand, the state of my heart and mind, and thus, bear that in mind as we conduct our negotiations here today. For as we say in Hausaland, while a dog's bark sometimes seems to be for no reason, it does so in order that people not forget that it is still a member of the neighborhood."

"Esteemed *Ozo* titled men, elders, Mazi Chidimma's family, relatives and friends, a wise child was once asked, 'why are your parents greater than yourself,?' and the child replied, 'because they gave me life.' Then, the child was asked, 'why are you greater than your parents?.' The child thought for a moment and then said, 'because it is through their offspring that our parents achieve immortality.'"

"I must confess that I did not set out initially to marry your daughter, Ngozi, or any other Igbo woman for that matter. I made a conscious choice to study in a university in southern Wazobia, but not necessarily to marry outside the confines of my own people and region of the country."

"Your daughter, Ngozi, struck me like a bolt of lightening whose chance of striking an individual is as improbable as oases in the great Sahara are infrequent. Allah smiled at me, however, when she found room in her heart to accommodate me--a completely smitten, love-sick stranger."

"It was from Ngozi's mouth that I first heard the words that opened up a whole new vista to me. She once said to me that it is her firm opinion that there is an inverse relationship between intelligence and prejudice. The more intelligent a person is the less prejudiced they are likely to be; and the less intelligent a person is the more prejudiced they are likely to be."

I found the idea intriguing, though I continued to view the proposition with a healthy dose of skepticism. I, therefore, queried her some more over the logic behind her proposition. Her answer was indicative of everything that is keen, attractive, refreshing and admirable about your daughter, Ngozi. She said that intelligence tends towards *rationality*, and prejudice tends towards what she called *symbolic emotionalism.*"

"Whether or not her proposition is entirely or partially true, a light bulb went on in my head that has never gone off ever since. From then on, in addition to her other many qualities, I felt like I had found a soul mate. That is why my soul yearns to be united with its mate; why I most humbly, but most desperately, ask for her hand in marriage."

Here before Mazi Chidimma's eyes, was the undeniable evidence of a *real 'ausa man*, in the person of Mohammed, who had come south to the renowned University of Ibadan and made the mark, fair and square. There was no *federal character,* as the contentious quota system in Wazobia is called, involved here. No case of grandfathers opening doors for unworthy beneficiaries. What do you do with this kind of compelling, intrusive evidence?

Do you ignore the inconvenient evidence and pretend it does not exist? Do you relegate it to the trash heap of *'exceptions that prove the rule'*? Or do you acknowledge the simple truth it tells by its own brilliant testimony? The truth that Mohammed is but an example of the potential dormant among all folk, waiting, likes smoldering cinders in a blast furnace to draw igniting breath from the bellows of a master blacksmith. The bellows of opportunity, of circumstance. The bellows of their *chi,* of *akalaka*--the handmark of *Chukwu* on each person's palms.

"Finally, esteemed *Ozo* titled men, elders, Mazi Chidimma's family, relatives and friends," Mohammed went on, "permit me to close by making what might sound more like a political rather than a romantic case for Ngozi and I. Permit me to make a case for Wazobia's ethnic-children commingling their blood. Contrary to what many skeptics fear, if we commingle the blood of our peoples, we will not loose the defining patent of history and culture that sets us apart from one another, nor stray from the different paths we choose to explore in life. Instead, we will become a mighty river with many tributaries."

"If we commingle the blood of our peoples, our children and their children, and their children's children, will reap a rich harvest of life more abundant. They will reconcile Wazobia, and perhaps even the whole of Africa, with herself; by laying an organic and sturdy foundation for the erection of the House of Wazobia fully at peace with itself. Thank you for hearing me out"

Mohammed's father was pleased with the work his son had done in his opening remarks. He had dazed the hunting prey with a glancing blow, now it remained for him to deal the animal the decisive blow. It remained for him to pull out the big gun.

EIGHTY

During the long journey to Isiobodo, Alhaji Futa Toro had decided on a plan of action. But he kept it to himself, not even sharing it with his son, Mohammed, who was sitting right next to him in the back seat of the car. For as it is often said, a real man keeps secret what he plans to do in the privacy of his heart.

He had decided that he would do something quite unexpected and powerful at the negotiations for Ngozi's hand in marriage at Isiobodo. He was convinced that his plan will be effective. That it will have the element of total surprise and that it will resonate among Ngozi's people for a long time to come. He is aware that as a people, the Igbo place a high value on the art of conversation and oratory. That they have a penchant for the dramatic. Yet, Alhaji Futa Toro felt that not even that cultural bent of theirs will have prepared his prospective in-laws for what he has in store for them.

Alhaji Futa Toro got to his feet, his tall, lanky frame clad in the flowing robe of his *baban riga*, giving him an aristocratic poise. Mazi Akajiaku got up as well and moved closer to Mohammed's father, but Alhaji Futa Toro told him in Hausa that his services will not be needed. Mazi Akajiaku was puzzled but returned to his seat. Silence gradually eased out chatter and took full control of the livingroom.

Alhaji Futa Toro adjusted his *konkosa* in the 'one thousand five hundred' fashion of Wazobia, and then, cleared his throat. Slowly, gently, with the polish of burnished gold, Alhaji Futa Toro began to speak in clipped, impeccable Oxford English. This surprised Mazi Chidimma, who had thought that the man's English would leave much to be desired. Still, the best was yet to come.

Alhaji Futa Toro greeted the gathered clansmen; craved their indulgence over his ignorance of their traditional customs of wine carrying, claiming it a mistake of the head and not of the heart. Pointing outside, he listed the gifts he had brought as his family's token of friendship and appreciation, except for one item. He left out the white Arabian thoroughbred from the list of gifts he recited for Mazi

Chidimma's clansmen, for reasons that will become evident as the day wore on.

Alhaji Futa Toro then paused and adjusted his *konkosa*. A master of the garb himself, he sensed the psychological readiness of the audience for the unfolding of his plan--the opening of the well kept secret in his parcel. Without warning, without the slightest hint of the direction his talk was going to take, Alhaji Futa Toro thrust his clenched fist into the air and bellowed in flawless Igbo:

"Ndi Igbo, kwenu!"

The stunned audience answered with a "Ya!"

"Ndi Hausa, kwenu," Alhaji Futa Toro demanded again.

The audience politely replied with an even louder "Yaa!"

One last time, Alhaji Futa Toro bellowed, "Wazobia, Kwezuonu!!"

The audience thundered "Yaaa!!!," their mouths still hanging open from shock.

As the saying in Igbo goes, the snake lies like a helpless rope for the man with a knife. Alhaji Futa Toro was like the man with a knife and his stunned audience, like the snake. Even Mazi Nnayelugo, the wit, whom most people call *ga ga no ogwu*--one who threads precociously on thorns, was paralyzed.

As if his opening ploy was not enough, Alhaji Futa Toro proceeded to speak in almost flawless Igbo. The only hint that the speaker of the language is not Igbo, was in the accent that rolled round certain syllables and cut sharply into the edges of phonemes. Otherwise, the grammar flowed with the ease of a rapid stream.

"Ndi Isiobodo," Alhaji Futa Toro continued in near-perfect Igbo, relishing the powerful impact his stunt was having on his hosts, "we have a saying in Hausaland that, it is impossible to know how sharp the blade of a man's sword is until he unsheathes it."

"There are few, indeed, who knew all these years, that I could speak Igbo until this very moment. Not even my beloved son, Mohammed, was aware of that fact. Today, I have unsheathed my sword, and you can all testify how sharp its blade is."

"However, we are not here for a battle or to cut up the carcass of *nama* like a butcher does. We are here for something far more important; something far more binding

276

and healing. Therefore, my ability to speak Igbo far from being a sword, is more like a set of numbers with which I am able to decode the combination lock of the door to the strongbox of the soul of your nation."

The gathered elders and relatives, but especially the *Ozo* titled men, nodded their heads approvingly at Alhaji Futa Toro's masterful play on words. This is the very stuff of which their daily bread of conversation is made.

Alhaji Futa Toro, now fully in his element seemed unstoppable.

"The esteemed people of Isiobodo, this young man sitting here," Alhaji Futa Toro said, pointing to Mohammed, "is the reason I am standing here before you today. Ordinarily, people rightly think it is a father who shows his son the way to manhood and wisdom. Yet, a time comes, when a man's child becomes his window to the world, his guide."

"Even as I speak to you now, I have not yet set eyes on your daughter, Ngozi. I do not know what she looks like. If I saw her on the street, I would pass her by for I have no idea what she looks like. Yet, my deep-seated love for my son, the compelling case he makes for his love for your daughter, Ngozi, and his sheer determination, are the reasons that changed my mind and softened my hardened heart over the matter of their betrothal and brought me to Isiobodo today."

"Otherwise, I tell you with all due respect and sincerity, nothing would have made me, a devout Muslim, agree to the prospect of mingling our blood with those of unbelievers. Now, thanks to my son Mohammed, I see life through different lenses."

Mazi Nnayelugo, tried to get up to say something, but *Ozo* Madubuike firmly hushed him up. Alhaji Futa Toro continued.

"If you look at *efi-Igbo*--Igbo cow and Hausa *shanu*, you will notice that they look different from one another. *Efi-Igbo* is stout, jet-black in color and usually, hornless. Hausa *shanu*, on the other hand, comes in both black and white, has long horns, and often, has humps on its back."

"Yet, both types of cow produce milk for the sustenance and growth of their offspring. The meat from both types of cow is tasty when used to cook all types of food or roasted over naked fire. Their essence are the same though their superficial appearances differ."

Ozo Okechukwu got to his feet, adjusted his red cap, cleared his throat and responded to Alhaji Futa Toro and his entourage.

"Eh, Alhaji Futa Toro, I greet you. Among the esteemed ranks of *Ozo* titled men, we have two standards of oration that must be met before one can be considered an *okwulu ora--*-one who speaks on behalf of the community. First, the literary elegance of the person's words must be as sweet to the ears as honey is sweet to the tongue. Second, the truth the person speaks must be sharp as well as strong enough to cut down a big tree."

"We are impressed with your eloquence. One could have easily mistaken you for an *Ozo* titled man, given the ease with which eloquent words of wisdom role off your tongue. Yet, not only are you not an *Ozo* titled man, you are not even Igbo at all. It goes to show that what our people say is true, that in this world what is in one person's house can also be found in another person's house."

Ozo Madubuike got to his feet.

"Alhaji Futa Toro, I join *Ozo* Okechukwu in saying to you that you have spoken well. Far better, in fact, than any of us here had anticipated. We had feared that your tongues may be too heavy in your mouths or that our ears may be tone deaf to your language, thus, impeding effective communication between us."

"As you have noticed, we took the precaution of having an interpreter present here today in the person of our brother, Mazi Akajiaku. But to our pleasant surprise, we have had no use for him."

"The fact that you can speak our language took us all completely unawares. It is also flattering to hear you speak our language with such ease. You have, indeed, made your way far deeper into the soul of our nation than would have ever been the case had we been both tongue tied by our mutually unintelligible languages."

"Yet, Alhaji Futa Toro, language, like a cooking utensil, is a tool. The availability and quality of a woman's cooking utensils cannot tell you how well the food she cooks will taste. I have been to a few of the big and expensive hotels in Wazobia, where they have the most modern cooking equipment,; yet, the taste of the food they dish out is not worthy of being served a good and loyal hunting dog, let alone a human being. But ask anyone here what mouth-watering dishes the *umu ada* of Isiobodo put out everyday for their families, cooking with simple aluminum and earthenware pots!"

"I say this in order to point out that while we admire your tool--your ability to speak well and to speak our language, we are ultimately more interested in the taste of the food you cook."

The gathered clansmen filled the air with praise names for *Ozo* Madubuike as he sat down."

Ozo Okechukwu got up again and began to make his way through another path of thought.

"In Igboland, we have a pertinent question that is often posed in order to rhetorically make the point of the importance of a man's pride in himself. The question is asked: *if another man's house is bigger than yours, is his home also bigger than your own? For all good homes are the same size and a proud man is always more concerned with how good his home is, rather than how big his house is.*"

"Alhaji Futa Toro, the Chidimma family home is good, and as such, we care nothing of the size of another man's *house*. All we care about is how good another man's *home* is as well."

The gathered clansmen showered *Ozo* Okechukwu with praise names as he sat down.

Alhaji Futa Toro paused, rose to his feet, reached into the deep pocket of his *konkosa* and retrieved two pocket size books. One was a Bible, the other, a Koran. He placed the two books next to each other on the coffee table in the middle of the livingroom.

"Esteemed *Ozo* titled men, elders, Mazi Chidimma's family, relatives and friends, these two holy books--the Bible and the Koran, are branches of the same tree of knowledge. The roots of that tree are fastened to the same soil. They draw life-giving nutrients from the same soil. The fruits that fall off the branches of that tree can only fall so far from that tree of knowledge."

"I say to all of you gathered here today, that if we fail to rise to our common humanity, if we fail to partake of our shared humanity and national community, then, we effectively relinquish any rights to the bountiful fruits that fall from the branches of that tree of knowledge."

"Therefore, let us courageously raise up the great walls of the church-mosque of our country, upon the unshakable foundation of the living truth in these books, and may he or she who breaks that covenant, be condemned to eternal damnation."

The audience moved by the evocative words of Alhaji Futa Toro, answered in a mighty chorus, "Ise," which in Igbo means *Amen*--so be it.

EIGHTY ONE

When they neared the point of negotiating the bride price, *Ozo* Okechukwu got up and said to Alhaji Futa Toro and his entourage.

"The young woman your son, Mohammed, seeks her hand in marriage, is what we call *nwanyi eze*--a woman fit for a king. She is the *ada*--the first daughter of the Chidimma family, therefore, before we get anywhere near the substantive issue of the bride price, we will need to see a demonstration of your appreciation of her high value and uniqueness, through a symbolic gift that can not be found anywhere around these parts; something which, if it were in the old days, your son, Mohammed, would have had to journey across the proverbial seven rivers and seven forests, to find."

Alhaji Futa Toro smiled to himself, for he had thought of this contingency. It was the reason he kept the white Arabian thoroughbred off the list of gift items he recited to Mazi Chidimma's gathered clansmen. Now, he tabled that gift item like a good hand in a poker game.

"Esteemed *Ozo* titled men, elders, members of the Chidimma family, friends, we have already crossed the seven rivers and seven forests, and what we brought back as a symbol of your daughter's high value and uniqueness is indeed rare and precious and can not be found anywhere around these parts."

Alhaji Futa Toro turned with a flourish to his son, Mohammed, and said to him in Hausa, "*Mohammed, je ka ka kawo dokin a nan. Ka ja shi zuwa cikin daki. Maza-Maza.--* Mohammed, go and bring the horse. Bring it right into the livingroom. Hurry up."

"Bring it right into the livingroom, Baba?," Mohammed asked his father with a puzzled look on his face.

"Yes, Mohammed, you heard me right, bring it right into the livingroom."

A few minutes later, Mohammed returned with the magnificent beast, urging on the neighing horse by pulling gently on the gold-embroidered reins on its bit. The hooves of the great stallion click-clacked on the tiled floor of Mazi

Chidimma's livingroom. The horse whinnied loudly, steam issuing from its flaring nostrils as the noble beast reacted with panic at the strange company of the gathered men and the even stranger surrounding of the livingroom.

The Arabian thoroughbred reared up on its hind legs with the power and majesty of a show horse, and the gathered clansmen fell back in awe, for very few of them had ever come that close to an *iyiya*--a horse. Only the venerable *Ozo* titled men stayed their ground. They could not afford the disgrace that cowering from an animal that a mortal being like themselves tamed would bring. For among their people it is said, that whatever one man can learn to do there are other men who can learn to do likewise.

Alhaji Futa Toro had made his point eloquently. One could not have brought a rarer gift to Isiobodo than a horse. For a combination of the tropical rain forest and the *tse tse* fly, have made the horse a stranger to these parts.

EIGHTY TWO

Bringing the Arabian thoroughbred to Mazi Chidimma's family as a gift made quite an impression on Mazi Chidimma and his clansmen. Ngozi's father began to warm up to the suitors and allow himself to entertain the very real possibility of them as *ndi ogo*--in-laws.

When the excitement from the dramatic entrance of the horse died down, Mazi Chidimma got up and walked slowly over to where Alhaji Futa Toro was sitting and greeted him; not in the ordinary manner of everyday greeting, but in the locked arms of *Ozo* titled men, distinguished elders and revered warriors in Igboland.

Alhaji Futa Toro knew then that he had successfully crossed an important bridge. Yet, caution and diplomacy were still highly advised, for as the chameleon is credited as having said, those who do not understand him wonder why he threads so gingerly. But he is careful with every step he takes so as not to mistakenly set foot in someone's farmland.

The time for negotiating Ngozi's bride price arrived. Alhaji Futa Toro had come prepared for what he assumed would be an expensive bride price. He had in the trunk of his Mercedes Benz the equivalent sum of 20,000 United States dollars in Wazobian currency. If need be, he was prepared to muster even more money. For it was prior to coming to the Chidimma household that ambivalence would have had a place in the scheme of things. Having come, all ambivalence must now give way to family honor and pride.

Let it never be said that a descendant of the Futa Toro family, brought down shame upon his family name because his arms were not strong enough to lift up a load that he freely elected to carry. For a sensible man must size up a load against his own strength, before throwing down the gauntlet to his challengers.

Ozo Okechukwu got to his feet and cleared his throat.

"Eh, Alhaji Futa and his entourage, I greet you all once again. If this were a secondary school examination, I would say that so far you have come through in flying colors. If it were a cross-country foot race, I would say that you are well ahead of the others and in sight of the finish line."

"But this is neither a secondary school examination nor a foot race, although at times it might seem like it is. Instead, it is more like a kind of identification contest in the dark or with blinders over our eyes. We are feeling each other out in order to determine what we look like without the aid of proper vision. For our people say that marriage can often be like *afia akpa*--a grab-bag sale. When you put your hand inside the bag, one is never sure what they might come up with."

"However, the bride price is neither an insurance policy nor the cat's eyes that can see in the dark. It is merely a symbol. A token of the value we place on our daughter. A token of the effort put into raising our daughter into a fine young woman. A token of how strong your son's arm is. For I am sure that in 'ausaland, you would not raise a thoroughbred horse, such as the one you brought to Isiobodo today, in the hope that a cripple will ride it on the day of the big race."

"Great horses are raised for and ridden by great men. So also, great women can only be the brides of great men. That is why we call such women in Igboland, *nwayi eze*--a woman fit for a king."

"In accordance with Igbo tradition, the members of Mazi Chidimma's *umunna* will go outside and huddle among themselves for a while to discuss how much they want as bride price for their daughter, Ngozi. When they return, they will whisper in my ears the terms they have set for you and I will relay the same to you."

"If you find that the weight of the load they place on your family's shoulders is too heavy, you can whisper in my ears and I will convey the same to Mazi Chidimma's *umunna*. We will go back and forth in this manner, until we reach a mutually satisfactory conclusion to the matter; or, God forbid, we disagree and have to go our separate ways."

"You might well wonder why all the whispering back and forth when we are all sitting in the same room and can speak out loud for all to hear?" Well, it is our custom that we do not haggle out loud over a human being as though we are trading *efi Igbo* or other kinds of merchandise at *Afia Uwa*."

EIGHTY THREE

Mazi Chidimma's *umunna* ceremoniously huddled together for a brief period, for they had long ago decided on what they would ask as dowry from Ngozi's suitor. Alhaji Futa Toro was surprised at how short a time their deliberations took. He correctly surmised in his mind that they were going through a formality and that the decision had been made much earlier than now.

Mazi Chidimma whispered into *Ozo* Okechukwu's ear and he nodded in acknowledgment. When the members of Mazi Chidimma's *umunna* all resumed their seats, *Ozo* Okechukwu got up and cleared his throat.

"Eh, Alhaji Futa Toro, Mazi Chidimma's *umunna* have reached a decision. They have asked me to tell you that they want a big bride price for their daughter. A very big bride price, indeed. For as I said to you earlier on, she is a woman fit for a king."

"Well, *Ozo* Okechukwu," Alhaji Futa Toro cut in, displaying a bit of impatience, "how big a bride price are they asking for?"

"Eh, Alhaji Futa Toro, they want a very big bride price for their daughter indeed, however, they do not want it in the form of money."

Alhaji Futa Toro was caught unawares. He had brought all that cattle. He had brought many bales of Kano cloth. He had brought more *gworo*--kola nuts, than they can finish in several years. He had brought an Arabian thoroughbred and he brought the equivalent of 20,000 United State dollars in Wazobian currency, and now they do not want money at all, but something else for the bride price?

His patience was beginning to wear thin. No matter how precious their daughter may be, she can not possibly be worth an arm and a leg. He braced himself for what *Ozo* Okechukwu had to say.

"Eh, Alhaji Futa Toro, Mazi Chidimma's *umunna* say that they want your family to bring them more *nku*--firewood, than the forest in Isiobodo can yield. They say that they want the firewood cut into logs the length of a man's arm, tied up in neat bundles of no more than fifty and stacked up for as high as the human eye can see."

"They say that they will make one major concession to your family. You do not have to bring them all the firewood today or even tomorrow. They say that your family can take its time. Whenever you finish completing the task is all right with them."

Ozo Okechukwu sat down with a mischievous twinkle in his eyes. He could tell from the look of dismay on Alhaji Futa Toro's face, that while he had managed to open the door to the strongbox of the Igbo nation with the right codes of the combination lock of their language, he was not familiar with all the contents in the strongbox. For if he were, he would have discerned that they were baiting his son with this ruse.

Alhaji Futa Toro fidgeted in his seat. He had not planned for this outrageous request and had no answer to it. Surely it was their polite way of saying no to his son's attempt at gaining their daughter's hand in marriage. They are diplomatically shutting the door in his face. After all his effort; after overcoming his own prejudices, spending so much money and indulging them in the revelation of the knowledge of their language, they throw this in his face as though none of that matters.

These people are a cold, egotistical and heartless lot. He leaned over to his son, Mohammed and whispered in Hausa, *"Ka san da watakila za mu bar wajen hannu banza saboda suna neman kudin auren da mu aje ba-za su kore mu da garin"*--"prepare yourself for the possibility that we might have to leave empty-handed, for they have made an impossible request of us in the form of a bride price. They may as well be telling us to get *thehellout* of their town."

Mazi Chidimma's gathered clansmen let Alhaji Futa Toro and his entourage stew. The *Ozo* titled men, always eager at one-up-manship, waited to see the nimble-footed Alhaji top this last act of theirs. But Alhaji Futa Toro had been bested and the wind had gone out of his sails. However, what happened next was beyond the expectation of anyone in the gathering, even the venerable *Ozo* titled men.

Mohammed got up and cleared his throat. His father almost jumped to his feet to pull his son back to his seat, but he controlled himself, for he felt that he had done all that he could humanly do.

286

"Esteemed *Ozo* titled men, elders, Mazi Chidimma's family and friends, Baba; I greet you all most humbly and profusely once again. In Hausaland, we have a saying that a prosperous farmer says that why he ceases hoeing at dusk is not because he is tired, but because the sun goes down on him, leaving him with no light with which to work. But if you give him daylight without end, he will hoe without resting."

"If any one of you will be so kind as to lend me their axe and show me which side of Isiobodo's forest I may begin my cutting, I will do my best to see how much firewood I can cut today before the sun goes down on me. At first light tomorrow, I will begin again."

"I promise not to stop cutting firewood in Isiobodo until your forests are no more and your landscape is as exposed to the three siblings of sun, rain and wind, like the part of Wazobia from whence I come."

Mohammed began to take off his *konkosa* as though preparing to get to work. At that point, the *Ozo* titled men rose to their feet in unison and said to Mohammed, "Our son, you have spoken and acted like a man. We were merely testing the depth of your love for our daughter. We now see that your love for her is as deep and expansive as the Imo River. Come and sit among your in-laws.

Mohammed walked over to where Mazi Chidimma's *umunna* were sitting, embraced Ngozi's father and took a seat among them amidst a thunderous applause.

EIGHTY FOUR

No sooner had all the knots in the string of negotiations over Ngozi's bride price become untangled, than some one slipped out of the livingroom to tell the *umu ada*--the daughters of the Chidimma extended family, gathered in the backyard that all was ready for Ngozi to make her much anticipated *debut* in the livingroom.

All day long, the *umu ada* carefully put Ngozi through the betrothal rituals required by Isiobodo custom and tradition. At mid day, the *umu ada* accompanied Ngozi to the the banks of the Imo River, where she washed herself, not with Lux soap or any other imported or modern manufactured bath soap in Wazobia; but with traditional Igbo bath soap--*ncha nkota*, made locally from palm oil and palm kernel ash since time immemorial.

Next, they oiled her body to a gleam from head to toe with shear butter. Then the women meticulously drew elaborate patterns on her legs, arms, midriff, shoulders and face, with *uli*; and made special markings under her eyes, wrists and ankles, with *nzu*.

They forced the large, heavy ivory anklets called *odu*, through both her well-oiled feet. Four sets of smaller *odu* bracelets were also squeezed through each of her oiled hands. A secret mixture of sweet-smelling seeds, flowers and herbs, was dabbed all along her inner thighs, under arms, between and underneath her breasts as well as behind her ear lobes. Immediately, the concoction began to emit a powerful but most pleasant fragrance that goes to the head the same way strong medicine goes to the blood.

Ada Ukwu, the *eze nwanyi*--first lady of the Chidimma *umu ada*, walked to the middle of the tight, protective circle of women where Ngozi was standing in splendid nudity. In her hands, Ada Ukwu held three lengths of finely woven white *akwette* cloth. Also hanging from Ada Ukwu's right arm were twenty long strings of jade waist-beads known as *jigida*. On Ada Ukwu's left arm, were four large, scrupulously burnished brass bangles. Each brass bangle represents one of the four great Igbo market days--Eke, Orie, Nkwo and Afor. One of the younger women in the circle, came forward to assist Ada Ukwu with dressing Ngozi up.

The first length of akwette cloth was tied firmly around Ngozi's waist. Gently, they put each string of jigida over Ngozi's head, shoulders and arms; rolling the string of beads slowly down Ngozi's mid-section and waist, until they came to rest on the swell of her hips one on top of the other, looking like a bead-skirt.

Next, Ada Ukwu and her helper, tied the second length of akwette cloth across Ngozi's bosom, securing her breasts like a bra. After this, they carefully expanded each of the four large brass bangles at their gaps and slipped them around Ngozi's slim, exquisite neck. Finally, they tied the last of the three lengths of akwette cloth like *ichafu*--scarf on Ngozi's head. All the while, the gathered women sang mellifluous songs in the background that could have melted the heart of the most battle-hardened warrior.

Beginning with Ada Ukwu, each member of the *umu ada* of the Chidimma extended family, came forward and gave Ngozi two pieces of advise. The first they said out loud so that all gathered there can hear. The second, they whispered in Ngozi's ear. That second piece of advise is meant for Ngozi's ears only. It has sometimes been claimed that the advise spoken out loud and the one whispered in the ears of the would-be bride by the *umu ada*, are often exact opposites of one another. The first being merely for public consumption, while the second—-the whispered one, contains the truth of what her advisers have in their hearts.

When the members of the *umu ada* finished with the ceremony of the advise, all the gathered women observed a great hush--a moment of silence in honor of the Imo River goddess--the giver of life.

From the livingroom, one could here the beautiful singing of the *nkwa umu agbogho* and the *umu ada* of Isiobodo as they accompanied Ngozi from the backyard into the livingroom. Ngozi looked more beautiful than at any time Mohammed remembers and looked more beautiful than anything Alhaji Futa Toro had imagined. Perhaps, this is Allah's will, he thought to himself with a satisfied smile on his face.

EIGHTY FIVE

Preparations for Chike and Bisi's *white wedding* had been a most hectic affair. Here were the first children of two proud and wealthy families about to get married across ethnic or *tribal* lines, and determined to impress upon each other their importance and economic means.

For Bisi's family, since she is female, the point of their lavish material contribution to the wedding was to send a loud and clear message to Chike's family on the extreme value they place on their daughter. Nothing, it is believed in traditional circles in Wazobia, increases or decreases the stock value of a young bride quite like how her own family sends her to her husband's house.

In the case of Chike's family, the unspoken purpose of their own lavish expense on the wedding, from the traditional *Ibu mmaya*, to the church wedding, was to convey in no uncertain terms to Bisi's family that although their daughter comes from a great family, she is marrying into an equally great one. It was also meant as a kind of public testament that his family is fully capable of not only looking after Bisi and her offspring, but in maintaining her in the opulent life style she is accustomed to.

Between the Olatunji and Nwafor families, they had managed to come up with a guest list of nearly three thousand people. Due to the sheer number of people, they had to rent the National Theater in Lagos for their wedding reception - a place designed to seat about six thousand people quite comfortably.

For the church ceremonies, they also had to obtain use of the National Cathedral and managed to get the Archbishop of Lagos, Right Reverend Aloysius Makonji to officiate. By the time all the expenses for the wedding had been tallied, both families had collectively spent over two million naira.

In the course of the feverish preparations for the wedding, Chike wrestled with the question of whether or not to send Azuka an invitation. Will she consider it insensitive of him or will she consider it courteous of him to send her an invitation to his wedding, he thought to himself? He knew that she would have heard of what a number of people were already calling the wedding of the century, and that his invitation to her, were he to send one, would not break the news to her for the first time.

Just one week before the wedding, Chike made up his mind to invite Azuka and personally mailed the invitation the very same day. When Azuka received Chike's wedding invitation in the mail, she sat for a long time in the privacy of her room, staring at the beautifully gold-lettered words on the invitation card. Tears streamed down her cheeks as memories came flooding back.

How dare Chike send her an invitation to his wedding, especially after all that transpired between them? Did he really expect her to be happy for him and his *ofe mmanu* bride? She flung the invitation card violently across the room, cursing Chike in the most vile words she could think of. As she raged at what she thought was Chike's impertinence, a devious thought lit up in her head like a light bulb.

Instead of staying away from Chike's wedding, why not go to the wedding and really make a mess of things for him? "Sweet revenge," was how a romance novel she once read described it. That same romance novel also said that all is fair in love and war. She would attend the church ceremonies and during the mass when it comes time for the priest to ask whether anybody in the congregation knows of any reason why these two can not get married, she would shock everybody by getting up and spilling the beans in full view of the esteemed congregation.

Azuka's mood became lighter as she rummaged through her wardrobe, trying to decide on what to wear for the occasion and whistling the once popular tune in Lagos, "if you marry taxi driver, I don't care,....if you marry lorry driver....I don't care...."

EIGHTY SIX

The cavernous building of the National Cathedral filled up slowly with the invited guests to Chike and Bisi's wedding. The V.I.P.s and members of the Medical Students Association of the University of Ibadan, took up the first twenty pews on both rows of the Cathedral. The city of Lagos had assigned one hundred police men and women, on foot, motor bikes and horseback, to assist with traffic and crowd control.

The church ceremonies were supposed to begin at eleven thirty A.M., but everybody knew that they would be doing very well indeed, if the event started at one o'clock. The Archbishop himself, whom experience had taught well how untimely Wazobians tend to be on occasions like this, had not even bothered to leave for the Cathedral from his diocesan residence as late as twelve noon.

Azuka, made sure to get to the Cathedral early. In fact, by eleven o'clock, she was already seated in the church. The reason she came so early was to make certain that she gets a seat nearer the front section of the great Cathedral. That way, when she stands up to deal her ultimate blow of embarrassment, it will have the full dramatic effect. She hoped and prayed that the news media, especially the television people, would be there to capture the spectacle in Technicolor.

Azuka pictured in her mind the look of horror that would be on Chike's face when he sees her raise her hand and rise to her feet in the middle of the church service to publicly rip away his mask of piety and morality. The thought gave her such an inner feeling of gratification, that for the first time since she conceived of the plan, she became a little afraid of herself.

Yet, she steeled herself to the mission ahead. This was no time for doubts or cold feet, she thought to herself. She must act with the same ruthless single mindedness with which Chike himself had dumped her nearly three years ago, despite the fact that she was three months pregnant with his child.

The great pipe organ in the left hand corner of the altar section of the great Cathedral stretched out long, melancholy, almost mournful notes of exquisite ecclesiastical songs. Some from the great European tradition of Gregorian chants and others from the sumptuous harmonies of Wazobian church hymns. It filled the inside space of the Cathedral with a robustness that compels a deep sense of piety and awe. The crowd flowed into the church, the invitees being mostly dressed in beautifully tailored African clothes.

Twice, within a space of twenty minutes, the congregation came to its feet before the celebration of the mass commenced. The first time, the Archbishop, along with his retinue of two other bishops, four priests, two deacons and six altar-boys, made their way into the Cathedral by way of the aisle, proceeding at a slow dignified pace until they reached the altar. They settled into their well-rehearsed positions, with the Archbishop and the other two bishops sitting on chairs that looked like the thrones of kings.

In the course of this short drama, the great pipe organ purred on in a solemn and subdued tone, stopping only when the high priests were seated. A heavy silence hung over the church. Minutes later, the congregation came to its feet once more, this time in honor of the arrival of the bride. Bisi and her bridal train made their way down the same aisle the Archbishop and his retinue had just come. Once again, the pipe organ heaved a long, powerful sigh of musical relief in the form of an entrance song, heralding the entrance of the bride.

Chike and Bisi were picture perfect. Chike wore an immaculate white chiffonaise *agbada*. The elaborate spidery web of embroidery work done on the front and back sections of the *Konkosa*, completely hand-woven. The elaborate and intricate detail of the embroidery work commanded attention and admiration. It had cost about twenty thousand naira to make.

Bisi wore a beautiful flowing white wedding gown that gathered closely around her waistline, accentuating her slim, firm midriff. The dress billowed outward from the waist, flowing all the way down to her ankles. The bodice looked almost as if it had been knitted, its strapless style showing off much of Bisi's shoulders and the upper parts of her breasts.

The same material used to make the bodice of the dress was repeated in the sleeves, which came all the way to her wrists.

The train of the dress flowed endlessly behind her, with six bridesmaids supporting it in their hands. The accompanying male escorts for each of the six bridesmaids, a flower girl, a ring-bearer, the best man and the members of the immediate families of the Olatunjis and Nwafors completed the entourage.

Soon after the bride, bridegroom and their entourage seated themselves, the Archbishop rose majestically to his feet, extended his right hand to an altar-boy and accepted his scepter, which symbolizes his sherperdship for Jesus. His rich baritone rumbled through the electronically amplified loudspeakers as he said, "In the name of the Father, the Son and the Holy Spirit," making the sign of the cross as he spoke.

The Archbishop went through the elaborate liturgical rituals at a deliberately slow pace and dignified manner. Sunday services at Wazobia, especially "high masses," celebrated by a venerable personage such as the Archbishop - and at a wedding at that - are expected to start late and end late. Nobody was in any hurry.

Eventually, the service reached the part when the bride and bridegroom step up to the altar and stand before God and man to exchange their marriage vows. Azuka's heart began to pound. The moment of truth was about to arrive.

Meanwhile, Chike and Bisi were facing the altar and the Archbishop, backing the congregation. Azuka could make out the back of Chike's perfect frame. His six-foot one frame and chiseled triangular torso filled her field of vision, displacing all other people and things in the church and in her mind. Memories flooded her mind. All the emotions she experienced in the course of their short but tumultuous affair surged up within her like a riptide.

She remembered vividly the rapture of their first night together and the subsequent emotional agony she suffered when he so unceremoniously dumped her. She recalled his insistence that she have an abortion. The clinic, the doctors in their white lab coats and the white-uniformed nurses. She remembered the needles, the endless probing and prodding, the terrible feelings of loneliness and guilt. She recalled the events at her aunt's place, the indescribable pain she felt over loosing the baby and the morbid process of doing away with the fetus; and she knew that she had to go through with her plan to embarrass Chike at his wedding. It was the least she could do.

The booming voice of the Archbishop jarred her back into the present as he uttered the fateful words.

"...If there is anyone in this church, who knows any reason why these two cannot become husband and wife, let him speak now or forever keep his peace."

The Archbishop observed a customary pause, for no one ever really expects that anybody would actually say anything in protest. It had never happened before, not even in the course of the long and checkered experience of the Archbishop himself. There had only been an incident once when a woman fainted at this same point in the wedding ceremony. But, nobody could tell if her fainting spell had been brought on by joy, despair or purely medical reasons.

A slender brown arm stuck out above the heads of a sea of dark faces, followed by the wake of a rumbling murmur from the congregation. With the bride and bridegroom standing right in front of the Archbishop, they were blocking his view of the congregation so he could not immediately tell what the murmur was all about.

One of the Archbishop's co-celebrants leaned over and whispered into the Archbishop's ear. Although quite surprised by what he was just told, the bishop calmly asked Chike and Bisi to move to the left of him. They did and turned to their side, from where they too could now see the slender brown arm with its index finger pointing to the heavens.

Chike recognized instantly who the arm belonged to. There was a huge lump in his throat. He could not believe that Azuka had such a vindictive streak in her. It had been nearly three years since their encounter, what more did she want from him?

"Yes," the Archbishop thundered, "stand up and let your voice be heard."

With slightly trembling legs, Azuka slowly stood up. Another murmuring wave washed through the congregation. When it died down, the Archbishop's voice boomed through the loudspeakers again.

"Yes, young woman, what is it that you'd like to say to this congregation? Do not be afraid, speak up."

Meanwhile, Azuka's field of vision had once again become filled only by Chike. Their eyes met and locked, speaking a private language only the two of them could comprehend. They stared at each other for what seemed an eternity. Bisi nudged Chike on his left arm with her elbow and muttered under her breath, "What on earth is going on Chike? Who the ....is that woman and what does she want?"

Chike lied. "I don't know.

EIGHTY SEVEN

The silence in the church was so thick, it was as though everyone in the church held their breadth and every conceivable motion ceased. Chike was nearly at the point of collapse, for he needed no soothsayer to tell him what it was Azuka raised her hand about. He could feel his entire body breaking out in cold sweat - the kind that comes involuntarily, no matter what the atmospheric temperature is.

How would he live down such a monumental disgrace Chike thought to himself? Would he be able to show his face in this community ever again, free of ridicule and shame? How would he explain matters to Bisi? What would he say to his parents? He had to hand it to Azuka, he thought to himself, she surely picked the ultimate setting to extract her revenge. He felt a familiar impulse to simply bolt and run away from the whole situation. But he knew it would solve nothing and might complicate matters even more. For one thing, people would see his running away as a clear admission of guilt. He stayed.

By now, Azuka had stood up to the full view of most of the members of the congregation and they awaited her comments. Minutes seemed like hours. In the meantime, a church warden rushed a cordless microphone to Azuka. She gently accepted the microphone from the warden after he tapped on the bulbous spongy foam-covered head of the instrument a few times to test it, producing a *toom...toom...toom...*sound through the powerful loudspeakers.

Azuka's mouth became completely dry with stage fright. Her tongue felt lime it weighed a ton in her mouth. She felt like someone who had swam out too far from the banks of a river. Going back was as much a task as going forward, and yet, if she did neither, she would drown. The only thing she had to cling unto in the middle of that metaphorical river was the inflated rubber ring of her rage. A pure, unadulterated, exquisite rage.

"Your Lordship," she managed to blurt out in a slightly tremulous voice, "My name is...."

At that very instant, a commotion erupted in the middle of the Cathedral around the right hand row of pews. It appeared as though people were trying to wrestle someone down. Several church wardens converged on the scene from various parts of the church. The melee continued for another ten minutes. Eventually, four church wardens bodily carried a man out of the church.

Apparently, what happened was that at the very moment Azuka began to speak, the man who was later evacuated had an epileptic fit. The coincidental occurrence of that man's epileptic seizure at the very moment of Azuka's impending testimony, seemed virtually miraculous, for the disruption it afforded radically transformed Azuka's mood and the telescoped attention of the congregation on her. As the commotion progressed, Azuka sat down and, minutes later, slipped out of the church *in cognito.*

EIGHTY EIGHT

Azuka sat down heavily on a wrought iron bench in the courtyard garden of the Cathedral. She was still hyperventilating from the excitement inside the church a few moments earlier. The anxiety of the moment of her would-be testimony and the commotion that simultaneously occurred in the church had stolen her thunder and mitigated her determination to continue with her mission of vengeance.

As she meditated quietly over what transpired in the church, Azuka gradually began to realize that in order for her to be free, truly free of imprisonment by her own pain and anger - she had to let go of her rage. Not necessarily to forgive Chike, but to let go of her own self-consuming rage. Forgiveness implies absolving him of the responsibility of his commission or omission. That, of course, she could never do. Letting go, on the other hand, involved the willingness to allow a situation she can not change to take care of itself, even as she gets on with her own life.

Since she had earned a bachelor of science degree in biochemistry at the University of Lagos, Azuka made up her mind to go abroad, preferably to the U.S.A., to train to become a Registered Nurse. She had heard rumors that there is a great shortage of nurses in that country and that the pay is good. She would throw herself into her work and allow the experiences of a new environment as well as new challenges to help her lay to rest her painful past with Chike. She got up, made the sign of the cross, walked to the street corner, hailed down a taxi cab and headed home, determined to make good on her decision.

As the cab sped its way to her parental home, Azuka remembered the comments of a certain Wazobian political leader. Once, when that leader was asked a rather tough question regarding something that happened in the country's past, he replied by saying that he would rather look forward than backward. For if God had wanted us to look backward, he would have given us eyes at the backs of our heads. Since God did not give us eyes at the backs of our heads, but rather only at the front of our heads, he would have to presume that that is the direction The Maker intended us to look.

EIGHTY NINE

As the commotion in the church died down, the catchiest noticed that the young woman who had been standing ready to speak had disappeared. He quickly made his way to the pew where she had been sitting, only to be informed by people who had been sitting next to Azuka that she had left the church. The catchiest hurriedly conveyed that information to one of the altar-boys, who relayed the same to one of the Archbishop's co-celebrants who, in turn, whispered it into the Archbishop's ear.

In a steady, almost grim voice, the Archbishop repeated his earlier call for anyone who had anything to say about the couple, as though the drama of the last few minutes had not taken place at all.

"If there is anyone in this church, on this day, at this time, who has any reason why these two should not be pronounced husband and wife, let him speak now or forever keep his peace."

The Archbishop's voice rumbled through the loudspeakers and a great hush fell over the church again. A full five minutes went by in total silence - the longest five minutes in Chike's life, to be sure.

The Archbishop proceeded with the exchange of vows, finally saying the following words, to Chike's greatest relief:

"By the powers vested in me as the Archbishop of Lagos, I do hereby pronounce you two husband and wife. What God has put together, let no man cast asunder."

The entire congregation, quite uncharacteristically, broke into a mighty applause. Chike turned to Bisi and kissed her full on the mouth. The deed had finally been done, and sealed by God.

After the newlyweds returned to their pew, the Archbishop continued with the rest of the mass. He went through the gospel, homily and communion with a new zest in his voice. Forty-five minutes later, the Archbishop ended the service with the words, "Go in the peace of the Lord, the mass is ended."

The Archbishop and his retinue made their exit, an exit that was just as ceremonious and dignified as their earlier entry. The newlyweds and their entourage followed, making their long drawn-out exit to the clicking and flashing of hundreds of cameras and the great pipe organ playing the tune, "Here comes the bride."

NINETY

Even now, it seems like only yesterday. The wind howled like a sonorous gong sounded in the echoing shaft of a disused mine. Lips cracked suddenly from the dryness of harmattan, oozing blood. People's hair had dusty hues and those wearing clothes that were once white, had brownish appearances as though they had not been properly laundered.

Everywhere, there was dry desolation. The very air was acrid, dust-laden and several degrees cooler than the usual temperature. In the marketplaces, the sale of petroleum jelly was brisk. Ugulu had returned once more to declare himself lord of all he comes in contact. It had now been nearly three years since Chike and Bisi got married and Bisi was in the throes of childbirth.

Their marriage had gone on reasonably well, if one discounts the incessant inquisition of relations, especially from Chike's side of the family, asking after why Bisi had not "taken in." Some even went so far as to suggest that some wicked members of Bisi's family who were not happy with her marrying an Igbo man, had put *juju* on their marriage to make certain she does not bear fruit. What those relations did not know was that Chike and Bisi were practicing strict birth control methods.

Being both doctors, they knew only too well what to do to prevent an unwanted pregnancy with iron clad certainty. They had merely postponed Bisi's conception in order to accumulate more money in preparation for the avalanche of financial expenses that would come with the birth of children. So they let the imagination of their relatives run riot, knowing fully well that it was founded solidly on ignorance.

Towards the end of the third year of their marriage, Bisi's stomach began to show. At the fifth month of pregnancy, one could have sworn that Bisi was at least eight months pregnant. Her stomach looked quite distended and she complained regularly of discomfort in trying to find the best position to sleep.

On one occasion during this period, Chike traveled to Egbe to see his grandmother, whom he had not seen since Bisi became pregnant. In the hurly burly of Lagos life, both Chike and his father forgot to tell her that Bisi had become pregnant. When Chike arrived at his grandmother's place, she was sweeping the front yard of her compound with an *aziza*. Chike's grandmother sweeps her front yard every other day without fail, leaving regular wave-like patterns on the sand-covered grounds of her front yard.

At the sound of an automobile entering her compound off the narrow dusty road that runs like a central artery through all the interconnecting hamlets of Egbe, Chike's grandmother raised herself from her bent-over position, re-tying her wrapper more firmly to her waist as she tried to make out who was coming to her abode. The tires of Chike's car traced two equidistant lines across his grandmother's front yard, messing up the neat symmetry of her wavy *aziza* patterns.

As his grandmother recognized Chike's car, her face lit up like a candle. She beamed with obvious joy at seeing her grandson. They went through the elaborate greetings and repeated hugs. Eventually, they made their way into her cottage, where she immediately began to prepare 'okoto' for Chike. Chike accompanied his grandmother to the kitchen and sat on a chair in the left corner of the kitchen at the side of the door that leads into the storage room.

His grandmother sat on a low wooden stool, her wrapper pulled up to her knees, as she used an *aka odo* to ground *akawu*, *ose*, *nnu* and *yabas* together in the *ikwe*. Later, she will mix in some palm oil and Cray fish to serve as the gravy for the *akpu*, *ukazu*, *nkpulu aghara*, *mangala* and, perhaps, *okporoko*, which she will toss together like salad.

Chike was quite sure of the path the conversation with his grandmother will take. First, she will ask after his health, then she will ask after the health of his parents, then she will ask after Bisi, especially whether she has become pregnant. Her mood for the remainder of his visit will depend largely on the answer she gets to that last question. If the answer is negative, she will sulk through the rest of his stay. She will act correct with him, doing and saying all the right things, but her melancholy will remain palpable through it all.

Chike let her go through her litany of inquiries, until she got to the main question of interest to her - whether Bisi was expecting a baby or not. As soon as Chike answered in the affirmative, his grandmother went into a near delirious state of joy.

She pranced about with an agility surprising for an eighty two year old woman, slicing through the air with her right hand as though she were cutting branches off an imaginary tree with an *ogbu adana*. She thanked her *chi*, praised the ancestors and made jeering remarks and facial expressions at her supposed "enemies."

She repeatedly did the *nto* expression at her "enemies," a facial expression that involves putting both index fingers directly underneath each eye and pulling down the skin as you simultaneously stick out your tongue. She hugged and kissed Chike several times, thanking him for a job well done as though he had completed a major public works project that few others were capable of handling.

NINETY ONE

Although Chike had recovered from the strain of the long night of Bisi's labor, and they now had twins - one a manchild, the other a girl. The night before their birth, the situation had been touch and go.

The gynecologist, a handsome Wazobian lady doctor, had said to Chike, as Bisi's labor pains seemed each time to increase a thousandfold, that she had suspicions that the baby was in a "breech" position, and that they might have to perform a "Cesarean section" on Bisi. Chike knew what she was talking about, for he was a doctor himself, though not a gynecologist. Droplets of sweat stood on his forehead like tiny imitation glass beads, as he nursed fears for Bisi and the baby's safety.

He must have walked up and down the corridor of the labor ward a hundred times or more. He feared the worst. As he awaited the outcome of the doctor's feverish efforts and perhaps the hand of fate, his imagination practically ran riot. He imagined his child taken from Bisi's womb stillborn, or Bisi dying from the task of child bearing, and even worse, both mother and child giving up the ghost.

His harried mind began to wonder into familiar superstitious crevices. He imagined that there might be a cosmic retribution, a kind of nemesis that God may be planning to visit on him for so avowedly seeking the termination of Azuka's pregnancy. Here at last, Chike thought, was his rendezvous with destiny.

Were there portends of some poetic justice involved here?, Chike thought to himself. The sheer irony of life struck him as he continued his anxious wonder. A few years ago, he would have given anything to get rid of a pregnancy, yet now, there was nothing he would not give to save this one. How much difference the seemingly benign variables of time and space make in our lives is often so easily glossed over.

It turned out not to be a baby in a breech position after all, but actually twins. The baby boy Chike and Bisi gave the name *Adelaja*, a yoruba name which means "*a crown is added to my wealth,*" and the baby girl, they gave the Igbo name, *Nkiruka-- -that which is yet to come is greater* or *the future is bright and promising.*

Later that night, as Chike watched the two infants suckling their mother's breasts, a smile slowly spread across his face. Tears weld up in his eyes, but they where tears of joy and pride, not tears of sadness. At that instant, a remarkable coincidence took place which seemed to have a supernatural dimension to it.

The telephone rang, and it was Mohammed calling from The University Teaching Hospital in Kano. He sounded thoroughly exhausted yet happy. Ngozi, he declared with evident pride, had just had a baby boy. Yes, the labor had also been difficult like Bisi's, but Allah be praised, all has turned out well.

Chike's mind went back to the powerful sermon Father Balogun preached last Sunday. It was as if some higher power had taken possession of Father Balogun that Sunday. He spoke with a rare eloquence that had Chike completely enraptured for the nearly hour-long sermon. For time matters little when words are sweet.

The most poignant parts of that sermon remains etched in Chike's memory...

> "Every one keeps talking of the Second Coming of Jesus Christ. Yet, in the current state of our world, if he comes again, many would not recognize or associate with him any more than when he first came.
>
> If he comes again, as a Jew, but still preaching a faith different from that of his own people, they will still not accept him as The Messiah. In all probability, if he comes again as a non-Jew, especially if he comes again as an Arab, he might not be able to live and work in the state of Israel.
>
> If he comes again carrying the "wrong" passport, he would be an illegal alien in many countries of the world. If he comes again, born of the "wrong" nationality or "race," he will be discriminated against, and perhaps, even be subjected to "ethnic cleansing." If he does not speak English or speaks it with a "foreign" accent, it might count against him in some parts of the world. If he is poor, does not have a college degree, and is not computer literate, he will not be able to find a decent job.
>
> If Jesus comes again and chooses *socialism* over *capitalism*; or turns out to be a spirited *environmentalist*, the great Multinational Corporations of the world, might line up against him."

Father Balogun paused dramatically, reached into the left hand sleeve of his vestment, retrieved a clean white cotton handkerchief and slowly wiped the sweat pouring down his face and neck and resumed his sermon.

"My brothers and sisters, if Jesus Christ were to come again, many would not recognize or associate with him. If he were to come again as a woman, many might not care to hear what she has to say. If Jesus Christ comes again physically unattractive or handicapped, many might not pay him or her much attention.

But alas, I say to you my brothers and sisters, that Jesus Christ may already have come again--at least four different times, and hardly any of us have taken notice. He came again in the person of Mahatma Gandhi; he came again in the person of Martin Luther King, Jr., he came again in the person of Mother Theresa; he came again in the person of Julius Nyerere; he is still among us in the person of Nelson Mandela.

Instead of taking notice of the "Jesus" we see among us, of his image and likeness reflected in our midst; we keep waiting for the Second Coming, like the proverbial ostrich who says he cannot see anything with its head firmly stuck in the sand." "My brothers and sisters in Christ, what we need most but lack most, is FAITH. Faith in God, faith in our- self; faith in our fellow human being; faith in a future made more secure and more abundant by our determination to make the life of Jesus Christ our own way of life..."

Father Balogun concluded his extraordinary sermon with a passage from the Bible. He quoted from the Gospel of Luke 17:6. The words are still fresh in Chike's mind.

"If ye had faith as a grain of mustard seed, ye might say unto this sycamine tree, Be though plucked up by the root, and be thou planted in the sea; and it should obey you."

The mustard seed with its pungent power, is used as condiment in food to add spice to bland palates. Perhaps, Chike thought to himself, perhaps, the beautiful ones have at last been born, remembering the title to Ayi Kwe Armah's novel. Wazobia's mustard seed, as in the Holy Bible, has been planted and is finally taking root in the rich soil of the regenerative faith of her youth.

GLOSSARY

Wa	Yoruba for *come*
Zo	Hausa for *come*
Bia	Igbo for *come*

English translations of some Igbo, Yoruba & Hausa Words

Word	Language	English translation
Ugulu or Okochi	Igbo	Harmattan—Dry Season
Ani	Igbo	Earth (Goddess)
Ite-ona	Igbo	Earthenware pot
Ogbueke	Igbo	Killer of Pythons
Buba	Yoruba	Dressy Traditional African clothes for women
Agbada	Yoruba	Formal traditional West African clothes for men
Onilegogoro	Yoruba	type of traditional Nigerian head scarf for women (literarily: the owner of a tall building)
Nka bu Chukwu anafu anya	Igbo	This is the God we can see
Oyibo	Igbo	White person
Okoto	Igbo	Cassava dish served cold
Ukazu	Igbo	A kind of green vegetable
Nkpulu Aghara	Igbo	Garden egg
Onye ocha torotoro	Igbo	A white person with a neck that looks like that of a turkey
Dogo turenchi	Hausa	Big English Words
Agu	Igbo	Tiger
Oji-Igbo	Igbo	Kola nut indigenous to Igboland
Gworo	Hausa	Kola nut indigenous to Hausaland

Nama	Hausa	Cattle
Onugbu	Igbo	Bitter leaf
Asoke	Yoruba	Traditionally woven Yoruba cloth
Akwette	Igbo	Traditionally woven Igbo cloth
Bata	Yoruba	Business name of a shoe company in many parts of Africa
Omo	Yoruba	Brand name of a detergent manufactured and distributed in Nigeria and other parts of West Africa
Mkpi	Igbo	He-goat
Akara	Yoruba	Bean cake
Akamu	Igbo	Corn cereal served hot
Ogbo	Igbo	A calabash cup
Ibu Mmaya	Igbo	Traditional wine-carrying for consummating a marriage.
Ofe Mmanu	Igbo	"Oily Soup" ---a derogatory term for Yorubas
Konkosa	Igbo	The top section of the Agbada
Aziza		Traditional broom made of a bunch of raffia sticks tied together in a bundle
Aka Odo	Igbo	Pestle
Ikwe	Igbo	Mortar
Ifunanya	Igbo	Love
Akawu	Igbo	Sodium Potash
Abuba Ugo	Igbo	Feather of Pride
Ako nu uche	Igbo	Common Sense
Ose	Igbo	Pepper
Nnu	Igbo	Salt
Akpu	Igbo	Cassava
Mangala	Igbo	A Type of Smoked Fish
Okporoko	Igbo	Stock Fish (Igbo).
Ogbu adana	Igbo	Machete (Igbo).
Chi	Igbo	Personal god (Igbo).
Nto		A kind of "take that" sign in Igbo Culture
Umunna	Igbo	Kith & Kin.
Utaba	Igbo	Tobacco Snuff
Uko	Igbo	Attic
Alo	Igbo	Advice/Wisdom
Ogodo	Igbo	A kind of loin cloth worn by wine tappers

Adanchi	Igbo	Midget
Gwodogwodo	Igbo	Giant
Ichiko Alo	Igbo	Caucusing--putting heads together
Ichafu	Igbo	Head Scarf.

English Translation of the Igbo Poem

Igbo	English
Ndu bu onyiye.	Life is giving.
Ndu bu okwukwe.	Life is faith.
Ndu bu akwa anyi na kwa.	Life is the crying we do.
Ndu bu ikuku anyi neku.	Life is the air we breath.
Ndu bu ochi anyi na chi.	Life is our laughter.
Ndu bu ichiko alo.	Life is putting our heads together.
Ndu bu ndidi.	Life is Patience.
Ndu dika akwukwo ofia,	Life is like vegetation that
Neso ebe nine.	grows every where.
Ndu bu ebisie, ka awuo nu udo.	Life is such that after we have lived, that we may die in peace.
Ndu bu isi.	Life is most important.

List of Igbo Proverbs/Sayings In the Novel

He who brings kola brings life

The kola nut that came from the King has returned to the king's house

If men urinate together, it produces a richer lather

If you see a toad running in broad daylight, be rest assured that something is chasing it.

No matter what the eyes see, they can never cry blood.

A boy who has been handed live charcoal fire on a cold harmattan morning by a neighbor, does not want the wind to extinguish it before he reaches his mother's house.

There is no point searching for something you can find on the floor of a house in the uko--loft.

When two kegs of good palm wine meet each other, they try to out-foam one another

A person who forgets when and where they got caught in a rainstorm is unlikely to remember who sheltered them from the same rainstorm

Whatever the kind of food one prefers, water is universally
needed to cook all types of food.
Good things never run out in this world

List of Characters in the Novel

1. Chike
2. Bisi
3. Ngozi
4. Mohammed
5. Chike's father--
6. Chike's mother
7. Bisi's father--
8. Bisi's mother--
9. Alhaji Futa Toro--
   Mohammed's father
10. Mohammed's mother
11. Mazi Chidimma--
    Ngozi's father
12. Ifeoma Chidimma--
    Ngozi's mother
13. Reverend Father
    Balogun--the Yoruba
    Priest
14. Reverend Father
    Okoro--the Igbo Priest
15. Babatunde Olatunji--
    Bisi's Uncle
16. Alhaji Qaria--the father
    of the three girls
    Mohammed's father
17. would have preferred
    his taking a bride from
    among
18. Bisi's little niece--the
    bearer of bad news.
19. The White Missionary
    in Isiobodo
20. Fatumata--
    Mohammed's former
    girlfriend
21. Osagie
22. Tunde
23. Hadiza
24. Ada Ukwu
25. Mazi Nnayelugo
26. Mazi Tobeolisa
27. Mazi Akwa Akwulu
28. Mazi Obiagu
29. Mazi Ikejiuwa
30. Mazi Ngala
31. Mazi Akajiaku
32. *Ozo* Okechukwu
33. *Ozo* Akaike
34. *Ozo* Obiora
35. *Eze Ozo* Ojemba Ewe
    Ilo
36. *Ozo* Okenihe
37. *Ozo* Obolo Dihe
38. *Ozo* Osisi di mma na
    Anu Akulia
39. *Ozo* Mba ana balu Agu
40. *Ozo* Wa Orji na milu
    Ora

Printed in the United States
210247BV00005B/120/A